D.J

Wildhorse Creek

Kerry McGinnis was born in Adelaide and at the age of twelve took up a life of droving with her father and four siblings. The family travelled extensively across the Northern Territory and Queensland before settling on a station in the Gulf Country. Kerry has worked as a shepherd, droving hand, gardener, stock-camp and station cook, eventually running a property at Bowthorn, near Mt Isa. She is the author of two volumes of memoir, *Pieces of Blue* and *Heart Country*, and a novel, *The Waddi Tree*. Kerry now lives in Bundaberg.

The Waddi Tree

'McGinnis has an ear for the colloquialisms of the bush and keen eyes when it comes to realising the landscape.' THE AGE

'Heartbreaking one moment but full of hope with the turn of the page.' ADELAIDE ADVERTISER

'This latest work by Kerry McGinnis should be on every school and book club list of recommended reads, right across Australia… McGinnis builds an epic that will touch all hearts and inspire others travelling the many hard roads in life's quests.' BENDIGO ADVERTISER

'A very readable book…written by someone whose heart and soul are inspired by the vast, unforgiving and sometimes terrible country in Australia's north.' SA LIFE

Heart Country

'McGinnis has the eye of a painter; she writes as she sees and the land comes alive.' WEEKEND AUSTRALIAN

'What makes this book stand out – apart from its compelling narrative of a vanishing way of life – is its lyrical description of the country and the elements that shape each season.' AUSTRALIAN BOOKSELLER & PUBLISHER

'A rare insight into the difficulties of life in the Australian outback during the 1940s and '50s.' WEEKLY TIMES

Pieces of Blue

'Lyrical, humorous and moving, *Pieces of Blue* is a family history that lingers after the reading is done.' THE AUSTRALIAN

'This is a beautifully written collection of fragments, vivid but tantalising snapshots of McGinnis's life.' SYDNEY MORNING HERALD

'McGinnis relates the saga of her childhood and her growing up years with verve.' TOWNSVILLE BULLETIN

'Kerry McGinnis's personal – and personable – story offers insights into an Australia unknown by urbanites. And into the human values and verities that underwrite life there.' THE AUSTRALIAN

'It is the author's word pictures of the sights, smells and sounds of the bush, and her perceptive rendering of the characters along the way, that make *Pieces of Blue* a book to be treasured.' SUNSHINE COAST SUNDAY

MICHAEL JOSEPH

Published by the Penguin Group
Penguin Group (Australia)
250 Camberwell Road, Camberwell, Victoria 3124, Australia
(a division of Pearson Australia Group Pty Ltd)
Penguin Group (USA) Inc.
375 Hudson Street, New York, New York 10014, USA
Penguin Group (Canada)
90 Eglinton Avenue East, Suite 700, Toronto, Canada ON M4P 2Y3
(a division of Pearson Penguin Canada Inc.)
Penguin Books Ltd
80 Strand, London WC2R 0RL, England
Penguin Ireland
25 St Stephen's Green, Dublin 2, Ireland
(a division of Penguin Books Ltd)
Penguin Books India Pvt Ltd
11 Community Centre, Panchsheel Park, New Delhi – 110 017, India
Penguin Group (NZ)
67 Apollo Drive, Rosedale, North Shore 0632, New Zealand
(a division of Pearson New Zealand Ltd)
Penguin Books (South Africa) (Pty) Ltd
24 Sturdee Avenue, Rosebank, Johannesburg 2196, South Africa

Penguin Books Ltd, Registered Offices: 80 Strand, London WC2R 0RL, England

First published by Penguin Group (Australia), 2010

1 3 5 7 9 10 8 6 4 2

Text copyright © Kerry McGinnis 2010

The moral right of the author has been asserted

Cover and text design by Karen Trump © Penguin Group (Australia)
Cover photographs by Getty, Masterfile and PhotoLibrary
Typeset in Fairfield by Post Pre-press Group, Brisbane, Queensland
Printed and bound in Australia by McPherson's Printing Group, Maryborough, Victoria

National Library of Australia
Cataloguing-in-Publication data:

McGinnis, Kerry, 1945–
Wildhorse creek/Kerry McGinnis
9781921518157(pbk.)
A823.4

penguin.com.au

FSC

Mixed Sources
Product group from well-managed
forests and other controlled sources
Cert no. SGS-COC-004121
www.fsc.org
© 1996 Forest Stewardship Council

KERRY McGINNIS

MICHAEL JOSEPH
an imprint of
PENGUIN BOOKS

For Judith, and the Morialta girls

Prologue

The boy came awake shivering in clothes that were sodden with damp. He woke gradually. First he was aware of the chill, then of the pain in his feet and the stiffness of his limbs. Next the pressure of the hard earth against hip and shoulder, and the by now familiar aching gripe of his empty belly. And then his brain caught up and the full realisation of his plight, which sleep had temporarily drowned, surfaced again.

He lay still for a moment, his body holding the foetal curl it had unconsciously assumed in sleep. The spiky branches of the bush he lay beneath were a green lacework beaded with little diamonds of dew. It was dawn, but not yet sun-up, and a smoky stillness lay over the little hollow he had chosen last evening. Not smoke, he saw, but mist. It accounted for the damp. Raising his head he saw again the small creek, the fence with split timber posts, and the sentinel line of gums fringing the pale curl of the dirt road. And not a yard from him, frozen in the act of chewing, a rabbit, fur bespangled with dew, its whiskers a-tremble as it took his scent.

The boy knew before he moved that it was hopeless. But he made the effort, lunging even as the rabbit stamped convulsively and fled. He ran the sharp end of a branch into his hand for his pains and swore feebly as the blood dripped. Tears overran his dark eyes. *Like that's gunna help?* But despite the angry jibe at himself he couldn't stop. Fifteen years old, he sat on a log by the creek hugging his knees and blubbered from hunger and helplessness. Finally he sniffed and smeared the wet from his cheeks. He was on his own and bawling wasn't going to get him a feed. According to what he could figure from the inadequate school atlas in his rucksack he was somewhere in country Victoria and there were many miles to go before he cleared the state border. He couldn't rest until that, at least, was behind him.

Mechanically he drank from the creek, struggled to his feet, pulled his load over his shoulders and stepped onto the empty road. He was scared down to the soles of his ill-fitting boots but while he could lift his blistered feet he intended to put distance between himself and what lay behind. And to pass the time he would find a new name for himself, to take with him into a new life. Something plain and simple that nobody would remember. Pain stabbed his blistered heel and he thought of Bill Martin, whose boots he now wore, and of the ten dollars the old man had raked from his pockets and pressed into his hand when he'd dropped him off on the bus route. The echo of his words still rang in the boy's mind.

'Keep going, son. Find yerself a life. It couldn't be worse'n what you've got here.'

2

That decided him. He would call himself Billy – Billy Martin. He spoke it aloud in the bird-haunted quiet of the empty road. Like a promise that neither the old man's cash, nor his kindness, would be wasted. And with it a silent vow to himself that no matter how hard or long the way, he was never going back.

One

The first mailrun of the year was always a matter of uncertainty. Keith Guthrie, chucking the heavy canvas bags on at the South-bend post office, wondered if he was even going to make it beyond the town limits. One year his first run had ended on the far side of the Common, and they'd bogged two trucks pulling him out. But that was the Gulf Country for you. Parts of Africa probably had better roads and the seventy-two–seventy-three Wet just ended – if indeed it had, he thought, cocking a jaundiced look at the sky where the fat, white clouds still hovered – had been a big one. In fact he couldn't remember a bigger – unless it was Cyclone Hannah way back in March fifty-one. It had flattened the town and drowned enough cattle to stock a small property. Small by Gulf standards that was – say five or six hundred square miles of country.

Thank Christ he hadn't been driving the mail then. He wiped his hand down his beard and took another squint at the clouds, his thin rake-like form canted easily against the door of the old Bedford. At least he had no weight today – just enough for traction in the mud.

All the heavy stuff – the kero drums for Rainsford Downs, a bag of spuds and another of wheat for Mount Ixion, and a thumping great box of parts for Wildhorse Creek – could wait another week, two if he struck trouble this run.

It was chancy bloody country and that was the truth of it – impassable bogs, washed-out creek crossings, former gutters gouged into ravines to hang up your back end. Sometimes in low-lying spots you found the track itself, rough as guts at the best of times, stripped clean away, grass and all, leaving the bare bones of clay and rock to jar your back teeth loose. He was mad to be still driving it after all these years. But, he reflected, settling himself in the seat, he wasn't alone in that. Half the buggers in the country were off their trolley. Had to be, to stay.

'Course (his thoughts ran on) it was mostly individualism in need of pruning. (Keith when not driving the mail was a passionate gardener.) What did a man want with such country? Or, more to the point, *think* that he wanted? All he actually got was isolation, extremes of climate and bloody hard work.

He glanced at the young hopeful sitting beside him. Another one heading out for his first season on the big runs. The wild, unfenced northern country was a magnet for young stockmen. They held the funny notion that it was romantic – but at least this was a quiet one, not busting his ears with questions like most of 'em did; hardly opened his mouth since they'd met. Keith squizzed him again, seeing a light-built lad of what he'd call average size, with dark hair showing under a ringer's hat. Average sort of face, too. On the thin side, the brown eyes a bit careful and the shadow of a mo on his upper lip, so at least he was shaving – twenty maybe and knew it all for a bet. To Keith's cynical eye the stock camp fodder that made up the bulk of his passengers looked younger every year. Well, a gate opener was company, someone to chew the fat with on the long track.

'What did you say your name was, son?'

'I didn't.' The young man turned his head to meet the shrewd gaze above the startling spread of beard. 'But it's Billy Martin.'

'Right. New to the area, eh? So, where're you heading?'

'Wherever there's work. Bloke at the pub said riding the mail was the way to go.' He adjusted the quarter window so that the blast of warm air played on his heated body. His skin was slicked with sweat and he used the flat of his hand to wipe his dripping cheeks. 'It always this hot in April?'

'Ah, it's just a bit of humidity,' Keith dismissed the heavy air though he lifted his arms to ease the weight of his sodden shirt. 'Big Wet. Road's only been open a week – good chance we won't get no further than the Mount. That's the first stop. End of the line's Brancaster and they'll be wetted in for another month. It's only a spit from the coast there – they'll have had sixty, seventy inches I shouldn't wonder.'

'Yeah?' Billy sounded impressed by the figures. 'That's some rain. Big place?'

'Average. 'Bout fifteen hundred miles. They're a mad lot of buggers any road – you wouldn't wanna work there.'

'That right? What makes them mad?'

'Dunno. Something in the water, maybe.' Keith changed down

to charge a patch of wet-looking track, a manoeuvre that flung his passenger about as the back end of the vehicle fishtailed violently until they were through.

Billy righted his hat and rubbed the elbow he'd banged into the door and twisted to look at their tracks. 'Bit soft – you get bogged much?' Long thin puddles lay alongside the track, the grass beside them a brilliant green. The passing countryside was a mixture of broken plains and light scrub thickly smothered in feed yellowing at the top where the seeds had formed and were drying. Here and there an area of deeper colour showed up quaggy acres of swamp and gilgai holes. A vehicle body abandoned in the grass displayed a large evangelical sign along its rusted side: JESUS SAVES, it read. Underneath in smaller capitals some wit had added: WITH THE ANZ.

'Don't even think about it,' Keith warned. 'This is just a trial run. First dodgy stretch I'm turning back. I'm paid to deliver the mail, not bust me guts in a bog.'

'Still, must happen sometimes.'

'Damn right. This country's a proper bastard. It'll bog you, perish you, ruin you. Freeze your balls off in winter, roast your eyes out in summer, and that's without the dust and the flies. You wait – the plagues of Egypt's got nothing on it.' Keith warmed to his theme. 'It's the arse end of the continent. You find yourself stuck somewhere needing a bit o' wire for repairs and there ain't a fenceline within a hundred bloody miles. And as for somebody coming by!' He snorted disgustedly.

'I heard it was big – open-range country.'

'Yeah. Not a boundary fence between here and the coast. There's horse paddocks, of course. The country's rotten with brumbies – there's some now,' His chin jerked sideways and leaning forward Billy saw them through the driver's window, an indeterminate mass of galloping bodies, mostly brown and bay, off in the scrub. 'And the odd holding paddock for bullocks. Well, that's how it's been. Be changing though when the government gets this disease control program going.'

'What's that then?' Billy instinctively ducked as they charged through a long sheet of water and a muddy spray arced across the windscreen.

'Bugger!' Keith switched the wipers on to scrape the reddish mess aside. 'Oh, some campaign the Primary Industry mob's starting up – testing cattle for disease. TB and brucellosis. Point is the stations are gunna have to fence to implement it. It's not gone down too well with the cattlemen.' He lifted a hand from the wheel to brush his beard. 'See, when it started in the inside country they all reckoned they'd be exempt out here. This country's too big for testing, they said. And how were they gunna control the scrubbers – that's wild cattle, to you – and what about the wild pigs? Seems they can carry tuberculosis too. Talked 'emselves into thinking it couldn't happen round here. But the government's going ahead with it. So you mighta got here just in time, son.' He waved an expansive hand at the landscape. 'Before she's all cut up and nailed down just like everywhere else.'

'Take a bit of doing though, won't it?' Billy ventured. 'Whose country are we driving through here?'

8

'Right here? The Mount. Axel Cooper's place.'

'What size is it? Do you know?'

'Yep. Twelve hundred.'

'Square miles,' Billy affirmed, doing sums in his head. The result caused him to whistle. 'That's a lot of fencing wire.'

'Not as much as they'll need on Rainsford Downs,' Keith said with relish. '*That's* twenty-seven hundred. And we're just talking the boundary. They've gotta have internal fencing too. So they can hold tested cattle apart from the untested stock when they're mustering. You can see why the graziers are a bit upset.'

'So how many stations are we talking?'

'Round here? There's Mount Ixion, that's the Coopers. Family property. Wildhorse Creek – the Reillys have got that. Rainsford Downs, comp'ny owned. There's Rumhole – belongs to Ken Walker. Plover Creek, 'nother small joint, and Brancaster which – ah, shit!'

'What's up?' The truck was slowing on a bend. Billy craned forward to see the spread of water before them. It must've rained quite recently for the tracks of the vehicle they'd been following had vanished. He could see where it had negotiated the wet patch, but now only the tops of the deep wheel tracks where it had cut into the mud were visible. The rest were under water. 'You going through?' he asked as they came to a stop.

For answer Keith switched off and climbed out, staring slowly about him as he stood and rolled a smoke. Billy got out too. It was cooler in the open. He pinched his shirt away from his body while his ears were assailed with the strident hum of insects. Bush flies mobbed him but he could see, and hear, a dozen other species from dragonflies to cicadas drilling the warm air with their noise. He trod experimentally to the water's edge, feeling the mud slide and give under his boot. The top few inches were very soft. Keith meanwhile had circled to the left where a dozen blackheart coolibah trees were scattered through grass that came to his waist. His disreputable felt hat hung over his brow as he stamped and pondered, skinny hands astride his hips over which his khaki shorts seemed in danger of slipping. When he had seen enough he returned to the road, wading out of the grass like some skinny water bird, his boots clogged with mud. Then to Billy's bewilderment he pulled a billycan from inside the spare tyre and proceeded to fill it from a drum lashed to the headboard.

'Get a fire going, will you, son?' he said. 'Might as well have a cuppa. Bit more sun on the road won't do it no harm at all.'

They drank it squatting on their heels in the long shade of the truck. The cicadas sang shrilly and the engine ticked as it cooled. Mosquitos hovered and Billy, contemplating what he could see of the wet track, ventured a question. 'You gunna go round it, off road?'

'Can't think of a better way to end in the shit.' Keith flicked the dregs from his cup and smeared a mosquito in a bloody trail across his wrist. 'Straight through. This bit of road's got a fair bottom to it. We'll put the tracks down first, but. You wanna hop up and chuck 'em off?'

Passengers were obviously expected to work. The tracks were heavy sheets of holed metal more than the width of a tyre and as long as the truck. They positioned them astride the water, which Billy saw had shrunk to a surprising degree while they waited. The steel was hot and the edge of it cut into his hands as he slithered and slipped behind Keith, trudging steadily ahead. He waited then in sodden, muddy boots, while the mailman returned to the truck, revved the engine and charged through. Prying the tracks free of the suction of the mud and reloading them was hot and dirty work. Keith drew off another billycan of water which they took turns to pour over each other's hands before throwing the remainder over the dirty windscreen. The wipers shifted most of the mud and they were ready to continue.

'How long you been driving the mail?' Billy asked.

'Too bloody long,' Keith grunted.

'So what happens if you get bogged?'

'Dig yourself out. And if you can't,' he jerked his thumb at the roof of the cab where a portable transceiver was locked into sturdy brackets, 'give the nearest station a shout. One of these days Main Roads'll make it this far and turn this goat track into a proper highway. I should live so long.'

'They probably felt the same further south,' Billy said, 'but I noticed a fair stretch of built-up road coming north from Windsor Creek, and a big plant working on it. There's another one heading for Normanton. Beef Roads, the signs say.'

'My eye. Defence Roads they are. Just like the Stuart Highway was, back during the war. Suits the government to pretend they're doing something for the voters, that's all. I reckon Vietnam's finally made somebody in Canberra look at a map and they seen what little access there is up here. That where you from then – the Creek?'

'I worked on a property there. And over the Tablelands before that,' Billy said. A corner post caught his eye and he jerked his thumb, 'What's the fence?'

'Horse paddock. We're coming up to the Mount. See you chain the gate good. Cooper's kinda fussy 'bout his horses.'

'Right.' Billy reached for the doorhandle, swung down and stood a moment with the muddy truck behind him, reading the metal scroll inset in a frame in the centre of the gate: *Mount Ixion Station. Cooper and Sons 1913.*

He pushed it open wondering, with a grin for Keith's opinion of the present-day road, what sort of goat track it must have been when the sign was first erected.

Two

Axel Cooper, owner and boss of the Mount, was a tall man with square shoulders and a hard, even-featured face. He was dressed in work pants, yard boots and a pressed cotton shirt with the sleeves rolled back against sun-browned skin. He shook hands, his eyes assessing Billy from hat to boot heels.

'Much experience, son?' He had brown eyes under straight heavy brows.

'Five years,' Billy said and watched the brows rise.

'You must've started young,' Cooper said dryly. 'What's that make you now?'

'Twenty.' Billy played his trump card. 'I worked with Ivy Henson for three of them.' He permitted himself a smile. 'She reckoned I should mention it, if I made it out this way.'

Axel's face cleared. 'In that case – Ivy wouldn't carry a no-hoper. She still got that black gelding? Horse called Magic. He just about was too, when it came to drafting.'

'Alive and well,' Billy confirmed, 'so – you got a place for me?'

His new boss nodded and waved a hand. 'Dump your gear in the quarters then come across to the yard. We're drafting up the working strings.' To Keith he said, 'The track's not too bad. I was out past Benson's Hole yesterday and kicking up dust on the red country. Here's Rachel coming – she'll take the bag. There's a cuppa in the kitchen if you want it.'

'Brewed up on the way, thanks.'

Billy shook hands with the mailman and hoisted his swag onto his shoulder, eyes already on the low white-painted building that was the men's quarters. It was one of many. He identified the Big House by its fenced garden, and saw a child coming through the gate, a mailbag swinging in her hand. She was lame, he saw with a stab of pity, then a horse whinnied and was answered by another and he forgot everything else in his eagerness to get among them. They'd said at the pub that Axel Cooper bred the best in the district. He shoved the door of the quarters wide enough to dump his gear. Dusting off his hands he strode out for the yards, the mail truck now heading back out to the road, already forgotten.

The horses, moving within the weathered rails amid a tangle of manes, and dipped and snorting heads, were all he could have hoped for. Billy's love was horses, a passion that Ivy Henson, the sixty-year-old ex-Gulfite had helped foster during their time together on her small property on the Tablelands. *They never let you down*, she'd said, understanding right from the first meeting with the skinny withdrawn boy he'd been back then that too many people already had. She'd had good horses, Ivy, but these were their equal – at least in looks. Billy, distracted by the fluidity of moving thoroughbred limbs, gave himself up to the pleasure of studying them, sparing little attention for the other men he would shortly be working with.

Of these, Garry Downes, the head stockman, was the most important, a slow-spoken man who blinked repeatedly as if his pale-coloured eyes bothered him. He looked Billy over as they shook hands, his own big-knuckled grasp surprisingly limp.

Garry had pointed out Ben, the owner's son. He'd nodded at the figure struggling to shut a heavy timber gate that had sagged on its hinges and said, 'That's Ben. There'll be another couple of blokes joining us in a day or so. They'll be coming out with the cook when he sobers up. Used to be a hotel chef till the drink got him.'

'Right.' Billy went to put his shoulder under the gate for the hoof-churned soil of the yard was deep and soft.

'Thanks.' Ben snagged the chain, hook facing up, Billy noticed, and reached through the squared timber bars to shake hands. 'Ben Cooper. Where you from?'

'Billy Martin. Windsor Creek way. The boss just put me on the books.' Ben was the taller by a couple of inches and broader through the shoulders. He had a pleasant, open face and a faint look of his father about him.

'First time in the Gulf then – how d'you like it?'

Billy grinned and let his eye fall lovingly on the restless horses. 'With nags like these it'll do me fine.' He saw Axel Cooper's shape silhouetted against the rails as he climbed into the yard and nodded. 'Looks like we're wanted.'

'Yeah.' Ben's tone was expressionless and the flicker of interest that had lit his face faded. He turned to plod through the heavy soil towards his father and Billy followed. But before he went he reversed the hook so that it pointed down, ensuring that any pressure applied to the chain – such as a horse hitting the gate – would not jerk it undone. It was an automatic reflex that would prove symptomatic of his job at the Mount, and, after a while, its greatest irritant – that of fixing up Ben's mistakes.

It was several days before the real work of mustering started. During that time Hans the camp cook arrived with the Burch boys, as Henry and Dan Burch seemed to be universally known, for all that Henry, at twenty-five and the older of the two, had five years on Billy. They were cousins, not brothers, lean and affable young men with corded forearms and little flesh on their rumps. Hans, a morose man in his mid-fifties, was short and tubby, with a heavy German accent and thinning hair. He swore in his native language and was very easy to upset. He had once been, according to the mechanic, who also shared the quarters, an officer and gentleman in the German navy – until his capture on the first day of the war. 'Screwed up his life. No chance of being a 'ero then, see?' The mechanic had rolled his eyes. 'Don't worry – you'll hear all about it first time he's got grog in.'

Tiny, the station cook, shared their accommodation but Garry Downes lived with his wife and child in the only cottage on the property. The men ate in the kitchen and, apart from Ben and his father, Billy saw no more of the Cooper family, which he learned included Axel's wife and two daughters. The elder Daphne, according to Henry, was a stuck-up cow. 'Rachel's not a bad kid, but. Got more gumption than the other two rolled together. 'S'families for you. The wrong 'uns get the looks or the nous – what can you do?'

Billy, uninterested, grunted an answer. Henry's tongue ran constantly and critically about the district, naming strangers in whom he had no interest. You got used to all sorts in stockcamps – the whingers, the know-alls. Henry himself seemed to be related to half the countryside, including the Coopers. He was cousin to Ben, and therefore also to Rachel, who bobbed suddenly into his path out of a low-eaved building as he returned from the yard the evening before the camp went out.

She wasn't a child. That was his first confused thought. She was small with no shape to speak of, but the face and form beneath the brown curls belonged to a young woman at least his own age. His eyes were drawn irresistibly to the heavy brace and boot she wore on her right leg and when he looked guiltily away he caught the faint flush that rose to colour her sallow skin, but she spoke equably, with no sign of discomfort.

'Hello. You're the new man. I'm Rachel. Dad said you're a horseman.'

It was Billy's turn to flush, but with pleasure at such praise. 'Did he? I'm glad he thinks so. Billy Martin.' He hesitated to offer his hand, saying lamely instead, 'You've got some beautiful horses here.'

'The best.' She spoke proudly. 'My grandfather started the stud. You want to see the stallions? Come in for a minute, I've got pictures of them all.' She jerked her head and he followed her into a room set up like an office. His gaze took in the desk and filing cabinet, and a shelf of books that seemed to deal mainly with the breeding of thoroughbreds. He ran his eyes over the titles before turning to the framed photographs about the walls.

'Ixion Pride,' she said, coming to stand beside him. 'He's our current sire. They're some of his get in the horses you'll be riding. Before him,' she pointed, 'the bay horse there, he's by Relay Point, who was a top racer in his time. And that one,' she turned awkwardly to indicate the earliest photograph of all, a black and white enlargement showing a dark, upstanding horse with ears pricked at the camera, 'was sired by Emborough, who won a string of races in Sydney, in the years between the wars. He was my grandfather's first sire.'

'Thanks for showing me.' He nodded at the picture of the grey stallion, 'There's one in my string, a gunmetal blue called Musket – he's got to be by him. Same head, same stance.'

'From a mare called Blue Sally,' she said happily. 'He'd be four, five years old now.'

'He's got a full mouth.' Billy nodded, referring to the growth of a horse's teeth. At five years all the adult teeth were grown. He was impressed by her knowledge and she saw it.

'Just because I don't ride,' she said defensively, 'it doesn't stop me being interested.'

A brazen clatter from the direction of the kitchen saved him from the need of answering this. 'I'd better go. Tiny's hell on blokes coming late to meals.'

Treading rapidly towards his dinner he reflected on the surprise she'd turned out to be. Maybe Henry had the right of it. If Ben showed just a tenth of her interest he might at least be able to recognise the horses in his own string, and not be caught out, as he had been that morning, bridling one of Billy's.

Three

It became obvious very quickly to Billy that Garry Downes was a worrier. He double-checked everything. That gates were shut, fires extinguished, and jobs completed. The constant scrutiny was irritating although Henry, when he mentioned it to him, shrugged it off.

'He's a bit of an old woman, Garry, but he's run the camp here for years. My uncle likes him. And to say truth,' he added, squinting ahead at the open plain they were riding across, 'nobody else'd put up with a hopeless bugger like Ben.'

'He doesn't seem to fit the mould,' Billy agreed. 'Nothing like the boss. Doesn't Axel have any brothers either?'

In answer Henry gave a satisfied grunt. 'I thought so. Swing wide – there's cattle ahead.' They began to trot and he turned his head, the sun glinting on the new-grown stubble on his jaw. 'There was Clem, but he died from a horning in the yard at Benson's Tank. Years ago now. Here we go, they've seen us.' He suddenly shot ahead to turn the lead of the string of cattle presently lumbering into a gallop. Behind him Billy gathered in the rest, alive to the pleasure of day, the feel of the horse beneath him, the wide plain running on to a horizon bounded by clear, pale sky, and the rich hue of the cattle, plodding now through the thickly clumped Mitchell grass from which the green was rapidly fading. A light wind plucked at his shirt and fluttered his hatband, and Henry's bay snorted and shook his head, rattling the bridle rings.

Billy watched the tiny birds swaying as they pecked on the grass stems and thought on what he'd learned. As a child he'd failed to understand the forces dominating his life and had suffered for it. So studying those whose lives impinged upon his own had become a habit and from his first day Ben had presented a conundrum. He was no stockman and never would be. And not all his father's thinly disguised anger nor Garry's patience would make him so. But perhaps the death of Axel's brother was the reason for their efforts?

The Cooper heir was pleasant enough, Billy silently admitted, just a pain to work with. You could be sure there would be horses missing when it was Ben's turn to get them up to the camp of a morning. And, working stock in the yards, that it would be Ben who bobbed up to block them at the mouth of the crush when you needed them to run, or who failed to chain the gate of the forcing pen behind the cattle after they'd all spent twenty minutes getting them into it. And he was no better in the open with a mob. Even the patient Garry had done his block and sent him back to ride on the tail after he'd set the lead spiralling in upon itself for the third time in one day.

It was a mystery to Billy how he could complicate so simple a task as driving cattle, or care so little for the beautiful horses he rode.

'D'you race any?' he asked as they unsaddled one evening. 'I would, if I was you.' He patted his own mare and rubbed the itchy patch of sweat behind her ear where the headband had rested. For his part Ben simply pulled his bridle free and turned away.

'Not likely. That's the old man's bag.' There was a sullen set to his features. 'A horse is a horse – who cares how fast it goes? I get enough of it when he's training.'

'So,' Billy hoisted his saddle to carry it to the rail, 'who does his jockeying?'

Ben shrugged, lifting his own. 'My cousin Dan, if he's around. He's a lightweight. Or there's always a couple of amateurs come to the meetings – like Simon Reilly. His family's got Wildhorse Creek. Dad likes his riding.'

Billy had never attended a bush meeting. He swung his burden over the rail, wincing as the stirrup hit his knee. It was almost dark for the days had shortened as May drew to an end. Hans's fire glimmered behind the windbreak and there was a savoury smell of cooking meat. 'When are the Races? I'd like to go.'

'July. And don't worry,' Ben said dryly, 'you will. Only two things the work stops for here – the Races and the Wet.'

'Sounds good to me.' And then because he found the other's attitude so strange he asked curiously. 'What d'you want to do, Ben? Blind Freddy can see you hate stock work.'

'You think a little thing like that matters?' Ben dumped his saddle and strode off, the drag of his spurs in the dust providing an angry underlining to his words.

'So quit,' he called but if he heard, his companion gave no sign. Billy shrugged. He supposed it was dead easy to hold a job when your father both owned the property and employed your immediate boss. He reckoned it would be a salutary lesson for Ben to try it on his own – say, under the aegis of Billy's last boss at Raebell Downs. His lips quirked thinking about the big, ginger-headed man – Ben wouldn't last two minutes with him.

'What's so funny?' Henry asked, reaching past him for the tea billy.

'Nothing.' He forgot Ben's problems and shoved his pannikin across. 'Here, seeing you're on the job.' Behind them the noise of the yarded cattle bellowed up to a brilliant display of stars but the men about the fire, long inured to it, scarcely registered the sound. Billy was, however, vaguely surprised at the wintry bite of the wind. He had expected it to be warmer this far north.

The next time he was in at the homestead he asked Rachel about her brother's obvious discontent. He had grown into the habit of dropping in to her office to say hello whenever the camp returned to the station. He had still to meet her formidable mother whom even the irrepressible Dan, with the lisp caused by two missing front teeth, described as a tartar.

'He hates the place,' she said shortly. 'That's why.'

'So why does he stick around?' Billy was genuinely perplexed.

'The poor sap thinks it's his duty. To Dad and the property. Four generations of Coopers on the property and he's the last male.' She closed the ledger she'd been working with. 'Dad ought to join the twentieth century. You don't see Ken Walker making an opera out of the fact there's only girls to follow him – supposing he manages to hang onto Rumhole long enough to die on it, that is.'

'Who's he?'

'Our northern neighbour. A real battler. Got about as much idea of stock as Ben, but he muddles along. Runs the place with just his wife and daughters. If that's what you call keeping a menagerie and never being able to muster your working plant. Ken's hopeless, but at least he faces facts – unlike Dad.'

'I see.' Uncomfortable to hear criticism of his boss he studied the hand-drawn wall map that showed the shaded boundary lines of the property, the blue of the Rainsford River that ran through it, and the spiky lines – like railroad tracks, he thought – of the half-dozen paddocks. The name *Rumhole Station* was lettered in outside the boundary on the north-east corner, while along the western edge the same fine hand had written *Rainsford Downs*.

'Your work?'

'Yes. Surprised?'

She was, he decided, amazingly plain, save for the sparkling intelligence that showed in her best feature, the bright, pansy brown eyes. 'Not really. It's just—' he hesitated and she cocked her head.

'What?'

'Well, it's a pity that you're not—'

'Whole, you mean?' For the first time there was an edge to her voice.

'No, of course not! I was going to say you should be Ben, that's all. You care for the place, the horses – and he doesn't. If you want to know you remind me of Ivy Henson. Her and her husband – they had a property somewhere round here once. She—' he struggled for words to express his thoughts, 'it was like she grew out of the land. I never met anyone who could do so much with stock. It was like they *wanted* to do what she wanted. And she loved her horses.'

'Like you.' There was a hint of sympathy in her smile.

'Yeah, well,' Billy straightened defensively, 'a man's only as good as the horse he rides. Makes 'em worth looking after. Not that Ben doesn't. It's more like they bore him – like office work would me.'

She sighed. 'Poor Ben. We got the wrong bodies, he and I. It's tough on him too – and Dad. Another son might have evened things out. As it stands I expect Ben'll end up with the place when Dad dies and either run it into the ground, or put it on the market as soon as probate's cleared.'

'Aren't there plenty of nephews?' Billy asked. 'Henry for instance.'

Rachel spoke with finality as she tidied the papers on the desk. 'His name isn't Cooper. And that's what matters to Dad.'

Four

The bullocks went off in June, the drover taking delivery of the thousand head on a blustery Sunday morning when a bitter wind whipped dust from amid the golden clumps of Mitchell grass, and blew the horses' coats awry. The drover's men rode hunched into their saddles with the collars turned up on their jackets. Their hands and lips were cracked from cold nights and chilly dawns and beards shadowed their cheeks.

Henry, watching them leave, spoke philosophically. 'Just shows, don't it? There's always some poor bugger worse off than you. How d'you fancy turning out at midnight for a two-hour watch with the temperature 'round zero?'

Billy, to whom the remark was addressed, grunted in reply. He was still annoyed about missing the previous day's drafting. He had been looking forward to trying out his horse, Musket, on the face of the camp as Axel and Garry selected the bullocks for the sale herd. It was fast, skilled work holding a large mob in the open while the camp-horses did their work. No true cattleman drafted fat cattle through a yard and every young stockman aspired to the skills that camp-drafting called for.

Instead, he had spent the day driving the truck into the station then fuelling and cleaning Axel's own station wagon in order to transport his womenfolk to a meeting in the Southbend hall. It was with growing consternation that he'd received his orders.

'But,' he stammered, 'the drafting. Why can't Ben do it? I was gunna have a go on my grey—'

Axel Cooper's brows had twitched at that. 'Ben's place is here.' His tone was short. 'Garry tells me you're reliable, so prove it – stay out of the pub. My wife'll tell you when she's ready to start.'

Billy's lips compressed. He let the grey go then yanked the tuckerbox down from the truck tray along with everything else that Hans would need in his absence. The truck body normally served as his kitchen. He'd just have to make the best of it as Billy himself would. There'd be other chances he told himself; all the same the thought of Ben making a balls of a job he'd been itching to try was galling.

So was the frustrating wait that ensued at the station for having presented himself on his return, at the Big House – hastily showered and shaved, his hair slicked wetly back beneath his hat – Daphne, the plastic rollers on her head tied in a scarf, told him sharply to return at two o'clock.

There was nobody around. A cock crowed from the sheds behind the meat-house but for the rest the station might as well have been a mausoleum, slumbering under the pale winter sky. Billy ate lunch in the kitchen with the taciturn cook, then sat on the steps of the quarters watching the mill blades turn and the lazy flight of black cockies between the gums, his mind back at the camp. He shifted his spine against the door jamb and cracked a twig between his fingers, wondering what sort of a fool Ben was currently making of himself. Nothing spoiled a stockhorse quicker than a rider who didn't understand his job. Which Ben certainly didn't. In a way – because he'd been at it, Billy knew, since primary school – it was a bigger mystery than the conundrums surrounding his own existence. Resolutely he put that thought aside for he'd long accepted that there was nothing to be gained by dwelling on his grandparents' treatment of him. *Let it go*, Ivy had advised. *It's behind you now.* She was right, he thought and not for the first time. Three years in her company had taught him she mostly was.

Dismissing the unprofitable train of thought he dwelt instead on Daisy, the red-flecked grey mare Ivy had owned. The black gelding Magic had been well known as a performer in the local shows, and even from Axel's comment, out here, but Billy had fallen in love with the grey.

She had a touch of Arab in her – plainly visible in her lean head with its short ears and slightly dished face. He remembered the feel of her nostrils whiffling against his throat in chilly dawns. And the brusque tickle of her whiskered jaw against his palm. She'd be waiting in the yard, stamping and nickering as he pulled the rug off, her breath a foggy plume in the wakening world. Looking back now with an understanding broadened by time and distance he supposed that she'd been the medicine, as much as Ivy's brisk kindness, that had turned his world around, allowing him to overcome the sense of worthlessness that he had carried with him on his long flight from the south.

Daisy, with her bounce and life, and the flow of muscular power beneath her satin skin. Astride the throne of her saddle he'd felt like a king. Like someone with a future worth seeking, to whom the past no longer mattered. And the drum of her feet against the earth was a song of praise that only horsemen knew. Remembering it now put things into perspective for him and he was suddenly sorry for Ben. He stood up, settled his hat and went to fetch the vehicle. Time to collect the women and get moving.

Margaret Cooper was a tall, big-boned woman. She sailed magisterially down the homestead steps, followed by Daphne, the scarf replaced by a fluff of honey-brown curls. Rachel came behind, more slowly, to lever herself into the front seat beside him. He waited behind the wheel, seeing from the set of her shoulders that she didn't want to be helped.

They drove in silence. It was a nice vehicle, quieter and more comfortable than the camp truck, or Keith Guthrie's rugged old Bedford. The road was better too, for the council grader had been at work and the narrow, rutted wheel tracks Billy remembered from his arrival had become a smooth highway. From time to time cattle strung across it heading into the river to drink and at the Six Mile, where a track came in from the south-west to join their road, they passed a man driving a plant of horses.

'They'll be Sam Harris's.' Rachel returned the horseman's wave. 'He always takes the Rainsford bullocks.'

'He's a drover?' Billy eyed the jogging horses. There were

thirty-odd, he judged, bays and browns with a creamy in the lead and a couple of skewbalds on the near wing. Two of the horses wore packs and all looked to be in good condition.

'Yes. And that,' she narrowed her eyes as the horses vanished behind them, 'is the Reillys' truck. Pull up, Billy.' Her face and voice were suddenly animated. 'I want to say hello.'

He let in the clutch and slowed beside the old green international just as Mrs Cooper spoke behind him. 'Why are you stopping? The meeting starts in five minutes.'

'Somebody's broken down.' Billy had spotted the blown tyre on the back wheel. He killed the engine. 'I'll see if he needs a hand.' Then the pair of boots belonging to whoever was jacking it up wriggled and a moment later their owner scooted out from under the body of the truck. It was a girl, dusty and dishevelled. She raked her hair back and resettled her discarded hat before getting up.

'Hey, Jo!' Rachel called as Billy pushed his door open.

Margaret Cooper's head appeared suddenly between them, her words frosty with displeasure. 'There's no time to stop. And no need; we're already late. Let her brothers deal with it.'

Rachel said, 'Mother! There isn't—' but Margaret Cooper's voice overrode the protest.

'Drive on. And do you think you could go a little faster?'

Billy, who'd been exercising the greatest care with his boss's vehicle, slammed the door shut again and twisted the key in the ignition. He hadn't seen anybody else at the scene and driving past without even the offer of assistance went grievously against the tenet of all bush behaviour. He covered the final six miles into town at twice the speed of the past twenty and his passengers had barely disappeared into the hall before he was swinging the nose of the Toyota back the way he had come, defying Margaret Cooper's instructions to wait in the shade at the back of the hall until he was needed.

The girl was hatless again. She'd grabbed the sideboards for balance and was jumping on the handle of the wheel brace trying to shift the nuts with her weight. Billy got out and self-consciously cleared his throat. 'G'day,' he said. 'Sorry about driving off like that but it wasn't my doing. Let's have a look and I'll get that undone for you.'

'Thanks.' She stepped aside and picked up her hat, giving it a cursory smack against her jeans before fitting it on. 'I'm Jo Reilly – in case the old bat didn't tell you.'

'Billy Martin.' They shook hands. 'You got a spare?'

'On the truck. I'd have been right, you know,' she added as if feeling the need to assert her independence, 'only Cub seems to have welded those damn nuts on.'

'He sure has,' Billy grunted, feeling the jar as his boot slammed against the brace. 'Rachel wanted to stop – not that I wouldn't have anyway. It was the old girl who wouldn't – on account of some meeting in town.'

'No.' There was a derisive glint in the girl's blue eyes. 'I mean I daresay she said that. But she just doesn't like Reillys – or the fact that Rachel's mad about my brother Cub. She's been shoving a spoke in *that* wheel for years. Somebody ought to tell her she's got nothing to worry about. Well, would you want her for *your* mother-in-law?'

'Uh – no.' Both feet on the brace handle, Billy essayed a little jump, his eyes taking in the play of expression on her face. She was his height, the vivid blue eyes were level with his, the fair, dusty hair now covered by the broad-brimmed felt hat. She had good teeth, even features, and a smooth tanned skin. She would have been pretty if not for the puckered scar like a large shiny dimple in her right cheek. He was wondering what could have caused it when the wheel nut's resistance suddenly gave and the handle spun under his boots, leaving him nowhere to stand.

Jo was laughing as he picked himself up, rubbing his tailbone. 'Sorry.' She primmed her mouth, the blue eyes still brimful of mirth. 'At least you shifted it.'

'Let's hope the rest are as easy,' Billy said in an effort to regain his dignity. She had a good figure, slight but rounded, and small, capable-looking hands, the backs of them scratched, the nails broken short as happened if you rode a lot which, stealing a glance at the well-worn boots on her feet, he guessed she did.

He said, 'You have got a wheel chocked?'

'Of course I have.' She watched him fit the brace again and jump on it. 'It's in gear too.'

'Good.' The second nut gave and after that the others were quicker. 'How far are you going?'

'It's a hundred and fifty to the Brumby. So I'll be late home tonight.' Seeing his puzzlement she added, 'That's shorthand for Wildhorse Creek. How long have you been in the Gulf, Billy?'

He grinned. 'Shows, does it? Only since April. Still learning the district. What about you?'

'We were born here. Not Simon, he's nine years older. Blake only shifted to the 'Bend the year before Cub and I came along.'

'They're your brothers – Simon and Cub? Who's Blake then? It's hard,' he said by way of excusing his curiosity, 'trying to get hold of a district. You related to everyone too, like the Coopers?'

'No. There's just us. Blake's my father. Cub's my twin. And I'm only stuck here because we need the fuel.' She nodded at the half-dozen drums behind the headboard of the truck. 'Cub had a fall yesterday or he would've collected it. The others are reading a test.'

By now Billy knew this meant putting cattle already tested for TB back through the yards to check the results. A lump at the site of the injection meant a reaction to the drug, in which case the beast was slaughtered. A post-mortem then established whether the disease was present. Frequently there was no proof, in which case the reactor became an NVL – a suspect beast but one with non-visible lesions. In the camp they derided the system. As Henry said, it did a helluva lot for the industry if you had to kill your herd to prove it wasn't diseased.

'Getting many NVLs?' He'd replaced the wheel with the spare and was squatting beside it securing the wheel nuts.

'A few.' She gathered up the tools, dumped them behind the seat, and squinted at the height of the sun. 'I'll bet she doesn't know you came back – Ma Cooper. Is she gunna make a fuss when she finds out? I mean she's really not keen on us. And of course she can't believe Cub's not interested in Rachel. Thinks he's after the station.' She cast up her brows. 'We went to school with her, for Pete's sake!'

Billy was intrigued. 'What's that got to do with it?'

'Put it this way. *I* wouldn't marry anybody I shared a classroom with. Not in Southbend anyway. Boring as . . . Seriously, you're not gunna lose your job over helping me?'

'I doubt it. Anyway I work for Axel, not his Missus. Besides, there's plenty of work. I can always try somewhere else.'

'Well, try us first,' she smiled at him, extending her hand in a friendly shake. 'And thanks a lot, Billy.' A gust of wind took her hat and she snatched it from the air. Her smile stretched the scar in her cheek and she turned her head as if suddenly conscious of his eyes upon it, to rake her thick hair back and jam the hat on it again.

'I will.' He almost wished then that Mrs Cooper *would* get him fired. In an effort to hold her a moment longer he said, 'Catch you at the Races, maybe?'

She laughed. 'I dunno yet. Sports Day comes first anyway.'

He watched the rounded swell of her hips as she stepped up into the cab and a moment later the engine turned over. She waved and he stood there as she drove off, dust rising like a veil over the back end of the heavy truck, and wondered if the load was graded all the way through to Wildhorse Creek – the Brumby, he reminded himself.

Turning it over in his mind as he stood there in the settling dust, a slight smile curving his lips, he thought the name was emblematic, somehow, of Jo. There was as great a difference between her and the pampered Cooper girls as there was between Axel's thoroughbreds and the hardy wild horses that roamed the scrubs and plains of the fenceless Gulf.

Five

Ben had said the work stopped only for the races and the Wet, but Southbend's annual Sports Day was another such occasion.

The station truck transported half a dozen horses into town before daylight, along with most of the station personnel. Tiny was the exception. Drink was his downfall. But he'd been on the wagon for six months now and was manfully determined to stay there. He'd spend the day baking bread, he said virtuously, and any silly bugger that turned up at breakfast with a hangover would get no sympathy from him.

Billy, his mind on meeting Jo again, had been looking forward to the day for several weeks now. He'd never attended horse sports before, much less ridden in them, which, Henry had assured him, he would be expected to do.

'Axel likes everyone to take part,' he said. 'That's why he always sends a truckload of horses. Great sense of community, my uncle. *All* the Coopers have, come to that. If they don't exactly run the district they give it a good shove along – *especially* my aunt. The old man,' by this, Billy now knew he meant Axel's deceased father, 'sponsored a coupla races. And it was *his* old man started the Jockey Club, so you might say it's bred into 'em.'

'I don't mind having a go,' Billy said, 'but what at? What d'you do?'

'Oh, the usual stuff – round the pegs, walk, trot and gallop, the Gretna, billycan race. It's a good day. Everybody turns up. There's a bar on the course, and the old girls in the Country Women's Associ-ation put on a dance in the evening. You wouldn't miss it for quids.'

'Sounds okay.' Billy considered his current mounts. 'Might load the roan, he turns like a dream; he's not fast though.'

'Speed don't matter much,' Henry said. 'You gotta fancy yourself a bit to enter the only race. It's a killer. Bareback down to the river and return. You seen the gullies on the riverbank? The burr's shoul-der high too. Any road, Simon Reilly always wins it.'

Billy's ears pricked. 'He's the jockey?'

'Yeah. Rides for my uncle – among others. He's not bad. They're a pretty wild bunch the Reillys, but they can ride – even the girl.'

'Jo?' There was a secret pleasure in saying her name.

'Oh, you know her?'

Billy shrugged, 'We met. Maybe she'll be there tomorrow?'

Henry nodded. 'Like I said, everybody comes. Remember to cash a cheque when you get into town. You'll need cash for the nomination fees.'

'I will.' He hesitated then decided to ask. 'What d'you mean by calling them wild – the Reillys? Are they reckless – or what?'

Henry blew out his cheeks. 'They've got a bit of a name about the place. Old Blake mostly. Ex-con and a pretty tough old bastard. Nobody's got much time for him. He took that place up eight, ten years ago and hasn't looked back since. Him and his boys been helping themselves to their neighbours' calves from the word go. Poddy-dodging,' he elucidated. 'You musta heard of it. Oldest game on the open range. Pinch an unbranded poddy from your neighbour's cow and stick your own brand on it. Keep the two apart till it's weaned and it's legally yours for all anyone can prove to the contrary.'

'Oh.' Billy digested this. 'Is it a common practice?'

'Depends on the owner, don't it?' Henry squinted down at the cigarette he was rolling then ran the tip of his tongue along the edge of the rice paper. 'Me uncle hands 'em back. 'Course you could say he can afford to. Not everyone's so honest, but. 'S'risk the cockies take in open-range country. I mean it's not like you've even gotta trespass to get 'em. No fences to keep the stock on their owner's land so they're free to roam onto yours. In the long run, though, it's six of one to half a dozen of t'other.'

'How d'you mean?'

'Simple,' Henry struck a match on his belt and inhaled comfortably. 'Say you've got a place alongside of Ken Walker's joint. You pick up his cattle in your muster and brand a few of his calves while you're at it. Shove 'em off somewhere to wean and you're a few head to the good – on'y meanwhile, he's doing the same by yours. Just like killers really. Come the end of the year it works out pretty much the same.'

A killer, in station parlance, was the beast butchered for meat, dry cows mostly that, because they were not rearing calves, were the better conditioned – and not every station killed their own brand. At the Mount, however, they did not kill out of the 'Stranger Paddock', the euphemism for neighbours' stock.

'Sounds like there's more than the Reillys could be called wild,' Billy sought to cover the mild shock the disclosure gave him.

'Ah, it'll be ending now with the fences going in. And like I said, not everybody does it.'

'I see,' Billy said lamely, 'well, it explains what Jo meant when she claimed the boss's wife doesn't like them.'

'I shouldn't think she really likes anyone,' Henry grinned. 'She don't even like *me* – and that shows you. 'Course the Reillys aren't what my dear aunt would call *respectable* either. Blake's wife left him, years ago, and the kids were dragged up anyhow – mostly, when Blake wasn't around, by a mate of his, an old half-caste bloke. They *were* bits of tearaways, but no worse'n me and Dan – or any other kids really. They used to sweat horses on the Common – borrow whatever took their fancy and ride hell out of them. The owners never did anything about it 'cause they were scared of Blake. He was a bare-knuckle man back then – a fighting machine. And a drinker. Lay out anyone that crossed him then finish it at home on the wife and kids. So they said, anyway. But they stuck with him so I reckon that's just talk. Still, the wife went. But then, who knows about women?'

Billy made the expected response to this well-worn sally, adding, 'I'm surprised they've hung onto the property if he's a grog artist.'

Henry shook his head. 'Not any more. Quit about the time his wife left, according to my old man. He had the fuel depot in town then and knew everyone – not that he'd of sold much to Blake.

Back then most of the droving was done with pack-horses. Why the interest anyhow?'

'No reason,' Billy shrugged. 'Just getting a handle on things. Everybody seems to know everybody else – even if you don't set eyes on each other above a coupla times a year. I'm just trying to catch up. Takes a while to learn a district.'

Henry laughed, his big-nosed profile sharp against the darkening sky. 'Yeah, well, thing to remember about this one is that most everybody's related. Not the Reillys, though. But it ain't safe to pick a fight with them either 'cause there's still Blake to contend with.'

Next morning they were in Southbend a little after sun-up but others were there before them. The racecourse was on the Common at the northern end of town and the trucks and horse floats scattered about showed where those with greater distances to cover had camped overnight. A working bee was already in progress thatching the roof of a makeshift bar and that of the horse stalls with fresh boughs, and hammering in a complicated pattern of steel pegs on a graded section of track. Billy pitched in with the others. The balding, freckle-headed publican was there supervising the erection of the bar, and an overweight policeman had parked near the gate and was slouched against the door of his vehicle. Billy noted him in passing but he'd long outgrown his fear of the police.

'Lazy sod that Sam Bullen,' Henry said as the two of them carried a table past the man. 'Runs the gambling in town. Hey, you gunna lend a hand, Sam? Told you,' he added when he was ignored. 'He'll stand around all day without lifting a finger – because he's on duty. Offer to buy him a drink and see how fast he forgets the fact.'

There was a copper heating at the rear of the tea stall being organised by a large fat woman with fading red hair who was assisted by a girl, obviously her daughter. 'Vi and Casey Walker,' Henry said, the first of many new names Billy was to hear that day. Between unloading metal chairs and helping load a zinc bathtub behind the bar with great slabs of chopped ice, he kept an eye peeled for the Wildhorse Creek party and was at last rewarded with the sight of Jo coming at a run through the gate leading a pretty piebald mare with a cropped mane and neatly shaped tail. She wore a checked shirt and a creamy-coloured felt hat above tight-fitting jeans and a new-looking belt. The piebald flicked nervous ears, moving in startled shies, her tail at half-cock. Billy tumbled his freezing burden into the tub and wiped his hands on his jeans. He turned to go and felt a tap on his shoulder.

'Half a mo, young fella.' It was the publican, whose shoulder had suddenly acquired a pink and grey bird that put up its crest and screeched at the younger man.

'Shut it, Bluey,' the man reached a spatulate finger to stroke the bird, which made a chirring sound in its beak. ''Fore you go mate, we need another hand for the grog.'

'Yeah, sure.' Billy turned back. It took four of them to transport the huge cooler of canned beer and the crate of bottles from the truck to the shed and by then, Alex Cooper's voice was ringing through the megaphone, calling contestants for the first race. Setting aside his first impulse to speak with Jo, Billy jogged to the stalls where the roan Fidget was waiting.

39

Six

It was an instructive day. Billy soon found himself caught up in the general high spirits and hilarity of the occasion. The events were conducted in heats to accommodate all those who wished to enter, and it was simply a matter of watching the first heat run off to learn what was required.

None of the tasks seemed too demanding of skill or effort for a competent rider – but all were complicated by the increasing restiveness of mounts unused to crowds and excitement. Galloping a hundred yards, then jumping off and remounting an excited horse while holding a full billycan of water and beating everyone back over the starting line without spilling it sounded easy – until you tried. Billycans were lost, dropped, trampled underfoot. Dan's horse bolted with its ears pinned flat, and others bucked or shied into the rails. Billy made it back with two inches of water remaining but the race went to a slower rider whose billycan was slightly fuller.

Girls as well as men rode. He saw Jo Reilly on a long-backed bay gelding with four white socks, a thin girl with fiery red hair on an ugly grey gelding, and the redhead from the tea stall riding a high-headed black.

In the Gretna there were more spills than ever, few station horses being accustomed to carrying a second rider. While men were thrown, or clung cursing to the cantles of bucking and bolting mounts, Jo Reilly, in the saddle of her piebald, with the slim dark-haired figure of her elder brother behind her, came home the winner.

Afterwards she found Billy by the rails, rubbing a bruised leg, for he and Dan had fared no better in the race than the rest.

'Billy!' Her face was animated, the blue eyes brilliant under the clear winter sky. 'I saw you a while ago. This is my brother Simon. Was that you on the roan? What'd you *do* to it?'

Billy looked pained. 'Me? Nothing! It was Dan. The idiot was wearing spurs. He hit her with them too.' He thrust out his hand to encounter a sinewy grip. 'Billy Martin.'

'Jo told me.' His eyes were grey, the cheekbones high in his lean face. 'Thanks for helping her out the other day.'

Billy shrugged. 'That's all right. Anybody would've.'

'It was you that did.' Simon's gaze slid to the leg he was favouring. 'As to Dan – you'll know next time.' His smile was a fleeting thing, slow to dawn and quickly gone. 'I never yet met a Burch with any horse sense.'

'Never mind, there's still the peg races,' Jo said. 'Have you put your name down for them?'

'You bet. She might play up carrying double but she can turn on the edge of a coin . . .' Billy began but Jo was looking beyond him.

'I've gotta catch Cub.' She darted off, calling over her shoulder, 'See you later, Billy.'

Disappointed, he watched her fall into step with a larger, masculine version of herself, down to the same cream-coloured hat. Their heads vanished into the crowd – there must be, Billy thought, counting the kids who seemed to be everywhere, close to a hundred people present. It was a vast increase on his daily encounters with the same half-dozen the stock camps and homesteads supported. It created a kaleidoscopic effect that the purposeful bustle did little to dispel. Then the megaphone crackled into renewed life and it was time to line up for the next event.

At least the peg races – figure of eight, bending and flag – were less rowdy. Billy placed second in the first, beaten by Axel Cooper riding his camp-horse, and found himself being congratulated by Rachel as he led the sweating Fidget from the course.

'Well done!' She wore a pink dress and a wide-brimmed hat beneath which her pansy-brown eyes sparkled excitedly.

'Thanks.' He grinned, 'She's a good mare. Lightning in her feet.'

'I like that,' she said, 'that you give the horse credit.' She smiled at him. 'There'll be a prize giving at the dance – you'll qualify for a ribbon – are you going?'

'Doubt it. Not much in my line, dancing. What about you?' He bit his tongue then but the words were out. He studiously avoided glancing down at the brace and heavy boot but felt himself flush as if he had.

'Everybody goes,' she said composedly, 'even the little kids. Anyway you could learn – to dance I mean. Didn't they have them wherever it was you grew up?'

His face closed, the brown eyes, a darker shade than hers, suddenly hard and wary-looking in the soft sunlight. 'I daresay. But I never went.' Abruptly he pulled the mare away, heading for the stalls behind the grandstand. When she saw him again a little later he was lining up with the rest of the early lunch crowd to buy a hamburger and tea, served in a foam cup from the now furiously boiling copper.

The bareback race was the last item of the day's program. 'And a good thing too,' Jo said. She'd returned with her twin in tow to find Billy, and the three of them were seated in the shabby grandstand, drinking stewed tea and eating rather dry buns in which the margarine had melted, while the last of the under tens foot races were run off.

'How's that?' Billy asked.

'They'd knock too many riders out if they ran it earlier. Be down on their numbers for the other events.'

'Cynic,' Cub protested. 'It's not that bad. Might get a sprained wrist or two from busters, and somebody broke his arm one year. That's hardly wholesale slaughter.'

'What about Eddie Gleeson? He broke his leg.'

'His own fault. Who's he kidding – at his age?' Cub retorted. 'Anyway he couldn't ride it in a saddle let alone bareback.'

'So have you tried it?' Billy asked.

The thick, fair brows rose. 'Do us a favour, mate. At my weight?

43

Against Simon? You'll see what I mean. 'Course you haven't seen him ride but he's magic with horses old Si. He's won the last three Crystals. Do it again today too, with the mare he's brought down.'

Billy was turning the odd name over in his head, 'Why's it called that?'

'For the prize, which is a piece of crystal,' Jo explained. 'And *that's* because it's run to honour Crystal Blackson who built and ran the first hospital in Southbend way back in the eighteen hundreds when the mines started the first time. She saved a lot of lives and wound up dying of typhus in nineteen oh two, I think. The Jockey Club dedicated the race to her, but it's not run to proper rules so they changed it to a novelty event in the Sports program. You'll hear it called the Ladies Race, too. That's a sort of local tradition. The riders wear their girl's scarf – kind of like the old knights were supposed to – carrying a lady's favour. If you haven't got anyone – girlfriend, sister, mother – then you can't keep the prize if you win because it's meant for a female.' She smiled, the scar a white dimple in her cheek. 'Old Si's got me three prizes so far. I'll show you the best place to watch it from,' she pointed her cup at the egg and spoon race going on before them, 'soon as this lot's done.'

'I'll be in that.'

A little redhead in sturdy boots won and Jo jumped up. 'They're getting ready for it now. Sam Bullen's the starter. There's Dan pulling his saddle off – he must be going in it too.'

'The bloke's a nutter,' Cub said. 'How many ringers get their teeth kicked out? He's the only one I know of. There're five-year-olds with more sense than him.'

'What does that make your brother, then?' Billy asked. 'How many times did you say he'd won it?'

Cub grinned. 'Point is, mate, Simon knows what he's doing. Just wait, you'll see.'

'Not if we don't shift ourselves.' Jo stood up. 'C'mon, before somebody else grabs our possie.'

It was a good vantage place that she led them to – a mound of dirt once pushed up as a makeshift loading ramp, its rawness cloaked with a cover of grass. From this elevation they could see halfway down to the Rainsford, a matter, Billy estimated, of a couple of furlong.

Across the heads of the crowd rapidly forming beside the road, Cub was counting the riders as each horse appeared. 'There's Si, and Dan; that's Scratchy on the chestnut, dunno the long bloke but he'll be lucky to make the start the way his horse is going. 'Nother stranger, big bloke too – what?' The call had come from behind and he turned to see Rachel smiling hopefully up at him from the foot of the mound.

'Can you give me a hand, Cub? I want to see too.'

It was the first time Billy had ever heard her ask for help, although the slippery nature of the dry grass probably made it very necessary. She was holding her hat on with one hand, her brown eyes fixed on Cub, who said something under his breath, then jumped down to assist. Billy, facing forward as the starters formed a line across the road, saw Jo roll her eyes, then a ragged yell went up as the horses thundered away.

Jo was finishing Cub's count. 'Eight, nine, ten!' she yelled as they flashed past. 'Si's in front. Dan's at the back – he was almost off then.' Rachel had joined them and her excited voice chimed with the rest as the crowd below was swelled by latecomers from the bar clutching beer tins as they ran. The air was full of dust and through it came a last glimpse of the riders vanishing into the bushy bauhinia scrub and waist-high burr where the erosion gullies known as breakaways seamed the river's flood banks.

'Dan's off,' Jo shrieked as a riderless horse cantered into sight, reins dragging.

'Two of 'em have taken the road.' Cub shook his head. 'They're out of it then. Yep, there's another one off. The big chestnut, I think, baulked at a jump. Spurs aren't allowed so the horses get a bit of a say in what they will and won't tackle.'

'How,' Billy said practically, 'do you know they all go the full distance? To the riverbank you said – but which part of it?'

'The water's edge. All four feet in the water, that's the rule. And Misery Jones is down there checking they do. The storekeeper,' he added, by way of explanation.

'Here they come!' Rachel shrieked, grabbing Cub's arm as the first of the returning riders burst into view. Dan appeared at the same moment, limping out of the burrs. The megaphone boomed urgently and the crowd pressed back as the lead flashed towards them in a thunder of brown and bay. Two of the riders were hatless, and the sleeve of one's shirt flapped loose where it had ripped on a passing branch. The foremost rider was crouched as if glued there, over the withers of a dark horse whose shoulders were sheeted with sweat. He flashed by too fast for Billy to see who it was.

'Is that him?' He had to shout to make himself heard.

'Yes!' Jo was jumping with excitement.

She grabbed her twin who bellowed, 'Told you! He did it,' at Billy. Then heedless of the footing both plunged down the mound and ran for the judge's stand where, once the riders succeeded in slowing their excited mounts, the winner would claim the race.

Billy, about to follow, caught sight of Rachel and recognised that without help, she would be unable to descend from the mound.

'I'll give you a hand down, if you want,' he said gruffly.

'Thanks.' She had looked, for an instant, almost frozen by her plight, and he was glad he had offered before she had to ask. Once before, soon after meeting her, he had volunteered assistance with a gate, only to be told firmly that she was lame, not helpless, and had been careful since not to re-offend. But she probably felt her crippled state more keenly today, with so much physical activity about.

'Thanks,' she repeated thinly, when they were on level ground again. The crowd had broken up, and here and there about the grounds kids were being rounded up and horses unsaddled. 'Time to leave. I'd better find Mum.' She hesitated, 'If you run into the twins again, tell Cub I'll see him at the dance.'

'Yeah, sure.' And it was only as he watched her limp away in search of her mother and sister that he remembered what Jo had said of Rachel being 'mad about Cub'. It explained why she had rolled her eyes at the other girl's appearance, as well as the stricken look he had momentarily glimpsed on Rachel's face at Cub, and his sister's precipitous departure. He felt suddenly sorry for her – but not sufficiently enough not to be glad of the excuse she'd given him to seek out the twins again to deliver Rachel's message.

Seven

By day's end Billy, Henry and the rest of the men were back at the Mount, unloading the horses and saddlery in the last light. They ate a hurried meal in a gale of shouted talk and reminiscences, filling in the details of their outing for Tiny on who had been present, and who had won what, and then headed for the bathroom. Dan wasn't returning for the dance. His knee had blown up like a football when he fell in the gully. He could scarcely walk, let alone dance.

'You coming, Billy?' Henry asked. They were going in his vehicle. The head stockman and his wife would travel in their own, while the Coopers, including Daphne and her fiancé – a young estate agent up from Harditch, three hundred miles to the south, would be following later in the evening.

'Might as well.' Hurriedly applying polish to his boots, Billy wondered at his decision. He'd be a fish out of water, but he hadn't hesitated when Jo had asked if she'd see him there. She could probably, he thought gloomily, dance like a ballerina. Girls seemed to learn that sort of stuff – at least the only girl he'd ever taken out before had never tired of trying to drag him to the Saturday night hops in Rockhampton where he'd worked briefly, as a strapper, in a racing stable.

The Southbend hall was in fact nothing so glamorous, being a large tin shed with a raised wooden floor and a narrow supper room partitioned off down one side. Banks of louvres, firmly shut against the chilly winter night, provided ventilation in summer, and the entrance was through double doors above the steps. The walls were hung with streamers and balloons and on a raised dais at the far end a woman on a piano and a man playing an accordion provided the music.

Billy paid at the door then stood about feeling self-conscious. The bench seats along the wall were filling up with family groups – everything from obvious grandmothers to babies. Children chased and shouted along the room's edge and a small ginger-haired girl of about ten scowled from the end of a bench to which a puppy was tied. He recognised her as the sturdily booted winner of the last novelty race. Amused, Billy watched the little play of events. The puppy lay against the girl's feet, chewing happily on the tongue of her shoe, while she resisted the efforts of several adults – including the large woman from the tea stall – to have it taken outside.

'I see you made it,' a voice said and his heart gave a quick leap of recognition as he turned to see Jo shining beside him. Her blonde hair looked freshly washed and she wore a wide-necked green dress that showed off her tanned arms. She smiled and passed on, saying something to Cub who had entered with her. Debonair in a white shirt and tie, his hatless head gleaming under the lights, he reached for her hand and they joined the half-dozen couples already circling the floor. Billy studied them enviously as the room filled and the volume of chatter rose.

More and more couples stood up as the music changed to a livelier beat. There seemed to be equal numbers of women and men but only a handful of girls, and the flock of young men with their greased hair and sunbaked skins kept them busy. Jo moved from partner to partner without pause, the fair hair and green dress a magnet for Billy's eyes. So busy was he watching her that Rachel's voice in his ear made him start in surprise.

'I thought you weren't coming?' The flower pinned in her brown hair matched her dress. She still wore the brace and boot but her sound foot, clad in a dainty sandal, tapped to the music.

Billy shrugged. 'Changed my mind. Bit dull being alone.' It crossed his mind then that he'd spent most of his life that way, making acquaintances but never friends – except for Ivy. And that had been a gradual thing, nothing like the sudden pull that Jo's company exerted. He felt suddenly glad to see his boss's daughter. They had nothing in common beyond a shared interest in horses, but he'd feel less of a dork sitting with her than by himself.

'Who's the kid with the ginger hair? The one dancing with the little skinny bloke? She's got a pup with her – it's tied up to the bench over there.'

Rachel raised her brows. 'I can well believe it. Ken Walker's youngest, Ants. That's him dancing with her now.'

'Ants?'

'Short for Antoinette. *All* the Walker girls have fancy names,'

Rachel said tolerantly. 'I reckon Vi, that's his wife, knew they'd never have a bean, but names are like dreams, aren't they? Dead cheap. See Ben, there? Well that's Charlotte Gwendolyn going round with him,' her flicked finger indicated the thin, fiery-headed rider of the grey whom Billy had noticed earlier that day. 'Of course they call her Charlie instead. And the oldest girl's Kathleen Caroline shortened to her initials, so she's Casey. That's her with Cub,' Rachel said, and Billy could not decide if it was pain or envy he heard in her voice as his gaze sought out and identified the two. It was the other girl from the tea stall, generous figured and happy faced, her hair the same ginger as her younger sister's. 'It was a waste really – the fancy names – they're never used.'

Billy frowned remembering the map he'd seen. 'How come they're so hard up if Ken owns Rumhole?'

'Huh! Him and the banks, you mean,' Rachel said dryly. 'What he owns is a mountain of debt. He's not even a cattleman – just a trucker who switched jobs. Now he's got to fence the place I don't know how he'll manage to hang on.'

Billy's thoughts had shifted. 'What about Blake Reilly? Henry was telling me about him. Is he here tonight?'

She shook her head. 'He could be over at the pub, but he doesn't come to town much.'

The dance ended and across the clearing floor Billy saw Axel Cooper making for the dais. In the shuffle of movement about the benches as people reclaimed their seats, somebody trod on the pup's tail, eliciting a high-pitched yelp that cut across the rising hubbub. With awkward haste Rachel got up.

'Damn! I forgot to sort the prizes. I better get over there.' She hobbled away. Billy, watching the Reillys drift together on the opposite benches, seized his chance and sauntered across the floor, lengthening his stride as the seats about them were taken. There was a space left beside Simon. He slipped into it and was greeted by name.

'Enjoying yourself?' Jo asked. Her blue eyes were sparkling. She sat between her brothers with the girl called Casey on the far side of Cub. He introduced his partner.

'Hi, Billy.' She had a freckled face and wide hazel eyes. 'I didn't see you on the floor.'

'Can't dance.'

'Casey'll teach you,' Cub volunteered. Then Jo hushed him as Axel coughed and began speaking.

The prizes were given out to good-humoured or ironic applause. Everybody knew what they'd won and Rachel, deft in the background, had the right ribbon or envelope to hand as each name was called. Billy paraded self-consciously across the boards to collect his own sash that he immediately folded small and shoved into his pocket. The last of all to be given out was for the Ladies Race and Simon, neat footed in light shoes, as opposed to the boots worn by most of the males present, had gone to the dais to receive his prize – a miniature crystal bowl.

'This is getting monotonous,' Axel Cooper declared with bluff good humour as he presented it and shook hands. 'That makes four in a row by my count. When does somebody else get a chance?'

Simon leaned forward to accept the prize, which brought him

52

close enough to the microphone to allow his rejoinder to be heard by all. 'Any time they're better than me.' No smile accompanied the words. They fell into silence and he'd turned away before Axel began belatedly to clap. A few others joined in but the applause quickly died. Jo glanced at him as he took his seat again, lips twitching and one eyebrow raised.

'Whoops! You dropped a clanger there, Si. They didn't like that one bit.' She lifted the lid of the box containing the bowl and admired her prize. 'Oh, nice. Far too good to waste on anyone round here.'

'Stuff 'em!' The words were softly said, then Simon breathed out sharply and seemed to relax. 'Ah, it's not worth it. Who needs their approval, anyway? I'll still get the rides, and they'll still ask you to dance. Let 'em think what they want – they always have.'

Billy, a party to the low exchange, swallowed his surprise. Knowing how yarns grew in the telling he had only half believed Henry's account of the Reillys' standing in the district, which the day's events had seemed to contradict. Nobody had shunned them. And neither Jo nor her brothers had lacked partners all evening. But he had become conscious of a certain aloofness about them. A willingness to ignore others and gravitate together, as if their own company suited them better than that of their neighbours.

Something changed in Billy's perception. They had lived among these people for years. Hadn't Jo, in fact, claimed it as the twins' birthplace? But they were outsiders still – as he himself had always been. The knowledge forged a link as strong as any attraction he felt for the friendly scar-faced girl getting up again to dance, this time with Ben Cooper, who ignored her brothers as if they didn't exist. The girl, Casey, had risen too and to Billy's alarm was reaching purposefully for his hand.

'Come on, then,' she said, one foot restlessly marking the beat. 'Cub said to show you how it's done.'

Eight

By daybreak the stock camp was back at the Number Three yards, dopey and out of sorts from the late night. They'd had two hours' sleep – at the most – Billy thought before they were dragged out again for breakfast and the drive to the camp where cattle waited in the holding paddock for their test to be read. He stuck frozen hands in his pockets and yawned, shivering in the predawn chill. He supposed it beat working on a fenceline.

They had passed the fencers' camp on the way out, a huddle of vehicles about the pale shape of a fly-rig. Light from the campfire had glinted on the nearby wire dump and the formless shape of men squatting around the fire as they ate.

There must be dozens of contractors building fences across the country, Billy thought. The stations had no choice in the matter for paddocks were the only way to quarantine tested cattle from the bulk of the untested herd. And only tested cattle, with the tail tag to prove it, could be sold, and then only to the meatworks. So the graziers had either to comply with government requirements or lose their income. Little wonder then that the BTEC program was so unpopular with cattlemen. Apart from the massive expense of implementing the necessary infrastructure, such control lowered the already depressed beef market, for when there was but one outlet for the grazier's product there could be no competition. It was the biggest change the country had seen since cattle first trod the Gulf soil – and there were plenty of pessimists to see within it the destruction of the northern cattle industry.

That seemed an unlikely outcome to Billy. There was nothing but cattle in the north after all – and a bit of ore, he supposed. They ran fourteen thousand head on the Mount alone, and, according to Dan, about thirty-five thousand on Rainsford Downs.

'Yeah?' Billy was impressed by the numbers. 'What about Wildhorse Creek?'

'Who knows?' Dan grinned, showing his missing teeth. 'Not something a Reilly'd be telling you, given how quick the herd's grown.' This was a dig at their poddy-dodging prowess. 'But they'll make out okay. 'S'little blokes'll like old Ken over at Rumhole'll be wiped out. He wants to sell anything he'll 'ave to fence and test. So what the banks don't own already, the agents soon will.'

'The vets are making a quid, any road,' Henry said. 'Sam was talking of buying a plane the other day. He's already got his licence, said he spends more time driving between jobs than working these days. He wants to get there quicker. Makes sense, I suppose.'

Sam Carson was the veterinarian handling the testing at the Mount and on half a dozen other properties as well. Dan hawked and spat dust from his throat then wiped his mouth on his dirty sleeve. 'He's making his fortune while silly buggers like us wear out our tailbones for next to nuthin'. You gunna open that gate, Ben, or you waiting for 'em to knock it down?'

At about the same time another conversation that would concern Billy was taking place between Simon Reilly and his father. The elder Reilly was a big man, flat bellied still despite his years, with thickly muscled shoulders and heavy forearms. He moved lightly for a large man but with deliberation too. There was no discernable warmth in his flat delivery or hard glance, though the fact never seemed to ruffle Simon who had long since ceased to expect it.

The two, squatting on their heels in the shade of a dinner camp tree, were drinking tea and studying a rough map Blake had sketched with a stick in the patch of dirt between them. It showed the projected outline of two paddocks, both of which hinged upon the erection of a stretch of boundary fencing between the Brumby and Rainsford.

'There's a stock yard already in place for both of them,' Blake said, 'and water enough. Besides, doing it this way a quarter of each paddock gets paid for by Rainsford.'

'Half paid for,' Simon objected. 'We'll have to foot our share of the boundary.'

'Try listening,' Blake growled. 'The way we'll do it – I'll make Bennett a proposition. Rainsford buys the material and we stand the fence.' He gave a bark of amusement. 'That ought to suit the bugger. He's wanted us fenced off from his stock since he got the management of the joint.'

'He ought to go for it,' Simon conceded. 'All the same, two pad-docks – it's a lot of work. We'll need to put somebody on the books to get it done. Even then the Wet'll beat us. Just clearing the line alone . . .' he let the words die.

'Like who? You find somebody,' Blake grunted, 'and I'll hire him. But I don't like your chances.'

It was true enough. None of the local men had ever approached Blake Reilly for a job, nor until now had they ever needed them as the four of them were sufficient to work the place.

Simon stirred the map with a twig then snapped it between his fingers as he looked up, his face clearing, 'There's someone – new to the district. Young bloke I met at the Sports. Billy – Martin, I think. He's got a job at the Mount. But we don't need anyone till the stock work's done. When the season ends it might be worth try-ing him, see if he'll come.'

'If he'll work.' Blake stood to clap his quart pot back in its cradle and scrape dirt over the fire. 'Money'll be tight enough from now on without carrying some useless bugger.'

'He's not that,' Simon said confidently. 'There's the look of a worker about him. Good hands on a horse too.' He unhooked the reins and gathered them either side of his mount's neck, grey eyes suddenly thoughtful. 'You know Bennett at least should be happy with BTEC – even if nobody else is.'

'He's got rocks in his head then,' Blake grumbled. 'Fencing might make him feel better about having us on his boundary but in the long run it'll cost the company more than if every man jack in the district was getting his poddies.'

'There's that angle too, but it's not what I meant. There's just no point now, is there, in pinching them? Not when you could be introducing disease onto the place from your neighbour's herd.' His quick grin flashed and was gone. 'Bit of a joke when you think about it. The government does nothing for this part of the country, never has, and now, purely by default, they're gunna do away with poddy-dodging. I wonder if Bennett's worked that out yet?'

Now that winter had receded the daylight came fractionally earlier with each dawn. Billy, heading down to the stables next morning, sniffed appreciatively at the cool air, which smelt faintly of dust and heavily of nectar from the flowering gums behind the quarters. The flying foxes quarrelled in them all night long and he, for one, would be glad when the blossom dropped. Amid the taller river timber a smudge of mist hung like pale smoke between the branches. The diesel sounded its background throb from the engine shed and beyond the station complex where the horse paddock spread across the open plain two brolgas stalked, dove grey against the whitened grass.

Gaynor nickered softly as he entered the stable, turning large, dark eyes upon him. As always he admired the lean beauty of her head, and the elegant grace with which she moved. She'd been purchased the year before at the Brisbane Yearling Sales, and her breeding, he knew, was of the best. Axel had named her for both her dam Gay Star and her sire North Wind whose blood, he had told Billy, could be traced back to the great Tulloch. Billy, who cared nothing for that, simply loved her for her bay beauty and kindly nature.

'Hello girl. How's the lady today?' He ran a hand up her neck crooning gentle love words as he held the bridle for her to take the bit. Sometimes Axel came down for the morning training session, but not always. He liked it best when there was just him and the mare alone with the dawn. She wasn't a stock horse, of course, but she was eager and responsive to his hands. It was no hardship to hack her about the paddock to settle her before taking her through the prescribed training routine.

Perched on the tiny racing pad, so different from the normal stock saddle, he patted her proudly again. 'Ah, you'll eat 'em up come Saturday week. Leave the whole field for dead, won't you?' Gaynor snorted softly, ears flicking back to the sound of his voice.

The Coopers, father and son, were waiting when he brought the mare back. Billy took his feet from the irons, slid down, and pulled the pad from her sweaty back.

'Went like a dream, boss,' he said. 'Hi, Ben.' Bending, he picked up Gaynor's near front foot. 'I thought so – heard it clacking. Shoe's loose – it's worn through. You want me to tack another on?'

To his surprise Axel shook his head. 'That's all right, Ben can do it. She's his now. If he's running her he might as well shoe her – hey, son?'

'Yeah.' Ben caught Billy's expression and his smile was wry. 'She's my birthday present. We're celebrating with a barbecue Saturday night. Everyone's invited, Billy, so tell the blokes, will you – just in case they're planning to head off to the pub?'

'Okay, thanks. Well, happy birthday, Ben. You want me to keep on with the training then, boss?'

'Of course. She's used to you – and Ben's a bit heavy.'

And he's likely to fall off, Billy thought uncharitably. He walked back to the kitchen where the bell had already rung for breakfast, trying to decide if he was more flabbergasted by Cooper's casual disposal of the beautiful mare, or jealous of his son for being the recipient.

For once it was a short day. The vet arrived and the cattle, already yarded, were run back through the crush where the skin under their tails was checked for the telltale lump that heralded a positive reaction. None occurring, the mob was taken back out to the Number Three paddock and the men were home and unsaddled again in time for a very late lunch, with the rest of the afternoon to themselves. It was the usual pattern. Few stations paid overtime but a run of long days were made up for by a considerate boss, with time off in lieu.

Billy did his washing, polished his boots, and sought out Tiny for a haircut. The massive cook had trouble fitting his fingers through the scissor loops but he cut hair like a professional. Admiring the results in a hand mirror, Billy thanked him and brushed off his shaven neck. Then finding himself at a loose end he wandered down to the stable where Ben was replacing Gaynor's front shoe.

The mare was playing up, eyes rolling whitely as she jerked at the hands holding her foot. Ben swore and dropped it to grab the reins as the mare backed restively into the corner of the open-sided stall. 'What's wrong with you?' Puzzled, he gave her a perfunctory pat while the shoe, secured only by one nail and that not fully driven in, flopped about loosely. Billy watched him pick the foot up again, not running his hand down her leg to soothe her as he would have done, but snatching impatiently at the pastern so that she jerked nervously away. In doing so her rump touched the wall and she bounded forward, sending him sprawling on his back in the stall.

Billy laughed. He couldn't help himself; it was at once so comical and so typical of Ben's way with horses. He put his hand on the gate and swung it open. 'Here,' he said, 'she knows me. I'll tack it on for you.'

Ben's face was red – from exertion or mortification, or both. The half-driven nail had torn the flesh between thumb and forefinger as he fell and blood dripped onto the wet patch on his jeans that had made contact with a pile of fresh dung. Hissing with pain he sucked at his hand, turning on Billy with sudden uncharacteristic fury.

'Mind your own bloody business, why don't you? You might be Dad's blue-eyed boy but, little though you may think it, I *am* capable of shoeing a horse! So just bugger off and let me get on with it.'

Billy shrugged and went. Afterwards he would ask himself what else he could have done, but he always came up with the same answer – nothing. Except perhaps not to have laughed. He salved his conscience with the thought that it was as much Axel Cooper's responsibility as his – he should have known better than to entrust the task to his son. Still, Billy could've gone back himself, and might've, but for that crack Ben had thrown at him.

Of course it would be easy to be jealous of anyone reasonably competent, he supposed, if you were as driven and useless as Ben – but that didn't make the accusation any more palatable. Repeating Dan's mantra to himself, *Not my business. I just work here, mate,* he'd left. And what followed was, in a way, inevitable.

Nine

When Billy entered the stables next morning he knew the moment he clapped eyes on Gaynor that something was wrong. There was no whicker of greeting. Instead the mare stood listlessly, head down, favouring her near front foot. Billy dropped the bridle and stooping to examine it, found the fetlock swollen, and hot to the touch. She flinched when he bent it, jerking back with a little snort. He lowered it gently and she scrabbled for balance on three legs.

'Whoa, girl. What's up?' Perplexed he ran his hands down her near cannon while she trembled and snorted against his hat. 'I dunno. Let's get that shoe off, then we'll get the boss down. How's that, eh?'

It was the work of a moment to fetch the tools although it took patience and a good deal longer to rasp through the crimped nail ends and pull the shoe free. Gaynor whinnied with pain as it came off. A fine sweat dampened her neck along the line of her mane, and Billy saw that her previous evening's feed was untouched.

He spent a moment gentling her with hands and speech before

stooping again to recapture the foot. 'There, steady lass,' he murmured, 'not gunna hurt you. I'll just have a look.' One handed, he fumbled his stock-knife free and used the back of it to scrape away the dirt and powdered dung to verify what he'd already guessed. Black blood oozed from a nail hole positioned too far in from the rim of the hoof. It had gone in at the wrong angle. Ben, the useless bastard, had pricked her – nailing into the quick of the hoof instead of the painless shell. And then left her standing on it all night.

Billy drew a deep breath as if air could quench the anger within him, and set the foot gently back to earth. He put the bridle and pad away, dumped the tools back in the little side shed where the feed was kept, and then set off for the Big House.

Axel met him at the gate, a tall figure in moleskins and cotton shirt, looking well pleased with the day.

''Morning, Billy.' His brows rose momentarily. 'Anything wrong? You're not through with the gallops already?'

'Haven't started.' It was an effort to get the words out. 'Where's Ben?'

'In the kitchen I should think. What—'

'The mare's in the stable – you should have a look at her.' Billy spoke without pausing in his stride. He went through the low gate, crossed the scrappy lawn worn by the to-ing and fro-ing of many boots to the kitchen door, and yanked it open. The breakfast bell had not yet rung. Tiny was at the stove, his back to the door, and Ben and Garry were cutting their lunches at the table. They both looked up as he entered and Garry's eyes suddenly narrowed.

'Hey, what's up with you?'

Billy had his gaze fixed on Ben. 'Who gave Gaynor her feed last night?'

'I did,' Ben said blankly. 'So what?' He cut a slice of beef and laid it on the bread.

'So how was she?'

'Okay.' He shrugged, mystified. 'Why wouldn't she be?'

'You mean you dumped the stuff in her feeder and didn't even check, you useless bastard,' Billy yelled, his anger spewing forth like lava. He had never hit anyone before but he did now. There was a meaty smack, a cry of mingled pain and astonishment, and Ben's nose blossomed scarlet. He staggered and fell. 'I'll tell you how she is,' Billy roared, following him down with another punch that found, not Ben's jaw as he had intended, but his shoulder, 'she's crippled, that's how she is. Because you can't even nail a shoe on without making a balls of it.'

Somebody was shouting, and Ben, recovering, punched furiously upwards, his knuckles stinging Billy's ear. He shook his head, blocking another punch, more by luck than instinct, and was hitting back when an irresistible force pulled him upright and spun him around in a complicated hold that made it impossible to move.

'You gunna calm down?' Tiny's breath was in his ear.

Ben was rising with Garry's help, holding a tea towel the latter had grabbed off the table, to his nose. He looked groggy, Billy saw, as well as angry and guilt stricken. *And well he bloody might.* All the same the spurt of rage within him suddenly peaked and Tiny, feeling the slackening of his muscles, let him go.

'What the hell d'you think you're playing at, Martin?' Garry shoved Ben down onto the bench, his usual placidity broken. 'Busting in here like a cyclone—'

'Save it,' Billy said tersely. 'I'm quitting. You might have to put up with him,' he added contemptuously, 'but I don't. I'll tell the boss to make up my time.'

Ben stood unsteadily and Billy tensed himself, but attack was the last thing on the other man's mind. His voice came thickly through the reddened cloth, 'I never meant – she's not seriously hurt, is she?'

Too angry to recognise the horror in the thickened words Billy said cruelly, 'No worse than a hawk with its wing torn off. But I shouldn't let it worry you. The station's got plenty more.'

The mail was not due for another two days, so Axel himself drove Billy the thirty miles into Southbend. He had collected his cheque at the office, the first time he had set foot in the Big House in the six months he had worked on the property. Axel had said little beyond telling him he'd run him to town then asking him if he was certain he didn't want to work out his notice.

'No. Dock my pay.' Billy just wanted to be gone. Despite telling himself that it was none of his business now, he added, 'Will Gaynor be okay?'

'Well she certainly won't be racing next week.' The set of Axel's mouth hardened. 'I caught Sam before he left town – he'll be back here tonight and he's bringing a tetanus injection and some antibiotics. That should stop the infection.'

'I hope so.' Billy pocketed his cheque and abruptly turned away. 'Thanks boss. Sorry if I've left you in the lurch. I'll get my gear.'

Rachel was approaching the steps as he descended them. He had no desire to talk to her but grunted a terse greeting as he made to pass.

'What's going on?' She caught his arm, her dark eyes wide. 'Tiny said you were leaving?'

'That's right. Getting a lift into the 'Bend this morning. I suppose I'll see you round town sometime.'

'But – what happened, Billy? Why—?'

'Go look in the stables,' he answered bitterly, 'and ask your useless brother.' Shrugging free of her hand he headed for the quarters where his swag was already rolled.

In Southbend Axel Cooper pulled up at the pub but left the engine running. 'This do you?'

'It's fine.' Billy got out and, hefting his swag onto his shoulder, nodded unsmiling to his ex-boss. 'Thanks for the lift.'

'I'm sorry to lose you,' Cooper said unexpectedly, 'but I understand.' It came as a shock to Billy to learn that the man shared his feelings. He had expected him to be angry, yes – the mare was valuable property, after all – but not to care so deeply, to be outraged to his soul, as he himself was.

'Thanks,' he said simply. He stepped back and the vehicle rolled away, swinging in a wide turn to head back the way it had come. Billy dumped his swag in the shade and sat on it considering his options. He didn't regret his actions, he told himself, but he was still out of work, and as it was mid September, the season would soon be ending. The storms, precursors to the Wet, could, everybody said, start as early as November. After that he'd have to find something in town – not a very likely prospect – or head back to the coast.

Many off-season ringers found employment over summer in the meatworks or the mines, but, whilst knowing it to be unlikely in the present climate of low prices and BTEC demands, he fancied something permanent on a property. His best chance for that lay with a company station. Something like Rainsford Downs. And there was no point in waiting on Keith Guthrie's old mail truck when he could dispatch a message from the pub's radio and get, if he was lucky, if not an immediate reply, then one no later than tomorrow. Settling his hat Billy went into the pub to see Oscar Davies about sending a telegram.

It was mid afternoon before the answer came back. Billy had a beer and a sandwich lunch at the bar, making desultory conversation with his host. The publican was as bald as an egg, save for a few hairs above his ears, and his head sat like a ball between big shoulders and wrestler's arms. His hands were large too, with thick fingers, and his hazel eyes looked out from a high-coloured face. He moved slowly favouring a gammy knee, a tea towel slung over one shoulder and Bluey the galah mostly riding the other.

The bird was a pest. It sidled along the bar top, claws clicking on the wood, to dip its beak into patrons' glasses.

'He's a terror on the 'ops,' Oscar said fondly, watching him, 'ain' cher, you old bastard?'

The galah shrieked and flew back to its owner's shoulder where he nibbled gently at his ear. 'Bastard,' he squawked, lifting his wings, 'Who's a bastard, eh?'

'You are,' Oscar retorted, putting up a hand to scratch his crest. Bluey crooned and leaned into his palm, eyes half closed in ecstasy. Billy yawned, wishing the bookie at Rainsford would switch on and pick up his message.

The return telegram when it came was short and to the point. *SORRY STOP NOTHING DOING STOP BENNETT (MANAGER)*

Sitting on the riverbank where he'd gone for a walk, Billy skimmed pebbles across the dancing sheen of the running water and considered his options. The calm peace of the river distracted him. It was pleasantly cool in the shade of the giant figs, the only sound to break the murmur of moving water that of birds quarrelling over the immature fruits in the branches above him. The flood banks showed how high the river rose in spate. He'd like to see a Wet out, witness at first hand the flood and fury Ivy had spoken of. And abruptly, his decision was made. He'd hang about. Something was bound to turn up.

Sam Bullen, the policeman he'd met on Sports Day, was in the bar along with a couple of crocodile shooters whose battered four-wheel drives, both carrying aluminium boats, were parked outside. Thin, bearded men in salt-faded shorts, they had the skeleton of a huge crocodile head wired to each bull bar, the teeth as thick through as Billy's thumb.

'There y'are,' Oscar said as he stepped into the room. 'Message come through on the blower. Blake Reilly from the Brumby wants a word. Said he'd call back at six.' He nodded at the clock. 'Just on that now. Through the door there – radio's down the end. The call sign's 4BX.'

'Thanks.' Seated before the wireless Billy made the call and was almost blasted from his seat by a gravelly voice replying. 'Wildhorse Creek, standing by.'

'Billy Martin here. You wanted a word?'

'Blake Reilly. You still after a job?'

'Yeah.' Billy's pulse leapt. 'Yeah, you got one going?'

'I'll give you a start, then we'll see,' the heavy voice said curtly. 'Be on the mail. You'll be met at the box. Over and out.'

As easy as that. Billy shoved the chair in and walked jauntily back into the bar in search of the mailman. Oscar caught his eye.

'Get through okay?'

'Yeah. I'll roll my swag out tonight but I'll need a feed. That okay? And where do I find Keith Guthrie?'

Ten

They were gone from the 'Bend by daylight and the sun was up by the time Billy got down for the horse-paddock gate at the Mount. Only Tiny met them. The stock camp was out, he said, and the boss away in Harditch at a producers' meeting. Heading out again, Billy craned his neck as they passed the stables and was rewarded with a sight of Gaynor moving slowly across the yard, favouring her leg. Then they were over the grid into the horse paddock and running through known country until they crossed the creek marking the boundary between the Mount and Rainsford Downs. It was all new country from then on and Billy settled back to enjoy it.

Rainsford, when they reached it, was set in a valley beside the river it was named for with a sweeping view of open plain fringed with distant trees and the purple bulk of a range. The station complex was large and included a gravelled airstrip paralleling the road in, and a tennis court behind the men's quarters. The Big House was painted white and rose on piles; a broad verandah ran around it and palms flanked the steps.

'Yours is the next stop,' Keith re-settled himself behind the wheel, fishing in his shirt pocket for his tobacco.

'We cross the river again here?' Billy eyed the jungle of palms, scrub and vines along the banks.

'Nah. She swings away to the west. Next big water's the Verity and then the Wildhorse. She's a running creek too. Bugger of a thing to get caught behind because most of the water along the border country drains into it. Keeps her up for days when she floods.'

'Pretty country,' Billy said approvingly as they reached the timber, his gaze sweeping over the white trunks of carbean, and a scatter of bauhinia just coming into new pink-tipped growth. The feed was brown or parched white but the cattle looked strong enough still, though far from fat. Beyond the range clouds had built but he judged them to be more decorative than useful. It was too early in the year, and not yet hot enough for rain, despite the warmth of the day, but then it was spring – except, Billy reminded himself, there were only two seasons in the Gulf – the Wet and the Dry.

'It's not bad here,' Keith conceded. 'Bloody rough on the Brumby, but. Most of that stands on end and feeds wallabies. Brancaster's worse – tidal creeks, big crocs and salt flats.'

Billy grinned. He suspected that Keith's dour outlook was a show he put on to conceal his deep kinship with the country. Ivy had been like that, going on and on about the drawbacks of the land she'd left in a tone so wistful that it did nothing to conceal her longing to return to it.

Their next stop was the mailbox at Wildhorse Creek. It was a forty-four-gallon drum lying on its side, on a stand made of four posts. Half of the near end of the drum had been cut out, and hinged into a flap that closed down like a door. It stood alone at the road's edge beneath a beefwood tree. Billy pulled his swag down from the load and swapped over the mailbags.

'He'd said I'd be met.' He cocked his head at the narrow track leading off into the scrub but the air was still, undisturbed by the faintest hum of an engine. 'How far to the station?'

'Twenty-odd mile.' Keith struck a match and the scent of tobacco mingled with the smell of bulldust.

'I can tramp it if I have to.' Billy offered his hand. 'See you round.'

'Yeah.'

The battered Bedford vanished. Billy sat down on his swag, prepared to wait – as he had often done before. He had deliberately obliterated the past from his thoughts, or as much of it as he could, but his present keyed-up expectation, balanced by the need for patience, reminded him forcefully of waiting at the bus depot, nerves a-crawl with hope and dread, the day he'd run away from his grandfather's farm.

Except, he reminded himself, that his boots hadn't fitted then, and beneath his shirt, the flesh of his back had been raw with the buckle cuts of his latest flogging. He'd been quite certain somebody would see him there; that either a cop or the old man himself would come to seize him before he got away. When the bus finally nosed into the kerb he'd been the first aboard though his legs had trembled so badly they would hardly carry him up the steps. And he hadn't drawn a full breath until the town was receding behind him.

Impatient with his wool-gathering, Billy slapped the fly crawling over a scratch on his hand and stood up. Maybe he'd drop Ivy a line tonight. Tell her about his new job and ask her about the Brumby, and Blake. One thing Billy had learned during his time in the Gulf was that nothing was private. Doing business over the public medium of the wireless saw to that. People's ages, their finances, medical histories, and who their creditors were was the everyday gossip of the land. It was therefore surprising that he'd heard so little about his new boss's business.

Five minutes later Simon arrived.

'So you got here.' He was in the Land Rover, his movements sparse and quick as he shook hands, worn cotton shirt patched with sweat. 'I got held up by a broken wire in the horse paddock fence.' It wasn't an apology but a statement of an attitude Billy would become very familiar with. On the Brumby no job was left to a more convenient time. If the fence was down you repaired it, if the tyre was flat you fixed it. Nothing was anybody else's task if you were on the spot.

'Sling your gear on. Cooper finished his mustering already?' It was indirect but Billy answered the unspoken question anyway.

'I pulled out. How much is left to do here?'

'Plenty. But the stock work's just the half of it. Done any fencing before?'

'A bit.' As the vehicle picked up speed Billy had the feeling that that might be about to change.

Simon confirmed it. 'We've a truckload of posts and wire all waiting. There's maybe a week's tidying up with the stock work then we'll start. We'll go through till the rains begin – that could be Christmas, or even later. Depends on the Wet.' He slammed the brakes on for a rocky gully and a wallaby squatting beside it bounded away across a tumble of rocks. Following it, Billy's eyes roved across scrub and scree, and the bony spine of a low range. It looked bloody awful country to be driving steel posts into – but he'd wanted to come. A week or two on the fence line would soon tell him if he wanted to stay.

The Spell paddock lay between the main road and the station. Wildhorse Creek ran through it and on the far bank lay the horse paddock and the station complex with the homestead backed onto the creek. There was a large vehicle shed and two smaller ones, a mill tower and tank, a fowl house and engine room and a little hut beyond the garden fence. The cook's quarter, Simon had told him as they walked through the gate and up the path leading to the kitchen. It sat alone, separated by a covered walkway from the rest of the house – to reduce the risk of fire, Billy knew, kerosene fridges being notoriously unstable in this regard.

A brindle bull terrier with a white chest met them at the gate, the hackles rising along her spine. Billy stopped dead. He'd worked on another property with a dog – a red heeler bitch that'd eat you for breakfast. He had the scars to prove it. She'd even, he remembered, bitten the boss's wife.

'She's okay,' Simon said. 'Sit, Belle. Let her get your smell.'

Billy suffered his hand to be sniffed and then licked but was very conscious of the click of the nails on the path behind him as they continued to the foot of the house steps. Simon pulled the screen door open. 'You can bunk on the verandah when we're home. Dump your stuff and come and meet the cook.'

He was an old half-caste called Suds whose wrinkled face was the colour of saddle leather. Over sixty, Billy guessed. His hair had thinned and silvered, and red veins showed in the yellowed whites of his eyes. Tobacco stains browned his teeth and his inner lip was very pink, incongruous against the darkness of his skin.

'There's some tea,' he indicated the big enamel pot on the hob. 'Help yerself. Cake on the board there.'

'Thanks.' Billy did so. 'Where's everybody?' Simon, murmuring that he'd catch him later, had gone off – presumably to put the vehicle away as Billy had heard it start up again.

'They'll be home come dinnertime. You play crib, boy?'

'A bit.' Card games were a popular pastime in station quarters.

'Good-oh.' Suds pulled a tobacco tin from his pocket, his tongue touching slyly on his upper lip. 'What about poker?'

'Nope. Euchre's more my style. How big's the property? You been here long?'

'Long enough.' The old man finished rolling his cigarette, struck a match to it, then pulled open a drawer in the table's edge to produce a crib board and pack of cards. He shifted the teapot aside and the dark eyes flicked Billy's way. 'Give you a game?'

Seeing that questions would get him nowhere, except perhaps, across the cook, Billy put curiosity aside. 'Why not?' He cut the cards to decide the dealer, gazing around at the unlined walls and uneven flagstoned floor on which the bench he was sitting on rocked when he moved. 'Fills in the time.'

Belle's tail thumping on the concrete pathway beyond the screen door heralded the Reillys' arrival. It was mid afternoon by then and Billy, taking his ease on the bed on the verandah, lifted his head from the cradle of his linked hands to look through the lattice that served as a screen between house and garden. He rolled easily to his feet, picked up his hat and went out and down the steps to meet his new boss.

His first thought was that Blake didn't look that scary – then a closer study of the man's eyes and the hard planes of his face changed his mind. Blake Reilly had an intimidating presence. It wasn't just size or muscle – Billy had met big men before – but an implacability of purpose that showed in his very stance, and in eyes that were colder and of a paler blue than Cub's. Eyes that wanted to make you drop your own. Billy held them with an effort and extended his hand thinking suddenly that it looked slim – girlish almost – compared to the other man's.

'G'day,' he said. 'Glad to meet you. I'm Billy Martin.'

'I worked that out.' Blake's hand made no effort to meet his. Instead, he reached to pull his hat off, and scratch, with his unoccupied fingers, amid his thatch of pale hair. Feeling foolish, Billy lowered his. The others had walked past into the kitchen and Blake stepped after them, dropping words as he went. 'You can make a start tomorrow. We'll get the paperwork squared away when I've had a feed. You got that billy boiled yet, Suds?'

'Nah, I'm cutting hair,' the cook answered crankily, and to Billy standing in the open door, 'Make up your mind, boy – in or out – on'y shut that bloody screen.' Feeling like a spare wheel on a twenty tonner, Billy stepped in. He was thinking he'd had friendlier welcomes when Jo called a greeting, and Cub added one of his own.

'Si told us you'd got here. Make the most of this arvo – last chance to loaf. Cooper must've been working you hard if he's finished his mustering. You want some tea?'

'Yeah, thanks. And, no, he hasn't. There was a row – I pulled out.'

'Who with?' Jo's eyes ran over his face. 'I don't see any bruises.'

'Ben's got them. Useless fool crippled a little mare I was training for Alex. 'Course he didn't mean to,' Billy admitted honestly, 'but I knocked him down.' He shrugged, 'After that, well there wasn't much choice but to quit. I wanted out anyway.'

'Lucky for us then,' Cub put in, 'that's if you're any good on a fence line. What'd Cooper have to say about it?'

'Not a lot. He was pretty mad about the mare. He'd entered her for a race in Harditch this Saturday.'

'No – about you clocking his son.'

'Oh that.' Billy, remembering Gaynor's whiffle of pain as the shoe came off, and the glimpse of her this morning, halting her way across the stable yard, felt his anger kindled anew. 'I reckon he'd liked to have done it himself.'

Eleven

In summer, dawn was the coolest time of day. The pearly light that would later change to a brazen glitter lay softly over the land as the white trunks of the carbean trees about the quarters were touched by the first rays of the rising sun. It was the time of day Alex Cooper loved best. Standing at the top of the homestead steps, looking across the garden to the sheds and stables and paddock beyond, reminded him of his boyhood.

At such times he felt the ghost of his brother Clem beside him. The skinny kid he'd swum and scrapped and worked with down through the years, who'd stood beside him on many such mornings enjoying, as Alex himself always had, in a boy's inarticulate way, the pride and satisfaction of place that came with being a Cooper, and owning the Mount.

Today Alex trod down the steps without pausing, his brow creased in a frown, and crossed to the stables. The antibiotics weren't doing their work. He'd known that since the previous day but the whiff of putrefecation that greeted him as he approached the lame mare confirmed his fears. Sick at heart, he looked at the grotesquely swollen leg and shoulder. Gaynor's whole body had puffed up with the poison in her blood. She was dying on her feet. He'd seen blood poisoning once before and knew that nothing now could save her. Anger at Ben churned in his guts and his hands unconsciously clenched into fists. An accident he could understand, but this was the result of more than a moment's carelessness. It was at best, stupidity, at worst a careless disregard for the animal which, given his own feeling for horseflesh, he found impossible to forgive.

With the blood hammering in his head Axel strode to the vehicle shed and fetched from his Land Rover the .22 rifle he carried for shooting pigs. He put his hard palm on the filly's forehead then gently stroked the puffy swelling over what should have been the hollow above her eye, as he shielded her glazed sight and brought the rifle up. 'Sorry, sweetheart.' He clipped the words out, swallowed hard and pulled the trigger, stepping back as Gaynor dropped bonelessly at his feet.

He worked the breech to eject the cartridge, slammed it closed and headed back to the house, face dark with the fury that was eating at him. Ben was on the verandah seated in one of the cane chairs pulling on his boots.

"Morning,' he called, glancing up, then something in his father's face made him stand. His Adam's apple jerked as his eyes flicked to the rifle and he said uncertainly, 'You've been to the stables? How is she today?'

'Gaynor you mean? The filly you neither wanted nor valued — you're asking about her?' Axel's voice cut like a whip and Ben paled.

'She's dead. A lump of carrion, rotten with septicaemia – that's how she is right now. Through *your* carelessness. Because you haven't enough bloody nous to tell the difference between a horse in pain and one that's playing up. Jesus Christ!' he roared. 'A first-year jackeroo would know that.'

'I'm sorry,' Ben said wretchedly. 'I was just – impatient, I guess. And then later I didn't notice.' Loathing himself he added bitterly, 'I suppose anybody else – Billy for instance – would've.' Involuntarily he touched his nose where, after five days, a trace of bruising still remained.

'Yes,' Axel said grimly, 'you're right about that. He's a horseman that lad; and the pity of it is that he's not my son. But you are going to learn, boy – you can be absolutely certain of that! You've got a duty to this place and I'll not see you shirk it. Garry's not been tough enough on you, but that's about to change. You can start by shifting the mare's body.'

Despair flooded Ben, washing away the guilt he felt over Gaynor's death. He wished he could stand up to the angry man confronting him. *Just tell him*, Rachel's scornful tones rang in his head and he did try. 'Dad,' he said desperately, 'I don't want—' but got no further.

'I don't give a damn what you want,' his father shouted. 'I paid three thousand guineas for that filly. That's three thousand bloody good reasons for you to make amends for her death! It's time you learned that nobody's going to carry you in this world. From now on you'll do the job right – the first time. And you can start by getting down to the shed for a vehicle and shifting that carcass. Have I made myself clear?'

Ben was defeated. A sense of hopelessness filled him. He picked up his hat, clearing his throat as he headed for the steps. 'Yes,' he said. His future was sealed. If there had ever been a chance to get his father to consider his own wishes, it had died along with Gaynor.

Twelve

On the Brumby, Billy and the twins were taking the horses back to their Wet season spelling paddock on Verity Creek. It wasn't a paddock in the proper sense, Cub explained, more a lucky accident of nature. A large valley fenced with the natural barrier of the range and bisected by Verity Creek.

'*Another* running creek?' Billy was impressed.

'No, just seasonal. But the gorge holes are huge and the middle one's not bad either,' Jo said. 'And there're lots of springs under the cliffs.' She looked at her twin, 'The valley's about – what? Fifteen square miles. Big enough for the workers anyway.'

'About that,' Cub tossed a stick at Carter, the black gelding that had stopped to browse on a beefwood. 'It's a handy paddock.'

'I'll say if there's no wire involved.' Billy moved cautiously on Freaky – he'd learned not to trust the bay pony that had more tricks than a bag full of monkeys.

'As to that there's probably a mile or so. Mostly short stretches to close up a gap in the range. And a couple of creek crossings. It's not exactly the Mount,' he said with ill-disguised pride, 'but range country has its uses. We'll get our paddocks a damn sight cheaper than the neighbours.'

'And here we are,' Jo said. 'There's the gate, next to the bloodwoods. You want to get it?'

'Yeah, 'course.' The discussion had distracted him and he momentarily forgot his caution. The narrow track wound between stands of weathered sandstone and on every side the ranges rolled away, darkening to purple in the distance. Up ahead of the plodding plant horses a skein of trees seemed to stand on the world's rim, branches backdropped by sky alone. Eyes everywhere he kicked the bay, cantering up beside the track to get around the lead. The horses swerved obediently away and without a second's warning the bay snatched the bit, dipped his right shoulder and spun, heaving Billy head over turtle into bone-jarring dirt.

He got up spitting, to the sound of the twins' laughter, and reclaimed his hat. Placid as a milking cow, Freaky stood waiting, reins in a puddle about his forefeet, delicately rubbing an eye on his knee. It was his second victory that day. Billy, who had plumed himself on his horsemanship, gritted his teeth. He had ridden spirited horses, and even a few that bucked quite well, but this was his first encounter with an out and out rogue.

Flushing with mortification, he swore and opened the gate. Bad enough to have the little mongrel get rid of him twice in the one ride, but in front of Jo – his self-esteem plummeted. He'd wanted to impress her and here she was treating it like a joke.

'He's got a natural ability that boy.' Cub, damn him, was

grinning at him like an idiot. 'Flies like a bird.'

'I noticed,' Jo giggled, blue eyes dancing at his discomfort, 'straight into the ground. You call that ability?'

'Very funny.' Billy knew he was expected to take it in good part, but his pride was hurt, and also his knee. He limped to open and then shut the gate behind them, before looping the reins on his mount's neck and swinging up. 'Just you wait, you little bugger,' he said fiercely. 'One of these days . . .'

Freaky snorted, unconcerned.

The pad descended steeply over ledges of stone then down a loose slope where pebbles skittered ahead of the moving horses. The angle of the sun left the floor of the valley in shadow and painted darkness under the forest of broad-leaf ti-tree that hugged the curve of the range to their left.

'Big Spring,' Jo said, the joke apparently over and forgotten. She pointed towards the scrub with her whip. 'It rises under the cliff there – masses of water. See the green? Wherever you find that along the range there's water.'

Billy nodded. Behind the drab olive of the melaleuca thicket the brighter green of taller trees showed through. Bloodwood, he guessed, and myrtle, maybe pandanus. 'We camping there tonight?'

'Not likely. Too wet. And there's rock pythons in there'd swallow you whole. The horse paddock's our camp. We'll pick up a few fresh nags tomorrow then head home.'

'And start fencing?'

'Yeah,' Cub said. 'Sorry you didn't stay at the Mount?'

'Not yet,' Billy answered truthfully, gazing around at the

spectacular scenery, 'the country's more interesting. And,' his eyes ran approvingly over the plant, 'you've got a few decent nags as well.'

'Not counting Freaky,' Cub suggested, straight-faced.

Billy's knee gave a painful twinge and he grimaced. 'You're not wrong about that.'

There was no heavy machinery on the Brumby. They used an old Fordson tractor at need, and with this they now cleared the line for the new paddock, felling the larger trees and doglegging the line at the dictates of the country. In places the run of the cliffs aided them for much of the sandstone range rose sheerly, guaranteeing a stock-proof barrier.

It was hot, and grew hotter as the weeks passed. They sweated gallons under the fierce sun, and their arms to the elbows where their rolled sleeves ended changed from an ordinary brown to a deep mahogany burn. Blake set a stiff pace – up before the dawn and back to camp on headlights, with a lay up over dinner camp taken in whatever shade offered along the line.

His boss, Billy mused, was a bit like a savage dog. All right as long as you didn't get too close, or do anything to annoy him. Blake had no small talk, and seemingly no interest outside the current job. Billy, over a dinner camp once, remembering that he'd been a drover, had asked him about his trips. It was a mistake he didn't make again. Blake had studied him for an unnervingly long time before speaking. 'Why? What business is it of yours?'

'Well – none.' Billy had shrugged, feeling suddenly uncomfortable. 'I mean – you don't want to tell me, that's fine. It's just something I've never tried myself, that's all.' The pale, hard eyes boring into him reminded him suddenly of the bull terrier Belle, standing four-square before him, hackles up. He looked away, wishing he'd never raised the subject. To his relief Blake had taken him at his word, picking up a month-old *Country Life* that somebody had stuffed into the tuckerbox against the hour there'd be time to read it, and letting the matter drop.

'What's it with him?' Billy asked curiously afterwards. 'I've seen gabbier fence posts.' He and Cub had a roll of barbed wire on the bar they carried between them, the wire unspooling behind them as they walked. 'I heard he did time once – is that true?'

'Yeah,' Cub shifted his grip. 'Before Jo and I were born. Armed robbery. Suds reckons the cops framed him.'

'What's he got to do with it?' Billy was surprised.

''S where they met – in the clink. I suppose Suds knows him better'n anyone. Better than we do, anyway. He swears it was a put-up job. Some cop getting square over a fist in the face during a pub brawl.'

'I see.' Billy digested this. 'Still, water under the bridge now. It must be long forgotten.' Although he himself had heard it from someone, so that was wrong.

'That's what you think.' It was as if his companion had read his mind. 'They never let you forget. Not around here, anyway.' They had reached a corner post. He tied off the wire and they started back for the next run. 'We'll strain 'em when we've run them all out,' Cub explained. 'What about your family? What was your old man like?'

'I dunno,' Billy said baldly. 'My mum either – she died when I was a baby. I lived with her parents then on their dairy farm. Cleared out when I was fifteen.'

'That's pretty young.' For once Cub sounded surprised.

Billy shrugged. 'I survived.' He remembered the cold, and the hunger pangs, and the night in the shelter shed when he'd brained with his own frying pan the pervert who'd fed him. He'd mistaken his interest for kindness, but once free of his grasp had fled in terror across the frosty football field, to huddle on a freezing park bench until daylight. 'It had its moments but all in all it wasn't so bad. I survived,' he repeated, while reflecting privately that had it been ten times worse, it was still better than the beatings and abuse he'd left behind on the farm.

October was a month of fierce electrical storms that produced little or no rain. The lightning strikes started fires in the ranges but to Billy's surprise they were let burn unchecked – not, he thought, that you'd have much hope of stopping them. Their glow filled the starry nights, and the morning air would be full of drifting ash and the scent of smoke. Kite hawks followed the fire fronts and the cawing of crows became part of the hot, discordant pattern of the month.

'Fires are good,' Simon said. 'They clean out the ticks and the old sour feed. They thin the scrub a bit too, and the spinifex. You let that build up and you'll get a really bad fire. Apart from being a hazard, old spinifex is useless. It's dry and tough and the stock can't eat it.'

Ivy, Billy remembered, had said it was highly combustible. It also had a distinctive odour when it burned and he grew accustomed to smelling it on the wind; and to the look of the dusty, smoky skies, and the burn of prickly heat on his body as the work progressed. With a bit of luck they'd get most of the fencing up before the Wet came. He'd be glad to see the end of it except that it would also mean his job on the Brumby was over. But maybe Blake would have him back next year. He'd ask him before he left.

The storms started in December. The skies were no longer brazen but bloomed with cloud, and thunder muttered at daylight when the wind came cool and fresh with the scent of rain. Tropical storms burst over them, the water pouring from the sky, as if from upended buckets. If they were caught on the line their hat brims drooped within moments, and shirts were moulded to their bodies. The rush of water across the parched earth swept up sticks and leaves and old cowpats, and five minutes later every surface and gully was awash.

They measured the results in an empty jam tin and Jo kept tally – eighty-seven points overnight, fifty-three one afternoon, two inches the day they bogged the tractor. That cost them an extra day of waiting while the ground developed a crust before they could begin digging the stranded machinery out.

Cub was annoyingly cheerful about the delay. 'Makes a change from stringing wire. I don't reckon we're gunna get much further on this job anyway.'

He was right; the brilliant sky and burning heat of the sun might be forcing green shoots from the sodden earth at an astonishing rate, but more rain was coming. The knowledge of it throbbed in the repetitive calls of the rainbirds, and could be felt in the hush of still dawns broken by the strident racket of channel-billed cuckoos. On the second morning after the tractor was dug out Blake called it quits.

'Time we were out of it.' A cool little wind fluttered his hat brim as he stared at the sky above the northern range where rafts of grey cloud had appeared.

They packed swiftly, with the ease of long practice. It was raining on the range when they broke camp, the distant clouds now a long grey curtain. Billy snuffed the smell of it, carried to him on the light wind. The suffocating heat had gone and for the first time in months he felt cool.

'Wet's coming,' Jo said, slamming the Rover's tailboard shut, and he sensed in her bright tones and quickened movements the same anticipation he felt in himself.

They were home by early afternoon, the rain now not far behind them. Thunder rumbled as they unpacked and Billy, lugging gear into the shed behind Blake, seized the opportunity to ask him about a job in the stock camp next year.

He divested himself of the tools he was carrying, putting each in its place, then turned in his deliberate way. 'Why – you quitting?'

'I –' Billy lifted his shoulders, 'well the job's over – isn't it? I thought I'd be drawing my cheque after today.'

'Depends.' In the gloom of the shed it was hard to read Blake's face. A handful of rain pattered tentatively onto the tin roof. 'If there's somewhere you've gotta be, fair enough. Otherwise you can put in the Wet here. No wages. Just do enough round the place for your keep, and if next month's dry we'll finish the fencing. Wages for that, then you're off the books again till the stock work starts.'

'Suits me,' Billy said. Inside his heart was singing. Not only had he not wanted to leave but this way he'd get to experience a Wet. 'Thanks,' he said fervently. 'I'll pull my weight. You won't regret it.'

'You know how to work,' Blake growled, 'so I don't expect to.'

Billy couldn't believe he'd heard the words. Then rain thundered like hailstones on the roof and Blake was splashing through it to reach the vehicle's cab where the windows lay open to the storm. He followed grinning, careless of the wet, unable to believe the old bastard had actually paid him a compliment.

Thirteen

Oscar Davies leaned on the pub bar, Bluey on his shoulder, and watched through the open door as the bush mob arrived for the annual Town versus Country cricket match. Traditionally it was the final gathering before the monsoon shut the district down. After that he'd have only the town drinkers, and the occasional visitor from Mount Ixion or Rumhole – while the roads stayed open – to tide him over. Although according to the grapevine there wasn't much cash to spare at the latter.

Behind him the motor of the coldroom hummed, a background to the brisk whirr of the fan whose breeze blew pleasantly about his head and shoulders. Parked out front was the Coopers' station wagon with its tinted windows, the ramshackle old wreck of a Land Rover Ken Walker drove, Sam Bullen's police vehicle, and a Toyota with several men on the back which, after a moment's considera-tion, he tagged as belonging to Rainsford. This was confirmed when the blocky figure of Lionel Bennett alighted from the driver's seat, followed by two women of substantial size. 'The missus and the cook,' Oscar murmured. Bluey, accustomed to this habit of speaking his thoughts aloud, crooned and nibbled his ear. 'And there's old Misery.'

Across the road he watched the storekeeper padlock the shop door and tread his careful way to join the group. Always careful, old Misery. Tight with a quid and rumoured to still own the first one he'd ever earned. He was the town's unofficial banker, and half the district, Oscar estimated, owed their livelihood to him. He himself was no exception – Misery had held a lien on the pub for years. And the way things were going – with cattle prices at rock bottom and the stations employing only half the usual number of hands – that wasn't likely to change. The town lived off the stations. Certainly their cash kept him going in fuel and grog and the other necessities of his trade. But lately, listening to the worried tones of his customers, he'd started to wonder when it would all fall apart.

Ken Walker for one was already in deep shit. He'd be the next one calling on Misery. Oscar wondered if the man would accommodate him. It would be chucking money away. You couldn't get a nicer bloke than old Ken but he, personally, wouldn't put him in charge of a chook raffle. '*Not* a good business prospect,' he told Bluey. But there was no telling with Misery. Oscar, who privately expected never to clear his own debt, and had been as astonished as he was gratified by the lifeline the old storekeeper had thrown him, wondered anew what prompted the man to loan where he did. Maybe, he mused, a finger idly fossicking amid Bluey's crest feathers, he wanted to be tied into the community. The penny-pinching

93

old sod had to be lonely. He had no family as far as Oscar knew and lived in a couple of rooms behind the shop where, with Sam Bullen's connivance, he ran the local gambling school.

Here his wandering thoughts were interrupted by the arrival of another mud-splashed vehicle pulling in beside the rest. 'Like the joint's a bloody car park,' he muttered. 'That'll be the Reillys. At least old Suds oughta be good for a beer or two.' He caught a glimpse of the young fella who'd gone up there a couple of months back. Probably finishing up and needing accommodation until the mail ran again – which could be a week the way the weather was. Business was definitely looking up. Whistling cheerfully, Oscar set up a couple of glasses in readiness, planning the salads he'd serve with the barbecue he was putting on for the crowd presently gathering at the school. His cook was having the day off but he had always liked messing about in the kitchen. It'd be a chance to try out that new mustard dressing.

Hearing boots on the verandah Bluey gave voice to his routine utterance, 'Who's a bastard?'

'All those silly buggers out there,' Oscar informed him. 'Cricket in this weather? They need their heads read. G'day, Suds, what can I get you?'

Billy had never played cricket. He had stuck to this denial despite Cub's disbelieving protestations. 'We're not talking ovals and coaching, mate. Surely you musta knocked a ball around in a paddock somewhere after school? Strike me blind! Even Rachel Cooper fielded before she got polio.'

'You've got a funny idea of dairy farming,' Billy told him. The truth was that kids from other farms *had* played but for him, it had never been worth the belting that would've resulted from being late for the afternoon milking. And without that practice there was no chance of making the school team. 'Dumb game anyway – all that running back and forth.'

Cub shook his head sadly. 'No wonder Freaky throws you! Any proper-thinking horse would. Well if we're short a man you'll just have to have a go.'

Luckily for Billy's peace of mind the weather scuppered this plan. The clouds had been building since dawn into a sky that by midday was dark enough to pass for early evening. It burst apart over lunch with a ferocious crack as lightning struck a tree in the schoolyard. The barbecue and tables were set up, along with the spectators, on the concrete apron under the school building. While the white flash still dazzled the eyes, the wind struck, bowling over small children, plastic chairs, and the lidded dishes containing most of the food. Ken Walker's wife cast her large bosom and outstretched arms across the nearest table but the cloth rose around her and a tornado of paper plates, of cups, and plastic cutlery, joined the hamburger buns and salad bowls in a race across the paddock. Billy dropped the Coke can he was holding to grab his hat then yelped as something slammed into his spine. 'Bastard!' screeched the tangle of wet feathers that was Bluey as he was blown south after the salads, then the rain was in the shelter too, an almost horizontal sheet. While paper napkins fell from the air like wet confetti, Margaret Cooper's photographic prints of Daphne's wedding two months before were whipped from the hand showing them off, and whirled away across the paddock.

The cricketers had run for cover as the tree exploded, some to the vehicles, some to the carnage under the school. In the Reillys' case, both. Simon with the wipers on at full speed came roaring across the road, already running water, while Cub rounded up his twin and Billy.

'Come on!' he roared. 'We're leaving.'

They bundled into the vehicle that actually rocked from the buffeting of the wind against the canvas canopy rigged over the back. There was no flap to cover the rear so it was just as well they'd be travelling north, Billy thought. Then he remembered the cook.

'What about Suds?'

'He's got two minutes,' Simon yelled. 'Or he can catch the mail home.' Water sheeted up as he wheeled back to the pub and Cub leapt out hatless into the storm again. Suds must've seen reason for both re-emerged and a moment later they were on their way, the Land Rover slewing wildly in the greasy black soil, the rain a curtain that blotted everything from sight.

Billy's stomach growled regretfully. He should've moved faster and grabbed a bit of steak before the storm took it all. He was soaked to the skin and Cub, swaying opposite and clinging like him to the headboard, hair plastered to his scalp was, if anything, wetter. If they didn't get across the river before it rose they'd be marooned for they'd never manage to return to the 'Bend once the rain had time to soak into the black clay.

'Reckon we'll make it?' he shouted into the noise and drifting spray that filled their shelter.

Cub shrugged, blue eyes bright in the dull light. 'Don't see why not,' he bellowed, 'weather permitting.'

Billy grinned. It had been a stupid question. This must be what old Ivy had meant when she'd talked about Gulf rain. *This piddle – this isn't rain!* she'd said of those drizzly summer mornings when the moisture sifted down into the bracken they were chipping, falling light as thistledown on their heads and shoulders.

Neither was this. It was a deluge. Billy, struggling between delight and awe, wondered if Simon could even see the road – then as the vehicle tilted sideways in a sudden violent skid, decided he'd rather not know. Just as long as they kept moving . . .

At the horse paddock gate Billy climbed stiffly down and stretched under a sky brilliant with stars. Dust stirred under his feet but the red tail light showed the drying mud smeared on the vehicle. The storm had played itself out hours before and miles behind. At the house he gave Cub a hand to unload Suds who had roused to a state of fuddled wakefulness as they dumped him on his bed.

'Whersh this – whatsh happening?' He ran a hand over his face and moved a pink tongue around his dry lips. "Ad a drink somewhersh—' a gust of beery breath made Billy draw back and turn his head aside.

'Go to sleep, old man.' Cub lifted his feet up, removed his boots and clicked the light switch off. 'The old boy'll have a head in the morning. Half a dozen beers and he's silly as a wheel. Dunno about you but I'm starving.'

'I could fang a dead horse,' Billy agreed. 'Let's hope the boss has turned on a feed.'

In fact Blake had made a curry. He was sipping tea in the kitchen when they entered and hung their hats on the pegs beside the door. 'Where's Suds?'

'Sleeping it off,' Cub said shortly. Of the three younger Reillys only Simon, Billy had noticed, ever conversed freely with their father. It was he who spoke now.

'What's for supper? We left before we could eat.'

'Not that there was anything *to* eat,' Billy picked up a plate. 'Man, I never saw rain like it. And the wind! Never mind the tucker on 'em, it even blew the tables away. Except for the one that fat woman jumped on.'

'Vi Walker.' Jo heaped her plate and poured tea for herself and her twin. 'I was talking to Casey and Ken's got the story from somewhere that they're going to bring in a ruling soon to make the stations truck their sale stock out.' She was speaking, everybody understood, of the Department of Primary Industries, architect of BTEC and the current bane of producers' lives.

'They can try,' Cub scoffed. 'Strike me! Shows you how much the government knows about this country. You couldn't *get* a bloody cattle truck over most of the roads.'

'No, but it'll have to come sooner or later,' Simon said in his calm way. 'It's being enforced already further in – no movement of out-side stock on foot through properties that have been certified free of disease. I heard Cooper and Lionel Bennett chewing the fat over it. More to the point he's getting a new head stockman next season.'

Billy looked up. 'Why? What happened to Garry Downes?'

'Not Cooper – Bennett at Rainsford. Seems Poota Johnson had a heart attack.'

Blake roused his brows. 'What – dead?'

'No, but he's hung up his boots. Gone off to live with his daughter down round Biloela they said, so Bennett's looking for someone else. Reckons Poota was getting past it anyway. Chuck us a bit of bread over, Cub.'

In anybody else, Billy would've have called the look in Blake's eye nostalgic.

'Well, with the fences going up it hardly matters. Pity though. Any more news?'

Billy choked on a piece of meat at this blatant acknowledgement of the Reillys' predatory past. Jo thumped his back and he drank a mouthful of tea and wiped watering eyes. He was disconcerted as much by her knowing grin as the shock of choking on Blake's comment. She worked in the stock camp too. He had never thought of that before. She was as culpable as her brothers and Blake. All the same, it was strange how little it seemed to matter to him.

Fourteen

In January the monsoon trough drifted north and the dry, searing heat returned. Creeks that had been brown torrents grew calm and clean again; the filled swamps gave back reflections of clear skies, and the feed grew as though drawn from the earth by the brassy heat of the sun. Cicadas shrilled through the day and at night the frogs provided a background chorus to the thump of the diesel. The white ants swarmed in choking clouds, their shed wings lying in gauzy heaps about the empty homestead.

The Reillys and Billy were back on the fence line, where they worked until the rain returned. And when it did, it stayed. Quite soon Billy found that the Wet had lost much of its charm for him. The endless overcast days, at first restful to the eyes, grew quickly hateful and he found himself longing for a sight of the sun. Anything to break the grey, dripping gloom of his surroundings.

It was too wet to get out – and there was nowhere to go, only the quaking bogs of the ti-tree country and the raging boundary that was Wildhorse Creek. For all of them their world had shrunk to the enclave of the station complex. Physically they were completely cut off from the outside world. Only their neighbours' voices still came to them through the medium of the Codan transceiver in the office. They listened to the disparate tones emanating from fifty different properties scattered from the western border to the lower reaches of the Peninsula: rainfall, river heights, recipes, the birth of grand-children, the price of cattle – anybody could add their two bob's worth, Billy thought, and mostly did.

Rachel called them one day, chatting inconsequentially to Jo, who, being closest, had picked up the microphone, about rainfall and river heights at the Mount until coming to the point by asking for Cub.

'Ah—' Jo twisted about to roll her eyes at her twin cleaning his boots on the verandah. He frowned, shaking his head. 'Sorry, he's not here right now. Was there something I can pass on?'

'It doesn't matter.' The disembodied voice flattened, disap-pointment evident. 'Maybe I'll catch him later. I just wanted a word – wondered how his injury was getting on, that's all.'

Three days before Cub, working on the gates they'd been welding for the new paddock, had dropped one on his foot. She must have been listening when Suds had called in on the medical session about it, Billy thought. Given her family's attitude towards the Reillys and the public nature of the wireless, it couldn't have been easy for her to make the call – but then her character didn't lack steel.

'He's fine,' Jo was briskly concluding the conversation. 'We're all fine. See you after the Wet.'

Billy spoke reproachfully to her twin. 'Hey, it was nice of her to ask. It wouldn't have killed you to say hello.'

'Much you know.' Cub's irritation was plain. 'You fancy her so much you talk to her.'

'Of course I don't. I only said—' but Cub had stalked off.

Jo shook her head. 'It's a bit of a sore subject, Billy. She's been keen on him since school – and never grown out of it. She can't seem to accept that he's not interested.'

'Maybe he would be if he gave her a chance. I like Rachel. She's a nice girl. Worth two of Ben – and about six of her snooty mother.'

'Tell you what, you hook up with her then,' Jo suggested cheerfully as she opened the verandah door. 'Give Cub a break. He'd be your mate for life, I can tell you.'

Aghast, Billy stared after her. He told himself that she hadn't meant it seriously, but that did nothing to stop the flood of dismay filling him. Did it mean she hadn't noticed his interest? Or – even worse – was this her way of telling him she had and didn't return it? Humbly he supposed it might be. She was so rare – the word came on a spurt of inspiration – and he so ordinary. God, he thought miserably, how could he ever have imagined she'd find him anything but boring – *especially* since he'd done nothing but get himself thrown a dozen times (well, four anyway) by that misbegotten mongrel Freaky. Billy gritted his teeth, remembering the last time he'd hit the dirt. She'd laughed. Well, so had Cub – but it was the sound of hers that had hurt.

He smacked the back of his hand, smearing the blood-filled corpse of a mossie across his skin, and went gloomily off to the sheds to find something to occupy himself with until smoko. Rachel, he realised belatedly, probably felt much the same, but the knowledge didn't help.

The days passed in a desultory fashion made memorable only by the little incidents that occurred. Like the one when he and Cub, digging a trench for a water pipe, watched in perfect dryness, the rain beating down a hundred yards away on the garden and home-stead roof. He stood dumbfounded, but his companion saw nothing strange about it.

'Every storm's got to have an edge. That's it.'

Billy shook his head. 'Ivy said it was weird country.'

Stuff you'll never see anywhere else happens there. That's what she'd actually said. 'Like what?' he'd asked, and she'd told him then about the fireball she'd once seen birth itself from a lightning strike and bounce through the scrub, setting fires as it went. It had been a bad blaze – a fierce October fire driven by a gale. For three days she and her husband had fought a losing battle trying to save their horse feed. They gave it up only when it reached a heavy band of wattle scrub, and the burning trees began to explode.

'What happened?' he'd asked. And Ivy had flexed her brown, work-roughened hands as if she'd but that moment laid aside the shovel, the deep wrinkles about her eyes crinkling as she laughed.

'A horse-pad stopped it. Can you believe it? A foot of cleared ground – but that's the Gulf for you.'

The sun chose that moment to reappear from a cloud behind them, and a rainbow sprang into being across the falling rain. It looked close enough to touch and to complete the unreality of the moment two of the horses, one of them the grey mare Butterfly, came bucking and galloping up the track, to burst through the waterfall of coloured wetness, the mare's gleaming coat momentarily taking on the rainbow's hues.

Fat and playful, they circled, snorting, tails and head high, and Billy's horseman's heart went out on a sigh of utter content. 'Unbelievable,' he breathed reverently. 'Unbe-bloody-lievable!'

'It's a rainbow,' Cub said prosaically as he bent again to the trench. 'You gunna stand gawking all day or do we finish the job?'

March brought the first drying days with a wind out of the south-east, and the pronouncement from Blake that the season had turned.

'How can you tell?' To Billy it seemed a day very similar to the one before – or the previous week, come to that. The dew still dripped from the eaves and his boots were soaked, and spiked with grass seeds, from a trip across to the trough.

'The feel of it.' Blake rarely used two sentences where one would do. As the day wore on Billy noticed that the clouds seemed higher in a sky of softer blue, and that while it was still hot the sun's direct rays had lost their bludgeoning edge.

From radio gossip they learned that Ken Walker's chook house had succumbed in the night, collapsing on its squawking inhabitants, two of which hadn't recovered. They were having chicken for tea, Casey cheerfully reported, and you wouldn't *believe* the size of the white ants that had wrought the destruction.

At Plover Creek, a station south of the 'Bend, the mechanic, newly returned from the coast, was evacuated again by the flying doctor with suspected appendicitis. And Oscar Davies, gossiping with Axel Cooper, who'd called him to check up on road conditions, revealed that Keith Guthrie had flattened a bloke in the bar, and bust up half his glasses, over a political difference.

'*Keith?*' Jo said.

Billy too was amazed. 'Wonder what that was about?'

'Too much sitting around,' Cub offered. It was over three months since the mail had run. He stirred restlessly. 'The country'll be drying up enough to work down there pretty soon. We'll be waiting for weeks yet.'

'And the green'll stay in the grass longer up here.' Unperturbed, Simon continued to roll the edges of the red-hide whip-fall he'd cut. Billy, however, shared Cub's impatience to be back in the saddle and free of the confines of the home paddock.

Next day, down in the creek with Jo, he lay back in the cradling water, practising his new art of floating. He'd learned to swim over the summer and the more eagerly because the Wildhorse's swift stream was the coolest place to be. Belle, who shadowed the twins about the place, swam with them. Billy still didn't trust her, but he had to admit that she had a better talent for the water than he, and appeared to love the exercise. She would even, as Jo demonstrated, submerge her head to retrieve stones the girl dropped. Groping blindly on the bottom, the dog would emerge, tail wagging and piggy eyes alert, to lay them at her feet.

'Bet she couldn't get a really deep one,' he challenged, finning lazily. 'Chuck one under the log there and let's see.'

'She will.' Jo tossed the pebble and Belle lunged, the splash rising around her. Air bubbles rose as the water settled but the dog didn't reappear.

'Told you.' Billy stroked gently towards the bank watching the bubbles, expecting any moment to see the bitch's blunt head break the surface. Jo was peering into the creek, the expectancy on her face changing to alarm. Then with a leap she was in the water, trim bottom and pale feet briefly visible as she dove after the dog.

By the time she surfaced with Belle in her arms Billy was there to help haul her up the bank. 'A stick,' Jo panted, wet hair streaming as they knelt on the muddy bank. 'It caught her collar ring. Is she dead?'

'Squeeze her ribs.' Billy, with vague memories of resuscitation procedures, suited the action to his words, encircling Belle's ribs in a fierce grip. He was rewarded with a gagging cough as the limp body convulsed then vomited water. Encouraged, he did it again and saw the dog's slick brindle chest rise of its own accord. A few moments later Belle got dazedly to her to her feet, jaw hanging and legs unsteady. She snarled at Billy and tottered to Jo's side.

'Huh!' The disgusted exclamation was to cover his relief that his stupid challenge hadn't resulted in the animal's death. 'That's gratitude for you. I always knew she didn't like me.'

'She does,' Jo protested, fondling the dog's damp ears.

'Funny way of showing it then.' Billy slapped the two mosquitoes on his shoulder and shot to his feet to stamp and swipe at his bare legs.

'She hasn't bitten you yet,' Jo reminded him. 'And don't forget she's a Reilly too.' The words puzzled him but before he could respond, or even decide if they carried another message, a squadron of mossies attacked. Snatching up their footwear, Jo slapped and ran, Billy on her heels, with the half-glimpsed idea in his head that she had not been speaking wholly of Belle. But he wasn't sure – and grew less so as the seconds passed. Attempting to reconstruct the way she had looked, the tone of her voice, brought only the shiny flash of her scarred cheek curtained by strands of wet hair, and blue eyes above the canine yellow. Then his feet passed from shade to the scorch of heated earth.

'Yow!' Hopping, swearing at the pain, Billy hurtled up the last bit of pathway to the gate and the cool of the lawn beyond, everything but the fire on his bare soles driven from his mind.

Fifteen

The first mail of nineteen seventy-four arrived at the Brumby in three large canvas bags on the second of April. Keith Guthrie unloaded them along with his version of local news. His trenchant comments on the state of the road, the creek banks, and the bog he'd had to dig himself out of formed much of this. Springs had opened in places as the sodden country sought to drain itself and it was one of these, disguised by the waist-high grass, that had caught him.

The stock camps were working on the Mount and at Plover Creek, he said. And up on the Gulf coast at Brancaster, where they'd had seventy-five inches for the summer and the road was still under water, they were barging fresh supplies in from Cairns. Almost as an afterthought he added the news that the 'Bend was getting a new copper any day now.

'No kidding?' Simon dropped his foot down from the Bedford's bullbar and straightened. 'Sam Bullen quit? I thought he was there for life.'

Keith sniggered. 'So'd he. Silly bugger only went and let a

plainclothes cop into the poker game. Got himself arrested – along with Oscar, old Misery, an' the rest of 'em there. Sam was took outta town next day – the rest have gotta front court in Harditch in a month or two.'

'So how come you weren't there to get arrested too?' Cub asked.

'Sheer luck.' Keith smoothed a hand over his beard. 'Never b'lieved in it before, but there y'are. I was crook in the guts that night. Didn't go to the game.'

'Who was he – the undercover bloke? How'd he weasel his way into Bullen's good graces? He's usually more cunning than that.' Simon knocked a march fly from his arm and trod on it. 'Shouldn't he have recognised another cop?'

Keith shrugged. 'He didn't. The fella had been hanging round town for a week or more, staying at the pub. Coulda been anyone. He was always taking pictures – Misery's shop, the old headstones in the cemetery – had one of them cameras that print 'em out on the spot.' He grinned with a touch of malice. 'Took a beaut shot of old Bluey. Oscar had it pinned up behind the bar. Told me the bloke was writing a book and was gunna use it in it. Ready to swear by him, he was.'

Cub laughed. 'I bet he's swearing *at* him now.'

Keith got ready to leave. 'Ain't it the truth?'

'What about Rainsford?' Simon asked. 'Bennett get his new head stockman yet?'

'Yeah, turned up last month. Bloke called Harry Lucas. Big tough-looking yella-fella – from somewhere up the Top End.' He hitched at the shorts over his skinny hips and climbed into the truck. ''Ell on wheels – according to him. Gunna straighten the place out – or so he was telling 'em in the pub last night.'

Cub raised his brows. 'Bet that went down a treat. What was he doing in town anyway?'

'Waiting on men. Rainsford hasn't started its camp yet.' Keith slammed the cab door and started the engine. He drove off, raising a pale curtain of dust against the clear sky.

'Well,' Simon got behind the wheel and pulled his own door closed, 'sounds like Bennett's picked himself a winner. Wonder if he works any better'n he talks.'

'Who cares?' Cub used a mailbag for an elbow rest. 'There's been a few wanted to take on this country but in the end they all find out it's tougher than they are.'

'The old man might know him – or of him. He spent enough time in the Territory after all.'

Cub's lip curled in the habitual sneer that the mention of Blake always brought. 'Yeah. Remind me.'

'He was working, kid.' The older brother term slipped out unnoticed by either of them. 'You're a drover, you go away.'

'Yep. And come home to drink and knock the family around. You've got the job description right,' Cub agreed savagely. 'Why do you always make excuses for him?'

'They're not excuses. It's just that I'm old enough to remember – and you were too young to see the full picture . . .'

'Oh, I see it.' Cub bit the words off, his expression ugly. 'Every time I look at Jo I see it. And I'm not about to forget it. And all your talk won't make me think differently.'

Simon shrugged, 'Let's drop it then. But he might've run across Lucas somewhere. Wouldn't hurt to know what he's like.'

'What's it matter? We're not likely to see much of him.'

'He'll be a neighbour,' Simon said, negotiating a gutter. He grinned briefly, 'Now we've turned honest we could even try and get on with him.'

Cub's laugh was short and explosive, indicative of astonishment rather than mirth. 'Bennett would think we were doing deals. He'd sack him on the spot.'

Blake didn't recognise the name. 'Lucas – Lucas? Never heard of him. Yella-fella, you say?'

'According to Keith.' Simon helped himself to tea and began sorting one-handed through the pile of mail. 'What about you, Suds – you ever hear the name?'

'Not as I remember.' The cook scratched his white poll as if to aid memory. 'There was a white bloke – Jack Lucas. 'E managed a place down the Diamantina in the thirties. 'E'd be long dead, but.' He reached for an out-of-date *Country Life*, saying, as Cub had, 'What's it matter?'

'I don't suppose it does.' Picking three letters from the sorted pile, Simon dropped them in front of Cub. 'Here's your mail, and no prizes for guessing where *they* come from.'

Billy, sitting beside him, saw that they were all addressed in the same neat, sloping hand.

'That damn girl!' Cub scowled ferociously. He snatched up the letters and, crossing to the stove, grabbed the tongs. Lifting the lid he thrust the letters into the flames and stalked from the kitchen. Billy opened his mouth to protest on Rachel's behalf, then, catching the minatory glint in Jo's eyes, shut it again and flipped open a catalogue that had slid his way from the growing pile on the table.

As the Dry season advanced the pace of station life quickened. On the Brumby they mustered the brood mares, branded the foals and later worked in the breaking yard with the new crop of colts. Beyond the paddocks the valleys were drying and soon the stock camp was moving out to begin the first round of mustering. Billy, legs smarting from his first full day in the saddle, found that with the drying of the speargrass time had somehow done a switch. Before there had been too much of it, now there wasn't enough to complete the day's tasks. Every muscle in his body protested as he walked back from the yards.

'You've got fat and soft – like the nags,' Cub jeered. He was walking carefully himself, Billy noted, but let it pass, too tired to rise to the ribbing. He was constrained also by the lately mercurial nature of the other's moods. Cub's normal even temper had turned pugnacious, even surly at times, and a pleasantry ventured often met with a short answer. Had it been anyone else Billy would have demanded an explanation – but he could think of only one way in which he had offended. The twins' relationship was very special. If Cub had noticed Billy's interest in Jo it was only natural that he should resent it.

That the reason might lie in the dour figure of Blake never entered his head. Dismayed, he said nothing while silently acknowledging that Cub's protective instincts might prove a formidable and quite unanticipated hurdle, in his quest for Jo's heart.

Even so there were compensations. Billy found them when offsiding for Simon in the breaking yard with that year's colts. It was at once thrilling and deeply satisfying, he discovered, to catch and tame the wild-eyed three year olds, all snort and terror, into wary biddable mounts. Persistently calm and endlessly patient, he coaxed and drilled them into acceptance, first of his presence, then of the lead rope, the bit and saddle.

'You're a natural,' Simon said after the first week.

Billy flushed with pleasure at the compliment. It was the one thing Ivy's training had not covered for she kept only the three horses, of which the half-Arab mare, Daisy, had been his favourite. Squatting on his heels in the shade of a post he remembered her now, her lean, slightly dished face, stubby ears, and gleaming red-flecked hide. She hadn't been tall but was superbly formed, with a good barrel and depth of shoulder. And her paces had been perfection.

'*Can't beat the Arab blood for stamina.*' He could hear Ivy's light, dry voice saying it. They'd been riding somewhere at the time, on one of those mizzly Tableland days, with the wetness shining their waterproof coats and darkening Daisy's light hide. He remembered the way the drops had hung from the fence wires and dripped from the brim of Ivy's old hat. She never minded the weather. They had gone for miles through the gloomy timber and dank underbrush, the only sounds the clop of their mount's hooves and the carolling of a persistent butcherbird. Later, hunched in the lee of a deadfall over which lantana had spread, Ivy had used a handful of dry bracken taken from her saddle pouch to light the fire that boiled their quarts.

Squatting there, holding a sandwich in the shelter of her hat, she'd grinned like a kid and winked at him. *'Round here they think I'm a mad old chook – mucking around in the rain.'*

Billy smiled back at her now, remembering. Beside him Simon said softly, 'Something funny?' He had his hat tilted back to show the white line of forehead above where it normally sat and was chewing a grass stem, obeying his own rule of granting the colts a breather between lessons. Gives 'em time to think, he'd said, which made perfect sense to Billy.

'Just remembering a mare I used to ride.' He stood up, eyes going to the clean line of his filly's legs. 'She's a looker – what's her breeding?'

'Just station stock. But Butterfly's her dam – and it shows.'

'Ah.' Even Daisy paled by comparison. 'Now there's a mare I wouldn't mind saddling.'

'You reckon?' Simon's gaze was sardonic. 'She's a bit of a hand-ful. You'd better master Freaky first. Now,' he nodded at the filly, 'she's about ready for the long reins.'

Sixteen

Next day, coming in late for morning smoko, Billy was all but bowled over by the angry form of Cub stamping out of the kitchen.

'Hey!' he yelled, grabbing the nearest upright to steady himself, but the other bulled on his way, face like thunder, crossing the garden in angry strides. In the kitchen Jo seemed to be trying her best to become invisible. With eyes downcast she huddled into herself, not touching the half-drunk mug of tea before her. Simon was silent, wrapped in his own thoughts, and Blake sat as unresponsive as a rock, rolling a cigarette with deliberation, his hard face unreadable. Only Suds, dealing a patience game at the end of the table, seemed untroubled. But when he cleared his throat it was as loud as a shout in the tension-charged room. Moving warily from old habit, Billy filled his mug, helped himself to a slice of Suds' excellent brownie and sat down, watching the others.

Jo, he sensed, was afraid, Simon irritated, and Blake was just Blake. Who could tell what went on behind that iron visage? They were a queer lot – hardly a family at all; more like strangers thrown together. Not that he, Billy admitted silently, had much experience of family life – but enough to tell that Cub hated his father. Jo just seemed to fear him, and Simon was mainly indifferent to his presence – like a man who had learned to live with a savage dog. The property bound them together he supposed but presumably they could leave if they wished to. Not for the first time he wondered why Cub should choose to stay.

He lingered when the others had gone, sipping a second mug of tea. Wandering across to overlook Suds hand he spoke casually. 'What was that all about?'

'Somethin' – nuthin'. Same as always,' the old man grunted. 'Black's white far as the boy's concerned – long as 'is father reckons otherwise.' He slid the cards together and reshuffled and Billy knew he would say no more. If he wanted to find out he'd have to ask Cub.

A few days later while they idled in the shade of a dinner camp, watching over the mob and waiting on the others, he did.

'I suppose it's not my business,' he said carefully, 'but in the kitchen the other day – what was that all about? And why do you hang on here when you could get a job anywhere? A blind man could see you hate it.'

Cub, who was twisting a new cracker for his whip from hair plucked from brown Ditto's mane, took his time answering, almost as if he needed to clarify his own reasons.

'It's him – not the place, or the job. The job's fine. Besides, why should I leave? This is our home.' The twins, Billy had noticed, almost always spoke and thought in the plural. 'Just because I hate his guts doesn't mean I'm gunna walk away from the only good thing we've ever had. The Brumby's *our* land. Mine and Jo's and Simon's. When we're dead our kids'll work it. And *their* kids after them. They bloody better or I'll come back and haunt them. You don't put your sweat and blood into a place to have your descendants chuck it away.'

He knotted the horsehair, inspected the finished work and flicked the loose end of the whip-fall into his hand. Billy unconsciously tightened his grip on Freaky's reins. If *he* tried that he knew the bay would have him on his ear in two seconds flat.

'Well, it's Blake's land too, isn't it?' Billy persisted. 'So what's he done? Why do you hate him so much? I mean, right, he's not the chattiest bloke I've struck – but he's a fair boss. And Simon seems to get along with him okay . . .'

'Yeah, well, he's got a short memory,' Cub interposed bitterly. 'Blake's a mongrel, always was, and far as I'm concerned, always will be. It might suit Simon to forget the past but I remember every time he wasn't there – and all the times he was. And they were worse. Coming home drunk from the pub and laying into our mother – and us, when we were handy. You don't forget that. Why d'you think she cleared out and left us?' He demanded vehemently. 'It was his doing.'

'He doesn't drink now,' Billy objected. 'I've never seen him do so, anyway.'

'Maybe not. But take my word for it, he did. And if you think a scrub bull's dangerous, try Blake on the rum. Oh,' he added bitterly, 'we made a rare entertainment for all the old gossips in the 'Bend when we lived in town. For a while there Mrs Reilly's black eyes were their main topic of conversation. Then she left and they could talk about *that* instead.'

'That can't have been pleasant,' Billy agreed cautiously. 'How old were you? When she left I mean. My mum died when I was a baby, so I don't even remember her.' Although there were times when if he thought back very hard to the old stone farmhouse in which he'd spent his childhood, he was almost convinced that he did. Perhaps because he wanted to believe it, he thought. Still, any least bit of love shown to him would surely have stuck in his memory, for there was certainly none to remember after her death.

Cub, intent on his own bitter thoughts, ignored the question. 'Yeah, well, if they were giving out medals for bad mothers, ours would've had the gold.' He closed his knife and let the whip-fall, with its newly attached cracker, drop. 'Even animals don't abandon their young. And you know the really funny bit? Her leaving straightened Blake out. He quit the grog cold. I daresay the cops would've seen us put into care otherwise. But he'd already done it so his reform came a bit late.'

'Done what?'

'Jo – that scar on her face.' The blue eyes were as hard as Blake's own. 'That's his work. He swung a bridle at her when he was drunk and the bit bar went through her cheek. Could've knocked her eye out instead of just a tooth – could've killed her even. But what did he care?' Staring bleakly inwards he added, his voice filled with self-loathing, 'Mind you, I did nothing to stop him.'

This anguish caused Billy to pull from his own experience and say quickly. 'You can't blame yourself, mate. You have to put it behind you.' Ivy's words, differently phrased: *Hatred's a heavy load, son. It'll break your back and cripple you, too.*

'I'll do that when the old bastard's dead.' Cub said flatly. Argument would not persuade him so Billy shut up; in the silence their mounts' ears twitched and pricked towards the scrub.

'Cattle coming.' He picked the reins off Freaky's neck and a moment later Simon and the lead of the fresh mob trotted into the open. Keeping a cautious eye on the pony he headed over to block them up, moving automatically, his mind mostly on what he'd learned. It explained everything. He had seen how close the twins were to each other. In hurting Jo, Blake had done the one thing that ensured Cub would never forgive him. No wonder he couldn't stand his father! It was different, Billy supposed, for Simon, even though he was fond of his sister – he could seemingly forget, or overlook, what his brother could not.

Billy shook his head. It was ironic to have crossed Australia only to find a situation that was similar to his own early experience. In his case it had not been down to drink, it was hatred that had fuelled his grandfather's actions. And to that extent, although he knew Cub wouldn't agree, to him Blake's failings ranked well below those of Billy's own relatives. Grog and indifference made for poor parenting but it wasn't in the same league as hatred. At that moment a whip cracked somewhere behind him. Billy hipped about in his seat to see if it was Jo and the pony, sensing his distraction, dropped his shoulder into a twisty buck that shot him out of the saddle. His landing scattered the mob and brought an irate bellow from Blake.

'Quit arsing about for chrissakes! If you're that useless get some bloody glue on your strides.'

Heart athirst for vengeance, Billy banged the dust from his hat, and limped after the bay. At least this time Jo hadn't been present but he had no doubt she'd hear of it from her twin. Scowling, he swung back into the leather muttering dire warnings to Freaky, while feeling brief empathy for Ben Cooper.

They were branding at the station yards when their first visitor for the year arrived. Billy, working the back leg-rope at the ramp, heard Belle bark and glanced up to see the Land Rover pull into the shade of a cabbage gum. Through the blowing dust of the south-westerly he watched the tall, khaki-clad figure alight and nudged Simon.

'There's a cop come visiting.'

'So there is,' he looked across the yard but Blake, working the broncho horse, was riding over to the visitor, coiling the greenhide rope as he went, to dismount and hitch the mare to the post. Simon finished castrating the bull calf, and earmarked it while Jo applied the brand. Billy and Cub pulled the leg-ropes off and the beast lurched, blatting to its feet to bolt into the security of the cattle.

'Wonder what he wants?' Cub lounged back against the ramp where Billy and Jo joined him. Simon walked across to the two at the fence where Belle had taken up a threatening stance, bristling at the newcomer.

'He'd have to be Bullen's replacement,' Billy guessed.

'Yeah. But what's he want here? Bullen never got outta town —'less there was a party somewhere.'

'We'll know in a minute – doesn't look like he's getting the welcome mat,' Jo observed.

Billy couldn't hear the words but Blake's attitude was plain enough. He finished speaking and turned his back on the stranger; Simon spoke sharply to Belle, quietening her growls while the visitor hesitated then got back in his vehicle and slammed the door. Simon stood to watch him wheel the Land Rover about and drive off. Neither man lifted their hand. Blake, mounted again, was already riding into the cattle, catching rope in hand, as if there'd been no interruptions to the morning's work.

Cub raised interrogative brows at his brother.

'Frank Watson, senior constable,' Simon said. 'He's familiarising himself with his district – *learning the country* – is what he actually said. He's gunna be doing district patrols. Calling by every six weeks or so to "keep on top of any problems". You can guess how the old man reacted.'

'What'd he say?' Billy cocked his head and Simon's fleeting grin came and went.

'Said he'd have him for trespass if he set foot on the place again. And to go and *learn* somebody else's. Plus a few other things. But he's not the office type Bullen was. Apparently he's got a couple of his own horses – and a float to shift 'em about with. Said it proved a good deterrent in his last posting.'

'Calf-o,' Jo called then, as the broncho mare came surging out of the cattle, the catching rope swinging wildly from the antics of the weaner lunging at its end. Billy and the other two scattered to their positions. The leg-rope loops flashed to snare the offside feet; the ropes were drawn tight against the ramp rails and the animal fell. Cub yanked the slackened noose clear of its head while Simon and Jo moved in to do their part. It was at once as intricate and as easy as well-practised dance steps.

Afterwards with the calf bucking away and another on the way into the ramp, Billy, shaking out his loop, paused to wonder if the copper was really making his rounds, or had singled out the Brumby for a visit because of the Reillys' well-known predilection for their neighbours' calves.

Seventeen

Southbend drowsed in the pleasant warmth of May. The endless sky above the town was painted with thin, high striations of wind cloud, as if an artist had flicked a white brush over a pale blue canvas. Oscar, sweeping the pub verandah, paused to stare at the wide sweep of the Common where the feed, moving before the light wind, ran in unbroken waves to the horizon. It was turning colour as it dried, as was the large sea of pea-bush behind the racecourse. That was half a mile through and stood taller than a man, a mini scrub of crackling stems and rattling seed pods. Pity the bloke trying to push fresh cattle through that lot, he thought. The buggers would be off like the devil was after them. Oscar hadn't always been a publican; he'd spent more than a season or two in the stock camps.

He parked the broom and went to shift the sprinklers, startling the old goanna that lived in the bamboo clump. It was, in his opinion, the best time of year with the heat of summer over, and the bitter winter winds still to come. The dust hadn't got bad yet and the council (for a bloody wonder!) had the graders out on the road.

He could hear one of them now working upriver, the snarl of the diesel a constant vibration against his ear.

Straightening up from the tap he watched a fuel tanker power past, spreading its dust over store and pub alike, including his newly swept verandah. Another vehicle, a Toyota towing a horse float, followed it down the street and pulled into the pub beside the blue utility already there. Lionel Bennett and his new head stockman – Oscar searched for his name, Lucas, that was it, Harry Lucas – got out and strolled over.

'G'day, Oscar,' Bennett glanced back at the ute. 'Axel Cooper hasn't got himself a new vehicle has he?'

'Nah.' Oscar nodded to the dark-skinned man beside him. 'How you doin', Harry? Visitor owns it. Haven't seen Axel today. Why? You expecting him?'

'Yeah. Council's supposed to be meeting, but nobody's turned up. I thought they might be here.'

'Cancelled,' Oscar said. 'I heard the notices go out this morning. Didn't you pick up your telegram?' he asked, alluding to the wireless traffic.

Bennett swore. 'No. I was gone before the Base came on. Damn it! Well I suppose we can still get the horse. New stallion,' he explained as they stepped into the bar, 'came up on the train to Harditch, then out to the Mount. Brought the top price in the yearling sales three years back, and a good track record since.' His laugh was rich with satisfaction, 'Axel's set to lose a few now. Next year's Cup will be ours – I guarantee it.'

'You a racing man, Harry?' Oscar asked as he served the beers.

'I don't mind a bet.' The half-caste's voice was deep. He was solidly built, his shoulders padded with muscle, and looked to be light on his feet despite a slight thickening of the jowls and in the region of his middle. Flash bugger, Oscar thought, eyeing the trophy buckle and engraved leather of his belt. And the top boots on his feet. Not too many ringers could afford fancy boots like that. He wore a fawn hat at a cocky angle that spilled dark curly hair over the heavy brow ridge, and he had the broad nose and strong jaw of his mother's people. No disguising the abo there, even if his skin had been lighter. Pugnacity cloaked him in the thrust of his walk and the ready challenge of his look.

Oscar, who did his own bouncing, recognised the chip on his shoulder common to a certain type of half-caste. The ones that resented their Aboriginality, and any white man who dared to hint at it. He wouldn't fancy him as a boss, he thought. Always having to prove himself faster and tougher than the next man – he'd give those under him a hard time. Just went to show – there were worse jobs than running a business where expenses seemed always to exceed income.

He wiped the bar, his gaze switching to Lionel Bennett. 'Met the new copper yet?'

'Yeah, he called by. Said he was up at Wildhorse Creek and Reilly good as threw him off. I told him if there was ever a place – or a bloke – to watch, it was that one. It does seem as if he's gunna do his job, though. The copper. Which is more than you could say of Sam Bullen. Well,' he glanced restlessly at his companion, 'let's get moving Harry. We've already wasted half the day.'

They left, boots clumping. Bluey, sidling over to eye their empty glasses, ruffled his feathers disapprovingly and shat on the bar room floor.

Three days later Cub left the branding to the rest of them to drive out to the mailbox in time to meet Keith. During the season it was Suds' task to meet the mail, but there was horse feed, and a bag of wheat on today – at least there ought to be – and they were too heavy for the old man to handle. As it was he backed the 'Rover up to the rear of the truck, sprang up and pulled them onto his own vehicle before he'd done much more than greet Keith.

'Good-oh. That'll keep 'em chewing for a bit.' Cub signed the sheet with a flourish and exchanged mailbags. 'How far back's the grader?'

'Hasn't reached Rainsford yet. The other one's working south on the Harditch road.' Keith scratched his ear. 'Country's drying out, not much more'n a foot of water over the road at Crane's Creek.'

'Yep, green's almost gone from the feed here. What's the word from the council? Have they voted on the bridge for the Crane yet?'

'Nah – this month's meeting was cancelled. Oscar said Bennett turned up for it – but only because he hadn't heard it wasn't on. The only other bit of news is Rainsford's new sire. A good 'un too – according to them that's seen it. Bennett and his head stock-man picked it up from the Mount, Monday. Lionel's been talking him up – he's got every race for the next five years run and won with 'im already.'

'Racing.' Cub shook his head. 'Bloody country's mad with it. I'd sooner hear they had plans for the bridge. 'Course there's none of 'em on the council live north of the Crane – that's the real problem. They'd have built it years back if it was Rainsford being inconvenienced – or the Coopers.'

Keith grinned maliciously and licked the paper on the smoke he was building. 'Could try standing yourself next election.'

'Yeah,' Cub's blue eyes smouldered, 'if I thought it'd do any good, I might.' He tossed the bag he held through the cab window. 'You're an interested party – the creek's always holding you up – so why don't you stand?'

'Ah, well.' Flicking a match into life Keith grinned again. 'I've only gotta *start* with the mail, see, and I get paid. Don't matter to me if the creek's up. Money's the same – only easier earned.'

'Figures,' Cub grunted sourly. 'Well, some of us have to earn our living.' He got into the Land Rover, banging the door twice to shut it, and drove off.

The next to call was Sam Handley the vet. He came bumping slowly along the track, headlights spearing the dark, to the Pandanus yards where the Reillys were camped. He'd picked up the papers from the homestead and bread, which Blake received with a grunt of thanks. 'Tucker's on,' he waved a hand at the circle of carbide light on the table. 'Grab yourself a plate. What's the news from town?'

Sam, a short, wiry man with an easy manner, laughed as he settled on his heels to eat. 'The new copper's the news. Just about the only topic – in the pub anyway. Regular demon for the letter of the law. Oscar swears he's there with a watch checking his opening hours. I pulled in there for a drink before he closed this arvo and this streak of khaki misery comes into the bar to tell me the mud on my numberplate *renders it unreadable*. His actual words. Had to wash the bloody thing before he was satisfied. He even booked Ken Walker for a parking offence. Told him he was a danger to traffic and old Ken says: *What bloody traffic?* Then he cautioned him for swearing.'

Simon, sitting across the fire from him, chuckled. 'The copper's got a point, you know. I don't call pulling up in the middle of the road parking – and that's what Ken does.'

'He wasn't much better when he had the trucks,' Blake put in unexpectedly. 'I remember coming onto him one time just after the Wet. In that bit of black soil country on Plover Creek, it was. He was fetching up a load in the tanker. Anyway, the road was still tacky and the weight pulled him into the table drain. The whole thing tipped, spilling the fuel – you could see it floating on the water in the drain. The bloody fool was boiling his billy just across the track from it.'

'What'd you do?' Billy, listening, was fascinated; more by the fact that Blake was talking than by the actual tale, for he rarely opened his mouth, save to give orders.

'Backed up half a mile and camped till they sorted it out. Stupid bastard wanted to blow himself up it was his business.'

'He probably wishes now he'd stuck with the trucks,' Sam fed a stick into the fire. 'Talk round the district is that he's up to his eyes in debt.'

'Yeah,' Cub nodded. 'Casey said something about it last time we met. Their agents are bailing up on them. No more credit till they repay a bit of what's owing. I don't see how they can, really, what with the fencing needed.'

'And parking fines.' Jo sounded indignant. 'He must be a flaming pain, that copper.'

Sam rinsed his plate in the bucket of soapy water standing on the coals at the fire's edge, then yawned. 'I'm for bed. What numbers have you got for tomorrow, Blake?'

'Three-forty or so. Won't take long.' Blake stretched and Billy heard his shoulders crack. 'Everything okay at the homestead?'

'Ah, almost forgot. Your cook wants meat. I said I'd pass it on. G'night.' He walked into the darkness to find his swag as the rest of them sought their own. There were few late nights in cattle camps; they started too early for that.

Next morning the testing was finished before midday. Sam cleared the cattle dust from his throat with a hearty hawk and spit, then sluiced face and hands in the washing bowl. He was due at Brancaster that evening, he said, spreading sauce lavishly over his bread and meat.

Blake, washing behind him, looked up, face dripping with water. 'Good. I'll get a ride back to the station with you.' The twins had taken a cut lunch with them to paddock the tested cattle so only Billy and Simon remained. 'I'll take the truck into town for the fuel,' Blake told them. 'You'd better see about a killer too. It'll be the last chance before the Races.'

'Righto,' Simon dug a fingernail into his ear. There was a scum of dirt on his teeth and his eyes showed white in the powdered dust of his face. Billy, sniffing, smelt the sour stink of the yard on himself and his clothes. He rubbed a knuckle across his own teeth to clean them, and spat. Killing was his least favourite job, but you had to have meat.

Blake and the vet ate and left. Billy and Simon had a more leisurely meal in the shade of the bauhinia clump under which they had camped. There was no point leaving until the twins returned. And they wouldn't go after the killer until the cooler half of the afternoon. Idly, watching the points of sunlight splintering against the shifting leaves, Billy said, 'We going to the Races then?'

'Of course we are.' Simon lifted an eyebrow. 'I've got rides booked with Axel Cooper, and a trainer from Harditch. We always go.' He eased himself back against the scaly trunk of the tree behind him. 'There'll be a Stockman's Flutter – you oughta borrow a horse and have a go. Cub's too heavy but you're not.'

'I'd be in that.' Billy had an agreeable vision of himself coming in first under Jo's admiring glance. 'Maybe Axel'd have something I could ride. Where are we going to find this killer?'

Simon yawned. His hat lay brim up on the dirt beside him. He ran a hand through his stiff, sweat-dried hair. 'We'll have a look up the creek when we get home. Should be something there.'

But there wasn't. They searched until sundown before heading back to Suds' complaints served up with a meal of macaroni and onions.

'What d'you call this?' Cub poked it with a fork.

'You're the ones didn't get the killer,' the cook reminded him. 'I can't work with nothing. Put some sauce on it.'

Billy already had the bottle upended over his serving. 'Where's the boss?'

'He left. Said 'e'd camp down the road save a bit of time tomorrow. Prob'ly beat the tanker there an' have to wait anyway – but you can't tell him nothing.'

'The 'Bend's out of fuel?' Simon asked.

Suds shrugged. 'Like I said – the tanker's due. What you gunna do about the meat?'

Simon sighed. 'Give it a rest, will you? We'll find something tomorrow.'

Next day Billy and the twins had better luck coming across a young, dry cow on the stony flats beside the Eight Mile Creek. By the time they'd shot and butchered the animal the waning sun was laying long shadows across the ranges.

'We'll be in the dark again,' Billy groaned as they threw the last of the meat onto its bed of green boughs. 'I wanted to get my washing done and dry tonight.'

'Nine-to-five jobs that away,' Jo thrust her thumb southward in the general direction of Harditch. 'Anyway you can still do it after tea.'

'That's the truck coming,' Cub commented later as they passed the vehicle shed and saw headlights coming up the track. 'The tanker must've made it. Anybody remember the axe?'

'I picked it up,' Billy said. 'It's on the back.'

Light beamed out from the kitchen windows as they pulled up at the door of the meat-house, where a single bulb cast light enough to work by. Simon was waiting for them with the meat hooks.

'Take the bones and liver in, Jo,' he said, 'the sooner Suds starts on 'em the sooner we eat. We'll finish up here.' They hung the cuts of fresh meat to cool in the night air, and salted and stacked the rest. The hide was folded and rolled, wet side in, to keep it moist and pliable. Tomorrow morning Blake would make it into a green-hide rope. Or he might volunteer himself for the task, Billy thought. He knew how it was done; he'd just never put it into practice yet. *Can't hurt you to learn, son.* Ivy's words. It was amazing how often he had reason to recall the things she'd said to him. With a sudden rush of renewed gratitude he resolved to write her again. It had been a while since his last letter. He'd do it tonight – and let the washing wait until tomorrow.

The kitchen, when he reached it, was rich with the smell of frying meat. Billy sniffed hungrily as he hung his hat. Then gaped at the sight of Blake, seated at the table and chewing gingerly on a slice of liver.

'Jesus!' Simon, following behind, sounded awed. 'What happened to you?'

Cub, blocked by immobile bodies, stared over their shoulders and scowled. 'Obvious – isn't it? He's been on the grog again.'

'Wrong,' growled Blake. His right eye was swollen shut; there was a cut across his cheekbone, and a livid patch on his jaw. Even as they watched he winced and raised a hand to it, unwittingly displaying the bruised and broken skin across his knuckles.

'You look like you tangled with a truck, boss.'

Blake's bottom lip had been split. Billy could see the scab as it stretched in a mirthless grin. 'Say that mongrel Lucas and you've

132

got it right. Talk about a set-up. He was sweating on me from the moment I got outta the truck. Someone must've told him who I was. I stepped through the door and wham! Bastard king-hit me.' He grimaced and eased his side. 'That was his first mistake. I suppose he thought the rest'd be easy. Well, he's learned different now.' Slowly, as if every movement hurt, he pushed his plate away, and swung his leg over the bench before standing up.

'What happened?' It was Simon who asked.

'Got himself arrested. I hope that bloody copper's cooking's as bad as his timing. Five minutes later and I'd have finished the bastard off. He'd have been happy to lock me up too, Watson – only this time there were witnesses. And what's more, sober enough to know what happened.' He creaked erect, holding his ribs, and slowly made for the door. 'I'm turning in. Get the load off the truck first thing in the morning.'

'Wow!' Billy stared around at the others. 'He must be hell on wheels, this Lucas. The boss looks half dead.'

'He got himself home,' Simon pointed out. 'And he seems to have won. So what do you reckon Lucas looks like?'

'Sounds like they deserve each other.' Cub picked up a plate. 'Let's eat. I'm starving. Did you do any onions, Suds?'

Billy's hunger was temporarily blunted by curiosity. He appealed to the old cook and Jo. 'But did he say why? I mean you don't just hit a bloke for no reason. The boss reckoned he'd never met the man before.'

'It might've been meant as a warning,' Simon hazarded. 'When old Poota quit last year there was some talk that Bennett was gunna replace him with a hard man who'd secure his boundaries and pull the Reillys into line. At the time I thought it was just that – talk, something the town had hatched up. Now,' he shrugged, 'I'd say the talk was right. Bennett knows how hard it is to get a conviction for poddy-dodging, but it looks like his strategy's backfired. It'll be interesting,' he added mildly, 'to see what happens next.'

And *that*, Billy thought, was, even for the imperturbable Simon, the understatement of the year. Because while Blake seemed to have won this round Lucas didn't sound the type who'd neglect to try evening the score.

Eighteen

The fight was the talk of Southbend for the fortnight leading up to the Races, ousting even the piquant topic of the arrival of the town's new nurse, who turned out to be Misery Jones' niece.

'Never knew the old skinflint had a family,' Oscar Davies confided across the bar. 'Thought he just hatched out somewhere, a self-sufficient orphan. Sorta like one of them mallee chicks.' Pouting disapproval he stroked Bluey's feathers. 'Hardly proper birds at all – no nest, no parenting.'

'She's his sister's girl.' Keith Guthrie had his own ways of winkling information out of newcomers. 'First time in the north. Hasn't seen her uncle in twenty years.'

'Well,' Oscar said philosophically, 'summer'll show what she's made of. Turning up in June don't give you much idea.'

'Ah, she's young,' Keith put a protective palm over his glass as Bluey approached. 'Was a time the heat never bothered me, neither. 'Sides, she's a single girl – she'll have all the young fellas after her. Won't have time to worry about the climate. How'd your court hearing go?'

Oscar scowled; the topic was a sore point with him. Both he and the storekeeper had been heavily fined for their part in Bullen's downfall.

'Bunch of wowsers,' he said bitterly. 'Another offence'll mean my licence. Not that that's likely, mind you.'

'Not with the human bloodhound around,' Keith agreed. 'Jesus! I dunno what we're coming to – I done a tail light last trip; hit the back end on a post while I was unloading at Rainsford. And you know I pulled into the Mount to borrow one off Axel *and* fitted the bloody thing before I come back into town? He's got us all bluffed.'

'Bastard,' muttered Bluey, standing on one foot while scratching the side of his head with the other.

Oscar's fleshy lips stretched into a grin. 'You got that right, mate.'

'So has he been back – since the fight?' Keith prompted, reverting to their earlier discussion.

'Who? Lucas or Reilly? Haven't set eyes on either of 'em. Not a dicky-bird on the wireless neither. Maybe they'll come to the Races. He's an unsociable bugger, old Blake, but he mostly turns out for that. Dunno about the yella-fella – he copped a proper pasting. Might keep away if he thinks Blake'll be there.'

'Well,' Keith climbed off the stool and stretched his skinny frame, 'you can't say life ain't interesting. I'd better toddle.'

'Shout for the bar,' Bluey husked at his retiring back.

'Wouldn't exactly break him,' Oscar muttered with a glance along its empty length. He rinsed the glass, dried it and placed it back in the rack, then sought out his favourite chair on the verandah to await the next customer.

For the young men in the district the new nurse was as big a drawcard as the Races themselves. There was also a degree of curiosity about the next meeting between Blake Reilly and Harry Lucas. Everybody knew the details of the fight and, for once, sentiment was firmly on Reilly's side. There was a general feeling that the big yella-fella had got his just desserts. A local man beating Blake was one thing – a stranger trying it by underhand methods brought out the partisan in Reilly's neighbours. As that amateur philosopher Keith Guthrie succinctly put it: 'He might be a bastard, but he's *our* bastard.'

Fiona Forrest, the newest appointee to the hospital staff, was one of the few to differ for Lucas had not spent the night in the police station's single cell, but in a hospital bed. After being introduced to Simon at the racecourse the smile left her lips and she gave a little gasp of horror.

'You're the one who beat that poor man unconscious.'

'No.' Slim and grave he stood before her, the sun highlighting his cheekbones, shadowing his pale eyes. 'Do I look like I could beat anybody up?'

'What?' She paused her indignation long enough to really look at him, then doubtfully shook her head. 'He was big and strong looking so – no. But I'm sure they said Reilly.'

'Yes. Bloke called Blake.' Simon smiled his swift, seldom seen smile. 'Three times my size. Bit like a brown snake if you cross him. As for me I don't even know what Harry Lucas looks like – is he here today?'

'I haven't noticed,' Fiona glanced about at the crowd, 'but there are so many. And they all wear those cowboy hats.'

'Shame,' Simon said. 'Tell you what – if you do see him, will you point him out?'

'But – I mightn't know where you will be.'

'Unless we stayed together,' he suggested, waiting until her lips twitched before he smiled again. 'And if you want a flutter – back me in the third. The horse I'm riding's gunna win.'

'Oh, in that case,' her hazel eyes sparkled back at him. She had a lithe, wide-shouldered figure with a mass of dark curly hair tied severely back from the clean angles of her face. 'I will – and in return you can tell me who everyone is.' She nodded, 'Starting with the redhead over there.'

Billy had gone straight to the stalls to look at the horses, specifically Gaynor. Instead he found himself standing awe-struck before the bay stallion housed alone in the end stall. He almost didn't hear Rachel's halting approach until she spoke at his shoulder.

'Isn't he a beauty? That's Rainsford's new sire. His name's Hexagon. From Dancing Nan by a horse called Oblong with quite a record of wins in Sydney.'

'Hi, Rachel.' He drew in a fervent breath. 'My God, isn't he something? I've never seen anything to equal that.'

'Really? Not even your Daisy?'

'You can't compare a half Arab with—'

She was teasing him, Billy realised, catching her smile. Her scent was a flowery fragrance against the ammoniac reek of the stalls. He shook his head. 'If he's half as good as he looks he'll have the Cup today.'

'Not this year. He needs to be in the district twelve months before he's eligible to run in that. But yes, real competition on his breeding. He's entered in one of the open races. Did Cub come?'

'Yes, of course. We're all here. Simon's riding for your dad and Kenny Burke, the Harditch trainer. So is Axel running Gaynor today? I'll have a couple of dollars on her if he is.'

Rachel paused to stare at him. 'You didn't hear? We lost her to blood poisoning. Dad was so angry! He and Ben – well,' she cut herself off and limped forward again, 'never mind. Actually he's got a horse here today for the Challenge – Ben, I mean.' She grimaced. 'Dad's idea, of course. For the sake of the Jockey Club, he said, keeping the numbers up. But really he's punishing Ben because he doesn't want to ride – he's hopeless at gauging a race. Which Dad knows very well.' She stopped, looking vexed. 'I don't know why I tell you these things – I suppose it's because nobody else bothers to listen.'

You mean Cub won't, Billy thought. He felt sorry for her and to cover it said lightly, 'It's what friends do, isn't it – listen? Look, if it's any help I'll take Ben's ride. I sort of owe him one anyway – I feel bad about socking him the way I did. I knew as soon as I cooled down he wasn't trying to hurt the filly, he was just—'

'Being Ben,' Rachel finished. Her brown eyes were troubled. 'I wish he'd quit the place. He's so unhappy. He's a gentle person; he can't bring himself to disappoint those he loves. And Dad doesn't seem to *care*. I don't know how he can't see what he's doing to him. But he's set his heart on making him fit to run the station. Though it might as well be Daphne for all the chance he has of making it happen. She's pregnant by the way.'

'Oh, well,' he sought for an appropriate response. 'I suppose your mother's pleased – and you'll be an aunt. Look, I'd better find Ben and fix up this ride.'

'You could win,' she called after him. 'Jimrack's a sprinter.'

'Maybe. Only Simon's brought a mare down too, so I'll be riding against him. *She's* fast too. And he's a jockey.'

'Well,' she said consolingly, 'you've got more chance than Ben, that's for certain.'

The Stockman's Challenge was the last race on the program. It was ridden in stock saddles and was open to all save professional jockeys. Billy, cantering the leggy chestnut down to the start, patted the sweating neck and looked over the opposition. He had shaken hands with Ben and thanked him for the ride. The latter had shrugged it off, his smile a little twisted.

'You're welcome. More your scene than mine, mate. Win the damn' thing if you can.'

Billy intended to. And having done so he'd ask Jo to accompany him to the dance. But first he had to beat the opposition – which included Carnival, Simon's temperamental liver chestnut mare. *Spiteful as a bag of cats* was how Cub had described her. She was fast, Billy knew, but just as likely to drop her head as race – at least he hoped so, for realistically, given mounts with comparable speed, he knew himself to be no match for the older rider.

Henry Burch was astride a short-coupled bay with powerful quarters. The race was only three furlongs so staying power wasn't going to matter, but he'd need an explosive start to get the jump on the bay. Plover Creek's head stockman, whom he vaguely knew to be called Snowy, was an unknown quantity, as was the horse he was astride. And the same applied to the final contender, a stranger with a black hat, on an ordinary-looking brown mare.

They lined up, Simon to the outside holding a prancing Carnival. Henry's bay stood stolidly but Billy could feel his tension flowing into Jimrack. The pistol banged and the bay shot away like an arrow in flight, covering three strides before the chestnut's longer legs drove him level. They raced stride for stride then the taller horse began slowly to pull away. From the corner of his eye, Billy had seen Carnival rear as the gun fired. He grinned in wolfish satisfaction and settled himself to ride as he never had before.

The distance was too short for tactics. They went flat out for the winning post. Billy kept one eye on it and the other on the bay still coming up beside him. Snowy and Black Hat were out of it, Simon left somewhere behind in the dust. A surge of jubilation filled him – they were going to do it. The second furlong post fled by and the world receded as Billy's hearing dimmed. Everything moved in slow motion. Crouched on Jimrack's neck he had time to see the bobbing rise of the gelding's head, the slow flare of his nostrils, and the way his mane floated in the breeze of their going. The bay, clinging to his left flank, was tiring and slipping backwards. Henry, looking chagrined but determined, still hadn't given up. Billy's lips stretched in a grin of triumph.

Then, as if a bubble had dissolved, sound and sensation came crashing back. He felt the wind tearing his eyes, heard the thunder of hooves and the faint yells of the crowd, and with a sudden heart-sinking jolt glimpsed movement on his right where Carnival's head was drawing level with his knee.

Tucking his body flatter along the chestnut's neck he watched hypnotised as the mare crept forward. Jimrack, aware of her presence, lunged desperately giving his all but Billy, watching fascinated, saw the mare's head glide level with the gelding's neck. Another stride, two – he turned his head to see how close to it they'd come – and the post was there, was behind him. They won.

Simon slapped his hand against the mare's streaming neck as they pulled up far down the track, and grinned. 'Good ride, mate. Almost had you.'

'You're telling me.' Billy felt light enough to float from the saddle. 'Greased lightning's not in it, considering your start. Why don't you race her properly?'

'She's not registered. Long story.' Standing in the irons they trotted back up the course. 'What're you doing on a Cooper horse, anyway?'

'Another long story.' Billy threw the words over his shoulder as they reached the stand, eyes already searching past Rachel and her father for Jo. Ben was there too, looking genuinely pleased for him, and here came Bennett, the Club president, with the blue sash over his arm. Everyone wanted to congratulate him, although whether it was because a Cooper horse had won, or simply that he'd beaten a Reilly, he couldn't tell. Suppressing an impatient sigh he waited for it to be over. Having accomplished his goal he'd gladly skip all the palaver in exchange for five minutes alone with Jo.

But when he finally got his wish it was too late.

'The dance?' She held her hat, a creation of straw with an artificial flower pinned to the side. 'Sorry, Snowy Sanditon's already asked me. I'm going with him.'

'Oh,' Billy was flustered. This most obvious outcome was the one he had not foreseen. His face fell. 'I wanted – that is, I thought—'

She waited but he didn't complete the sentence. Seeing his disappointment she spoke with tart exasperation, 'You've had all day to ask me, Billy. If it comes to that you've had all month. I wasn't going to turn down a perfectly good invitation just in case you feel like issuing one at the last moment.'

'No, of course not. Sorry, I should've – well, have a nice time then.' Numbly he watched her walk away through the diminishing crowd. How well, he wondered, did she know this Snowy who was older (and taller) than he himself was? *And* a head stockman to boot. She'd never mentioned him, to his knowledge. Billy felt a sudden primeval urge to punch his lights out. There was one comfort – Cub would do it for him if he tried anything on. But that thought brought its own worry.

Kicking an inoffensive clod of black soil into pieces he scowled at the youngest Walker girl and strode moodily back to the camp they'd pitched in the timberline. Winning had been a waste of time. He might as well have come in last for all the good it had done him.

Nineteen

Next day the four of them were late getting back to the station as the dance had gone on past midnight. Oscar Davies had hosted a barbecue at the pub and from this his patrons had drifted either into the bar, or down the road to the hall. Billy had returned to camp to lie wretchedly awake picturing Jo in Snowy's arms, face alight as she gave herself over to the music. It could have been him if only he'd asked her sooner. Or maybe not. He stared up at the stars that seemed to shiver in the chilly night sky wondering, if he had asked her earlier, whether she would still have turned him down.

An hour or two later Blake returned, hauling Suds with him across the lumpy tussocks. The cook was dead drunk, plaiting his legs and expostulating blearily as he was dumped onto the swag that Blake kicked open.

'Stay there, you silly old bugger,' he growled. He turned to the fire and squatted, poking it together, and a moment later a flare of light outlined his hunched form. A loud snore shook the night from the direction of Suds' swag, quickly followed by another. Billy humped onto his side and pulled the pillow over his head to deaden the maddening sound, misery and jealousy taking up equal space in his heart.

Next morning, between the late night and Suds' hangover they made a subdued camp as they packed up and loaded Carnival for the trip home. Suds, groaning and sick, was bundled unsympathetically into the 'Rover with the twins, Billy electing to ride with Simon and Blake in the truck. Simon seemed in good spirits. He'd collected Billy's race prize, a miniature cup which now lay glinting on the dashboard.

'It was a good night,' he said, 'you should've come. Plover Creek's got a new governess; you could've practised your dancing.'

Billy made a bad-tempered sound that served as acknowledgement and it was Blake who picked up the conversational ball. 'Did Lucas turn up then? I didn't see him at the racecourse.'

'He wasn't there. I was talking to Nobby Elfston last night and he said Lucas stayed home. He's got no time for him, reckons he's a mongrel to work for – real standover merchant. He admired your handiwork, by the way – said it was a week before Lucas was riding again.'

Blake grunted. 'He coulda done it himself; the bastard's not so tough. Wouldn't be surprised if he tried something all the same to get his own back. His sort usually do.'

'Like what?'

'How do I know?' Blake's heavy shoulders lifted in a shrug. 'Fire's easiest.' His gaze swept the grassed land beyond the window. 'Or he might try forcing a fight on you or the lad. If it come to that he'd cripple you both.'

'Not me.' Simon slowed, changing down for a gully, head cocked sideways to listen behind for the mare's movements. 'I wouldn't fall for it. But Cub – yeah, he's hot-headed enough. I'll warn him, for all the good that's likely to do.' He frowned. 'Maybe it's as well he didn't turn up yesterday.'

'He bottled it,' Blake said, 'that's why. But I'm telling you I've seen brown snakes I'd trust further than Lucas. And you can pin that in your hat.'

They reached the Brumby in time for a late lunch in the kitchen where the stove had to be raked out and lit, and one of the kerosene fridges refilled. Belle, having upset her water dish, was whining on the chain. The garden drooped dryly awaiting the hose, and as soon as the vehicle reached the gate the poultry came flocking to be fed. It was truly amazing Billy thought how many chores the homestead generated. By the time it was all done and Cub had run the horses into the house paddock the day was spent.

Next morning, with the sun just tipping the eastern range top, they started back out to the camp. Suds had recovered from the drink, and Billy from his fit of pique. He and the twins went with the horses, while Blake and Simon drove ahead. It was fourteen miles across to the paddock where the sale cattle were mustered. The buyer was coming tomorrow, Billy knew, for it had been arranged since before the Races, so they could look forward to an easy day. Then, if a sale were made tomorrow, they'd shift the cattle back to the homestead yards before starting south to the trucking yards at the Mount. He'd never done any droving and was looking forward to the experience.

He hunched his neck into the sheepskin-lined collar of his coat for the wind was cold and the dust in its folds gritted against his skin. The twins were feeling it too; the end of Jo's red scarf was pulled across her face and Cub, riding on the wing, had one hand buried in his coat pocket. Dust brisked ahead of them down the track and if it hadn't been July, he thought, turning his eyes to the grey mackerel sky above, he'd swear it was building up to storm.

It was Cub's angry yell rather than the engine noise that alerted him to the camp truck's return. It roared up to the lead of the horses and stopped, sending the plant skittering right and left into the scrub.

'Block 'em up!' Blake's bellow easily overrode the wind. 'The cattle are gone. Some bastard's flattened the fence.'

There was no time for questions. Simon was there too; both of them snatched bridles from the load and were saddling up even as Blake issued his orders. 'Jo, take the nags on to the camp, and get that fence mended – there's wire at the yards, and a couple of steel posts. There could be a few head still in the paddock – we didn't stop to check. Billy, Cub – you're with me. They can't be long gone, though this damn wind won't help the tracking.'

'What about the truck?' Billy asked.

'Forget the bloody truck.' Blake yanked his Bates strap tight and reached for the iron. 'Getting them back's what matters.'

This task proved as difficult as Blake had feared. By the week's end, and despite all the country they had covered in their furious riding, they were still over two hundred head short of their original numbers. By then Blake's mood had settled into one of black fury aimed squarely at Harry Lucas.

'You don't *know* it was him,' Simon said unwisely as they unsaddled that final day after paddocking the last few head gathered. It was late, a sickle moon stood upright in the darkness overhead and the sight of the fire was welcome in the black chill of the night. Billy's legs were so stiff he groaned as he squatted to hobble the bay, Nellie. She snorted tiredly above him and he heard the links of the chain chink in the darkness as she moved off.

'Yes, by Christ, I do!' Blake said savagely. 'Work it out. The paddock was sound Friday night when we left it. We're gone for the weekend and by Monday the paddock's flat and the cattle gone. I told you he'd try something.'

'Yeah.' Simon warmed his hands at the fire, which lit the angles of his cheekbones shadowing his eye sockets. 'Logically it's him. Everybody else was at the races. So – what do we do?'

'You gunna get onto the police, boss?' Billy ventured. He'd expected Blake to do so when he first saw the wreck of the fence through which the Fordson tractor (left outside the paddock at the yards where they'd used it only the week before) had been driven. 'It's malicious damage – trespass too, I suppose.' It was certainly malicious – the tractor's ignition had been left on, and the front tyres slashed, so that they could neither start the vehicle, nor move it from where it had been left.

'It's a lot more than that, sonny.' Blake, who was easing the camp oven of stew from beneath its coating of ash in the oven hole, bared his teeth in a snarl, 'And nothing to do with any lousy copper.' He dumped the oven onto the coals to reheat the meal that had cooked in their absence. 'Anyone making that tea – or you gunna let the bloody billy boil away?'

Jo had gone back to the homestead with a message to postpone the buyer's arrival until tomorrow. He would find a smaller mob of bullocks which, if not exactly run to skin and bones, as Blake alleged, would, Billy thought, certainly weigh lighter than they had previously done. And they still had the droving trip to the Mount in front of them for while cattle buyers agreed a price on the station, they paid on delivery at the railhead. The trucks had also needed to be re-booked – but there was no way to recover the time they had lost.

Lucas's intervention had been shrewdly timed for they were past the turn of the season. Every day that passed now would see the breeders steadily losing condition as the protein failed in the dry feed as the year drew towards summer. Which meant they would wind up cutting the second round of mustering short, and that mattered quite a lot. Work undone, in the cattle industry as elsewhere, was money lost.

They had a good trip down to Mount Ixion with the bullocks. Eight days of steady progress as the mob fed south, first through the Wildhorse country, then Rainsford and finally the northern end of Cooper's land. And six bitterly cold nights under the white chill of the winter stars. But the watches passed uneventfully and the last night saw them in the station yards at Mount Ixion, ready to load at daybreak.

The only interruption to their routine was when Keith Guthrie pulled into their camp one sunset and even he had little news to impart.

'Nobody's home anywhere. Whole sodding district's gone to Harditch for the rodeo.'

'Of course, I'd forgotten it was on,' Simon said. The stations always gave their men time off for rodeo knowing they'd pull out if they didn't. 'Who's holding the fort at Rainsford then?'

'Lionel and his missus are still there. And the bookie and the mechanic. At Plover's Creek there's nobody but the cook. Even the Walkers went – and he's supposed to be broke. ' Keith shook his head in wonderment. 'How many ways can a bloke get thrown from a horse – or a bull, come to that? You seen one, you seen 'em all.'

'Let's hope Swenson hasn't lost his drivers to the broncs then,' Blake said. Swenson was the carrier contracted to cart the bullocks. Keith left without disturbing the cattle, now settled on the camp the other side of the truck. Billy, squatting by the fire, yawned and cocked his head to catch the faint sound of Jo's whistling as she took the dog watch. Tomorrow night they'd be at the Mount and they'd all get a full night's sleep. He wasn't sorry either. Droving was a different form of stock work, as Ivy had once told him, but for himself he preferred proper station hours.

At Mount Ixion they hobbled the plant outside the horse paddock, yarded the cattle and camped within hearing, tying a night horse up as a precaution. Bullocks, Simon said when Billy asked why the horse was needed, had been known to flatten even solidly built yards if they rushed. It didn't pay to be complacent. The distant thump of the diesel came to them in their camp and they could see the lighted windows of the homestead, although both the quarters and Garry's cottage were in darkness.

'Somebody's home, any rate,' Blake said. He hadn't mentioned Lucas in days, but nobody was deceived into thinking he'd forgotten him. Of course there wasn't much he could do about it right now, Billy thought. Not with Lucas away. But he had to come back sometime.

Axel Cooper arrived later, stepping out of the darkness into the circle of fire-shine that lit and hid by turns the faces of those about it. Billy saw and greeted him first.

'G'day, Axel.'

'Billy.' They shook hands and he nodded across the fire to the older man. 'G'day, Blake. Jo,' he tipped his hat to her, 'boys.' They murmured in answer and he squatted on his heels and held his hands to the blaze. 'Came to tell you Earl was on the radio earlier. He wanted me to let you know the trucks'll be on time.'

'Right,' Blake grunted, 'thanks.'

'The place looks pretty deserted,' Billy said. 'I suppose they're all in Harditch – you going too?'

'Not this year. Look, I've been wanting a word, Blake. We're starting up a branch of the Cattlemen's Union. Everyone's agreed that something has to be done to protect the industry. I wondered if you'd be interested in joining? We're trying to get representation from every property in the district. We need a show of unity right now. If the Cattlemen's Union is strong enough it can provide a voice for all the northern producers. The government's running mad at present, the way it's bringing in these reforms. They're ruining people – driving them off their land. We need a strong body that can lobby against moving too fast on a whole raft of issues. So right now we're canvassing for members. What do you say? Will you come along to the meeting?'

'Who's running it?' Blake asked.

'Lionel Bennett's got the Chair, I'm Secretary and Rachel's doing the Treasurer's job for now. There's an organiser from the state branch coming up—'

'You can count me out then,' Blake interrupted, spitting a shred of tobacco from his mouth while continuing to roll and tuck in the ends of the cigarette he was fashioning. 'I wouldn't stay in the same room with that bastard Bennett, and you can tell him I said so.' He pulled a burning stick from the fire and lit the smoke, his pale eyes hard and unblinking.

'Look,' Axel spread his hands, 'if ever there was a time to pull together it's now. Whatever your differences with Rainsford, can't you put them aside? We're talking peoples' livelihoods here.'

'Not mine,' Blake growled. 'It's only the no-hopers who've got themselves into debt that'll go down. And they shouldn't be in the game in the first place. You're wasting your breath. I'll join nothing Bennett's a part of.'

Axel Cooper rose to his feet. 'I didn't expect much else, so I can't say I'm disappointed. Goodnight then.' He left as quietly as he had come, boots soundless in the dust.

'Maybe we should join,' Simon said after a moment. 'At least we'd keep abreast of what's happening.'

'What are stock inspectors for?' Cub asked. 'All right for Cooper – he's only a spit outta town. It'd take us half a day to get to a meeting – and the rest to get home again. It's all time and fuel – and just for a lot of talk.'

'But if people are being ruined – I'm not talking about Ken Walker, he couldn't manage a kid's picnic let alone a property, but other people—' Simon began.

'You think running to meetings will stop that?' Blake rose to fetch his soap and towel. 'The lad's got the right of it, for once. They'd be better off staying home and working. Is there a tap anywhere round this joint, Billy?'

'Corner of the meat-house. They keep a hose there.' He watched Blake's torch bob away in search of it. The man had to be cast iron; he seemed as impervious to the cold as to everything else, including neighbourly appeals. But perhaps, Billy thought, it gave him satisfaction to be in a position to refuse the men who looked down on him.

They trucked the bullocks at dawn with a cold wind stirring the yard dust and the sky streaked with murky cloud. Despite Blake's knock-back the previous evening Axel came down to help.

'Few head down?' he enquired. 'Don't you usually send more?'

'Yeah.' Blake spoke shortly and it was Simon who explained about the flattened paddock.

Axel's eyes narrowed. 'Have you reported it? Can you prove it was Lucas?'

'I don't have to,' Blake said. 'I know it.'

'How?' Axel Cooper asked bluntly. 'Look, it's a task for Watson. That's what the police are for. Lay a complaint and leave it to them.'

Blake laughed. The sound startled Billy as he'd not previously heard him give way to mirth, however ironically flavoured. 'I'd sooner have pleuro in the stock than coppers on the place,' he said. 'You stick to the law, Cooper. Me, I'll settle for getting square.'

Twenty

The threat inherent in Blake's words stuck like a burr in Billy's thoughts. On the third day of the return journey, finding himself detailed off with Jo to drive the horses, he spoke to her about it. Since the furore arising out of the discovery of the sabotaged paddock he had scarcely been alone with her. In a way he was glad of it for it had saved him from what he felt would be the blunder of mentioning the dance. Now, nearly three weeks on, it was possible to fall back into old patterns of behaviour as if the invitation she'd refused had never happened.

'What Blake said about getting square, back at the Mount – what do you think he meant?'

'Something Rainsford won't like,' Jo answered promptly. 'It's an old trick you know – but mostly when there's a manager involved. It's the easiest way to persuade a company boss to shift a man that's seriously upset his neighbours. Bryant and May carry big sticks.'

'Who?'

Jo laughed. 'Slowcoach! Matches. They make matches, Billy.'

'Strike me!' His eyes widened in alarm. 'You don't think he'd burn them out?' The grass was sapless, dry as tinder, and the south-easterlies blew daily. A fire at this time of year would be a disaster.

She shook her head. 'Two can play at that game. We're vulnerable too. But whatever he does it's probably happening right now. He had to have some reason to want the boys with him this morning.'

She spoke with a casual unconcern that Billy could not share. 'Axel was right, I reckon. He should've gone to the cops.'

'Who'll do precisely nothing.' Jo brushed impatiently at a fly on her cheek. 'Besides, Blake hates the police. And even if he did – he can point the finger but it doesn't give them proof. Better to show Bennett that he's got himself a problem he can't afford. Anyway,' she lifted her shoulders, 'that's how it's done up here – people tend to sort out their own troubles.'

Ivy, he remembered, had once made a similar claim. Billy scratched his cheek where the stubble itched. 'I suppose I'll get the hang of it if I stay long enough,' he said dubiously.

'You will.' She smiled suddenly, the scar in her cheek dimpling as she did so. Looking away she said, 'You've had one Wet up here, Billy. Are you staying for the next?'

'Until I get a better offer. I like the place. I dunno about the people – you've got some weird ways,' he teased, 'but I daresay given another twelve months I'll think them normal too.' Her eyes creased up as she answered his grin with her own. Then he spoiled it all.

'That bloke Snowy – is he your boyfriend?'

'What?' Her cheeks flushed pink as she answered back sharply. 'Where did that come from?'

'You mean he is.' Billy felt his breath harden in his chest and he changed tack. 'Sorry. Not my business. He seems a decent bloke. I think Rachel told me his dad was a drover. She knows everyone, that girl.'

'Yes.' Jo was confused, her usual acid tongue stifled by Billy's change in tack. She wanted to kick herself for not denying the relationship that didn't exist. Instead to save her pride, she set herself to match Billy's apparent equanimity. 'You sound like you like her, Billy.'

'Is that so surprising?' Wounded pride changed his tone from nonchalance to detachment.

Jo, taken aback by his sudden coldness, leapt to her own conclusion.

'No, of course not. Pick of the bunch if you ask me. Listen – isn't that the truck coming?'

A few moments later it appeared behind them. Numbly, Billy trotted up the wing, turning the horses off the road. Cub, sitting by the window, leaned out to give him the thumbs up as he passed. He had no idea what he meant by it, nor, at the moment, did he care. If somebody had appeared just then to offer him a job at the other end of the district he would have accepted with alacrity.

But nobody did. Jo, biting her lip, spent the rest of the ride wishing for a subtle way in which she could disabuse him of her interest in Snowy. Not that he'd care, anyway, she told herself. No wonder he'd left it so late to ask her to the dance. Probably had to clear it with Rachel first. She was still preoccupied that evening and Cub found both his sister and Billy a disappointing audience when he recounted their revengeful exploit against Rainsford.

'Sounds pretty stupid,' Billy said shortly.

He was the only one to regard it in that light. Certainly Frank Watson didn't think it was stupid when, a week later, he paid another visit to Wildhorse Creek. They had commenced the second round of mustering by then but he had followed them out to Buffalo Camp, a lagoon at the end of the track, with nothing but a broncho yard and fly rig to mark it out from the surrounding bush.

That afternoon, riding on the wing of the mob of cows and calves they were bringing in to the yard, Billy was the first to spot the vehicle tracks. He waved Cub over and pointed.

'Who do you reckon that could be?'

'Search me. Not the 'Rover treads so it can't be Suds.' Dust hung in the air and clung to the blond stubble on his jaw. 'Guess we'll find out when we get there.'

They yarded up and headed over to the camp that was set in a thicket of forest ti-tree, a hundred yards back from the lagoon bank. The police vehicle had been parked to one side at a little distance, and in a manner to provide shade against the westering sun. Frank Watson, dressed in khaki and his official hat, waited beside it, squatting, stockman fashion, on his heels. He rose to his feet from beside the ashes of a small fire as they rode up and nodded a greeting.

Blake wasted no time on civility. 'You again. You're trespassing, copper.'

'It's official police business, Mr Reilly,' Watson countered. 'I came to see you. The old fella at the homestead told me where you were camped.'

'What business?' Blake swung down and hooked up his reins.

The rest of them followed suit and Billy got his first close look at Watson. He was tall and fit looking, his skin as browned as Billy's own. His hair, what he could see of it, was light coloured, as were his eyes, set either side of a longish nose. He'd played for the Town side in the cricket match last December, Billy realised, only he hadn't recognised him then out of uniform. He knew what he'd come about and was sure the knowledge was written on his face.

'I'm following up on a complaint from Rainsford Downs,' Watson said. 'It seems they're missing a few gates from their Crocodile yards. You know them?'

"Course I bloody do. Drive past them every time I go to town, don't I?' Blake said aggressively. 'I thought even you could've nutted that one out.'

'Well, somebody, sometime in the last month, didn't drive past. All the gates are gone. Lionel Bennett seems to think you might know something about it.'

'That's a drafting yard,' Cub said. 'Awful lot of gates. Steel too, weren't they?' He looked at Simon.

'Yeah, I seem to remember they were.' Simon rubbed his jaw. 'Take a bit of shifting, wouldn't they? You'd need a decent sort of truck.'

'As to that I don't think they were stolen. More – displaced. Most likely to the bottom of the Crocodile Hole. It's around forty feet deep they tell me. And that straight bank would make it dead easy – you'd just have to drop them over. By the look of the panda-nus I'd say that's what's happened. Not even very far to carry them. What do you think, boys?'

'Sounds the sorta thing that'd be right up his alley –

159

what's-his-name?' Blake snapped his fingers and appealed to his sons. 'That new head stockman of Bennett's?'

'Harry Lucas?' Cub supplied straight-faced.

'That's the one. Bastard that knocked down our paddock and let the bullocks out.'

Watson's eyes narrowed fractionally. 'Why would he do that? And how do you know it was him?'

Blake ignored the last question. 'Drown the gates, you mean? *If* that's what happened to 'em. Or sabotage me muster? Well, I dunno – could be he gets a kick outta vandalism. Maybe you ought to be asking him instead of wasting my time.' He turned his back, heading for the waterbag that swung at the mouth of the fly rig. Watson stared after him then turned abruptly back to Simon.

'You should have reported it.' He pulled off his hat to scratch his head, displaying a straw-coloured poll damp with sweat for the heat had returned with the month of August. 'How do you know it was Lucas – have you any proof?'

'What do you think?' Simon asked, and in a different tone, 'Have you?'

'No.' The policeman's lips seemed ready to quirk for an instant but were held firmly straight. 'All the same, consider yourself warned – all of you. I'll have a word with Harry Lucas. I want an end to this sort of thing before it gets out of hand.' He replaced his hat. 'I've seen you jockey, haven't I? At the Races?'

'I do a bit,' Simon admitted.

'Thought so. Picked you the moment you rode in. That was a nice mare you had in the Challenge.'

'Yeah,' Simon nodded. Cub held his tongue until the vehicle was rolling then guffawed and cracked his brother on the back with his open hand.

'What do you reckon he'd say if he knew?'

'Knew what?' Billy looked suspiciously at the pair of them, half expecting to find himself on the end of another leg-pull.

'Old joke,' Simon said briefly, walking across to the fire that Jo was fanning back to life. Cub, however, was happy to explain.

'You know Butterfly, that blue roan of Simon's?' At Billy's nod he continued, 'well she's half sister to Carnival – different dams but the same sire. It'd be what – seven, eight years ago – first summer after we bought the place. Old Si took a packhorse and two of our best mares that just happened to be in season and led them across to Bennett's stallion paddock. It's not so very far across country from Verity Valley. Anyway, the horse did the business, Bennett's none the wiser, and old Si wound up with a couple of well, *nice mares* – as the copper would say. Simon's always been nutty about horses,' Cub added tolerantly, 'bit like you, Billy – only he rides better,' he added, with a smile.

Billy shook his head. 'I don't think I'd like you lot for neighbours.'

'Ah, bit of give and take never hurt – especially if Bennett's doing the giving.' Cub ducked to enter the fly where the tucker table was. Billy followed, grinning despite himself. *Long story*, Simon had said when he'd asked why him he didn't race Carnival. It wasn't long at all, just complicated by the usual Reilly twist.

By mid October the mustering was done. The horses, which they were feeding, were still strong, but the cattle were half poor, the cows' strength leached away either by the calves growing within them, or those already at foot. The sun blazed a relentless heat on the land where the grass crunched underfoot, as brittle as straw, and about as nutritious. At night the dry storms thundered around them, the lightning strikes starting fires whose smoke stained the dusty sky. Dust was everywhere – in the air they breathed, on the clothes they wore, on the tired feed and even the surface of the shrinking waterholes.

They were camped up on Coronet Creek in the northwest corner of the property when Blake called it quits. It was the first time Billy had been there and he wondered that they bothered to muster the area at all. It was unprepossessing country – the waterhole a dwindling pool in a narrow, scrubby creek surrounded by gravel ridges and stands of fractured stone that would give a rock wallaby pause. Plenty of spinifex and the sort of girth-high, shrubby bushes that tangled a horse's feet, but very little actual feed. There were cattle there, he'd seen a pad snaking down the bank; also the barefooted tracks of brumbies in the damp sand. He wondered what they ate – but then you seldom saw a brumby in poor condition.

'What do you run out here,' he asked Jo as they saddled up, 'mountain goats?'

'You'd be surprised. We'll pick up some of those bullocks we lost – see if we don't.' She let the saddle flap drop and pulled the iron down from Flute's neck. 'There's a few scrubbers hang out here as well. We always leave this camp till last when the water's low, then hit 'em. We'll do better than you think.'

'Supposing you don't fall off again,' Cub said, looking at Freaky. 'Not a good choice, mate. He's got that look in his eye today.' He appealed to his twin, 'Don't you reckon he's got that look? Sort of cunning, but thoughtful – like he's sort of searching for the right place to dump him.'

Billy gathered the reins. 'Soak your head,' he invited pithily, 'see if you can shrink it to fit your hat.' Nevertheless, once in the saddle he kept a prudent grip on the pony's head – not that it had helped much in the past. But then, he told himself, the ground had never looked quite this hard before, either.

They found cattle at mid morning, just settling to camp in a wattle thicket. One moment they were shapes half seen in the shadow, the next they were on their feet and galloping, with nothing but the drum of their hooves and the slap of the parting scrub to mark their passage.

Billy had an impression of fleeing red and white hide, of half a dozen beasts large enough to be bullocks and, more immediately, a shiny cleanskin cow right in front of him as the rest of the mob fanned out and vanished into the wattle. Blood up, he yanked Freaky after her. The pony sprang into a gallop then slammed on the brakes and whipped his head down.

'Oh, you rotten bugger!' Billy roared. Standing in the irons he was already off balance. The saddle lifted under him, throwing his weight back and his legs up. Loathing for the horse was a snake in his brain. Already he was anticipating the rush of the ground, the jarring impact, and the inevitable humiliation of facing the others afoot. In a fury of rage he caught at the flying mane and slammed his right leg – adrift on a level with the plunging neck – down into the bay's shoulder.

He'd forgotten he was wearing spurs – and so, apparently had Freaky. The pony leapt again, but forward this time, jolting Billy back off his perilous perch on the cantle of the saddle. With nothing to lose he spurred him with both heels and the bay bent to his task and went after the cow. Sunlight glinted on her shiny hide and the strings of white froth from her muzzle as they turned her, then in a whirl of dust and thunder the rest of the mob caught up and Billy was too busy watching the wing he found himself on, and choosing a passage through the timber, to worry about his mount.

The broken scrubby land gave way to the flat ashy soil of a shallow valley dotted with silver leaf and swamp box. Here, in semi-open country, they pulled up to cool the slavering cattle before they overheated. Billy, sitting the lathered Freaky in the shade, saw they'd got about thirty head – nineteen of them cleanskins, the rest bullocks and dry cows, all in top condition.

'They live on the scrub,' Simon explained when he commented on it. 'The bullocks like that bit of country – it's always worth a look.' He glanced down at Freaky's shoulder. 'He's cut himself. Must've collected a stick in the scrub.'

'No.' Billy felt no shame. 'The little sod was trying it on again. I hit him with the spurs. Worked a charm.'

'Ah, well.' Simon's slow smile dawned. 'You've got his measure then. I wondered how long it'd take. He'll be okay now. Beat a rogue once and they chuck it in.'

It seemed too simple to be true but over succeeding days as they returned the bullocks to their paddock, branded the cleanskins, then took the plant back to the station, Simon's reading of the situation proved correct. On the last morning when they were leaving for Verity Valley to turn the horses out for the summer Billy, whose turn it was to get them up to the yards, did so, bareback, on the bay pony.

'Signs and wonders.' Cub saluted ironically as he trudged through the churned sand to swing the gates shut behind him. 'I daresay you'll be walking on water next.'

Twenty-one

The annual cricket match was a poor affair that year. The worrying state of the cattle market had closed down most of the stock camps earlier than usual so there were fewer ringers to make up the Country team. Even Mount Ixion, which normally retained their mechanic throughout summer to help with the windmills in the back country, had put off all their employees save for the cook.

'We'll just have to draft some of the Town side over,' Oscar Davies told Keith Guthrie over a beer. 'There's a fencing crew staying in the pub – I'll ask them. Might be one'll want a game.' Oscar himself was to be umpire, filling in for Misery Jones, currently away down the coast. 'Crook,' he said bluntly of his absent neighbour, '*bloody* crook, I reckon, to be shelling out for a quack.'

'Uncle Mal's not at all well,' Fiona Forrest told Simon. 'He's been coming up to the hospital to see the flying doctor on his clinic runs, and was told to get some tests done. Which sounds a bit ominous. It's why he went to Townsville.'

'Sorry to hear that,' Simon hooked his hand higher on the

upright he was leaning against, his eyes fixed on her face. 'Are you close?'

'Not really, but – he's family, and you don't get to choose that. I know what the town calls him. And my mother says he's still got the first five cents – pennies it would've been – he saved, but still he's sick and old—'

'Not that old,' Simon interjected.

'Seventy-three – and I'm a nurse,' she finished, 'so I care. It's what nurses do. Besides, apart from Mum I'm the only relative he has.'

'That old?' Simon scratched his chin. 'Just shows, living mean must be good for you. Still, like you say – you can't pick your family. Though some of us would be happy to try.'

'Yes.' Calm hazel eyes regarded him. 'But as long as you don't make the same mistakes – and you apparently haven't – it doesn't matter.'

'How can you know that?' he asked almost roughly.

Her smile was faint, but reassuring. 'Uncle Mal might be close with his money but he loves to talk – it costs nothing, I suppose. He's lived here fifty years and he's never forgotten anything, as far as I can tell. You'd be surprised what I know – especially about the Reillys.'

Wary all at once Simon said, 'So you've been checking up on us?'

Fiona smiled and her face beneath its wild nimbus of hair was suddenly pretty. 'Of course. I'm interested, and I thought, instead of the gossip, which never stops in a place like this, I'd go after the facts.'

He dropped his arm and straightened. 'Did you? And what are they – according to old Misery?'

'Nothing very dreadful, so relax.' With a mischievous smile she stuck out the fingers of her left hand while counting the points off with the other. 'Your parents split up when you were kids; your father's a brute – well I'd already worked that out after seeing the man he beat up – and you don't have many friends in the district. However,' she circled the little finger with the index one on her right hand, 'you've a name for being good toilers, you particularly are noted for horsemanship, and you run a tidy, solvent operation up there in the hills. That's how Uncle Mal put it. I asked where solvency came into it. And he said he'd never loaned you money – but he'd be willing to, if you needed it. Apparently he does that. Quite big sums too, from what he hinted at. Half the town seems to be in his debt. So,' she cocked her head, 'are you upset that I checked you out?'

'No. I – well, to tell you the truth I'm too staggered to – old Misery a moneylender? Yeah, he's tight with a buck but I never really believed he had dough. Not with a capital D.' He frowned, 'He's kept his lip buttoned all these years – why would he tell you now?'

'I think,' Fiona said judiciously, 'that it's his way of reaching out. Since he got sick he's come to see how – well, maybe not lonely, but – isolated he is. It was the evening of the day the doctor told him to have the tests done that he told me about the money. Oh, not straight out, you know, but hinting around. He's a strange old man; he was making contact, perhaps the only way he knew how – through giving me secrets.'

'And now you're telling me,' he said bluntly, 'why?'

She regarded him gravely with just a hint of a curve to her lips. She was, he thought, older than he'd first assumed – twenty-seven, maybe, or twenty-eight. A woman, not a girl.

'Because secrets shared breed trust and that makes for friendship. I want us to be friends, Simon, and at the rate of half a dozen meetings a year that could be a long process with you. You've a – cautious nature, I think. So I'm taking a shortcut – do you mind?' She had her answer in the sudden gladness that lit up his face and he watched her smile break fully as she gave a little whoop of relief. Casey Walker glanced behind her to see who had laughed.

'She's enjoying herself anyway.' Cub heard a touch of bitterness in her tone and sighed to himself. His hand hurt and he was sick of the Walkers' problems, which Casey had been telling him about for the last half-hour. Before that he'd put up with Rachel's fussing over the stitched finger that he'd sliced to the bone while cutting up meat the previous evening. With the painkillers wearing off and his patience at an end he'd been bitingly rude to rid himself of Rachel.

Cub sighed aloud this time and shut his eyes. All right, he'd kissed her once – maybe more than once – in his teens, but that was as far as it went. He'd just wanted to be able to say he'd kissed a girl. It hadn't been the blinding first love that she seemed to have dressed it up as. For him it had been simple curiosity, and a desire to get one up on Jacky Burch whom he'd spent most of his school life hating. Truth to tell, her lurching gait and withered leg repulsed him. And if that made him a bastard he was sorry – he just wished she'd realise that he wasn't interested.

Casey's voice was suddenly frigid. 'I'm sorry you find my problems so boring.' There was a clatter as she jerked herself out of the folding chair. 'I daresay you lot have got no worries. You've pinched enough calves to keep the Brumby going no matter what happens.'

'Casey,' Cub flushed and struggled to sit upright. 'I'm sorry. I wasn't – I was thinking about something else.'

'And that makes it better, does it?' she said furiously. 'I should never have told you! And if you breathe a word to anyone about it I'll – I'll—' She rushed off without finishing the threat.

'That's the second one,' Jo said as she came up behind him. 'What on earth are you saying to them?'

Cub shook his head. 'She was telling me her troubles and I switched off.' He grimaced with dissatisfaction. 'Put it down to the red hair.'

'And what are her troubles exactly – a love affair?'

Cub snorted and held his hand. 'Like she's gunna tell me that? They're losing the place. Ken's up to his eyes in debt.'

'Oh. Sounds like everybody's having a rotten day. Rachel looks as if she's been crying. And Billy's getting around with a face like thunder.'

'He doesn't like cricket. Besides, it's really too hot to play. Must be forty degrees out there.'

Privately Jo thought that it wasn't the cricket but the fact that the Plover Creek head stockman had turned up. His presence had surprised her, for surely the stock work was finished, but he was staying on for December, Snowy had explained, caretaking the property while the boss and his family were away over Christmas.

He'd been flatteringly persistent in his attentions and Billy had got the steer by the hind foot, in the annoying way men had of jumping to the wrong conclusion. She exhaled sharply, watching her twin.

'Come on.' He was pale under the tan, his brow beaded with sweat.

'Where to?'

'Nancy's place.' Nancy Waring, wife of the town's mechanic, was the local hairdresser. She ran a salon in her front room that was patronised by all the local women. 'I'm getting my hair cut. Her place is cool and quiet, and she's got a canvas lounger on the verandah. You can't play so you might as well be comfortable. And it'll keep Rachel out of your hair.' She was fairly sure that she had been wrong about Billy's professed interest in the Cooper girl, but if she wasn't – well she wouldn't be there to see either.

Billy stood near Ben in the patchy shade of a bloodwood in the corner of the schoolyard, watching the slow movements of the men around the pitch. He knew very little about the game but supposed he was an outfielder – or was that baseball? Ben seemed just as uninterested, kicking at the dirt and fanning himself with his hat. There was no wind and the ball came nowhere near them; the sweat dripped, the flies buzzed and boredom was the biggest part of the game. Billy abandoned his post and wandered closer to Ben.

'I didn't notice your father in the mob back there,' he jerked his head at the school building.

'He's on holiday,' Ben said. 'He and Mum have gone down to the Blue Mountains. Dahpne's there – she's having a baby sometime this month.'

'I thought she and what's-his-name lived in Townsville?'

'Yeah, they do.' Ben sleeved his flushed face. 'Shit it's hot! Only Warwick's got leave and they've gone down to his people for the birth.'

'I see. Who's left on the Mount then?'

'Just me and Rachel – and old Tiny. What about you? You heading off somewhere?'

Billy laughed. 'Yeah – turn right for the fencing camp. Until the rain comes anyway. After that I'll see. But the way things look,' he waved at the burning blue stretched above them, 'we could run out of wire before the Wet even starts.'

'Yeah,' Ben agreed morosely, 'sooner the weather breaks the better. I'm running my butt off getting round the paddocks to check the waters. Lucky there's been plenty of wind for the mills – until today.' He wiped his face again, 'What idiot decided to play this game in the tropics, any—'

A roar erupted and both looked up to see the ball curving to the earth a dozen feet to their right. 'You playing – or propping up the bloody scenery?' the irate voice of their captain yelled. Ben jogged to recover the ball and hurled it, but his aim was wide and the triumphant batsman made it to the crease.

'Ah, shit.' There were days – and Ben seemed to have more than his share of them – when you couldn't get anything right.

The dance that usually followed the match was abandoned by mutual consent. It was too hot for anything as energetic as dancing even if there had been something better than Cynthia Davies' amateurish piano playing on offer. The Reillys, having the furthest

to travel, were the first to leave, Rachel and Ben, with the responsibility of locking up, left last.

'We ought to organise taped music,' Rachel said thoughtfully
on the way home. 'Bands are the biggest expense of every ball. And
Aunt Cynthia is a disaster. You can't tell a hymn from a tango when
she's playing it. Shouldn't you have the lights on?'

'D'you want to drive?' Ben demanded roughly. 'Jesus, Rachel!
I dunno why Dad didn't leave *you* in charge. *Shouldn't you do this?
Haven't you done that? Have you forgotten something else?* I can see
perfectly well, and so can the wallabies. If you want me to hit one
the best way is to dazzle it with the lights.'

Rachel held back a retort. Ben was like a bear with a sore head
these days and the heat only made it worse. A quarrel now would
be easy after the day she'd had. It had been folly holding the match
in such weather when people were bound to be (excusably) irri-
table. She bit her lip, remembering her own tears and the cause
of them. It wasn't Cub's fault; but she was a little put out that Jo
hadn't let her know by radio that the accident had happened. You
couldn't expect a man to make a fuss about his hurts. He'd only got
angry because she'd embarrassed him in public with her concern.
If she'd just waited until they were alone – well, she'd know better
next time.

They slowed for the grid that marked the beginning of the small
stud paddock where the station bulls were bred. It was fenced off
from the river, water being pumped out to an earth tank by the
windmill faintly visible in the gathering dusk. The day's heat seemed
to be distilled in the smell of the dust that caught them up as they

crossed the steel grid and before she could stop herself, Rachel asked, 'Have you been checking the water here?'

'For Christ's sake!' Ignoring its grinding, Ben slammed the gear stick forward and ripped the light switch on. It had grown darker in the last few minutes and almost immediately he had to stand on the brake to avoid the wallaby that had stopped in the middle of the road, transfixed by the high beam. It gave him time for his irritation to subside and he said more moderately, 'In case you haven't noticed it's been blowing like the clappers for the last week.'

'Sorry,' Rachel said meekly. She could have pointed out that with mills, wind didn't necessarily mean water, but he was right. He was in charge and she should just let him get on with it. She was too much like her mother, not trusting others and wanting to run everything herself. Shifting uncomfortably on the sticky vinyl of the seat she wondered, for the first time, if Cub thought so too. Billy had once told her she was bossy, she couldn't remember for what reason, only that she'd dismissed the idea. Just because she could make decisions and see what needed doing . . . She bit her lip again. She even sounded like her mother! No more interfering, Rachel vowed. From now on Ben wouldn't hear another peep out of her.

Twenty-two

Just before noon the next day Ben Cooper stood on the platform of planks that formed a makeshift ceiling over a section of the large machinery shed. Because of his closeness to the galvanised iron roof, only a foot above his head, the sweat was literally dripping off him. It stung his eyes and made his hands slip on the rope but he was nearly done. Below him the grader and the bulldozer rested.

The platform had been built for storage, and for a large part of the preceding week he'd been occupied with storing the unused stationary engines up there, enjoying the challenge of working out the leverage, and the positioning of the blocks and tackle, to achieve it. It was a task he felt suited to, unlike the rest of it.

A sob caught in his throat and he squeezed his eyes shut, feeling the sweat-slicked rope slide in his palms. Jesus! Why *hadn't* his father left Rachel in charge? He knew. It was a test of his ability, his fitness to fill the role for which he'd been bred. Axel must have thought that with the place shut down even Ben couldn't mess up, but he had. And it made it worse that the stud paddock was only five kilometres from the homestead.

'Oh, God!' He rested his forehead against the coarse hemp that hung bar-straight from the roof beam, thinking about the futility of it all. He must've clocked up hundreds of miles running the waters on the rest of the run, but the paddock where the small herd of expensive stud cattle bred bulls for the station was watered via a pipeline from the river. He'd passed the mill every day, its blades whirring merrily, and had never once turned off the main road to drive the four miles out to check that the earth tank was full and the water was reaching the trough. He'd not even thought of it until Rachel's question last night.

Billy's bitter accusation came back to him: *you never even checked, did you?* That's what he'd shouted when he'd crippled – killed, really – his birthday filly. He hadn't meant to but it had happened. He hadn't meant this latest disaster to happen either, but it had. Once again he'd failed not only the station but also his father who had entrusted its care to him.

'I'm sorry, Dad,' he muttered as he finished knotting the noose. He lifted it over his head. 'I tried. I really did. But the bloody mill was broken down.' Of course he should have stopped and examined it, but he hadn't. And next time it would be something worse – though what could be worse than a paddock of perished stock? He was a failure and what he was about to do was best for everyone's sake. He felt briefly sorry for his sister left to deal with it all until his father's return, but she was strong – stronger than he'd ever been. His last thought before he stepped off the platform was that for once in her life, Daphne might come up trumps and birth a son for the property.

News of Ben Cooper's suicide was known in Southbend almost from the moment Frank Watson returned with the body. Rachel's telegram to Axel, *Most urgent you phone me at post office stop leaving for town now stop Rachel*, had been heard at Rainsford and the Brumby, but it wasn't until Keith turned up on Wednesday with the mail that they learned the rest.

'Hung himself,' he said succinctly. 'In the grader shed.'

'My God. Poor Ben.' Billy shook his head at the horror of it. 'Jesus! It's less than a week since we saw him at the match. Why'd he do it?'

Keith struck a match to his cigarette. 'The yarn is he perished the stud herd. They reckon the pump packed up on the mill and he never noticed.'

'That'd be right,' Billy said. Knowing Ben it was inevitable. He glanced at Cub standing silent beside him. 'What about Rachel? How's she coping? Is her family back yet?'

'Arriving tomorrow. She's at the pub with her aunt. Oscar's gone out to the Mount to run the waters and keep an eye on things. Me and Nev already fixed the mill. Christ!' Keith shook his head, the cigarette burning unheeded between his fingers, 'all it wanted was new buckets. Ten minutes to get the nut unscrewed and change 'em, that's all it took. And the poor bastard killed himself for that.'

He hadn't checked, Billy thought, but let it pass. He said, 'On your way back tell Oscar if he needs a hand for a coupla days I'll come if he lets me know. Or if Rachel needs help or . . .' He tailed off, unable to think of anything concrete he could offer. 'Would you do that?'

'Yeah, I'll pass it on. Thanks, son,' Keith said as if the offer had been made to himself. Shaking his head he pushed himself off the sideboard he leaned against. 'It'll come hard on Cooper, his only boy. Four generations on the place and it ends like this.'

'Yeah,' Cub agreed soberly, as they were heading home again, 'I suppose there'll be an inquest. Who would've thought the silly bugger'd do a thing like that? There's got to be better ways to solve your problems.'

But dreadful though it was, the shock of Ben Cooper's death was soon to be overtaken by Cyclone Tracy's horrifying devastation of Darwin on Christmas Eve. By the time the news trickled out the old year was ending with little in the way of rain in the Gulf. Ironically, by the end of January 1975 Brisbane was flooded.

'Seems everybody's copping it but us.' Simon switched the radio off, bringing instant relief to everybody's eardrums. Billy wondered if suffering the crackle and roar of static was worth it for the patchy bits of news they managed to pick up.

'We'd get better reception if we stuck a twenty-foot aerial up on the high ground,' Cub said, echoing Billy's thoughts.

'That'd last until the first blow.' Simon yawned. 'And when push comes to shove I'd sooner have poor reception and some solid shelter against the time a cyclone hits us, than the other way about.' His words sobered them all. They'd heard the details of Tracy – the destroyed city, the death toll. It was a staggering natural disaster, even for a country where nature ran to extremes. Many of the victims fleeing south for refuge had passed through Harditch.

February arrived with brassy skies and isolated storms that ran a creek here or filled a swamp somewhere else, but never completely closed the main roads. Sometimes Keith Guthrie's mail truck ran a day behind schedule but it still ran, and the wireless gossip was dominated by talk of the weather: when and if the monsoon would come and the prospects for the new season if it didn't.

One of the benefits – or you could call it a drawback – of a dry summer was that it had enabled them to finish their section of the Rainsford boundary much sooner than would've been possible given a normal Wet.

It had taken a month of brutal labour to stand, and string, and strain the miles of fencing but it was done. There was now a gate five miles south of the mailbox to delineate where Rainsford Downs ended and Wildhorse Creek began. Billy, shoving it open for Cub to drive the laden truck through, glanced both ways along the cleared line to see the sun sparkle on the new wire, and felt a measure of satisfaction for a job well done.

It had been hard toil in the killing summer heat, but that fence would stand for the next fifty years – he'd guarantee it. Whistling he headed back to the cab, testing the ropes on the load as he did so. The front wheel rested in a puddle. Stepping wide to avoid it he pulled himself up into the seat beside Jo.

All three were returning from a trip to Harditch – an unexpected bonus at this time of year. Now that the boundary job was done he could have gone away for a break, but to be truthful he had barely considered it when Simon asked him if he was planning a holiday.

'I'll stick around,' he had answered. He mightn't be sure what his next move should be with Jo, but instinct told him that leaving wouldn't help.

Others had gone – Simon himself took a fortnight's break, departing on the mail with the vague intention, he said, of perhaps heading down the coast.

'Not unless old Misery's niece is going too,' Cub commented. 'First time I've seen Si really stuck on a girl.'

'About time, isn't it?' Jo responded. 'He'll be thirty this year.'

Rachel had also gone. She'd looked very different when they ran into her in the street. The soft curls that had framed her face had been cut into a glossy bob and instead of her trademark wide-brimmed hat and pastel dress she wore a trim shirt, and pants that covered the leg brace. Her face looked older, as if marked somehow by her brother's death, and there was an air of greater reserve about her – at least in her greeting to Cub, making no more of meeting him than of any other neighbour.

'It seems that everybody's in town this week.' Jo's gaze scanned the lobby of the hotel behind her. 'Are Axel and your mother here too?'

'No, I'm travelling alone – off on holiday actually. What about you lot?'

'In town for supplies,' Jo said, adding uncertainly, 'ah, how've you been, Rachel? We were so sorry about—'

'Yes, thank you,' firmly Rachel cut her off, 'and for your card. We appreciated it. How're you doing for rain at the Brumby – getting much?'

'No.' Cub cleared his throat. 'Could be a light year – too early to call yet though. Heading down to your sister's, are you?'

'No,' she said coolly. 'I'm off to Cairns for a couple of weeks. Well,' she glanced at her watch. 'I have to fly – literally. Catch you after the Wet.'

'Take care,' Billy said, but she'd already turned away, a small, indomitable shape; leather shoulder bag dipping with each limping step she took.

Staring after her Jo said, 'It was her that found him, you know. No wonder she looks different. How would you ever get something like that out of your head?'

The inquest had only just ended. There had been a private cremation ceremony in Harditch for the family, which meant half the district – if they had all gone, Billy thought. This was his first encounter with any of the Coopers since the tragedy and he wished now that he had sent Rachel the letter he had written at the time, and then screwed up as inadequate. Jo had added his name to the card, however. *From the Reilly family, and Billy*, it had read. She had suffered a similar uncertainty, asking, 'What else should I put?' but none of them had known what to say.

They continued on their way down the street. Billy's thoughts were still on Rachel when Cub nudged him, indicating with an infinitesimal jerk of the chin the swaggering gait of the half-caste coming their way.

'Take a look – that's him.'

'Who?' Billy saw a thickset man who could have been either side of forty, and was dressed in jeans, a flashy shirt, and top boots. The light-coloured Stetson and the sheen of sweat on his face made his skin seem darker. He opened his mouth to repeat the question just as the man turned into the door of the pub that took up the remainder of the block.

'Harry Lucas,' Cub said. 'Simon and I ran into him on the road one day last year. It was when the carrier brought the wire out for the boundary and got dry bogged. We had to unload it to get him out – remember? Anyway that was him – the mongrel that lost us those bullocks.'

'We've picked most of them up since,' Billy said practically. '*And* you lot deep-sixed their yard gates so I reckon you're about square. Not counting the belting Blake gave him. Are we leaving today or not?'

'Yes, we are,' Jo said. 'Soon as we've loaded up. I'm not planning on sitting out the Wet in a bog.'

Nothing had seemed less likely then but before the month's end Cyclone Harriet came sweeping in from the Timor Sea to effect a dramatic change. Simon had returned by then, and even Suds, grumpy and hung over from a stay in the 'Bend, made it back on the last mail before Harriet hit.

She came blowing in from the Gulf, driving clouds ahead of her like dingoes harrying sheep. They were low, grey clouds packed one atop the other, stretching from horizon to horizon, menacing in their silent approach. The air was still at ground level, and heavy with humidity. Only the clouds moved, covering the blue like a lid was being pulled across it, and bringing with it the first heavy plops of falling rain.

Blake and Simon had been on the homestead roof all the previous day when the warning of Harriet's approach was first broadcast so the corrugated iron was as secure as screws could make it. In the saddle shed Billy and Cub hung the packs and riding saddles from the rafters and stacked the ropes and bridles above them.

Billy eyed the finished job and then his companion. 'What sort of a flood are you expecting?'

'It's a narrow valley, mate. And the water rises fast.' He dusted his hands. 'You ever notice that yellow line Oscar Davies has got painted round his pub wall about on a level with the bar?'

'Can't say I have. Why?'

Well we had a blow back in the sixties – and mind you the 'Bend's a lot flatter country than this so the water spreads more than it can here. That paint job marks the flood height.'

'No kidding?' Billy was impressed. 'Half the town must've been under. What about the store? That's lower than the pub.'

'Oh, Misery had his shop prepared; lost his shed though and everything in it. The stations downstream were finding all sorts of stuff for months after. Billycans, baking dishes, tyre tubes – you name it. The Walkers got a coffin. Got tangled in the netting fence around the Rumhole homestead. There were three of them according to Misery, but the other two never turned up. Ken's gave him quite a turn because the lid was screwed down – he thought it came outta the cemetery.'

Billy chuckled. 'I'll bet. What'd he do with it?'

'Shoved it in the chook yard for the hens to lay in. Wasn't good for much else.'

'Bit optimistic wasn't he?' Billy asked. 'Planning to sell coffins, I mean.'

'Oh it was old stock – left over from the mining days. He went into competition with the undertaker back when the town had one, but it didn't work out.' Cub picked up the ladder and made for the door. 'Come on. We've gotta get the diesel out of the creek and chop a week's worth of wood and stack it somewhere dry. Better make sure the lighting plant's got plenty of fuel too. They're not jobs you want to be doing in the middle of a blow.'

Above them a sudden gust blew rain like shotgun pellets against the roof. They rattled loudly for a few moments then eased again and through the open door Billy saw the tops of the timber swaying under the racing sky. The air had cooled and he shivered. 'Rain's coming.'

'Best we get a move on,' Cub said.

Twenty-three

Darkness came early under the heavy clouds, ushering in a cold wet night for it was raining solidly by then. The water thundered relentlessly on the tin roof, shooting straight over the tops of the gutters, where it was shredded to spray by the rising gale. The blackness howled outside, the wind on occasions rising from a roar to a whine but in the kitchen, where Suds had pulled the window shutters closed, all was cosy warmth – even if you had to shout to make yourself heard.

Blake had brought the wireless down from the office although nothing but static and the piercing hourly whoop of the cyclone warning issued from its speaker. Once, Billy thought he heard a voice but it was impossible to pick up actual words although the gabble (if such it was) evoked a sudden picture in his mind of other such rooms scattered across the vast hinterland, each with its handful of people, waiting out the dark fury of nature's force. A little frisson went through him, like ghostly fingers brushing his spine. There had not been time during the bustle of preparation to actually fear the cyclone, although so soon after Tracy he knew he should, but when the sturdy kitchen wall suddenly shook to the force of the wind, the first stirring of unease touched him. If the building went . . . He was suddenly glad of the wireless. You could hear nothing on it, and even if they could transmit a message nobody could possibly reach them, but while it ran they weren't entirely cut off from human contact.

By ten o'clock the lights were out and everyone was in bed – Billy in the kitchen, for the latticed walls of the verandah were no barrier to the storm. The rain was a solid roar of sound that all but drowned the shriller scream of the wind. The chimney had blown off and a mixture of water and steam sprayed over the stovetop. Using his torch Billy got up again to thrust another chunk of wood into the firebox and empty the large pot he'd positioned to catch the steady trickle of water. More burst in through the door carried on wind gusts until the flagstones ran with water, but he was dry on the bed, as long as the roof held.

He dozed fitfully, waking to empty the pot and marvel at the sheer quantity of water the sky could produce. It was as if an ocean was being emptied on them; his unease grew as he tried to picture the likely results on the country. Wildhorse Creek would be thirty foot high at this rate. He wondered how the chooks were faring in their pen. Suds had taken Belle back to his hut and he imagined the horses huddled somewhere in the paddock, drenched and battered, their rumps to the freezing blast. Because that was the other surprise – how cold it had become. Something crashed at the back of the house. He got up, undecided whether to venture out, and discovered that the flagstones were ankle deep in water. The rain was no longer just spraying in through the screen door but hosing under it in driving sheets.

The meat bags were kept in the store. He rolled two together, wedging them against the doorframe with a chunk of firewood. Another crash sounded from the direction of the creek and he jumped as something slammed into the kitchen wall. Above the roar of the elements he fancied he could hear the agonised scream of the mill head, its blades freewheeling into the storm. Shivering he used a tea towel to wipe his wet feet and crawled back under the blankets.

Later, voices and movement woke him. Blake said, 'What the hell . . . ?' and he sat up, blinking in strong torchlight, to see the sodden bags being kicked away from the door. Then the lack of noise struck him. The wind had dropped. Rain pattered gently, no more than a whisper on the roof. Unexpectedly the diesel thudded into life and in a little while light flooded the room.

'What . . . ?' Billy said.

'Rise and shine.' Cub was hatted and booted; Jo, similarly attired, was pulling a jacket over her shirt. 'The Wildhorse is over its banks,' Cub said cheerfully. 'The paddock's going under and it's floating the fuel dump away.'

Billy felt stupid with fatigue. 'The wind's stopped.'

'Eye of the storm,' Blake informed him. 'It's half three now and there's no telling how long the break'll last.' Simon stuck a wet head through the door and he shifted his gaze to him. 'How's it looking?'

'The shed's knee deep, engine room's—' Simon moved his hand

in a seesaw motion, 'bit higher. Okay yet – for a bit. But there's stuff spread to hell already. Tyres, fuel drums – anything that'll float or roll.'

'Better get busy then,' Blake said, leading the way outside.

The garden was awash, the paddock an unfamiliar sea in their torch beams. Beyond the gate Billy sank to his knees in cold water; bemusedly he shone his torch about and immediately espied the forty-four-gallon drums bumping and rolling in the current that tugged at his legs. They looked like a fleet of clumsy boats.

Jo grabbed the closest drum and Billy splashed past her to grasp the heavy rim of the next one and was momentarily stumped. 'What are we gunna do with them?'

'Stick 'em in the cattle yard,' Blake bellowed, his own hands full. Simon was at the shed backing a vehicle out. It churned slowly through the rising water that rippled in the headlights, making for the higher ground near the house.

It was hard work hauling the drums against the current. When all they could find was safe Cub shone his torch to count. 'Might be shy one. You realise we're gunna have to drag them out of here afterwards?'

Billy wasn't paying attention. 'Wonder if the chooks have drowned?'

'Suds'll see to them. Let's get after the rest of the stuff.'

The water was nearly thigh deep now. In the engine room the diesel had been shut down. Simon and Blake, working by head-lights, were getting a chain sling around the runners of the lighting plant to hoist it into the roof.

'How high do you think it'll come?' Billy's legs ached from the weight of the deepening current.

'Who knows? Rain's getting heavier.' Jo sagged against the upstream side of a tree. Her torch had dulled to an orange glow; she turned it upwards before killing it and Billy momentarily glimpsed the wet hair straggling out beneath the droop of her hat brim. She looked as cold and worn as he felt.

'Here, that's too heavy for you.' He took the tyre she was struggling with and shivered. 'You ought to be inside out of it, it's no work for a girl.'

'Oh, don't be so damn gothic,' she said crossly. 'Do you think I'm made of sugar? Just for that I'll have it back.' She grabbed the tyre and set off, pushing it before her, the rain beating dimples into the moving water caught in the fading glimmer of his torch. The battery was almost finished; he turned it off.

Cub was stacking gear in the vehicle shed. He seemed cranky too and Billy, tired, shivering in wet clothes that hampered his movements and smarting from his misdirected chivalry, wondered if all twins synchronised their moods as closely as Cub and Jo seemed to.

'What's wrong with you?'

'This bloody country,' Cub snarled. 'The new boundary fence? It's gunna be washed flat. We'll have to stand the whole sodding thing again.'

'Nothing you can do about it,' he said unsympathetically as rain erupted again onto the roof, and the wind, reborn in an instant, carried it into the shed to spray them where they stood. 'Here it comes again. Let's get back to the house.'

Suds had the carbide light going in the kitchen, in which nearly a foot of water lay. The screen door was propped wide and he was shifting the store contents onto the house verandah, itself damp but now rendered rainproof with a sheet of polypropylene covering the lattice. Water sloshed in the wood box and in the bottom of the cupboards, whose contents littered the table. A hen was perched atop the woodpile that had been transferred into the wheelbarrow, and five half-grown chickens huddled on Billy's bed.

'What the hell—?' he began indignantly.

'Gotta keep 'em dry and warm, boy, or they'll die.'

'I notice they're not in *your* bed.'

'Wouldn't last long if they was,' Suds cackled. 'Belle's there.'

Blake and Simon splashed in to join them at the stove, onto which the water was once more trickling. Billy automatically emptied the pot, straight onto the flooded floor.

Jo plunked her sodden hat onto its peg and pulled off her coat. 'It's coming from – snake!' Her yell brought their heads about in time to see the long sinuous body eel in, head up, through the door.

'Watch it! That's a red-bellied black.' Cub, being closest, seized a billet of wood from beneath the hen's feet and hurled it as she took off squawking, wet wings frantically beating the air. The snake darted aside in the water, striking as it went, its movements shockingly fast. The hen hit the tabletop, skidding across pots and pans and bowls, and with a hysterical shriek launched herself again, cannoning into Billy's chest. He swatted her away as Cub threw another piece of wood.

'That's no bloody good!' Blake roared. He hurried out the door to return a moment later with a long-handled shovel. As if sensing the greater danger it presented the black lunged at him, wet body glistening in the smoky light. Blake swung the blade, missed, and tumbling backwards hit the table, precipitating a shower of cooking pots onto Billy's bed. The chickens rose shrieking into the air. One alighted on the table while the rest smacked into the water.

The snake, meanwhile, had made the tactical error of sliding up onto the cupboard where its body was easier to see.

'Look out, it's doubling back,' Simon yelled. Blake smacked the open cupboard door shut with the shovel. Its head reared back then suddenly exploded into a mess of blood and bone.

'Jesus!' Billy roared. He'd leapt a foot when the shotgun blasted from behind his right shoulder. Jo, ejecting the spent cartridge, was quite composed as she laid the gun down on the table. Then, before he could say anything, something in the water touched his leg and he kicked reflexively, sending the struggling chicken flying. She hit the table leg and dropped like a stone.

'What'd you do that for?' Suds cried reproachfully.

Cub cracked him across the shoulders, his own shaking. 'Your face, mate! You looked like your last moment had come.'

Billy shook his head sheepishly. 'All I could think of was snake.' He watched the old cook scrabble after the floundering chicks. The hen was in the rafters, still shrieking, while outside the rain poured down.

'What's that bloody chook doing in here, anyway?' Blake demanded.

Suds bristled. 'Thought she was the broody, din' I? Turned out she ain't. How the hell's a man supposed to tell in the dark?' He filled an empty bottle from the kettle, wrapped a tea towel around it and thrust it, together with the soaked chickens, into a box, which he shoved at Billy. 'Here, seeing you done for the other one, yous can look after these.'

The wireless static was muted; behind it faint voices whispered in the dark. Somebody, somewhere had reception, Billy thought tiredly. Jo yawned and picked up the teapot.

'Be daylight soon. We might as well have some tea.'

Twenty-four

Dawn showed a grey world. Clouds, the watery valley and the drifting curtain of misty rain. The big poinciana behind the house was down in a welter of smashed branches – one of the crashes heard in the night. There were gaps in the windmill sails. They found one of the missing blades in the kitchen wall. It had cut through the iron to embed itself in the post behind it. Splashing, exclaiming, Billy and the others explored their changed environment. There was a tree branch down across the metal rain gauge, partially blocking the top, but the receptacle still contained a little over eight inches. As far as the eye could see across the valley it met with the shimmer of water.

'It's dropping though,' Cub said, 'nothing like as deep as it was.'

'How do the stock survive?' Billy wondered, staring at the stripped trees and downed timber. Wildhorse Creek was bankless, its waters a tumbling flood of roiling brown topped with great suds of dirty spume. As they watched another tree fell, its top swallowed by the flood, its roots torn free to the air. 'I can see how it got its name – the creek.'

'She's a bit of a bolter,' Cub agreed wryly. 'Nothing to what the Rainsford will be like though. I bet old Ken's up to his neck at Rumhole.' A hideous clanging broke out behind them as Suds beat the length of steel casing that served as the meal bell. 'There's breakfast.'

Blake had replaced the wireless battery with a fresh one and as they ate they listened to their neighbours recounting rainfalls, river heights and general destruction. There were several wirelesses in Southbend – the pub, the hospital and the police station all had one, and from these they gathered the news of the town. The river was out to the racecourse, several houses had been unroofed, the flagpole at the school bent in half, and at the depot the tractor Nev used to shift drums about had been bowled across the yard to finish upside down in his sump. Most of the big shade trees in town had been uprooted, outbuildings demolished, and there wasn't, Oscar Davies averred, a whole sheet of glass left in the 'Bend. The river height was nowhere near the record line painted in the bar but you could still drive a boat down the main street.

Plover Creek Homestead was minus its roof and overhead tank; its people wet but unhurt. Axel Cooper said briefly that they'd lost the mill head, and that an uprooted carbean tree had smashed a hole in the men's quarters. Then it was Casey Walker's turn, and to Billy's surprise she gave the Wildhorse Creek call sign.

Jo, who was closest, answered. Casey spoke rapidly, her voice coming and going. 'You all okay over there? I'm not sure how much battery's left. The charger drowned with the lighting plant. Over.'

'We're fine,' Jo said calmly. 'Bit of a flood, couple of trees down –

one fell on the gauge but we measured eight inches – could've been twelve or so. How about you? Over.'

'Flooded,' the girl said succinctly. 'The river looks a mile wide. It's about six feet deep downstairs, but Dad thinks we're safe enough up here. The dogs got swept away – apart from a couple of the pups that Ants snuck upstairs. We lost the chooks, God knows where the horses are, and the vehicles are under water. It's like being in a boat – and we've got that tied up downstairs just in case.' Her signal was fading, some of the words lost in transmission.

'You're breaking up,' Jo said. 'Catch you later.' She signed off. 'Looks like we got off pretty lightly.' The voices gabbled on, the stronger stations drowning those with weaker signals, while outside the rain stopped and a weak, silvery light – all they would see of the sun that day – seeped through the heavy layer of clouds.

Suds, who was stoking the stove, looked up. 'It's stopped. Which of you young fellas is gunna fix my chimbley?'

Billy stood. 'I will.'

'*After* you shift your bed. And the poultry.' The old man stared about at the mud and mess. 'The joint's a pigsty, and cyclone or not I ain't having that.'

As if making amends for its previous lack, the rain continued for the next ten days. Sunlight was a memory as the grey, overcast days dripped by. The world was full of the sound of trickling water – and just as well, Suds remarked, or they'd be bucketing the dirty stuff from the creek. The cyclone had shifted the five-thousand-gallon tank on its stand. Not much – it had been full at the time, and tied down to boot – but enough to crack the downpipe where it joined the tank, the contents of which had then drained away. They had repaired the pipe since, but it would be days before the pump could go back into the creek. In the meantime they stood buckets under the gutter spouts, or dipped from the swag-bellied tarpaulin they'd rigged in the garden.

In the kitchen, Suds, with an eye to the diminishing meat supply, banged down dishes of rice and macaroni, his fierce glare daring them to complain. 'We should've hung onto that snake,' Cub said, wrinkling his nose. 'It'll be a while before we get a killer.'

'Or anything else,' Blake smothered sauce on his portion. 'We'll be lucky to drive out of here before the end of April.'

'It'll be a good season though, boss.'

Blake snorted, his pale eyes kindling on Billy. 'Good? Yeah, there'll be feed – a lot of it rank and useless. The roads'll be gutters, washed down to the bedrock; the creek crossings are history, and the fencing buried. And if we don't get bushfires and Three-Day out of it you may call me a fool.'

Billy hid his surprise with a grin. 'I wouldn't dare. What's Three-Day?'

'A sickness cattle get,' Simon put in, 'and on top of that we'll have lost stock. There're bound to have been a few caught on the low ground. Probably some of the nags too.'

'Be worse down along the Rainsford,' Cub said comfortably. 'The stock there'll be standing in water for days, and pulling mud every time they move. Who was it said: *It never rains but it pours?*'

'I dunno,' Billy quipped, 'but it sounds like he might've been through a cyclone somewhere.'

In Southbend, one of the numerous Burch kids, a barefoot urchin in a ragged felt hat passed down from an older sibling, was earning pocket money at the hospital. The matron had paid him once again to slide through the netting that kept animals and inquisitive children from creeping under the building, to douse the standing pools of water with kerosene to prevent mosquitoes breeding there. Once the rain had stopped, and the river drawn reluctantly back to its banks, the insect life had come into its own.

With April ending the town was coming alive again. The roads were open, the mail trucks running, and the ringers returning to fill the stock camps. Not all of them were happy. There were many repairs to make before the actual stock work could start.

At Rainsford Downs, Harry Lucas kicked disgustedly at the trunk of the anchor tree on the bank of Cutaway Creek, to loosen the mud on his boots, then grabbed up the strainers and shouldered the remaining half coil of wire. That, thank Christ, was the last creek crossing. 'Well, come on!' he barked at the other men, 'we're not standing around this shit-hole all day.'

They were happy to comply for amid the saw-toothed pandanus and waist-high undergrowth the mosquitoes were something fierce. The head stockman's dark skin seemed to afford him some protection and, as a coloured man in a white fella's world, he'd learned to endure, but right now he was fed up. He was a head stockman for chrissake. He wasn't paid to bust his guts wrestling the cables of smashed creek crossings from under a ton of mud and logs. His hands smarted, his shoulders ached, and his boots were bloody ruined. He eyed them with smouldering resentment as he divested himself of his load.

Other men wore flat-heeled yard boots suitable for ground work but not Harry Lucas. His expensive top boots were a constant reminder to him of how far he had come from his start back in the Mission where his older, blacker brothers had always had it in for the little yella git his mother was so ashamed of. She claimed to have been raped by a white man but Harry thought it more probable that she had sold herself to him for grog.

As a kid he'd hated the white race quite as much as he did his black tormenters, and nothing much had happened since to alter his views. He had known from the beginning that the only escape from the Mission was through the white man's world, and his position of half-caste – neither fully black nor fully white – gave him the necessary foothold. By custom his colour entitled him to be treated as a white man – to eat in the station kitchen rather than at the blacks' table, to bunk in the quarters, and to draw full pay.

Custom might demand tolerance of his presence, but it didn't buy acceptance with many – for the bulk of his work-mates he was still, and always would be, something less than white, a yella-fella. And inevitably, in every camp or kitchen, somebody would call him on his colour, or his cocky walk, challenging his right to the tenuous place he had established for himself.

So he'd learned to fight – and to like it. It had felt good to pulp sneering white faces whose owners had been convinced that a bloody boong wouldn't, or couldn't, defend himself. His disdain for and resentment of the despised race he could never become a part of grew with each victory. They'd been rough men too, those he'd defeated, big, hard bastards with work-toughened fists, but he'd put them all down. All but Blake Reilly.

He'd taken beatings before in his fighting career but few as vicious as the one handed out by Blake Reilly – and that after he'd got in that first, unexpected blow that ought to have half crippled his adversary. To his own surprise Harry fought shy of a second match. He could absorb punishment with the best but there was something about the way the older man had kept coming, of the cold implacability of his advance, hinting at a murderous intention, which had put the wind up him. He'd known a horse or two like that and invariably they crippled or killed their riders. Shoot them, or leave them alone – that was the answer. But he couldn't apply either solution to Blake, the man who'd brought him down in a bar room full of his peers. The memory of it was never far from his mind: but there were other ways to make him pay.

Driving the narrow track back to camp he thought with satisfaction of the stroke he'd pulled last year with Reilly's bullock paddock. Of course what he'd really like to do was catch the bastard with cattle somewhere on Rainsford land. There'd been a lot of talk, in the pub and the camps, about Blake's poddy-dodging activities, but so far, despite having kept a careful eye on the boundary country during the course of his work, he'd seen no sign of the Reillys' presence. Which meant they hadn't been there, because if there was one skill his childhood had taught Harry Lucas, it was tracking. As an unwanted kid in an over-large and hungry family, it had often meant the difference between eating or not.

Harry's jaw clenched in determination, like a trap snapping shut.

He jammed the brakes on and the Toyota skidded to rest beside the fly rig, eliciting a curse from somebody on the back who hadn't been holding on. Oh, yes, at a time and in a manner of his choosing the old bastard would pay.

Twenty-five

The range country dried more slowly than the open downs. While the first of the year's breakers were being ridden out of the yard at Rainsford, Billy and the twins took the truck out across the valley in order to top up the wood supply, their last task at the homestead. Tomorrow they were leaving for Verity Valley to muster the horses and begin the season.

It was a beautiful day under the clear arch of the autumn sky, with the wattle coming into flower and the seed heads of the grass ripening in swathes of pale gold. The waterlilies were out in the swamps and as they paused to check the track, Billy watched a mother duck arrowing between the stems ahead of her flotilla of ducklings. He turned to catch Jo's eye and she smiled, her face showing the same delight he felt.

He said impulsively, 'It's worth it, isn't it? The heat and the hard yakka. Ivy said this country was magic. She was right.'

'That the old girl you worked for?' Cub banged his door shut. 'Come on, hop in. She was wrong, mate. What she meant was: you stay long enough you lose your marbles. You're as barmy as the rest of us now. Magic – I ask you? It's a duck.'

He charged across the track at the dried end of the swamp and climbed onto the rocky ground, then slowed to eye the flanks of a gravel ridge furred over with spinifex and dotted with the twisted forms of snappy-gum, their preferred firewood. 'Doesn't look too bad,' he said, changing down, 'but you never know. Hang on.'

But the ground held and shortly the truck was parked halfway up the slope of the ridge. Switching off, Cub got out and took the two axes off the back, proffering one to Billy.

'In a minute.' Billy nodded at the fissured rocks crowning the eminence. 'I want a look at the view first.'

Jo followed him, her boots occasionally slipping on loose stones. He grabbed her hand, pulling her up among the boulders until they stood side by side, staring out across the landscape, at the dark, winding line of the Wildhorse and the bright-coloured hollow of the valley, its grey–green scrub dusted here and there with the gold of the wattle. A breeze puffed pleasantly against their faces and Jo inhaled deeply, 'Smell that, Billy.'

He did, scenting wattle blossom, spinifex, and a tang like new-cut hay that was a mixture of green and drying grasses. There was aniseed too, from the little grey plant that sprawled across the stone and the clean, wild smell of the range. And behind it all, mixed with the high cry of a hawk, sounded the steady thud of Cub's axe.

'I love this time of year,' Jo's eyes were bright, like pieces of captured sky. 'And this view.' She waved a tanned arm to take in the distant smallness of homestead and yards, and the shine, like dull pewter, of the creek water. 'When I die I want to be buried here,' she banged her heel on the stone, 'overlooking the valley. To be a part of it forever. I'm gunna put it in my will.'

'The digging might be a bit hard,' he quipped.

'Seriously.' Her face was solemn. 'Do you think we can know anything after death, Billy? That there could be such a thing as a spirit?'

He shrugged, 'Who knows? I don't. Why?'

'Because if there is, I should like to think that mine would hang around here. To see the creeks run Wet after Wet, and watch the moonrise, and to know when the wildflowers came. Have you ever thought that not everybody finds their own country, Billy? Ben didn't – or he would never have killed himself. But we have – and when you saw the ducklings and said that about it being worth everything – I knew that you had too. Don't you think that makes us incredibly lucky?'

'Yes.' He remembered the lash of Gulf heat, the bitter bite of its July winds, the gasping humidity, and punishing insect plagues of its monsoons. 'I don't think anyone could be happy living out here, year after year, otherwise. You'd never stick it out. Ivy knew; she told me the country would claim me if I stuck around to let it. And I reckon it has.'

She opened her mouth to say something more just as Cub's bellow brought both their heads round. 'There's no hurry but are either of you planning on working today? God knows I've been trying but I can't get these damn logs to load 'emselves.'

Jo turned away and Billy, seeing his opportunity vanishing,

launched hastily into speech. 'Jo, would you – I mean, I don't know if Snowy will be there or – but the Sports are coming up and I wondered – will you go to the dance with me? If we get to them, that is.'

As he waited for Jo to answer, his words played over again in his mind and he wished he could reorganise them. What had made him mention Snowy? And what would she make of it that he had? 'I'd really like you to,' he added hopefully and at that she smiled.

'Okay then. Thank you, Billy. I will – if, as you say, we make it.'

That evening he sat down and wrote to Ivy. The letter would go out in the bag tomorrow so she should have it within a week he guessed. He had not been, by any means, a regular correspondent, writing only when the urge took him, which was usually when he had something he considered significant to tell her.

He had described the Brumby to her in previous letters, and his running battle and surprising victory over Freaky, and more lately the cyclone. This evening he simply wrote about Jo, telling Ivy a host of little things that made her what she was. The way she laughed, the exact colour of her eyes, and how the little whorl of hair in the middle of her forehead, where the part was, shone silver in sunlight. He sat for a long time, smiling occasionally as he wrote. It ran to several pages when finished, ending with her agreement to accompany him to the dance.

'Stone the crows! You writing a book?' Cub looked up from the cards he'd laid out. 'You're as bad as old Si – he's always scribbling away to that nurse in town. You got a girl somewhere too?'

Billy grinned. 'None of your business.' Cub never wrote to anybody and Rachel's letters to him had stopped. Since Ben's death she seemed to have forgotten him. That day in Harditch when she'd been leaving for Cairns she had scarcely spoken to him, as if her infatuation with him had died along with Ben.

The Sports that year were held on the last weekend in May. The council grader had not yet reached the Brumby boundary and the road was frightful, but at least the country was dry enough to allow driving around the worst sections. Cranes Creek, Keith Guthrie had warned them, was the biggest obstacle with most of the bank washed away.

'We'll probably have to unload the horses there. Reload on the other side,' Simon said. 'Keith reckons you need a good run at it to get out. We'll see when we get there. Are we all going?'

'Not bloody likely.' Blake finished his last mouthful of breakfast steak and pushed the plate aside. 'Give Lucas another go at the place? Whose to say the bastard won't torch the homestead this time?'

Simon looked worried. 'Would he be that big a fool? He got away with it once but if Watson's had a word with him . . .'

'It's not a chance I'm gunna take,' Blake growled. 'Have a look about when you get to town then get onto the pub's wireless and let me know if he's showed up there or not.'

'Good idea. Of course *not* being there doesn't necessarily mean he's coming here – but still . . . You coming, Suds?'

'Bet your life.' The old cook licked his lips. 'That first beer's gunna go down a treat.'

'Okay,' Simon nodded, 'so what horses are we taking?'

'Freaky.' Billy had decided this weeks before. The pony was handy and surprisingly fast, his size an advantage when it came to dodging and turning.

'Flute,' Jo said, just as Cub spoke.

'That bay mare of mine – Melody. What about you?'

'Oh – I don't know, something for the Crystal Race. I'll think about it.' Simon was frowning, his mind still on Lucas. As if there had been no interruption he said, 'I can't see the point of further sabotage. Presumably he did the paddock to get square for the belting you handed him. But anything more in that line will bring Watson down on him – probably lose him his job too, because Bennett must know we'd retaliate. Anyway, how does he gain by it? It doesn't make sense.'

'Doesn't have to.' Blake's tone carried conviction. 'It's personal for him. Bennett could sack him tomorrow but he wouldn't let it go. I've met his sort before. He don't like white men either. He's got a chip on his shoulder that would choke a horse. We haven't heard the last of him – and that's fair warning.'

Suds was hauling his bread bowl from the cupboard. 'There's corned meat cooked. And I'll bake you a coupla loaves to keep you going,' he said, bending a minatory eye on his employer. 'You just see you keep the joint clean. Wash up after yerself, and don't leave nothing out for the ants to get. I'd sooner stay 'ome if going means coming back to a mess.'

Billy, heading out the door to find and bring in the required horses, grinned, knowing perfectly well they'd have to tie the old man up to keep him from accompanying them.

In the event Blake was proved wrong in his assessment of Lucas; one of the first things to greet Billy and the twins as they pulled in behind the stalls at the racecourse was the sight of the head stockman climbing down from the cab of the Rainsford truck. Simon had to be aware of it too, as he had parked the truckload of horses immediately behind the other vehicle. He and Suds were up in the bed of it, sorting out the halter ropes and inspecting the damage to Connemara's leg.

It hadn't just been Cranes Creek that was difficult. Before they had even reached the creek one back wheel had dropped into a deep washout concealed in the grass that covered the road. The violent lurch of the vehicle had sent the bay mare crashing into the side of the crate where her leg had become caught between the slatted timbers of the side. She'd kicked herself free, scrambling to her feet, snorting and trembling, with blood on her skinned hock.

'You still gunna ride her?' Billy asked casually. 'Looks like it could be nasty.'

'I think it's okay.' Simon turned her carefully and led her down the ramp, chin on his shoulder as he watched her walk. 'She's not stepping lame. Long as she doesn't stiffen up.' He handed the bridle to Billy. 'Stick this on her and put her in a stall, will you? I'll run Suds back to the pub. Might even get hold of Blake now and pass the news on.' They'd loaded and left before the morning star had risen and it was still a little before eight, the time the morning radio traffic started.

Grasping Freaky's lead rope as well, Billy led them both away, Jo following with her black mare. In the stalls he inspected Connie himself, wishing the injury was a little worse. He was immediately ashamed of the thought but if Simon couldn't ride her then here was his chance . . . Billy didn't fool himself – he knew he couldn't compete with Simon, but if the older rider was safely out of it then his own way lay clear – or clearer; there would still be the other starters to beat. He would chance it, he decided. A bit of work around the pegs, or a knock in one of the other events, he thought hopefully, could easily worsen Connie's injury. And he had to do something to grab Jo's attention. Winning the Crystal for her should just about cut it.

Other vehicles were coming in to unload. The Mount Ixion truck was already parked off to one side, with Ken Walker's old junk heap beside it. The familiar ammoniac reek of dung and horseflesh greeted him as he shot the sliprails home on the stalls then turned quickly to where the girl was doing the same with Flute.

'Jo?'

'Yes?' She was lifting her saddle and raised an inquiring eyebrow above it.

He spoke rapidly before Cub caught up. 'I'm going to enter the Crystal Race this arvo. Can I ride for you?'

She looked astonished. 'On *Freaky*? What are you thinking, Billy? He's too slow!'

'He's nippy, and jumps well.' Billy defended his choice. 'The point is, can I? Will you give me your colours?'

She laughed suddenly, as if the madness of it appealed to her, and her blue eyes danced. 'Yes – why not? Only don't go getting yourself killed. The rest of the field will run right over a little runt like that.'

'They'll have to catch him first,' Billy said optimistically. 'Connie'll be the one to watch. That is if the mare's okay for it.'

'She looks fine. And he'll be keen to ride,' she added, 'because of Fiona. He hasn't said but I think he'll be carrying her colours today.'

'Oh, well.' Billy shrugged. 'A bloke can hope . . . I'll give it my best shot anyway.' The main thing was that she had agreed. He hugged the knowledge to himself. If he came in last – which he had no intention of doing – she'd still know that he was doing it for her.

Twenty-six

The day proceeded as other Sports Days before it. Smoke from the copper and barbecue behind the tea stall mingled with the dust of furious activity on the course, and the loud hailer competed at times with the sudden snarl of a dogfight or the shrieks of children running wild. People met and parted between events as the crowd constantly shifted.

This time around, Billy knew most of the district by sight if not always by name and moving through the day, between the refreshment stall, the bar and the jockeys' changing room – currently serving as an office where Fiona Forrest and Margaret Cooper were taking the entries – he kept an eye open for Snowy. It frustrated him that he didn't even know his suspected rival's last name. And when he eventually spotted the tall figure his heart clenched to find him in Jo's company. They were walking together, laughing, when he caught them up.

He greeted Snowy with a curt nod. 'G'day.' Then looked hopefully at the girl. 'Jo – I've entered Freaky in the Gretna but I need a partner. How about it?'

'Sorry, Billy. I've just told Snowy I'll ride with him. Anyway,' she added practically, 'with Freaky you really need somebody lighter. Why don't you ask Ants Walker?'

Billy repeated stupidly, '*Ants?*'

'Why not?' Jo asked reasonably. 'She's lighter than me and that's what you want in a short dash. There she is,' she pointed at several youngsters playing on the railing at the foot of the judges' box. There was no mistaking the Walker hair. 'Grab her before someone else thinks of it.'

'Hey,' Snowy protested good-naturedly, 'that's aiding the opposition – you want us beaten by a kid?'

Billy swallowed his sudden rage and turned away. After all the other man might have been referring to the Walker girl. Jo believed he was, repeating, 'Why not – if she rides well enough?'

As it turned out, Dan Burch riding double with a skinny half-caste boy won the event. Freaky, understanding he was expected to carry double, rebelled. And Billy was ignominiously dumped in the centre of the track and watched Snowy and Jo come in second, the tall head stockman's arms clasped firmly about the waist he himself had hoped to hold.

Afterwards, his enjoyment replaced with conflicting emotions, Billy joined Rachel in the shabby stands. It was shady and quiet, above the bustle of the crowd now lining up for hamburgers at the refreshment stalls.

'How've you been?' he asked. She was in pants and a tailored shirt again.

'Fine, thanks.' Her mouth sketched a smile and she spoke automatically, then her lips tightened and she shook her head. 'No, I'm not. Why do I go around saying that? I've been doing it all morning. People come up to me and ask, and I tell them I'm fine because that's what they want to hear. They look happier the minute I say it – relieved that nothing's expected of them. But I'm not fine at all – none of us are. Not me or Mum or Dad. The truth is my brother killed himself and I just don't know how I'm supposed to be. Sometimes I just want to scream I get so angry. And the rest of the time I'm either drowning in sadness, or guilt. You can't believe how *guilty* I feel.' Her brown eyes flashed. 'Sometimes I hate Ben for – leaving us like that. It's like he's escaped but only because he hung all his problems on me first. Mum's busy making him into a saint and Dad acts like he never existed. He ignores me when I try and talk about him. Give him twelve months,' she said bitterly, 'and it'll be like – "who's Ben?" So no, I'm not fine at all, Billy, but thanks for caring.'

'I'm sorry,' he said, feeling inadequate. 'It can't be easy – but it's not your fault. As for what Ben did – I think nobody can really *want* to kill himself. I mean it must've seemed to him to be the only way out.' He let his words drift into silence before adding hesitantly, 'People make mistakes. Only there's some – like that one – that can't be undone.'

'It was such a damn *selfish* thing to do,' she cried angrily, then sighing and changing the subject, 'What about you? I see you're still with the Reillys. Well,' she qualified, 'riding a horse with a Reilly brand on it anyway.'

He grinned unconvincingly. 'Trust you to notice that.'

Rachel was nothing if not perceptive. She said suddenly, 'You're in love with her, aren't you – with Jo?'

'Yes,' Billy said miserably, 'for all the good it's doing me.'

'I'm sorry,' Rachel patted his arm. 'It's not easy is it, with twins? Damn them! They're not like the rest of us. They only seem to need each other.'

'Yeah.' He was grateful for her sympathy but now he was the one anxious to change the subject. 'You eaten yet? What about I nip off and get us a bit of lunch? And you still haven't mentioned your holiday.'

'Okay,' Rachel said. 'I'll tell you all about it when you get back.'

A little later Jo found her twin sharing the shaded step of the jockeys' changing room with Casey Walker.

'Room for one more,' he said. 'Shove up a bit, Case.'

'It's okay, I'm not stopping. Hello, Casey. Just wondered if you'd seen Billy anywhere?'

'Over in the stands with Rachel Cooper. They're having lunch and a heart-to-heart.' He grinned and jerked his head back. 'Simon and Fiona are doing the same inside. Seems the world's full of couples looking for privacy. It's why we're perched out here like shags on a rock. What did you want Billy for?'

'Oh – it wasn't important. I'll catch him later.' Jo turned away. She'd been meaning to join him for the lunch break – just in case he'd minded her agreeing to ride with Snowy in the Gretna. Not that she could easily have refused, but boys never saw that, the stupid great lunks. It was all very well for them, she thought

213

indignantly – they only had to ask, whereas girls had to try and work it out through signals that, in Billy's case, were extremely confusing.

Of course she would rather have partnered him in the Gretna – if he'd only thought to ask her first. But she was too shy of disclosing her feelings (and too unsure of Billy's) to risk refusing Snowy – and everyone else that would have asked her while she was waiting on him to get round to it. Girls, being lighter, gave contestants a better chance in the race. That was the only reason Snowy had secured her promise but refusing him – and all the rest – would have made her preference too obvious. Which she wouldn't mind, she thought moodily, if she could only be sure of his. Billy's problem was that he never seemed to follow things through, a failing that was driving her crazy.

His contradictory behaviour hurt and bewildered her. Why ask permission to carry her colours if he was going to spend his time with Rachel? Or was she reading too much into it? Didn't he understand the significance of riding for a girl in the Crystal? It was permissible to race for your sister as Simon had done – but not usual. Perhaps he just wanted to win and needed a girl's name for his nomination to be accepted, and it meant no more than that? Even though she had as good as told him otherwise. Remembering her remark about Simon riding for Fiona, she felt her cheeks grow hot. If Billy had entered only to race then *that* was why he'd immediately latched onto Rachel, to nip in the bud any silly ideas she might be getting about him. Jo pressed a hand to her scarred cheek that felt fiery with the humiliation filling her. And after the race there was still the dance to get through.

The Crystal race was the last event of the day. Leading Freaky from the stalls out onto the main road, Billy's heart leapt to see Simon standing with Fiona beside the gate.

'I thought you were riding?'

'The mare's stepping a bit short. I won't risk her. Best of luck, mate. And watch out for Jacky Burch. That's him,' he nodded towards a stocky young man with the distinctive Burch features going past on a black horse. 'Let him alongside and he'll get his leg under yours and have you off.'

'Right, thanks.' Billy grinned nervously. Never mind butterflies, his stomach felt full of canaries. 'At least with you out of it I've got a chance.'

'You'll get yourself bloody killed,' Cub said coming up behind him. 'Since when've you been bareback champ anyway?'

'It's how I learned,' Billy said equably. 'As good as. There's not much to a racing pad.' His eyes moved beyond Cub to his twin, strangely quiet in the background. 'You got something for me, Jo?'

She passed him a folded, embroidered hanky. 'This'll have to do.' It seemed like she was about to add something, but instead she said quickly, 'Good luck. Be careful.'

Billy tucked it into his shirt pocket. 'I won't lose it.'

'I meant – the race.'

'Be bloody careful,' Cub said forcefully. 'Nobody's actually been killed – yet. But anything goes. Particularly with that little sod Jacky.'

'Simon's already warned me about him.' The canaries were turning into galahs. Billy nudged the pony into movement and grinned tightly at his supporters. 'See you at the finish line.'

Five others lined up with him. Henry and Dan Burch, a stripling called Hughie from the station the other side of Rumhole, and two others – one well over six foot and too heavy, Billy thought, to be riding any sort of race. The final man was Jacky Burch, Oscar's nephew, and another of the numerous Cooper connections. The starter wasted no time.

'You know the rules. All four feet in the river or you're disqualified. Wait for it – any moment now.'

Then the starting pistol went and they were off to a barrage of cheers and shouted advice.

The big man on the chestnut cut straight for the road, riding at a ferocious lick. The other four raced down the set of cattle-pads that led across the lower end of the deep breakaways eroded into the earth from the edge of the road cutting. Half a dozen of these paralleled the river's course and had to be crossed to reach it. It was the route Simon had always ridden – chancy, but sound, if a horse jumped cleanly and the friable rim of the breakaways held up. The lead rider held the advantage with the dust behind him and a clear view of the ground ahead. The way doglegged but it was still shorter than the road. But not as short as the route Billy had chosen.

'What's he doing?' Jo cried as the bay pony shot left towards the road. 'He might as well pull up now.' Freaky swerved around a clump of bauhinia and streaked away on a new line midway between the road and the riders on his right, and she caught her breath. 'He's not—'

'By God, he is!' Cub punched the air. 'Did you see that – he must've jumped his own length.' Freaky had left the ground as if jet propelled, in a wide, low leap that brought his hind feet neatly to the far side as his forequarters plunged ahead. 'That pony's like a cat. I thought he was mad to pick him, but he just might do it.'

'He'll kill himself.' Jo felt sick. The road curved left to reach the gravel bed of the crossing that lay upstream from the racecourse, while the pads doglegged right before angling back to the shallows a hundred yards downstream from where the road entered the water. Billy, by choosing to ride a straight line, was going where neither vehicles nor stock could, straight across the widest sections of the breakaways, which were ten and even twelve feet deep at that point. If Freaky missed his footing, or failed to clear a jump, his rider would end up in the bottom of one of them with the horse on top of him.

Crouching behind the pony's withers Billy was too busy ducking the swat of low branches and maintaining his seat to consider this. Freaky had thrown his heart into the race and was plunging dangerously fast down the bank, clearing obstacles and swerving around trees like a self-guiding missile. They cleared the last one and in a dozen strides were careering down the thirty odd yards of shingle bank.

The noise and wind of their own passage along with the thunder of blood in his ears blocked all other sound. Garry Downes, the Coopers' head stockman, there to check that the rules were kept, loomed out of the corner of his eye as they struck the shallow water where the pony skidded in a sheet of flying spray. He almost went to his knees. Billy dragged him up and round, and with a convulsive lunge they hit the shingle again. It slowed the pony's pace. He made the top in a series of plunges while his rider clung onto the mane to keep from sliding backwards. There was a yackia from downstream followed by a startled yell as a rider came unstuck through the shingle and a flurry of horses appeared in Billy's side vision. He slapped his open palm against the bay's lathered shoulder and yelled encouragement.

'C'mon boy, you can do it!'

Freaky was tiring. And one of the other riders had spied his route and was coming after him. It was the reason Billy had aimed for the road at the start, to throw them off the scent. Now there was someone on his tail. He dug his heels in and they flew the first three breakaways, but on the fourth Freaky's hind feet slipped and, for a horrible moment, his body hung downwards while he scrambled for purchase with his back legs before heaving himself out. A thunder behind heralded the other rider's arrival. Jacky Burch on his black. He powered over the jump, eating distance with every stride. A derisory yell floated back as Freaky lunged into a canter. Billy swore, knowing there was no point in continuing. No matter how game the pony was he simply couldn't outrun the black. Freaky, however, had the scent of challenge in his nostrils and leapt in pursuit.

They raced at the next to last breakaway and the pony jumped wide and low again, his hindquarters tucked well under. But Burch's horse refused. Perhaps he wasn't a natural jumper, Billy thought as he felt the lift and the thud of their own landing. The black had pecked in mid stride and stiffened his shoulders, skidding to a stop at the breakaway's edge. The suddenness of it sent Jacky straight over the horse's head. Billy's heart leapt – there was a chance!

'Go for it, boy!' He howled into the rush of wind and the sun-splattered kaleidoscope of passing leaves, 'C'mon, just one more!' He forgave the pony for every bruise his body and pride had ever suffered in the last two years as the bay pricked his stubby ears and sailed bravely over the last enormous gap, then dug in for the final run home through the scattered bauhinia. The field was coming, he could hear the hoof beats closing, but the road was near. He tore onto it, past the moving blobs that were people, breathless, hearing the cheers, hands slippery on foam-spattered reins, his back jolting in response to the uneven stride as he pulled Freaky in. He could feel the heat of the horse where their bodies touched and a wild, compulsive love for the tough little rogue filled Billy's heart. Behind him, like sounds in a dream, came the thud of hooves on gravel as the rest of the riders reached the road.

When he'd finally got the lathered pony settled Billy loosened his grip on the sweaty reins and walked him back to the judges' stand. Freaky's nostrils were wide as pipes, his bay hide turned black with sweat, but he stood quietly as Billy fished the scrap of lawn and lace from his pocket and held it up for all to see. He was so breathless he had to try twice for enough voice to shout the words: 'I claim the Crystal Race for Joanne Reilly.'

It earned him a cheer and a clap as he folded the token and put it away before cocking his leg over the pony's wither and sliding to the ground. He could still hardly believe he'd won. He looked for Jo and saw them all coming, faces expressing delight in his victory.

Cub whacked his shoulder. 'You did it! You and the runt. Congratulations, mate.'

'Yes.' To his surprise Jo's voice was cool with none of the enthusiasm he had expected. In a state of bewilderment he heard her say, 'Well ridden. You've done the station proud, Billy.' To Simon she added, 'I don't think Axel Cooper's gunna reckon it much of an improvement to have another man winning it for the Brumby, do you?'

'Probably not.' He blew out his breath. 'My God, Billy, don't try that stunt twice – or not with a different horse anyway. He only had to miss his footing . . . How'd you know he could jump like that?'

'Oh, he's good in the bush. Never goes round what he can scramble over.' Hurt and completely nonplussed, Billy watched Jo step aside to say something to Fiona. They laughed together, then Fiona called something to Simon and fluttered her fingers before both girls walked off with the dispersing crowd. Stupefied, he watched them go. His plan had worked perfectly. He'd won the race – for her, as she must very well know. And now she acted like he'd done it for the *station*?

If he lived to be a hundred he would never understand girls.

Twenty-seven

In the makeshift bar on the racecourse Harry Lucas stood alone amid the noisy drinkers, stubby in hand, brooding over the general dissatisfaction of life. If he'd had his way he wouldn't even be here today at this rubbishy excuse for entertainment, where the locals would sooner side with a bloke they actually hated than with an outsider. It had come as no real surprise that the punch-up with Reilly had won him no friends. These tin-pot towns were all the same. Reilly was a bastard but he was *their* bastard – that's how it went. It was an inverted form of pride, a situation where a stranger was on a hiding to nothing – damned whether he won or lost. And particularly so, Harry's lip curled in bitter recognition of the fact, when the stranger was part boong.

He gulped angrily at his beer. If it wasn't for his useless bloody boss he'd be up on the Wildhorse this minute hitting Reilly where it hurt. But Bennett had lost his bottle since the copper had come sniffing around, asking questions about flattened paddocks and missing gates. The jelly-kneed bastard had told him to forget it, that all he was ever supposed to do was give Reilly a pasting – and seeing he'd tried and failed, to leave him and his property alone, in future. Lucas ground his teeth. He despised Bennett, who didn't have the guts to do his own dirty work while disdaining those paid to do it for him. He'd just as soon chuck a firestick into *his* shed, he thought vindictively – and he would, if he could figure out some way of making it look like Blake Reilly had done it.

It was no more than a passing idea but it lodged in his head. Drink forgotten, he considered it. Maybe not the actual shed, or a fire, but some substantial damage to the station that'd cause a helluva stink for Bennett and place Reilly in the frame. Harry Lucas grinned to himself. He'd take his time and nut it all out. There was plenty to work with on a big company place. There were the buildings to start with and machinery worth thousands of quid . . . Even that bloody horse Bennett was so proud of cost more than a man could earn in twelve months.

He was thinking about that when the idea hit him, all laid out and ready to act upon. It was like watching his rifle sights settle on the imaginary point of the V between a beast's horns. The quick surge of satisfaction that came with knowing you couldn't miss. That was it, by God! Shoot the horse and the job was done. He only had to make it look like Reilly's handiwork and the whole damn district would be baying for blood. Lucas downed the rest of his stubby and grinned again. He'd teach 'em all. And just to start the ball rolling he'd go to their bloody dance too. He knew he wouldn't be welcome, but there wasn't a one of them with the guts to object to his face. Maybe he'd even ask Bennett's toffee-nosed missus for a dance. It'd be worth it just to see her trying to refuse.

The dance was a less formal affair than the Race ball. But there was no bar out the back as had been the custom in Sam Bullen's day. A uniformed Constable Watson hovered near the steps to the hall and those too inebriated to walk straight were turned away.

One ringer, still clad in the day's dirty shirt and jeans, was remonstrating with this ruling as the Reilly party reached the steps.

'Bloody wowser.' The man swayed on the heels of his riding boots. 'Supposed to be – free country an' a man can't – can't –' He lost the thread of his argument and Watson turned him firmly about.

'Sleep it off, Jimmy. Come back and complain in the morning.'

'Don'tcha worry. I bloody will,' the drunk slurred and set off on an unsteady course into the dark.

'Good,' Jo said crisply. 'I hate being mauled around by half-full ringers. When they've had a couple of drinks they all reckon they can dance.'

'Seems they're good for something then – coppers,' Cub said. He caught her hand and stepped onto the floor. 'Show 'em how it's done, shall we?'

Billy stood and watched them go. He didn't know if Cub was aware Jo was supposed to be partnering him; it hardly mattered. She was treating him as if he were a stranger. He'd returned her handkerchief, half hoping she would tell him he could keep it, but she'd taken it without a word. She'd dropped it onto her open swag and a few minutes later he saw the wind flick it away into the grass. Inwardly seething, he'd left it there.

Glancing around he saw Casey Walker sitting on a bench between her sister, Charlie, and Fiona Forrest and went across to them.

'Hi, Casey, feel up to some more practice with me?'

She stood up. 'Why not? Cub always has the first ones with Jo. Hey, I heard you won the Crystal!' Regretfully she shook her ginger curls. 'I missed the whole thing – just my luck. Fiona says Jacky Burch broke his wrist.' She spun under his raised arm then put a hand back on his shoulder and gave him a friendly grin. 'Know what? I reckon you're improving.'

'That's good,' Billy said and promptly trod on her foot.

She winced theatrically and laughed at his stricken look. 'Okay, maybe not that much – but a bit.'

He stood up with Jo but it was a bad choice for the dancers progressed in a circle, changing partners, and he kept losing his place. Later there was a foxtrot, a dance also new to him. It was hard to talk while following her instructions but he tried, anyway. 'What's the matter, Jo – is something wrong?'

'Apart from you having two left feet? Not that I'm aware of. Why?'

'How should I know? I'm asking you.' He lost the next move and plaited his legs, blundering into the couple behind them.

'Well, pay attention instead,' she said tartly. 'And concentrate, for heaven's sake.'

When the music stopped he saw her back to her seat. 'I think

I'll sit the next one out,' he said stiffly. He had scarcely sat down before Henry Burch was there sketching a larrikin bow before her. And after him came Dan, and then Cub again – Billy's glance swept the room without spotting Snowy's tall form. But Lucas was there, unmissable in a scarlet satin shirt, dancing with a pretty coffee-coloured girl whose features bore the unmistakeable stamp of her Chinese–Aboriginal parentage.

Then it was time for the prize giving – only this time it was Billy crossing the floor to receive the little box of crystal, his cheeks burning as Cub held thumb and forefinger between his teeth to let loose an uninhibited whistle. He regained his seat as the clapping began again for another rider then handed the ribbon-tied box to Jo.

'Thank you, Billy.' She made no effort to open it.

'Aren't you even going to look?' Fiona's eyes widened. 'I'm sure I would.'

'It's safer packed. I'll do it when I get home.' But her cheeks flushed and Billy saw Cub's head turn her way, his look one of surprise.

The dancing started again after supper. Billy, happy to escape the floor, let himself be co-opted by Vi Walker into loading the eskies and gas bottles onto the back of a vehicle parked behind the supper room. He was making his way back after washing his hands at the sink when the music was replaced by raised voices, one of them Jo's. She sounded furious.

'Take your hands off me. I told you no. En-oh. Isn't that plain enough?'

Billy shot through the opening separating hall and supper room and crashed into a couple drawing back, as others also were, from the source of the row. 'Sorry. Let me through please.' He pushed desperately between them.

'You stuck-up little bitch,' Harry Lucas snarled. 'What makes you so bloody special? Think you're too good to stand up with a yella-fella, do yer?'

Jo, equally angry and with the disastrous frankness that characterised her, answered clearly, 'When he's drunk, and has no manners – yes.'

Billy had reached her. He stepped between them, turning his back on the half-caste. Over Jo's shoulder he could see Cub coming, forging his way through the crowd, his look murderous. He must have heard every word. And behind him, a glimpse of the puggaree on Watson's hat and his khaki-clad shoulders. Jo's blue eyes blazed furiously, she was trembling with indignation. 'One more word,' she gritted, 'and I'd have slapped his filthy face. Do you know what he said to me?' Despite her outcry, she would never repeat the suggestion Lucas had made – particularly not to Billy.

'Keep walking,' he murmured. 'And it's okay, I just saw Watson. He won't let Cub do anything stupid.' He hoped it was true.

It was. Cub's rush was arrested by a hand gripping his biceps. 'I'll handle this,' the policeman said, 'you keep out of it.'

Cub tried to get past him and Jo, catching sight of them, ran across the floor to grab his other arm. 'Leave it – I'm okay. Do as he says, please!' she pleaded.

Held between the two of them Cub glowered at the half-caste. 'You hear me good, Lucas. You ever come near my sister again – you even *speak* to her – and you'll be picking bits of yourself outta the landscape for a week.'

'That'll do,' Watson said. 'Okay, Harry,' he leaned away from the smell of liquor on the other's breath, 'time to leave. The rules are plain enough – no drinkers in the hall. Outside or it's the lock-up for you.'

'I'm not drunk,' Lucas said truculently. Under the heavy brows his dark eyes glared. He was still steady on his feet and only a certain laxness in his posture and the burn of heat in his eyes hinted at the amount of grog inside him.

'You've had quite enough. Come along.' Harry found himself moving and struggled for the resolution to resist. 'You're making a show of yourself – interrupting the dance, insulting Miss Reilly.'

'That cheap little bitch! No better'n her gaolbird dad. Oughta be locked up, the pair of them. That's an idea. The old man ain't handy but you could shove her in the cells.' He leered, 'Lock me up too. I wouldn't mind showing her what she's missing.'

'Hold your tongue, man,' a new voice snapped, and with the slow comprehension of his condition, Lucas grasped that he had an escort besides the copper. Oscar Davies was there, along with George Hamilton, the wiry young bookkeeper from Rainsford, and his boss, Bennett. It was he who had spoken, his tone harsh with censure. 'I expected better from you. That's a white girl you're talking about.'

If he'd had one more drink Lucas could not have controlled the murderous rage this rebuke brought. He wanted, with a longing so strong he could almost taste it, to smash his fists into Bennett's face and pulp it to a bloody paste. His body trembled with the effort of restraint. All his life, he thought through the roar of the blood beating in his temples, it had been the same. The names, the insults, the casual ease with which the almighty whites despised him.

The Reilly bitch was not the first white girl to turn him down, but few had done it so publicly. She'd pay for disgracing him like this – as would the superior bastards hustling him from the hall as if they couldn't remove him too quickly from their exalted presence. They'd regret it – by God they would! Davies' pub could always catch fire. He grunted with satisfaction at the thought, his slack mouth hanging open.

Watson's grip on Lucas's arm tightened. 'You gunna spew, don't do it here.'

Lost in his fantasy Lucas ignored him. Oh, yeah, they didn't know what was coming to them. He remembered his plans for the Rainsford stallion. Bennett was gunna wish he'd kept his sorry mouth shut. *A white girl*, was she? Bloody little cock tease for all that – he'd seen her watching him. It'd be different if he'd got her alone. With his mind filled with a mixture of rum fumes and hate, Harry Lucas let himself be marched out of the bright spill of light around the hall steps, away from the music and laughter into the waiting dark.

Twenty-eight

Simon, being absent from the hall at the time, missed the sight of Lucas being escorted outside. He and Fiona had become engaged during the course of the evening, although he kept that news to himself until the following morning.

'So when's the wedding?' his brother asked when the congratulations were over.

'Next year, probably. Old Misery's dying. He's only got a few months – six at the outside they reckon. Fiona's going to quit her job and nurse him through it.'

'She any sort of a cook, this girl of yours?' Suds asked. His hangover had been a mild one; he'd even eaten breakfast and was presently mixing a batch of dough in the bread bowl.

A faint look of surprise crossed the prospective groom's face. He had obviously never considered the matter. 'I've no idea. I suppose so – girls cook, don't they?'

The old man cackled heartily. 'Fat lot you know. Worst cook I ever met was a woman – she damn near killed me. 'S'what started me cooking. *Wife, I says to her, either I rolls me swag or you gets outta the kitchen. I can't stand no more indigestion.'*

Jo stared. 'I didn't know you'd been married, Suds.'

'For a while,' he admitted. 'She run off with a shearer's cook in the end. Maybe she reckoned he could learn her something. All I know is *I* couldn't. That woman could burn boiling water.'

Blake greeted the news practically. 'You'll be wanting your own place. Don't expect too much to start with. Not till prices improve.'

'We don't,' Simon said briefly, 'she understands that.'

'Good.' He got up and went out, his boots ringing loud on the concrete walkway.

'Damned if I'd bring *my* bride home to any place he was inhabiting,' Cub said savagely but Simon was unperturbed.

'Fee will manage. Don't worry about her.'

Across the district the mustering continued. The cattle season was short, a time of frenetic activity with much to accomplish before the strength went out of the feed and the short days lengthened again to the heat of summer. The only interruption in the work was the occasional day at the homestead to change horses or pick up more supplies. Everywhere it was the same and if, Billy mused, riding with a week's growth of itchy beard behind the cows and calves they were currently driving towards the buffalo yards, you could get a bird's eye view of the district, it would consist mainly of dust.

Dust rising from the roads where the cattle trucks roared, and the stock inspector, and vet's vehicles darted between the stations. Dust billowing in red clouds above the yards where the branding and testing was done, and dust diffused across the sky, as it was right now, raised by the myriad hooves of the thousands upon thousands of head being worked across the country. It was everywhere, a faint pinkish colouration in the air that dimmed the shine of the eucalyptus foliage and coated the grass. Tasting it on his tongue he spat across his mount's neck. Then he sniffed and came alert, head up, nostrils flaring in earnest.

'Hey!' Jo was closest, and trotted across at his call, a man's handkerchief tied, bandit style as dust protection, across her lower face.

'What's up?'

'Smoke.' Billy's eyes narrowed, quartering the horizon. 'There – that faint column, far over behind the range. You reckon that's smoke? Or a willy-wind?'

She squinted. 'I hope not. Not at this time of year. That's about where the new paddock is.' Jerking the handkerchief down she stood in the irons, sniffing deeply. 'You're right. I can smell it too. It's a fire. How did that start?'

The matter was too urgent for speculation. A fire in early summer was one thing with the Wet close to hand. A fire in late June, with all moisture gone from the ground and no chance of regrowth until the rains, was a disaster. He spun his mount and hooked in the spurs. 'I'll tell Blake.'

The mob was almost a mile still from the yard. Blake's gaze swept the skyline while his horse fidgeted under his hand. His distance vision was failing as he could barely make out the grey smudge, but there was nothing wrong with his nose. 'Some careless bastard's let his fire get away,' he growled. 'Tell the rest – push 'em along. We'll have to get over there. If that's not in the paddock it's too damn close for my liking.'

Eventually, far faster than would normally have happened but still too slowly for their handlers' comfort, the cattle were yarded. It was past noon but nobody thought of lunch as they threw water canteens, shovels and the camp axe into the truck bed and took off. It was twenty miles back to the homestead and thirteen more across on the new road to the boundary paddock. Billy, riding up the back with Cub, eased his grip on the headboard as they spun onto the main road and for the first time risked standing erect. The smoke was all about them now, like a blue veil between the trees. Fortunately the day was still. The lack of both wind and heat would inhibit the fire's spread.

The fire was in the paddock but burning slowly, creeping rather than racing through the short golden feed that spread sparsely across the gravel slope where they met it. But that would change if it once reached the flat land and got amongst the tangled mass of knee-high swamp grasses there. Blake drove straight through the flames onto the safety of the burnt ground behind and led the rest of them in a charge upon the fire.

It took a couple of hours to shovel and beat out the last of the blaze. 'How big an area, do you reckon – a square mile?' Simon smeared a sleeve across his face and leaned on his shovel.

'At least – maybe two,' Blake said. 'Could've been worse. Question is how did it start? Let's have a look along the road.'

Billy, who was starving for a feed, groaned inwardly. But nothing would satisfy Blake until he had patrolled the perimeter of the fire.

'What's the good?' he groused, knowing it would make no difference. 'I mean, if it was a campfire that got away, how you gunna tell? Stands to reason it would burn all round it.'

Blake, driving at a crawl with his head out the window, was studying the ground. He stopped while Cub opened the boundary gate, continued for a hundred yards, slowed even more, then drove on, slowed again, and finally stopped altogether and switched off.

'There.' They followed him from the truck and then back down the road reading the sign. It was perfectly clear. Somebody had driven along there, pulling into the grass of the verge every so often to throw a match. Some of them had died for no burnt patches coincided with the swerve of the tracks, but two had caught – substantially, for at that point the vehicle had turned around just short of the boundary gate. Whoever it was had not actually been on the Brumby, but the prevailing wind was from the south-east. And there were more windy days than not throughout winter.

'It was deliberately lit.' Billy voiced what they were all thinking. All but Simon, who had continued on down the road and called back to them.

'Hey! Come and look at this.'

They went, only to be halted by his upraised hand. 'Don't wreck the tracks. Our firebug had a flat on his back tyre, see? I noticed the wheel wasn't running true, then it grabbed in the sand, there. You can see it's flat by the width. Here's where he got out to change it. Riding boots,' he fitted his own alongside them, ''bout the same size as mine. Whatever caused the puncture tore the tube up pretty bad because he slung it. It's there in the table drain, along with this,' he flourished a cardboard container, 'the box for the new tube. It must've been sent out on the mail because it's got the Harditch Toyota dealer's label on it. Addressed,' he held it out for inspection, 'to Rainsford Downs. No prizes for guessing who lit the fire.'

'Lucas,' Blake gritted. 'It's got his stink all over it.'

Billy trod carefully around the story written plainly in the stretch of red earth. He could see the smooth smudge where the man had lain to position the jack, the drag mark where he had removed it, the overlayed boot prints where he'd stood on one foot and used the other on the wheel brace to first loosen, and then tighten the nuts. A cigarette stub had been dropped nearby, and alongside it was the pockmark in the still congealed dirt where he'd taken a leak before getting back into the vehicle. He'd lit the fire on Rainsford knowing it must travel the short quarter-mile through the boundary. But in that case why leave behind the damming evidence of the box? Was it carelessness? Or did he panic when he had the flat in case he was caught on the scene?

Abruptly he knew. 'He did it on purpose. Left that,' he nodded at the incriminating label, 'so we'd know he did it.'

Simon frowned. 'Why?'

'I dunno. But it must be so. He's not stupid; he'd get the sack if Bennett found out he was setting fires on the station.' With sudden inspiration he added, 'The boss didn't report the paddock. Maybe he thinks he won't report this. That way he can burn us out without any comeback.'

'If you think that, you're as big a fool as he is,' Blake growled.

'That only makes sense if he means to pull out,' Cub objected.

234

'Maybe he has. He might've come out and lit the place up then driven back to the station and quit.' A little stir of wind fluttered the air and he looked down at his feet. 'He can always say it was an accident. By the time anyone gets out here the tracks will be long gone.'

'Or,' Jo said, 'maybe he's already *been* sacked. Bennett was pretty annoyed with him for that business at the dance. So he lit the place up to get square on him as well as us.'

'No.' Simon shook his head. 'It's over a month since the Sports. In any case you can't sack a man for getting drunk. Not in his own time. Besides, if he wanted to hit the station why not a match in the bullock paddock? A bit of bush country's not gunna matter. It's the paddocks that count.'

'So – what next?' Billy asked. 'You gunna report it, boss?'

Blake shook his head. 'The bastard's up to something – I can feel it. He's boxing clever here. I think we'll keep shut about the whole thing. Anybody asks, you act surprised. Not that we're likely to see anyone but the vet – and the buyer. He's coming Thursday.'

'Keith will notice it.' Billy remembered the mailman's quick eyes.

'The tracks will be gone by then. And the burn's not large. I'll get Suds to pump him – see if he can find out anything.'

'Like what?' Simon asked.

'How the hell do I know?' Blake scratched his whiskery jaw where the stubble clung, pepper and salt grey, and frowned. 'He's trying *something* on. Maybe he wants us to hit back. For all I know he could have the Stock Squad lined up to muster us. He'd only have to catch us trespassing in a Rainsford paddock and it'd be excuse enough.'

'But they wouldn't find anything,' Jo objected.

'Might. If Lucas had already put 'em there.'

'Jesus!' Billy, hunger forgotten, jolted to attention. 'D'you think he'd do that?' The suggestion had shocked him but not the others.

'Of course he would.' Simon's tone was cynical. 'Anyone that'd burn a man out isn't gunna worry about planting a few cattle on him.'

'Well, hadn't we better check – muster the paddocks?'

'Have a bit of sense,' Blake growled. 'We've got cattle in the yard, and a mob of sale bullocks to shift. There's bugger all time to spare as it is. Come on, let's get back to the station for a feed.' He glanced at the sun, now sideways in the sky. 'As it is it'll be dark before we even make it to camp.'

Twenty-nine

Over the next few days they waited to see what, if anything, would happen. Nothing did. The yarded cattle were tested and branded. Blake drove into the station to meet the buyer, a weathered veteran called Kyle who represented Queensland Meat Limited, and whose greeting was followed by the question: 'When are you gunna get an airstrip out here, Blake? I could fly out in a quarter of the time that damn road takes to drive. You ever worry about getting somebody out after an accident? I forgot to pick up the waybills, by the way.'

'That's a bloody nuisance. We're right out of 'em.' Blake leaned across to shove the passenger door wide. 'Hop in. There'll be a cuppa tea at the camp.'

The bullocks were duly sold, then tail tagged and taken to the station where the pack-horses needed to be mustered from the spell paddock. Billy was despatched to Southbend in the Land Rover to collect permit and waybills from the police station, and returned with unsettling news.

'They know about the fire,' he said, entering the kitchen and reaching to hang his hat. The screen door slammed and he tossed the sheaf of waybills onto the table, around which the others had gathered for smoko. 'I got the mail, too.' He let the bundle of newspapers and letters slide from under his arm. 'It was while I was picking up the waybills. Watson asked did we have any proof that somebody on Rainsford tried to burn us out.'

'Yeah?' Blake's face didn't change but behind the pale eyes his brain was busy. 'What'd you tell him?'

Billy shrugged. 'That it wasn't true and asked him where he heard it. I said somebody had camped on the boundary and their fire got away but they put it out before it spread far.'

'Did he tell you who told him?' Simon was sorting through the mail.

'No. But I stopped at the pub for a feed and Oscar brought it up. I asked him where he heard it, and he said the story was going round that the boss reckoned Rainsford was to blame. Bennett's grader driver was in the day before and even *he* was saying it.'

'Well it wasn't me said anything,' Suds declared bellicosely. 'Keith told me there'd been a bit of a burn on the boundary, an' I said *been*'s a good word seein' as I'm too old to be chasing fires. And that was it.'

'We know that, Suds,' Jo pushed her mug along the pine tabletop. 'Can I have some more tea? I'll bet Lucas started the story himself.'

Blake grunted assent. 'The question is why?'

No answer presented itself and next morning at daybreak they left with the bullocks for Mount Ixion. It was an uneventful trip, their only contact a meeting with Keith Guthrie.

'We're missing the Races. They're on this weekend,' Jo reported when she returned from speaking with the mailman.

'Nah, he's got it wrong. They're always later.' Cub, perched on the convenient limb of a tree, was doing the dinner-watch over the camped bullocks.

'As a rule. But the cyclone damaged a couple of racetracks over east. Mount Morgan and somewhere else. Washed them right out so they cancelled their meets and that's brought everybody else forward. So ours is a fortnight early.'

'Can't be helped,' Simon said. 'I wonder if Cooper's been trying to get hold of me to ride for him? But maybe he won't be racing. It's only seven months after all, since Ben—'

'Oh, he is. Keith reckons Bennett's entered his new horse for the Cup. Axel's got two runners in it, and the betting's pretty lively already. So he'll be racing as usual.'

'Any other news?' Blake asked as he emptied the billy preparatory to packing up.

'Just that Misery's in hospital. The flying doctor took him out two days ago.' She looked at Simon. 'The old boy'll have a fit when he gets back. Keith said Fiona's painting the shop.'

Simon grinned and stood up, spurs clanking softly as he moved. 'That'll give the 'Bend something to talk about. That and our engagement should keep 'em busy for the rest of the year.'

Back home again the work went on. August brought a few days of overcast and freezing winds that changed suddenly and inexplicably to heat.

239

'Early summer this year,' Simon commented. The horses, worn down from work, were already shedding their winter coats.

'We're gunna miss the rodeo – again,' Cub lamented. After the late start to the season they were too far behind with the mustering to even contemplate a week off for the annual event. Blake was taking the truck into Harditch for supplies while the rest of them travelled to Verity Valley to muster fresh horses. Even Freaky, Billy noticed as he pulled off his shoes and removed his neck-strap, was starting to show his ribs and the bones in his rump. And the pony was a good doer, able to maintain his condition longer than most.

'We can get the nags you know, Si,' Jo said, tossing worn shoes into the drum outside the saddle shed. 'If you wanted to slip into the 'Bend I mean, and see Fiona. You won't get another chance for a while.'

He shook his head. 'She's not there. Misery's due home from hospital and she's gone down to bring him back. He's too crook to travel alone.'

'He must really be sick,' Billy said.

'The cancer's spread. Fiona says he mightn't even last the six months they gave him.'

'I think I'll miss the lousy old skinflint.' Cub pondered the matter. 'I mean he's always been there, carping away at the council for wasting money on this and that. Stocking the same old stuff in the shop – and that hasn't changed in forty years.'

'It has now,' Jo's eyes danced. 'Ten to one he'll need the hospital again the minute he sees it. Keith said it's about the colour of custard – and it's got a bright blue trim.'

'It was the only paint in the shop,' Simon defended his fiancée's choice.

Cub chuckled. 'So he picked it himself. That oughta recommend it to him, then.' He pulled the packs down and matched them to their bags. 'Right, all set. Whose turn is it for the horses in the morning?'

'Mine,' Billy said resignedly.

'Better catch something for the night paddock then and I'll let the rest out.'

They left at cock crow next day, the myriad hooves splashing across the ford in the grey light while a mist rose off the water, floating like a gauzy scarf amongst the timber where wallabies thumped away ahead of them, dark shapes in the red and brown of the swamp grasses. Simon, reining in beside his brother, said, 'Blake'll take some persuading but this summer we really ought to put in an airstrip.'

'You've been listening to Kyle Clements. He was banging on about that. We've managed till now without.'

'Because we've been lucky,' Simon said. 'Think about it, mate. We've never had a bad accident. But what if we did, or someone was really sick—'

'Like Fiona?' Cub scratched his nose. 'That's what you really mean, isn't it. Getting engaged has turned you into an old woman, Si.'

'Maybe. But we both want kids. You ever think about getting a pregnant woman or a sick baby out of this place? You know how long it takes and what the road's like.'

'True. Still – you want your own house, and now an airstrip – It's a lot of money all in one year.'

Simon shook his head. 'It needn't be. We find the right bit of country we could do all the clearing ourselves, then hire the council grader to run a blade over it. Somewhere here in the valley would be ideal.'

'Wrong side of the creek,' Cub objected. 'For the Wet I mean.'

'But close to the house. That's what matters – how far are you gunna drive in the Wet, anyway? And the creek's fordable most of the summer. I've given it quite a bit of thought.'

Cub grunted. 'Yeah – you're in love. What *I'm* thinking about is the work involved.'

'So? You'll have a family some day too. And speaking of that,' Simon said, 'Fiona reckons that Billy's keen on Jo. You think she could be right?'

Cub snorted. 'You think the sun's coming up tomorrow? Of course he is! Has been for ages. You mean you hadn't noticed?'

'No.' Simon looked curiously at him. 'It's okay with you then? I thought you'd be – I know how close you two are.'

'Why shouldn't it be? Billy's a good bloke. And he won't make any difference to us, you know.' In the face of his brother's mystification he added kindly, 'I can feel Jo, in here,' he thumped his chest, 'and she can feel me. Nothing's gunna change that. Why shouldn't she love someone else too? He's got my blessing if it's him she wants.'

'Don't you know?' Simon was surprised.

'What am I, a mind reader? She likes him, that's all I know. You worry about Fiona. How's she gunna get on with Blake? He's not the perfect prospect for a father-in-law, is he?'

Simon was confident. 'She'll manage quite well. She's not,' he smiled at some private memory, 'easily intimidated. Anyway, she won't have to live in the same house as him. Don't worry about Fiona. I'm not.'

'You should know,' Cub flicked his whip at Freaky, lagging on the tail. 'So, the program is we get the nags back, finish the mustering, get the ramp and gates done for the new yard, and put in an airstrip.'

Simon grinned. 'That's it – except you forgot the fencing.'

'Oh yeah – and that. Should be a breeze. Lucky we got an early start this morning.'

Two days later they were home in time to help unload the truck, Blake's return with the ration order having coincided with their own. The moon was up by the time they'd dumped the last of the empty cartons and were returning from garaging the vehicle. It was a couple of nights off the full and in its pallid light the skeins of flying foxes winging into the creek timber were plainly visible. Billy gazed up at them, wondering how far they could scent the nectar that drenched the night with the smell of honey. Then the kitchen bell shattered the steady thump of the diesel and he picked up his pace. It was a long way back to their dinner camp at noon.

Blake, pouring tea from the big enamel pot at the table's end, seated himself. 'We should be able to finish the shoeing tomorrow and get packed up—' he broke off as Suds thumped a large casserole dish down beside the tray of condiments. 'What's this?'

'Macaroni cheese.' The cook spoke with mordant satisfaction.

'An' plenty more where it come from. Told you, before you all bug-gered orf an' left me, we was outta meat. We still are.'

'Christ!' Blake said irritably. 'What d'you do with it, anyway? Orright, we'll get you a killer.'

Suds addressed the air above his head. 'Anyone'd think I was the only one round here et beef.'

'Just as well the days are getting longer,' Cub grumbled. 'Wouldn't be much use going to bed if they weren't.'

Notwithstanding, they had the horses in at dawn and by midday were busy with hammer and rasp. To save time they were shoeing their soft, white-footed mounts first, and putting only front shoes on the rest. The hind ones they could shape and carry with them to attach at their leisure.

'Whenever *that* happens.' Cub, with Banjo's front foot clamped between his knees, used the handle of the shoeing hammer to shove his hat back. 'Anyone sees it coming let me know. I'd hate to miss it.'

'God, you whinge, mate.' Billy, pushing a nail into a bar of soap to ease its progress into the hoof, suddenly lifted his head. 'Hey, vehicle coming. I wonder who that can be?'

They weren't left long in doubt. The four-wheel drive wheeled in towards the homestead gate then, as its driver glimpsed move-ment at the yard, turned sharply and continued on there. Belle growled from the shade of a post and rose, hackling until Jo called her sharply to heel.

'It's the bloody copper – again,' Blake said. 'What's he want this time?'

244

Frank Watson climbed out, slammed the door and stood staring at them across the rails, his look distinctly unfriendly.

He dispensed with a greeting and got straight to the point. 'Right, Reilly – where were you the day before yesterday?'

Blake capped the tobacco tin he'd opened, slipped it into his pants pocket and rasped the golden-tan flakes between the heels of his two palms. He had a cigarette paper stuck to his lower lip that waggled as he spoke. 'You talking to me – or them?' An inclination of his head indicated his two sons.

'You'll do for starters. I'll get round to them. Now don't bugger me about,' Watson's eyes were as hard as his tone, 'where were you Monday?'

'In Harditch.'

'And the day before?'

'What do you bloody think? Getting there of course.' He unstuck the rice paper and poured the tobacco flakes into it. 'What's—'

It was like offering meat to a starving dog. Watson's expression was one of unmitigated triumph as he cut Blake off with another question. 'So you admit you were on Rainsford – that you drove through the property, right? And this on Sunday last?'

'Of course I bloody did,' Blake snapped, his expression suddenly wary. 'You know any other way of getting to Harditch? What are you driving at, copper? What's this all about?'

'I wondered when you'd get around to asking.' The policeman's eyes narrowed and his jaw muscles bunched in anger. 'D'you often do that? Go around shooting horses?'

'What the hell are you talking about?' Blake barked, cigarette forgotten. 'I've been framed once by you bastards. What're you trying on now?'

'Yeah, what's this all about, Watson?' Simon stepped forward, light eyes watchful. 'Which horse? Shot where? And why should we have anything to do with it?'

'I'm talking about Bennett's new stallion – or has he killed more than one? He was gut shot in the paddock two – three days ago. Died about a quarter-mile back from where he was shot, just off the road. I'm taking you in, Reilly.'

There was a combined gasp from Simon, Billy and the twins but it was Blake who spoke. 'What – because I drove through the property sometime during the week? Grow up, Watson. That doesn't prove anything. Whyn't you simmer down first and ask yourself why the hell I'd do a thing like that?'

'Because you blame Rainsford for the fire you had on the boundary last month,' Watson shot back. 'How's that for a motive? You mightn't have reported it, but everybody heard who you thought was responsible.'

'And doesn't that strike you as interesting?' Simon asked. 'We not only didn't report it, we never mentioned it to a soul. And yet everybody heard that we blamed it on Rainsford. Don't you find that strange?' Watson's eyelids flickered and he pressed on, 'Somebody on Rainsford spread that story. Ask Oscar Davies. Actually, we blamed Lucas. But if he was spreading the yarn he'd keep that bit quiet, wouldn't he?'

Frank Watson frowned. 'Why would he point the finger in his own direction if—'

Blake shouldered his way back into the conversation. 'Because this was what he was planning, of course. Jesus Christ! Anyone with two brain cells could see it. Give us a reason to strike back, make sure everybody knows it, then slip out and blow the horse over. He was smart enough to know you'd fall for it. Not,' he added with heavy sarcasm, 'that that makes him very clever.'

A hint of doubt crept into Frank Watson's face. 'Is there any proof of this?'

'It's an educated guess, that's all,' Simon said. He told him about the tube box, adding, 'I know – anybody could have chucked it away, days or even weeks before.'

'And try this on, copper, I wasn't carrying a rifle. Took it outta the cab before I left.' Blake looked about at the others. 'Some of you must've seen me do it?'

'I did,' Simon agreed. 'It's on the gun rack in the office still.'

'And me,' Billy remembered. 'I was on the verandah when you came in with it.'

'Witnesses,' Blake snapped. 'You still think you're taking me in?'

Watson suddenly looked less certain. 'Don't push it.' His gaze swept over Billy and Simon, the grey eyes hard as glass. 'You'd better not be lying, boys.'

'Believe me,' Simon said flatly, 'if I thought he'd killed that horse I'd be the first to dob him in. This is down to Lucas.'

'So *you* say.' The policeman strode back to his vehicle, slammed the door and made a tight turn back onto the road, dust unfurling in a long cloud behind him.

Thirty

Axel Cooper bumped his solitary way along the boundary track in second gear. The black soil was gapped with deep fissures so the pace suited the road condition while allowing him time to inspect the fence. He pulled up once in the corner where a scatter of coolibah grew amid the now dry gilgai holes to shift a tree branch that had fallen across the top wire, and again a little further on to throw his weight against a leaning post that a beast had pushed against when the ground was wet. He did it mechanically, as he did most things these days. In the back of his mind was the vague hope that some day, if he kept performing the necessary chores, the interest that even the most mundane tasks on the station had once held for him would return.

Deep down he doubted it, but even if Ben's death had taken the savour from living he had to go on. The land came first and however little interest he now felt for it, good husbandry was ingrained into the very fibres of his being. The guilt he bore for his son's end was a separate thing, something that would never leave him. And alongside it, shocking amidst his grief, was a festering anger that life should deal him such a hand.

If he could only start over – with an effort Axel cut off the thought and with something like relief saw Ken Walker's colicky old Land Rover approaching along the opposite side of the fence.

The two men pulled up, switched off, and got out, exchanging greetings.

'Feed's going back,' Ken observed, squinting across the thinning flinders grass. He rasped tobacco between his palms. 'How're your dams holding?'

'Good enough so far.' Their talk touched briefly on surface things. Ken, glancing without seeming to do so at his neighbour, thought him aged and thinner – and no bloody wonder, losing his boy like that. If it had been one of his girls – Ken's heart contracted for a moment as he allowed himself to imagine it; there were worse things than being broke.

Axel for his part noted the front tyre worn almost to the canvas, the stooped shoulders and lined face of the other man, and the boot sole laced on with wire, and drew his own conclusions. Which were suddenly confirmed when Ken took a resolute puff on his skinny cigarette and spoke.

'Glad I ran into you today. We'll be selling the old place – sooner rather than later. That is,' he said heavily, 'if anybody still wants cattle country the way the market is right now. I thought – seeing as how our lands run together – that it'd make a handy addition to the Mount. Makes sense to get bigger, you know. God knows the big runs are doing best outta BTEC. It's the battlers like me goin' under. So,' he finished abruptly, 'I'm giving you first refusal. What d'you say?'

'Sorry to hear that,' Axel said. 'It's a damn shame. I'm tipping there'll be more than a few forced out before it's all over. You've got to question the government's timing of the whole thing, in the middle of the biggest recession the industry's had since the Great Depression.'

Ken nodded. The arguments were stale, the sentiments voiced a hundred times before wherever cattlemen met. But the truth they had all had to face was that however vast an area they controlled, the northern cattlemen were too few in number to matter at the ballot box. He said, 'So, had you thought about expanding?'

'What for?' The words fell bleakly into the stillness around them; for an instant Ken Walker glimpsed the naked pain behind Cooper's iron control. Then the man turned aside to grip the top wire of the fence, brown, scarred fists clenched around it between the barbs. 'I'll be selling up myself – eventually,' he said. 'What else am I going to do with it now?'

'Yeah, 'course. Sorry. I was thinking of my own troubles, not yours.' Ken cleared his throat softly. 'Life's a bitch.' Embarrassed, he raised his eyes to watch the tiny shape of a lark shooting up into the blue on wings of song. Animals hurting that bad you could shoot, he thought; men just had to endure. He cleared his throat again and changed the subject. 'Who do you reckon's responsible for killing that horse of Bennett's?'

'I've no idea,' Axel said heavily. 'That sort of thing usually happens near the towns – weekend shooters raising hell. But as a deliberate act?' He shook his head. 'Who would do a thing like that?'

'Not Reilly then? That's what everybody's saying – payback for some fire Rainsford's supposed to have set.'

'I seriously doubt it. Young Martin's still working there. He's got a real feel for horses. He pulled out of here over the accidental crippling of a horse, so I can't see him being a party to killing one. Or Simon Reilly, come to that. Even Frank Watson seems doubtful about it now for all he roared out to the Brumby breathing fire. Anyway,' he glanced at the sun, 'I'd better head back. How's your mustering going?'

'Slowly. What about you?'

'We're getting there; started our second round.' Axel looked up again at the cloudless sky, 'I hope the heat holds off a bit longer.' He climbed into his vehicle; the engine fired and raising his hand, he swung the wheel in a tight circle to regain the road.

Ken Walker stood watching his retreating dust. 'You poor bastard. And we think we've got troubles.' He shook his head, sighed heavily, then returned to his own vehicle, the stalks of the flinders grass crunching dryly under his feet.

By the end of September summer would no longer be denied. Little puff balls of cloud glazed each day's horizons while the condition was falling off working horses and breeding cows alike. It was the same each year but an ongoing worry for all that.

At the Brumby they had heard nothing more from Watson about the shooting of Bennett's stallion, although Keith Guthrie had made his position in the matter clear. Friendly chats were a thing of the past. He had to carry the mailbag but freight for the Reillys had a habit of being overlooked, or accidentally dropped off at the wrong destination. Tiring of the inconvenience of fetching it back, Blake finally sent a message to the depot to hold everything that came for the Brumby and send it out with the vet.

'Guthrie's cutting his own throat,' Blake snarled, despatching Billy to retrieve a bag of wheat over-carried to Brancaster. 'He needs more than the mail contract to survive. But if that's the way he wants to play it he'll not see another penny of mine.'

'That'd be another cent,' Cub said disagreeably. 'You wanna drag yourself out of the past, old man. The world changes.'

'Yes.' Blake looked at him, the planes of his face set. 'It does – and it's a pity that you can't too.'

'Oh stop it,' Simon slammed his palm down onto the table. 'I'm sick of listening to the pair of you bicker. The way I see it you can't blame Guthrie. He's been a horseman in his time. Besides, what have we ever done except despise the people who might've put in a word for us now? You can't have it both ways.'

'Are you bloody daft?' Cub seemed to have trouble finding words. '*They* despise *us*. They always have – thanks to *him*,' he jerked an angry thumb at Blake. 'Well, sod the lot of them I say. They want to believe we did it – let 'em. Because they're never going to change.'

'Then perhaps it's time we did,' Simon retorted. 'And not just to save fuel chasing after freight. This is the rest of our lives we're talking about. Okay, maybe we haven't been model citizens in the past, but it's not too late to start earning a bit of respect for ourselves.'

'Some chance!' Cub said flatly, fixing a bitter gaze on Blake.

Billy returned with the much-travelled bag of wheat and the stock camp resumed its labour. Most of the stations had bull-runners working, a new sub-industry for the big runs, spawned by the requirements of BTEC. A history of open-range grazing had led to a natural build-up of scrubbers on the big properties – wild cattle which, having been missed in a couple of musters, had gone feral, and lived apart from the main herd. There were hundreds of them in the seldom disturbed back country of the big runs: wild cleanskin cows, and bulls with murder in their heart and absolutely no fear of man.

In the open country it was possible to run the scrubbers in a vehicle hung about with tyres to protect against the bull's horns when they were brought to bay. The bull-runners used their machine's weight to knock the beast over, before leaping out to tie it down. It was then winched aboard the following truck, transported to a steel yard and trucked off to the meatworks. Bulls weighed heavier than bullocks and, even going as ground meat for the hamburger trade, fetched more in the present market than their castrated kin. It was dangerous work but worth it, even without a choice, for the Department of Primary Industries would move in and shoot scrubbers not cleaned out by the station. As possible tuberculosis carriers they had to be eradicated to comply with BTEC regulations.

On the Brumby, where the geography was too rough for such tactics, they used trap paddocks about the waters, and horses, to achieve the same results. Younger cattle, once trapped, would often settle and could be tested and paddocked. They were also more easily held in the coachers – quiet cattle the musterers ran the

scrubbers into to hold them. Cleanskin bulls were seldom as amen-
able, more inclined to charge the first rider they saw. They were
a frightening sight, spearing blindingly fast out of the dust, heads
down and withers humped behind wicked horns.

Up on Lancewood Creek in late October the Reillys were
shifting camp, the plant, pack-horses to the rear, moving listlessly
through the noonday heat. It was starved-looking country, Billy
thought – ashy grey soil that raised a pale dust under the moving
hooves, and low, yellowed-off scrub flowing like a dyspeptic river
between the conical-shaped sandstone hills. The thin spread of
dried grass was powdered white, the sky itself bled by heat to the
same pale colour, and the narrow gutter of the creek looked as if it
had never seen water.

There were, however, rock holes further along where the scrubbers drank and, judging by the tracks, the odd mob of brumbies, not
to mention everything else that crept and crawled and flew. Billy,
feeling the sweat run down his ribs, pulled irritably at the shoulder
of his shirt then slowed Crab's pace to accommodate Flute. Jo's
black mare was lame from a stone bruise picked up the previous
day. They ought really not to be travelling her but, left behind, she
would be lost to the brumbies. At least they were heading home,
Billy thought, as he clicked encouragingly at the limping horse.
Nightfall should see them back at the homestead – unless they ran
into cattle first, but that, at the moment, didn't seem very likely.
There was nothing but scrub hereabouts, and broken country fit
only for goats.

The thought had no sooner formed when the scrubber bull

came out of the dense wattle thicket to his right, bearing down on the plant like a runaway truck. He was big – that much Billy saw while time seemed to freeze about him – a dirty roan, with horns like lances and a dusty poll above little piggy eyes. His ears were tattered from fighting; there was an old gore scar on his flank and a cloud of buffalo fly about his shoulders. Crab shied violently, fighting the bit, and Billy's wits returned.

'Watch out!' he roared, as the tail of the mob burst apart in a stampede of panic. 'Behind you, boss!'

Blake's mount Walleye, a tall grey with one white eye, lunged forward as Blake jerked about in the saddle, inadvertently turning his mount side on as he did so. With time seemingly suspended, Billy was able to see everything at once – the dust pluming lazily behind Walleye's driving hindquarters, the violent dig of Blake's spurs into the grey's ribs as he comprehended the danger bearing down on them, and the horse's whinny of terror as the massive beast came on, head low and tail straight behind him. The horns, as thick around at the base as Billy's wrists, buried themselves in the grey's flank. Walleye's forequarters rose until all four of his feet hung for a second clear of the ground, then he staggered sideways and crumpled to the dirt.

Billy caught a flash of scarlet as the horns withdrew and slammed his own spurs home but there was no need to even try and draw off the bull. Blake, amazingly, had landed on his feet and within a hasty skip of a solid-looking emu apple tree. The bull made a half-hearted pass at the figure revolving around the protective trunk then, tail lashing after the style of a thwarted lion, vanished into the scrub, flattening any that impeded his progress.

'Jesus!' Cub had arrived at the same time as Simon and sat in his saddle staring at the fallen horse. Walleye stroked ineffectually with his forelegs in an effort to rise. Blood pooled on the thirsty earth and his breath came in grunting gasps. Shock caused Cub, for once, to speak naturally to his father. 'You were lucky to get outta that.'

'Don't I know it.' Blake cast an eye over the scattered plant. 'Somebody blocking up those horses?'

Billy hipped in his saddle, 'Jo's got 'em. Shall I get the rifle, boss?'

'No need. I'll pith him.' Blake had his stock knife out. He squatted by Walleye's head and pushed the short blade in behind the ear, severing the spinal cord. The grey shuddered, drew his hind legs up to kick once, then lay still. Blake patted the sweaty neck before wiping the blade on it. He snapped it closed then worked the bridle free, lowering the horse's head gently onto the hot dirt. 'Poor old fella,' he murmured, but so softly only Billy heard him. A moment later he was all business again, stepping around the horse to strip the gear off and calling a couple of them to give him a hand as the girth straps lay underneath.

'We must all be blind – we rode right past him,' Simon said, eyeing the wattle thicket. A bull alone at this time of year was not unusual, nor was the savagery of his attack. 'He must've been dozing and woke to find us on top of him. What horse do you want?'

'Opal will do,' Blake grunted, working the girth from under the heavy body of the grey. 'One horse crippled and another dead. It's as well we're finishing up for the year.'

Billy took the bridle and went to catch the black mare, mindful as always of her hind feet. She was a poor doer as a consequence of having knocked a front tooth out on a rail as a colt in the catching yard. It meant she never got the work she needed to quieten her. She seemed to be always in the plant, half poor, hard to catch and very willing to kick whoever tried it.

Jo, riding on the far side and now holding the restive plant together, saw him with the bridle. 'What's up?' She had, he realised, missed all of it. 'What started them off like that?'

'There was a bull camped in the wattle clump over there.' Billy jerked his chin. 'Came out of it like a runaway train and skewered Walleye. Fastest thing I ever saw.' He buckled the throatlatch while the mare sidled and blew down her nostrils at him.

'No wonder they bolted! What about the grey?'

Billy grimaced. 'He's dead. Blake pithed him. The bull got him in the flank with both horns.'

'What about Blake?' There was no anxiety in the question.

'He's fine. Landed on his feet and got to a tree. Jesus!' The enormity of possible consequences suddenly struck home. 'He could've been killed – any one of us could've been.' The trickle of sweat on his ribs was suddenly freezing and goose bumps lifted the hairs on his arms as he considered the speed of the near fatality. If the tree hadn't been there, or if Blake had landed badly . . .

'Well we weren't.' Jo dismissed his fears in her usual forthright manner. 'You know what they say – *might* and *maybe* make a very poor yard.' It was actually Cub who said it, but the twins used each other's phrases as easily as they did each other's towels. The lead of the plant was wandering again and she threw an impatient glance at him. 'Hurry up, Billy. Give him his horse so we can get moving.'

Flute, in fleeing with the rest, had done her bruised hoof no good and was lamer than ever. When they pulled up at the rock hole for a late dinner camp the mare lay down to get the weight off it, and stayed in that position until they were ready to move again.

'You better drop her off when we reach the gate in the paddock, save dragging her the extra distance,' Blake said. 'Catch her tomorrow when she comes into water and we'll feed her in the yard till she's right again.'

Billy grunted assent. It was too hot to talk. Riding on afterwards he daydreamed of the cool depths of the Wildhorse and determined to have a swim as soon as they got back. Just dive in and stay under until his lungs threatened to burst. A couple of feet below the surface and the water was cold enough to put a chill on your skin.

An impatient 'Hoy!' broke into his musings and blinking off the fantasy he saw that they'd arrived at the back of the holding paddock that ran down to the house. Blake stood dismounted by the open gate, waiting for somebody to grab the crippled mare and lead her through it.

Billy was closest. He slipped off Crab and with a hand on Flute's neck strap coaxed her up to the opening into the paddock.

'You can shut it,' Blake said, of the gate, as he slid a boot into the iron and reached to grab the pommel. His shoulder muscles bunched, dislodging the coils of his whip. It dropped down his arm to touch Opal's neck. She snorted, eyes and nostrils dilating, and backed up into the wire gate.

It happened in a moment. Later, Billy would recall that the mare

258

hated wire. Her reaction was as fast and startling as the scrubber bull's had been. Jamming her tail she squealed and lunged forward, breaking Blake's grip on the saddle. Hopping on one foot, the other still in the stirrup, he fell and Opal barrelled over him, a hind foot lashing back in a vicious kick as she bolted, wild eyed, with trailing reins, for the safety of the mob.

It was over in the blink of an eye. Cub, in the lead, yelled, 'What's going on?' as the pack-horses, their loads clanging and swaying, cantered by him, but Billy didn't answer. Blake's hat had bowled towards him and lay brim uppermost in the dust, exposing its sweat-stained inner band. He picked it up and ran the few paces separating them.

'Boss?' he said tentatively, and then louder, 'Boss!'

Blake lay as he had fallen with the whip handle under his shoulderblade and its thong snaked across his body. One boot pointed west, its spur rucked sideways, and a long smear of dust marked that leg of his jeans. His eyes were closed and his pale hair, darkened by sweat, was pasted to his forehead. He looked to be asleep. Under the soiled cotton shirt his chest rose and fell and the breath puffed gently from his slack mouth. He'd been knocked cold, Billy thought with relief. That was all it was. Then he saw the blood pooling, much as Walleye's had done, in the dirt beneath his head, and his heart sank.

'Oh, Jesus!' He dropped prayerfully to his knees beside him.

'Billy?' Simon had appeared, eyes narrowed, voice crisp. 'What happened?' Behind him his mount's head loomed like an inquisitive bystander's and Billy was suddenly aware of the twins' shocked presence and, in a niggly underpart of his brain, that he hadn't tied Crab up. If the horses moved off he'd clear out for sure.

'She knocked him down – Opal,' he spoke tersely, 'then ran over the top of him. His head – I think she kicked him.'

'Christ!' Gingerly Simon felt his father's skull, rolled a lax eyelid up and felt for a pulse. 'Maybe he'll come round,' he said without much conviction. 'In the meantime we'd better get him some help. I *knew* we ought to have an airstrip.'

'What's the panic?' Cub spoke roughly. 'A bang on the scone won't kill *him*.'

'Oh, get over it for a minute, will you?' Simon snapped. 'There's a good chance his skull's fractured. You ride home and fetch the Land Rover. Stick a mattress in the back. And have Suds call the flying doctor.' He considered for a moment. 'Tell him it's a head injury and we're taking him to the 'Bend.'

Jo spoke for the first time. 'Rainsford's closer.'

Simon shook his head. 'Be dark before we get there. Same with the Mount. But they do night flights into the 'Bend so there must be lights. Besides, the hospital's there. You better get the nags home and seen to, Jo. Billy can give me a hand here – we'll have to carry him to get him to the vehicle. The road'll be bad enough without bumping him across the paddock.'

Billy got to his feet. 'I'll let my horse go then,' he said, adding apologetically, 'I'll be as quick as I can, but I didn't tie him up.'

Simon had picked up Blake's hat and was using it to shade the unconscious man's face from the blast of the afternoon sun. He glanced up from his task. 'Take your time. He's not going anywhere.'

Thirty-one

It was after dark when the vehicle carrying its still unconscious burden reached Southbend. Billy, squatting on the rolled swag beside the silent figure, straightened his back with a groan as the wheels met the smoother going. Above him the tarp they had rigged to provide shade for the injured man billowed in the wind of their passage, but he no longer noticed. There was a pain between his shoulderblades from hours of crouching beside Blake's still form, and he was perishing for a drink. He knew there was water in the cab, and in the bag swinging from the bullbar, but pulling up would only have lengthened the time on the road.

Billy was there because Cub had angrily refused the task, fair brows drawn together in a scowl as he slapped the tailboard closed.

'Don't expect me to put myself out for him. He never did for us.' The growl in his voice could have passed for Blake's own. 'I wouldn't cross the road for the old bastard if he was dying.'

'For all we know he is,' Simon retorted tartly. Jo had hesitated, plainly not wanting to volunteer, then spoke reluctantly, 'I'll—' but before she could finish, Suds stepped forward.

'He's me mate. I'll go with him.' He glared at Cub. 'I thought better o' you, boy. You got your life in front o' you – wouldn't hurt you none to let go of the past. I'll get me boots.'

Simon touched his shoulder. 'It's okay, Suds, Billy'll come.' Diplomatically he added, 'We might have to carry him. He's a big weight and you haven't the strength for it now. Better you stick by the wireless in case there's a message.'

'Yeah.' The old man's mouth worked and he leaned over the sideboard to grip Blake's flaccid arm, his voice hoarse with feeling. ''Ang in there, mate – you'll be fine.'

They hadn't waited longer but had gone as they were, Billy with the spurs still strapped to his boots. He'd turned them onto his instep since and as the long slow miles passed with no sign of change in Blake's condition, his fingers found and spun the rowels, the tinny jingle of the movement a counterpoint to the rattle of the vehicle's tray and Blake's increasingly heavy breathing. The fidgeting helped calm his impatience for the journey to be over for it seemed increasingly plain that Simon's evaluation was correct – Blake *could* be dying. He was certainly gravely ill.

The words Suds had spoken to Cub played on Billy's mind. Flicking the sharp points of the rowels he thought about them, his eyes shifting between the spinning spikes and the comatose figure beside him. Cub had never made a secret of the antipathy he bore his father, and Billy had occasionally wondered at the older man's forbearance. Perhaps the old cook was right – the past could not be changed so it was better forgotten. Billy himself had managed it (though not without Ivy's help) and perhaps the time had come for Cub to do the same. Blake had got himself off the grog after all, and that couldn't have been easy.

Although wary of him at first, Billy had gradually come to feel a sneaking admiration for his hard-bitten boss. He was inclined to believe his assertion that he'd been fitted up for the robbery. But he'd done the time and put it behind him to apply himself single-mindedly to the task of building the property into a solvent business. Suds, Billy thought, was his only real companion. As a family unit his children might as well be hired hands like himself.

Darkness fell sometime during his musings. They hadn't even crossed the Rainsford yet because they were travelling slowly to minimise the bumps. Peering back up between the roil of pale dust and the edge of the tarpaulin he saw the first stars and twisted about to knock on the back window. Simon pulled up and leaned an inquiring head in under the edge of the makeshift canopy.

'I can't see him,' Billy explained. 'Turn the cab light on.'

'Okay.'

The dim glow through the back window cast just enough light for Billy to watch over his charge. With his knees wedged uncomfortably tight against the mattress to prevent it sliding on the corners, or when the track descended and rose again through the hills, Billy yawned and wished the journey ended. It'd be midnight at this rate before they even arrived – and when they did he hoped they'd get a bed at the pub for what remained of the night. Snuffing dust he put his hand down as he'd already done a dozen times, to fumble under the unconscious man's ear for the thready beat of his pulse. It was still there but the skin felt clammy and cold. Billy wondered if it was shock, for the night was warm. His nerves crawled with the need for speed. They were still an hour out from the Mount . . .

When they finally arrived the hospital was a blaze of lights and the flying doctor came down the steps carrying one end of a stretcher and a powerful torch. The matron was there, and Fiona, cool and professional in a pristine uniform. In a bustle of organised purpose Blake was carried up the steps, and out of sight down a passageway. The scuffed soles of his riding boots were Billy's last sight of him as he was borne away.

Restless and impatient he paced the waiting area, ignoring the hard plastic chairs. 'He doesn't look good, does he? I hope he's gunna make it.'

Simon, perched on a chair, had opened his stock knife and was cleaning his nails with the tip of a blade. 'You're full of surprises, Billy. There probably isn't another man in this town would agree with you.'

'He's all right,' Billy said defensively. 'I do realise he doesn't *want* to be liked. But he's always treated me fair.'

'You're right about that. Prison did it to him.' Simon thought about that statement in the calm way he had before adding, 'Mind you, he was a rambunctious lad before that – but in a different way. He always drank a bit and he liked to fight.'

Billy nodded. 'Cub told me.'

'No. Not the way he remembers it. That was after prison.' He snapped the knife shut. 'Up till then he never raised a hand to Mum or me. I was luckier than the twins. They were born after he'd turned mean. I've got the good memories to balance out the rest. There was a time,' he said unemotionally, 'when I loved him. He ruined that, but I still don't hate him. Not like Cub. He's too like him, of course, but apart from that he won't ever forgive what he did to Jo.'

'Her face? He told me.'

'Yeah, well, that's when it became common knowledge – not that it was exactly a secret before; nothing ever is in a town as small as this one. And soon afterwards our mother left.'

Billy twitched a calendar straight, noticing that there were only two days left in the month. 'How old were you?'

'Fourteen. The twins were five. They never really knew her – not the way I did. They've got this picture of a weak, scared woman who didn't protect them – but it wasn't really like that. They blame both of them: her for leaving them and Blake for, as they think, driving her away. They've never understood that she had to go.'

He stood up and began to prowl the room, tapping the backs of the plastic chairs and inspecting the pale blue walls where the calendar and a clock hung. The hands stood at twenty minutes to eight. Billy sat down, hitching a booted foot over his other knee. 'When she left – did she tell you she was going?'

'Yes.' Simon turned from his scrutiny of the clock. 'Just before school – on a Monday. She said the man she was going away with had told her she could take one of us. That's all he was prepared to house and feed. And because she knew she couldn't split the twins up she'd chosen me.' He shook his head. 'I didn't even *want* to go.

I knew it would end with this man the same way it had with Blake, because she was like that. I don't know how I knew that at fourteen – but I did. And I was tired of trying to protect her. But – she brought it on herself and it was Blake I felt sorry for. She *goaded* him, you know, and then when he finally lost it and hit her he'd drink to forget.' He shook his head as if to dispel the memories. 'I was a kid, Billy. I just wanted my dad back and maybe I thought if she went away, that I'd find him again.'

'Well, he's stopped drinking.' It was all Billy could think of to say. He hadn't heard Simon talk as much, let alone as intimately, in all the time he'd known him.

'Yeah. Maybe her going was what he needed too,' Simon said. 'Suds turned up soon after. He ironed our clothes and cooked our meals through the rest of the time we were at school.' His lips twitched, 'Mind you he got drunk every Friday night, but it only made him happy. It was an eye opener for me – a drunk that sang and brought lollies home for us.'

Heels clacked in the corridor and Billy sat up as Fiona came into view. She smiled at Simon and went to him, putting a hand on his arm.

'Sorry it's been so long. I can't stop. Just wanted to let you know that your father's in bed and comfortable. Doctor's staying with him for now. His blood pressure's low but when he stabilises they're flying him to Townsville. Tonight probably. The pilot's standing by. I'll go along if needed, and you know we'll do our very best for him.'

'I know you will. Thank you.' Simon rubbed absently at his jaw, his gaze troubled. 'Did he come round at all?'

'No,' she let her hand slide down to squeeze his fingers. 'He's in a coma, Simon. It's quite serious. Any skull injury is. They'll get a neurosurgeon to him as soon as possible. You look worn out,' her gaze shifted to Billy, 'you both do.'

'Yeah. Well, we can't do much here then. Best thing'll be to stay at the pub tonight and see what's happened by morning. I'll send old Suds a message too – he's bound to have the wireless on still.' He sneaked a look up the empty corridor and bent to kiss her lips. 'Don't touch me, sweetheart. I'm filthy.'

'All right then.' She straightened her cap. 'Go get some rest. We'll take care of him. 'Night, Billy.'

'Goodnight, Fiona.'

They walked out into the warm night where sheet lightning played through high-piled cumulus clouds, and yellow squares of light bloomed in the town windows. Billy stretched until his shoulders cracked then smacked at a mosquito on his arm.

'I could eat a horse,' he said, 'and it wouldn't have to be too well cooked either.'

'I dunno what time the kitchen closes,' Simon turned the key, 'but Oscar'll knock us up a feed. Hey and remember your seatbelt. Watson seems to have caught half the town driving without 'em.'

Thirty-two

There were vehicles in front of the pub, light, the sound of voices and the wonderful smell of frying spilling from the open doorway as they pulled up and got out. A dog was barking somewhere, and distantly a man's voice bellowed, '*Siddown* you yapping bloody mongrel!'

They walked up the path, and their boot heels clumped on the boards of the verandah so that the men filling the bar stools swung their heads to the sound. Keith Guthrie, Dan and Henry Burch, and a couple of younger men, one of whom Billy half recognised. Henry had a glass of beer and plate of chips before him. Billy's mouth flooded at the smell but before he could do more than nod a greeting, Oscar straightened up so quickly that Bluey, preening himself on his shoulder, put up his crest and squawked in protest.

'Out,' he said to Simon. His face was grim, his brows snapping together in a scowl that sent wrinkles climbing his bald head. 'You're banned. You, your brother, your old man, and anyone that runs with you.'

'What're you talking about?' Simon stared, astonishment changing quickly to anger as the drinkers deliberately turned their backs and addressed themselves to their beer. None of them had acknowledged his or Billy's presence. His voice roughened. 'Look, it's been a hard day. We've come for a feed, not this shit. So are you gunna serve us or not?'

'Told you, you're banned. Horse killers don't drink in my pub. They don't eat here either. Far as you're concerned the kitchen's closed – permanently. Now leave, or I'll have you arrested. I daresay Watson'd jump at the chance.'

'We had nothing to do with killing that horse!' Billy exclaimed, wounded and infuriated by the accusation and the contempt on the publican's face. The turned shoulders of the men he had worked with and competed against were even worse and he took a step towards them. 'Henry, Dan – for God's sake,' he appealed, 'you know I wouldn't do a thing like that—'

'Save your breath.' Simon grabbed his arm. 'They'll think what they want to.' He made for the door. Billy hesitated then swore and followed him out.

Outside, standing on the dark patch of lawn, with the soft whine of mosquitoes and the faint rumble of thunder in their ears, his anger boiled over. 'Jesus, Simon! You grew up here. There's gotta be somebody in the damn place will believe you. Sod it, I'm not gunna starve. I'll knock old Misery up.'

He stalked through the bent arms of the turnstile and across the road to the store but hammering on the darkened shop front brought no results. Rounding the side of the building he spotted a dim glow emanating from an old-fashioned sash window, its pane so coated with dust he could see nothing through it. He cupped his hands against the glass and was rewarded with a quavery cry.

'Who's there?'

'He's home anyway,' Billy said. Simon had followed him. He leaned past Billy's shoulder and tapped on the pane.

'It's Simon Reilly, Mal. I know it's late but we need a bit of stuff from the store. If we could come in for a min—'

With startling abruptness the window flew up and a moment later Misery Jones thrust the barrel of a shotgun through the aperture. Billy almost didn't recognise him. The big, slouch-shouldered, bear-like shape had shrunk back to bones, and the loose skin of his arms swung like a rag in the wind. His face had sunk in on itself, giving the effect of sharpening his nose and deepening the brown smudges under his eyes. The rest of his skin was grey and soft looking, like putty, but not his eyes.

'Clear off,' he snapped. 'Shop's shut to you lot. And this,' he gestured with the weapon, 'says it's staying that way.'

'For crying out loud!' Billy exclaimed. 'Here we go again.'

'Get used to it.' Misery's breath suddenly caught and the barrel sagged as he brought his elbow in hard against his body. When he could speak again he wheezed, 'You made your bed – sleep in it if you can.' He jabbed the shotgun at Simon, 'Know something Reilly? 'I won't see Christmas, but I wouldn't change places with none of you. I wouldn't want that much hate inside me.' Then his mouth opened suddenly and a moan was wrenched from him before he slammed the window down. They stood stunned, watching the light glimmer and fade, catching, through the cracks of the shrunken boards, the faint shuffle of his slippers as he left the room.

'He was using a candle,' Billy said stupidly. 'Too flaming mean to switch on a light.'

Simon ignored the observation. 'Well, they've all made it pretty plain how they feel about us.' He jerked his head in the direction of the vehicle. 'Come on. No point in hanging around. Let's go home.'

Next morning Blake's condition was described as grave. During the night he had been transferred to the base hospital in Townsville without regaining consciousness. There, X-rays taken on arrival had shown that he had a depressed fracture of the skull that was causing pressure on the brain and they were now awaiting the arrival of the surgeon to do something about it.

Simon, listening, keyed the microphone. 'So – he'll be okay when that's done?'

'Well,' the doctor – not the same one who had come to the 'Bend – replied. 'It's early days to be deciding that. Certainly his chances will be better once the pressure's released. Over.'

His voice echoed tinnily in the hot and boxy little office where Simon sat in the only chair. Suds leaned against the wall, his cigarette forgotten, while Billy and the twins crowded the doorway. Simon clicked the microphone again. 'How long should it take – before we know something, I mean? Over.'

'I'm afraid I can't say,' the doctor replied. 'Better, I think, to just wait until the end of the op. Perhaps if you were to call back this

271

afternoon we might have something for you, but I'm afraid I can't help you now.'

'So, what's new?' Cub snorted when Simon had switched off. 'Remember when Nev Farmer lost his fingers and they called in from the boat to ask could they be stitched back on? A different doc back then of course, but he didn't know either.'

'I assume they couldn't be,' Billy said, after a moment, 'seeing he hasn't got 'em today.'

'That's because the shark et 'em. He ran a trawler back then, old Nev. They pulled a shark in with the catch and it was flopping around on the deck and took most of his hand before a crewman kicked it over the side.'

Billy looked at him. 'Why ask then?'

'So he could figure out whether to sack his crewman or not. Nev reckoned they coulda got the fingers back out of the shark. Only the eager beaver with the boot never gave him the chance.' He puffed out a long breath and looked at his brother, 'So – you planning on going down to Townsville? It's a bloody long way.'

'Not today,' Simon said, 'but when he's come round after the op I'd better take a run down. Me and Suds,' he cast a glance at the old cook, 'you two as well if you want. Billy could look after things here for a day or two – couldn't you, mate?'

'Yeah, 'course.'

'You can count me out,' Cub said flintily. 'What about today then – we taking the horses over to Verity?'

'Let's leave it for a bit – at least until we find out what's happening with Blake. No sense rushing it when, by allowing an extra day, we could get those fillies out of the stallion paddock on the way over. But right now we can't be away from the radio that long.' Simon wiped sweat from his face. 'Wouldn't hurt to do a bit of burning over the creek though, and while we're at it look around for an airstrip site. What happened to Blake just shows how much we need it.'

'You're the boss,' Cub agreed. 'Mind you, it'll be a big job without machinery. We're not likely to finish it this summer.'

'We'll never finish it if we don't start,' Simon turned the radio off and stood up. 'And the first thing's finding the right stretch of ground.'

'Bugger me!' Suds interjected. 'What with Blake getting hurt and all, I plain forgot the mailbag. Truck'll be along this morning and the bag ain't out at the box.'

'I'll do it,' Billy said, turning his head with sudden resolution. 'Come for the run, Jo?'

She eyed him. 'You just want a gate opener.'

'Dead right I do. So – how about it?'

'Since you make it sound so irresistible – okay then, I'll come.' Her lips quirked in a grin and Billy's heart leapt but the moment they were in the vehicle and moving towards the bottom gate a crippling shyness seemed to rob him of the power of speech.

There was much that he meant to say and Blake's accident made it somehow more urgent that he did so immediately. Blake had been hale and well one moment and helpless the next. He would never forget the way he had looked or felt – the thready pulse below his ear as he lay, flat as a toppled tree, all the life and vigour gone from his frame. It could've been him. He shivered internally at the thought, like a tightrope walker glimpsing the drop below, and turned his face resolutely towards her. 'Jo—'

'Billy!' she squeaked, eyes widening. Her left arm was rising to shield her face; the other stiffened against the dash. 'Brakes!'

'Shit!' He jammed his foot down and they skidded to a halt a foot short of the steel bars. 'Sorry,' he said sheepishly, backing up. 'Wasn't watching.'

'Well please do.' She opened the gate, closed it again after the vehicle and hopped back in, the fair hair swinging against her cheeks. 'Maybe it would be better if you just pulled up and told me whatever it is you want to say.'

Taken by surprise he looked at her again as the vehicle coasted down the bank into the creek. 'How—?' The steering wandered with his gaze and the front wheel found a hole and dropped into it with a crash that stalled the engine.

'Hell!' He heard her giggle. They were sitting in the middle of the Wildhorse. He opened the door, saw the water purling past and closed it again. Swearing, he reached for the keys.

'Leave it.' Her voice sounded smothered. She had a hand over her mouth but she couldn't hide the laughter in her eyes. 'I didn't mean quite like that but at least we've stopped.' She turned sideways on the seat to face him and leaned forward. 'Why don't you just kiss me, anyway,' she said, 'and we'll sort the rest out later?'

'Jo?' He stared into her face, his gaze welded to the little puff of silvery hair growing in a contrary direction from the top of her forehead. Her lips were soft and pink, matching the colour in her cheeks, and there were two little creases at the corner of each eye. He watched her lids veil them in sudden shyness and needed no further invitation. Hoisting himself around behind the confining wheel he placed gentle hands either side of her jaw and brought his lips to hers.

She was the first girl he had ever kissed properly. He did it again, more thoroughly. Her lips opened and he tasted her sweetness as his tongue explored her mouth. She turned in the seat then to bring an arm about his head. His hat tumbled aside as hers had done and he felt her fingers through his hair.

'How did you know,' he said when they paused for breath, 'that I loved you?' He spoke in simple wonder and she laughed.

'Oh, Billy! How do you know the sun shines? Because you can see it and feel it, of course. Only I thought I'd very likely be thirty before you got round to mentioning it. Talk about a slowcoach! What were you waiting for?'

'I like that,' he was suddenly indignant. 'Every time I looked around you were with Snowy. You went to the dance with him; you even,' he remembered aggrievedly, 'went in the Gretna with him instead of me. What was I supposed to think?'

'A girl's got her pride,' Jo said defensively. 'Besides – you should talk! What about Rachel? I looked for you after the Gretna that day and you were eating lunch with her. Every time we went into the 'Bend you were with her. I thought – because she'd quit bothering Cub – that she must've fallen for you instead. And you certainly weren't ignoring her.'

Billy kissed her again. 'Dope. She's unhappy. She just needed somebody to talk to.' His heart sang as it all became clear to him. 'You knew I won that race for you. Even though you pretended not to.'

'Well I worked it out – finally.' She gave a little shiver. 'Promise me you won't ever do that again? I nearly died when I saw the route you were taking. I kept thinking – *if he's all right, if he doesn't fall, I'll let Rachel have him.* And then when you were okay I was just furious with you again. I wasn't very gracious to you that night, I'm afraid.'

'It wasn't much of a dance,' he agreed, 'with Lucas and all.'

'No.' She wrinkled her nose then tilted her head coquettishly, blue eyes glinting. 'When did you first notice me, Billy?'

'That would be the first time I saw you,' he said simply. 'Scooting out from under the truck that day when you had the flat. Remember? You were carting fuel.'

'You changed the tyre for me.'

'I couldn't believe it when Blake offered me a job.' He played with her fingers, smiling a little. 'And then I guess I just gradually became part of the family – which was good, I mean I liked it; it's the first time I've ever felt part of anything. But then you seemed to act like I was just another brother—'

'Well, what was I supposed to do?' Jo asked reasonably. 'Just assume I was irresistible and jump on you? Come on, Billy! I'd think we were getting somewhere and next thing you'd be ignoring me to off with Rachel – is it any wonder I gave up and went to the dance with Snowy? He's married by the way. Hush,' she added as his mouth opened in surprise, 'not very successfully I gather. His wife lives in town with the kids and his mother-in-law. A bit of a tartar according to him.'

'Oh well,' Billy said, prepared to forgive.

'At least you won't have *that* to worry about. Or me either. You said your mum was dead, Billy, but not what happened to her?'

'She was killed, run over by a car – I think.'

Jo's eyes widened. 'You mean you never asked?'

'I was two – well, maybe three – when it happened,' Billy grimaced, 'and the first thing I learned from my grandfather – apart from the fact that I wasn't wanted – was never to mention her name. He'd even scratched it out of the bible. There was a big family bible he read from every day. It used to live on the dresser in the kitchen.' He could see the room again as he spoke and shook his head to dispel the image. 'He was a religious crank, my grandfather – they all were. He belonged to one of those sects that believe in punishing backsliders. Anyway, when I was about twelve, I thought I'd sneak a look in the bible, see if my mother's name was written there. I didn't know what it was, you see. Still don't, actually, because he'd scored it out so thoroughly only the "C" was left. Mine wasn't there either. But he always said I had no right to exist.'

'Oh, Billy, that's dreadful. How could he do that?'

'Like I said, he was a crank – and a bitter old sod. She disgraced him by getting pregnant and he never forgave her. For all I know she might've thrown herself under that car. I wouldn't have blamed her but I – hoped she didn't. That she didn't deliberately leave me. One day I'll go back and find out how it happened – the accident – and her name and age. Even if the old bastard's dead there'll be records somewhere.'

'And your father?'

'I don't know. Somebody who offered her kindness, or escape – or what she thought would be escape?' It wasn't love. No man who loved her could have left her to face what she'd had to face. 'I can't be sure, Jo, but I think she was younger than us when she died. Maybe still in her teens. He'd have belted her too, you know, pregnant or not. *Especially* pregnant.'

'Poor girl.' Jo leaned forward and kissed him tenderly on the forehead. 'And poor you. I thought we had a rough time of it, but not even to know your own mother's name! I wonder what the C stood for? It could have been Cathy, I suppose, or Carol – maybe even Caroline. Caroline Martin, that's got a nice ring to it.'

'Um – the thing is,' Billy said, 'if it was, then it would've been Caroline Rasmuss. My name's not actually Martin. I mean it is *now*, because I made the legal change back in 1970, but before that I just called myself Martin. I didn't want anything to do with him – my grandfather – ever again. And,' he added honestly, 'I stole to get away from him. Not much but he'd have reported it. And I was underage. If they'd picked me up the police could've taken me back.'

'Sounds like a smart move,' Jo said practically. 'What about the Billy bit?'

'Ah,' he reddened. 'I was hoping you wouldn't ask. The real Billy Martin was my grandfather's cowman. I took his name. Mine's actually Wilhelm – my people were German settlers originally. Please, don't tell Cub.'

She laughed. 'His isn't much better you know. It's Jason. The Burch kids gave him heaps over it. We all used to listen to that radio serial, *The Argonauts*. Where Jason goes to find the golden fleece? They'd bleat at him in the playground. It sounds silly now but half the fights he got into were over that.'

Billy laughed. 'And I suppose you were right in there beside him, swinging at everything you could hit?'

'Naturally.' With one finger she traced a line down the side of his face. 'You know I love the way you do that. When you laugh your eyes—' she broke off in sudden consternation and sat up. 'Good God! We forgot all about the mail.'

Billy straightened and reluctantly let go of her hands. 'He'll have already been.'

'In that case . . .' Jo snuggled back beside him and blew softly on his sweaty neck. The soft hairs on his nape stirred and he shivered. 'Tell me more about your life, Billy, after you ran away, I mean. Where you went and what you did. I want to know everything.'

'Long story and a dull one – until I met you.' He kissed her nose and then the smooth scar tissue on her cheek. 'I'm cooking. What about I shift us somewhere into the shade first?'

Thirty-three

Billy, delirious with happiness, was hardly conscious of the passage of time. His thoughts, waking and sleeping, encompassed only Jo. But it was now three days since Blake's operation and the bulletins from the flying doctor reported no outward change in his condition. Since the pressure was removed from his brain his vital signs had improved but he was still unconscious. And not even the neurosurgeon could predict how long he might remain so.

In a rare state of indecisiveness Simon got up from the radio and ran a hand through his dark hair, 'Well, that doesn't help much. Seems he's no worse, but he's no better either. I suppose there's no point in hanging around. We'll take the horses over, and get those fillies fixed up. Maybe he'll wake up while we're gone. And when we get back I'll head down to the coast. Suds can keep checking on him. Or,' his gaze fell on his sister, 'you can. There's no real need for you to come, Jo. If you stay and he does wake up, you could ride across to bring us word.'

'Not on your Nelly,' Jo said robustly. 'I'm going.'

'It's geography, Si,' Cub explained. 'Haven't you noticed? Jo and Billy – the further they are apart the less use either of 'em is. I put it down to the magnetic pull of minerals in the ground. Geography.'

'That's geo*logy*, you moron.' Billy aimed a blow at his ear, missing but collecting his hat.

'Whatever.' Cub grinned, retrieving it. 'It means I get to run the nags, so you two better pack up. And don't forget a fishing line.'

They got away after an early lunch, leaving the still lame Flute whinnying over the fence after them as they moved off down the valley. The horses plodded slowly through scrub and whitened spear grass, unshod feet crunching gravel as they took the track across the range. Heat lay over them like a cloak drawing the sweat from both man and beast. The birds were silent and, at the turn of the track where the sandstone boulders stood, the shade lay black and sharp edged, tempting the leading horses to stop.

'Early storms coming,' Cub rolled his shoulders. The blue of his cotton shirt was marked with the white rime of his sweat, and his eyes were squinted almost shut. The sky was full of clouds, high, and shiny with glare.

'Not today,' Billy decided. 'Still, be nice – when we're home again, of course. Four inches say – a toupla days after we burn.'

'Two,' Jo said. It was a game they played, arranging the rain. 'In a good fast downpour to flush out the creeks; then another two within the week once the ground's wet.'

'Not before I get back from the coast,' Simon objected. 'I don't fancy squatting on the bank of some watercourse waiting for it to run down. Besides, you're forgetting we've still got to get the truck into Harditch for supplies. And that might be an interesting exercise, too.'

Cub looked at him. 'Why? It's only October. The country's so dry it'd take more than four inches to close the road.'

'Not that. Money. Or didn't it occur to you that we need Blake's signature to access the station account? We'll be paying for the fuel and tucker orders ourselves unless he wakes up soon.'

'Ouch,' Cub said. 'I hadn't thought of that.'

'And there's more,' Simon added. 'I suppose the wages can wait a bit but the vehicle registrations won't. Due in December. Then there's the rent and rates. And the operating costs for next year: vaccine, tail tags, trucking bills, yard fees . . .'

'Hang on,' Cub said, 'you're getting ahead of yourself. *Next year?* He'll wake up long before that.'

'He might not. According to Fiona some of them don't.'

Billy thought of the way Blake had lain lax and empty, first on the ground and then on the mattress, and shivered. 'For how long?'

Simon shrugged. 'Five years – ten. Until they switch the machines off, I suppose.'

Nobody had a reply. They rode in a silence broken only by the tread of hooves until Crab lunged at Tosser, ears flat, mouth open to bite. The brown darted sideways, kicking up, and caught the aggressor neatly under his chin. Billy heard Crab's teeth click forcefully together as he swerved away, shaking his head.

'Whoa-back!' He reined his mount across to turn the chestnut into the mob. Jo followed him and they rode side by side, murmuring softly until an exasperated yell from Cub brought their attention back to the job and they found themselves in the middle of the horses they were supposed to be driving.

That night they camped in the valley beside the stallion paddock, and were on their way again by mid morning. The stallion's mob, scenting the plant, had been within cooee of the fence and it was an easy matter then to yard them and draft the fillies off.

'Saved us a bit of time,' Simon said with satisfaction. 'We'll brand them later today.' He dug at his teeth with a bit of twig he'd split with his thumbnail. 'Means we can check the fences first and even pick up a few nags to take back.' They never had less than a dozen horses in the home paddocks over the Wet. 'Back tomorrow night, easy.'

'Not before I've caught a fish,' Cub said firmly.

It had rained in the valley. About a week before, judging by the growth of feed and the water lying in the little creeks. They feasted their eyes on the balm of green, while the horses spread hungrily, tearing at the sappy grass.

'Must've been two inches,' Simon said, 'at least. Who was talking about early storms?'

It was amazing the difference rain made. The ground had been swept clean of old tracks, and the bush of dust. The box leaves glittered in the sun and there were fresh red tips on the bauhinias. At the camp site the herbage lapped over the traces of old charcoal and down by the creek a million insects buzzed amid the paperbark blossom.

They took their time over lunch. The fire they built to boil their quart pots burnt to ash, and their saddle horses dozed in the shade, the light winking on stirrup bars and bit rings when they shifted. Billy, lying back on his rolled swag, his head beside Jo's, felt, through their twined hands, the steady beat of her pulse. The buzz of flies was loud in the somnolent noon. He heard the distant bawl of a beast and the strident, repetitive call of the koel.

'I wish that damn bird 'ud give it a rest,' Cub said, pushing himself upright and with that Simon rose too.

'Time to make a move. If you boys check Bolthole Gully and the range side I'll see to the horse paddock here. Don't forget to fetch the brands back so we can do the fillies. I'll get 'em drafted off while you're gone. If you see any fresh horses you can bring them too. You working, Jo?'

'Nope.' She was ferreting towel and toilet bag from her swag. 'I'm going into the spring for a bath. But I'll cook tonight.'

'Wait for the fish then,' Cub instructed. 'Man, the barra in that gorge hole are so big you need a winch to pull 'em out.'

'I'll believe it when I'm eating them.' Billy already had a foot in the iron and suddenly paused that way, one legged, beside the patient Slug. 'Hey, where are the tools?'

'In the cave with the branding gear. It's next to the spring. We'll get the fencing gear going past and the ropes and brands coming back. Well, come on. There's fish waiting to be caught.'

It was more rock shelter than cave, Billy thought, when they reached it. The bulge of the cliff-face had been undercut aeons before and a fortuitous rock fall since had brought a huge sheet of sandstone down to add a sort of porch roof to the hollow already there. It contained fencing and shoeing equipment including a very large anvil, which he gaped at in amazement.

'How the hell did you ever get *that* onto a pack-horse?'

'We didn't,' Cub said. 'It was here when we came. But there is a road into the valley, you know. It's quicker to follow the horse pad so we don't bother with it much. Here, grab hold of the pliers and strainers and I'll take the wire.'

They cut across the quaggy edge of the scrubby area surrounding the spring and struck out to the north, crossing the myriad little gutters that drained the range slopes and fed into the deep but narrow creek known as Bolthole. The rain had been widespread. They followed pads scoured clean of tracks and areas where fresh-washed sand ripples were scarcely marked even by the passing of beetle or lizard life. Ducks rose from a flooded claypan and as they moved deeper into the tangled scrub along the banks of the Bolthole, the midges hovered in clouds over deep deposits of drying silt.

The branch of a wild plum, a-spray with tiny white flowers, snatched off Billy's hat and he reined about, grabbing it before it fell. The strainers were slipping across his pommel. He hoisted them higher, senses teased by a familiar smell, and looking down instantly located the source – the green cowpat into which Slug had stepped.

It triggered a memory of something so commonplace he had not even noticed it at the time. The cry of the koel on the dinner camp and behind it the bellow of a beast, where no beast should have been.

'Hey!' But Cub had forged ahead, beyond hearing. Billy spurred into a trot to range alongside him. 'Hang about,' he said. 'Where'd the cattle come from?'

Cub frowned blankly at him. 'What cattle?'

Their voices and movement must have disturbed them for suddenly, deep in the blue–black shade across the creek, a dozen head scrambled to their feet. Cows and weaners, full bellied and sleek looking, muzzles lifting and ears fanning to stare before they took off. For any stockman a glimpse was enough to identify ownership. The cows all bore the Rainsford earmark but the weaners had none – they were cleanskins, ready for branding.

'Them,' Billy said, succinctly.

As one, they dropped their burdens, plummeted into the creek and went after them. Slug, acquainted with the spurs, surpassed himself and shot around the lead and the two horsemen sat for a moment staring at their capture. The cows, giving up the game the minute they were stopped, stared back. They were quiet enough; paddock cattle, used to being handled.

Billy heard the quick in-drawing of Cub's breath as he said what they were both thinking.

'They never got here by themselves.'

'If the crossing's down . . . ?' Billy hazarded and Cub snorted.

'They look like scrubbers to you?' His expressive face, wearing his anger like a thundercloud, was hardening as he spoke. 'Just suppose, for argument's sake, that you're a copper. And say somebody tipped you off to take a look in this valley. Which,' he added unnecessarily, 'is a stock-proof paddock that cattle can't wander into at will. And you come across a nice little mob like this – what'd you do?'

Billy's stomach clenched nervously. 'On your record I'd probably arrest you. Or at the very least impound the cattle and send for the Stock Squad who would certainly arrest you for stealing them.' He cast a nervous look about, eyeing the clumps of timber as if any one of them might hide two or three uniformed police. 'You think that's likely to happen?'

'Bloody oath I do,' Cub snapped. 'Dear God! He warned us – he said something like this could be on the cards. Jesus! I wonder how long since they were put here? You realise they could be on their way here right now? I'm talking about the cops,' he finished in case Billy hadn't understood.

He had, but was grappling with something else. 'Who?' he demanded. 'Who warned us?'

'Blake – when we found the fire. He said Lucas could be planning it then. But he wasn't – he did the horse instead. And we thought that was it. Well,' he finished grimly, 'it looks like it was only part of it. There was never any real chance of proving anyone shot the stallion, but to be caught bang to rights with Rainsford stock in our paddocks – oh, they'll get a conviction on that, all right.'

Forcing himself to speak calmly Billy said, 'We'd better get rid of them then.'

'Yeah. But hang on a sec. Let me think. The rain's good – it'll make the tracks easier to see. He must've swum them in through the gorge and they'll have to go out the same way.' Under the hat brim his blue eyes blazed with concentration. 'Means we're mustering south. And the road comes in from the northern end of the valley, but it hasn't been used since we built the horse yards. So it'll be overgrown and that'll slow them down. Okay, this is what'll we'll do. You get hold of Simon and I'll go for Jo.'

'And these?' Billy jerked his chin towards the cattle.

'I'll give 'em a start down creek. You get moving. And make it quick, mate. If we go down for this it could well put paid to the property.'

Right.' Billy's mouth was dry. Hauling Slug about he drove the spurs home and the brown horse, galvanised, leapt his own length and took off in a dead run for the camp.

Thirty-four

At the spring Jo tied her mount, Lady, to the branch of an ebony tree and picked her way through the muddy ground to the water's edge. The cliff rose sheer above the main spring hole, a large rock basin of indeterminate depth surrounded by a sprawl of ferns and moss. The ground was boggy for acres around while here and there the water surfaced through it in little rivulets and seepages, creating a dense mat of secondary growth under the broad-leafed bloodwoods, and the thickets of ebony and myrtle that crowded the base of the cliff wall. The air was rich with the smell of damp, and rotting humus, and heavy with the somnolent buzz of insects amid the flowering foliage.

She dropped her towel over a bush, laid her hat beside it and unbuttoned her shirt, then looked about for a flat rock on which to sit and remove her boots. She pulled one off, stuffed the sock in the top of it and was reaching for the other when Lady whickered behind her, the sound immediately followed by the noise of a hoof hitting stone.

'Hi!' she called indignantly. 'Clear off! I told you I'm having a bath.'

'Couldn't a timed it better then, could I?' The voice was gravelly, heavier than her brothers'. Startled, she jerked erect and spun about to see Harry Lucas smirking at her through the pricked ears of a snorty-looking chestnut.

Alarm edged into her mind. 'What're *you* doing on the Brumby?' She snatched at her shirtfront, holding it together as she fumbled with the buttons.

'Oh, this and that.' He stepped down from the horse and let the reins drop. 'I hear old Blake's not too good, eh? Serve the bastard right. Maybe a visit from the Stock Squad's just what he needs.' She backed away as he advanced, the rocks hurting her bare foot, clutching the boot she'd snatched up. She didn't like the open lasciviousness she read on his face, or the way his tongue came out to wet his lips. 'Don't go getting dressed on my account, girlie. We'll have a little fun first.'

Jo's breath caught and she almost gagged on the sudden rush of fear that filled her. 'You wouldn't dare!'

She could scarcely have said anything worse. Lucas's smirk twisted into a sneer. 'Because you're white, you little trollop? Too good for the likes of me, eh? Well, by God, we'll see about that. You're like Bennett and all the rest of 'em – think I should stick to the gins, huh? But you got the same equipment, h'ain't you? So let's try it out. We got the time; plus I owe you one for showing me up at the dance.'

He lunged, grabbing the sleeve of her shirt as she whirled about, stubbing her toe as she did so, but the pain went unregarded for there was nowhere left to run. In backing away before his advance she'd come up against a dense thicket of flowering bush. With flight out of the question Jo screamed at the top of her voice and swung the boot she held at his face. The heel of it caught the broad nose with all the strength she was capable of. It was enough to temporarily blind him but he was not a fighter for nothing. Snorting blood, Lucas lowered his head and kept coming and as she turned to run his hand closed crushingly over her shoulder. He pulled her about with enough force to rip the top buttons from her shirt.

'You little bitch!' There was blood on his teeth. His hand cracked across her cheek and a swift movement from one booted foot swept her legs from under her. She fell half into the bush that had blocked her and saw the triumph flare in his face as his hands went to his belt. He was going to rape her. Understanding and terror galvanised her actions. She drew breath into her body and as his weight dropped towards her she screamed again and kicked, not with the bare bruised foot crushed beneath his own, but with the sharp toe of the leather riding boot she still wore.

At the last moment his fighting instinct prevailed and he was already twisting his body to protect his most vulnerable part when the kick was launched. Without that defensive action it would have incapacitated him. He roared and rolled aside, freeing her foot.

The breath sobbing in her throat, she scrambled to her feet, clawing her way through the bush, heedless of the scratches inflicted on her bare arm. If she could get across the overflow of water from the spring to the far side of the large hole, she could dodge indefinitely from side to side. Fear leant her strength and cleared the blind panic from her brain. If Lucas thought the others were close by it might give him pause. She screamed her twin's name as she flung herself forward. Then quick as a cat Lucas was up and his muscled arms closed about her thighs.

'*Now* you little bitch!' He had her down, ripping at her middle to get at her belt, when her call was answered by a bellow of challenge packed with a fury to split stone.

'Get your hands of her, Lucas! By God, I'll kill you for this!'

Cub was off his horse and crossing the intervening space like a charging bull. Lucas, disoriented by his sudden appearance, barely had time to scramble up before the onslaught was upon him. Trembling all over and wincing from the pain of her crushed foot, the girl limped across to the rock she'd sat on before and with unsteady hands snatched at her sock and pulled it on, heedless of the mud. There was, she told herself firmly, nothing to cry about but for all that she had to grit her teeth to stop them chattering and to still the shaking that invaded her body. She could still feel his hands clawing at her and she dared not think what would have happened if her twin hadn't come.

So absorbed was she in combating shock that the grunting and smacking of fists on flesh only a dozen paces away seemed just a background to a dream. She smoothed the sock over her foot and with fingers that seemed stiff and unhelpful, found the tags and pulled her boot on. Eventually brought out of her daze, she looked up to see Lucas flat on his back on the ground. Cub stood over him, his shirt hanging awry, the high flush of temper still on a face marred with the marks of the fight. His chest heaved and his fists were bloody as he came across to where she sat.

'Jo, are you okay? Did he—?'

'No.' She spoke starkly, striving to keep her voice steady. 'He got his belt undone but that was all. But he was going to. He said – oh, God!' She squeezed her lids shut, seeing again the flare of lust and hatred in the smoky brown eyes. 'I'm all right. Truly. I kicked him in the goolies.' She bit back a giggle, knowing it would spiral out of control. 'But if you hadn't come . . .' She shuddered, her eyes darkening with sudden fear and he seized and held her protectively against him, as he had years before when they'd cowered in the bedroom listening to Blake stumbling home from the pub. 'How did you know?'

'I – felt it. I knew something was wrong. You said you were coming here and—' His voice shook suddenly. 'Jesus, Jo! I thought you were drowning.'

'I'd rather have been. He—' She pushed her face into his chest, shoulders heaving as the sobs took her. 'Oh, God! I was so scared. He said – I saw – he was going to—' With a great effort she stilled herself, lifting her head to smear the tears away on a brown wrist. 'But he didn't.' Her voice firmed and she was in control again. 'What's he doing here, anyway? He said something about Blake and the Stock Squad?'

'I'll bet he did. He's planted a mob of Rainsford cows on us. All with cleanskin calves following them. It's a frame-up – if the Squad turns up before we get rid of them we've had it. Billy's gone for—' There was the hollow knock of a stirrup on timber, then a rush of hooves as the other two completed his sentence by their presence. The sound stopped, at sight of the twins, then Billy was off his horse and running, stumbling through rocks and mud.

'Jo! Are you okay? What happened?' His frantic gaze took in her state: the muddy jeans and torn buttons, the reddening welt on her cheeks. He swung to look at Cub then his peripheral vision caught sight of the prone figure on the ground. Gently he touched Jo's face. 'Did he do that?'

'Yes, but it's all right, Billy.' She left her twin for the comforting shelter of his arms. 'All right,' she repeated, feeling the tension in his muscles. 'I'm okay, really. Cub stopped him.' Despite the calmness of her voice she trembled against him as he gently turned her face to inspect her cheek. She heard his breath hiss. 'I'll kill him for that!' He made to put her away from him and she gripped his shirt, two handed.

'No! It was just a slap – really. I'd smacked him in the face with my boot. Besides kicking him where it did most good.' She giggled again with a mixture of mild hysteria and relief before once again clamping down on her emotions. 'Then Cub knocked him cold. So all told – between Blake and Cub and me – he's not having a very good time, is he? But what's he doing here? Cub's told me about the cattle. You'd think he'd be long gone if it's supposed to look like we've stolen them.'

Simon had swung down and come to stand beside them. He gave his sister a searching look. 'You truly okay? I'd say he came back to check. To make sure we hadn't found them. Because they've been here a while – they're too settled for it to be otherwise.'

'Suppose we ask the mongrel?' Billy strode across to the recumbent form and bent to seize a fistful of shirt. He cracked his open hand across the dark, bloodstained face. Lucas was coming around for his eyes were half open and their fixed, smoky regard enraged him further. 'Wake up, you bastard,' he said furiously. 'Shamming it won't help you.'

He drew his arm back again, relishing the chance, but something in the figure's stillness, in the unwavering regard of the dark gaze, gave him pause. Then, as he stood there, a fly buzzed onto the man's face and crawled across the slack lips, its gauzy wings undisturbed by any puff of breath. Billy straightened and took a step back.

'Oh, Jesus!' It was a prayer. He swallowed hard. 'Simon! You better get over here. I think – I think he's dead.'

Shocked into immobility, the three of them watched Simon squat beside Lucas and examine him. The twins had drawn instinctively together again, her arm clutching his waist, and his, her shoulder. Billy felt neither jealous nor excluded. Theirs was an older, deeper bond, forged in the womb, different from the newer one of his and Jo's love. Shock had drained Cub's face to the colour of old bone.

'He can't be dead. God Almighty! I laid him out – I didn't kill him.'

'He's dead all the same,' his brother said. 'Oh shit!' He sat back on his heels, his face a study of consternation. 'What do we do now?' He rolled the dark head sideways to demonstrate. 'It wasn't your fault. He landed right across a rock. I think it broke his neck.

Take a look.' It was the first time Billy had seen Simon's equanimity destroyed.

Unwillingly they did so, seeing the short bar of sharp-edged sandstone fitting neatly between Lucas's shoulders and head. His neck had come down across it – like a guillotine in reverse, Billy thought numbly, as the enormity of their situation burst over them all. Helplessly he looked at Simon.

'What are we gunna do? Jesus! The cattle are bad enough but if they find us with a body – They'll do us for murder!'

'I know.' Simon's eyes were pinched half shut in thought. 'Even if Lucas set it up with them, they're never gunna believe his death was an accident. They won't *want* to. And right now we don't have a whole lot of support round here. I mean, take the whole damn district – who, out of it, is gunna give any one of us a character reference?'

'Rachel?' Cub dabbed at his split lip and winced, adding with mordant humour, 'I'm not even sure of that now. And Fiona.'

'And that's about it.' Simon stood up. 'We've got to get rid of the body.'

'Where?' Jo seemed the least affected of them all by the presence of the dead man. 'Can't we just leave it and get rid of the cattle first?'

'Too risky. The cops could turn up and arrest the lot of us before we got back to do the job. No, better do it now. We'll sink him in the spring hole – that's deep enough – but we'll need to weight him first.'

'Rocks.' Billy looked feverishly around for something not embedded in the mud.

Simon shook his head. 'We'd have to wire them to him. Too much chance they'd slip off.'

'Jesus, you're right – what then?'

'The anvil from the cave. We can put a twitch around the stem of the base. Nothing'll shift that. And the weight'll ensure he stays down.' He punched his fist gently and repeatedly into his other palm as he thought aloud. 'I can't believe this is happening! But we've gotta think it through. Let's see – he turns up missing they'll mount a search. That's the first thing – so they need to find something. I'll swim his horse back through the gorge, break a rein maybe, rough the saddle up a bit – make it look like he's had a fall. Given the country they won't think it too strange that he's never found.' He looked around at them, injecting confidence into his voice. 'It'll work. All we've got to do is keep our heads. Let's get that anvil. Jo, you grab the horses before they clear off, and,' he glanced cursorily at the bare-headed corpse, 'find his hat.'

Thirty-five

Throughout the time it took them to fetch the heavy anvil and set it down at the lip of the rock hole, while the three of them carried the horrible, lolling body across to lay beside it, Billy was conscious of time winging away. His fevered imagination turned every sough of wind into the rumble of a distant engine descending the face of the range.

Jo had followed after them to the cave to snatch up a light coil of the plain wire they used for fencing. She grabbed a hammer for they had no other way of cutting it. The pliers were back on the bank on Bolthole Creek where Billy had dropped them. Lady shied from the load, running giggle-headed to one side as Jo swore at her and then lapped the reins beneath her belly, conscious, like Billy, of the remorseless march of time.

At the rock hole the men squatted and knelt about the body as if partaking in some ghoulish rite. 'Good thinking,' Simon said briefly as he used the hammer handle to tighten the twitch around the narrow part of the anvil's base. He pounded the excess wire across the rounded end and then bent the flattened section until it snapped. Billy cringed as the metallic blows echoed off the cliff and cast a nervous look behind him.

'You got his hat?' Jo stood behind Cub, close enough to feel the heat of his body but looking away from the work of his hands.

'Yeah.' The wire that encircled Lucas's waist was threaded through both sides of the hat's crown.

'That's it,' Simon said. 'Get his legs over.' Cub thrust his boot against the anvil and there was a splash followed by a gurgling sound and an uprushing of bubbles. All three rose to their feet. For a moment they stood silent, watching the widening rings as the water rocked and slowly settled, then Billy bent to wash his hands, scrubbing them hard against each other in the dark water.

'Right,' Simon pushed his hair back and settled his hat. 'Let's get hold of those cattle. Cub, you cut for tracks north of Bolthole. The rest of us'll muster south. We'll meet at the gorge. And don't coddle 'em along. We want to be done by dark.'

It turned out to be an optimistic timetable. A full moon was rising over the range before Billy and Jo, sitting tensely in their saddles, heard the distant snap of the whip that announced Cub's coming. Simon had vanished into the dark mouth of the gorge leading Lucas's chestnut. Some thirty head of cattle, all they'd found, stood quietly in the moon shadows as they sat their saddles and fretted. The night wind sighed in the timber and their tired mounts shifted from hip to hip, or rattled the bridle rings as they reached to feed. The minutes stretched out until Simon had been gone for half an hour. As for Cub, they had not set eyes on him since leaving the spring.

'What's keeping him?' The question burst from Jo but there was no helpful answer Billy could give. He would come when he came. Nerves a-stretch, they sat on, listening to a cow's ears flap as she shook her head, the wail of a curlew on the flat behind them, and then, at long last, that snap of the whip again. The cattle heard it too. Billy saw a head lift in the amorphous shadow and gritted his teeth as a cow bawled. An answer came out of the darkness, the whip snapped again and they could hear the click of hooves as the little mob quickened its pace and trotted to join the rest. Moonlight gleamed on the sweaty hide of Cub's mount.

'How many?' Billy asked.

'Ten head.' His teeth glimmered in the pale light when he spoke. 'What've you got?'

'Thirty.' Abruptly Billy added, 'He couldn't have done it alone.'

'I thought of that. You'd need two men. So somebody else knows about it, but he's gunna have to keep his mouth shut, isn't he? We shouldn't have to worry there.'

'I was thinking, when they find out Lucas is missing, he'll have a fair idea where he went.'

'But not what happened,' Cub argued. 'How could he? And like I said, he opens his mouth, he dobs himself in. Where's Si?'

'Just coming.' Jo spoke softly, head cocked to the soft thud of hooves. Then Simon's roan was there, snorting softly as he chewed the bit. He peered at them, saw Cub and nodded.

'Let's go.'

It wasn't until the mob, bellowing noisy displeasure, was feeding reluctantly into the creek that Billy's tight-wound nerves began to relax. They were just a swim away from having made it. He could feel the others' relief in the sudden easing of tension about him. Even Simon stopped pushing to announce that the task didn't need four of them. When the tail was in and swimming, dragging a pewter-coloured wake of ripples behind them, he nodded to the twins. 'Billy and I'll take them. You two head back, and if you can pick up fresh horses on the way, all to the good. We have to get home tonight.'

'Tonight?' Cub groaned. 'Another thirty mile?'

'You better believe it. The cops can't see you, mate, not till the bruises have gone. Think about it. Lucas missing and you looking like a truck hit you. You don't have to be Einstein, do you?'

'Yeah, you're right.'

'So find us a coupla saddlers and we'll get a feed into us and go. Billy and Jo can clean up here tomorrow. It's gotta look like we've never been near the place.'

He turned the roan and Billy, with time only to touch Jo's arm in passing, slapped the reins on Slug's neck and followed him into the creek.

'Look after her,' he called to Cub, knowing there was no need, that she was safe with him; but it comforted him to say it.

They rested the horses at the far end of the gorge where the waterhole shallowed to debouch into a gravel-strewn creek bed. The cattle, painted silver and black by moonshine, waded out, hooves clicking on the stone, and drifted silently away to vanish into the scrub. Far off under the moon a dingo howled and from within the black cleft of the gorge the raucous cry of a bittern sounded.

Simon sighed and heaved himself back into leather. 'God, what a day! My boots'll be bloody well ruined.'

Billy, swinging himself tiredly into his own saddle, felt a sudden mad desire to laugh. It was such a typical Reilly utterance. To worry about a pair of boots when their entire future was at stake. If it came to that, down the gorge and back again wasn't doing his own footwear any favours but it hardly mattered when compared with what had gone before.

He said, 'Do you reckon we got them all?'

'God, I hope so.' Simon blew a long breath through his teeth. 'Maybe it won't matter. I mean maybe Lucas hadn't even called the cops yet – but we can't afford to assume that. In the morning you and Jo get whatever nags you can find, and drive them about over the tracks.' Billy saw his hat brim tilt as he scanned the now clear sky. 'Forty points of rain'd help, but outside that it's the best we can manage. Then grab half a dozen horses and get the hell out of the place.' The silhouette of his hat moved as he shook his head. 'I'm sorry you've been dragged into all this.'

'It was Jo he tried to rape,' Billy said, 'of course I'm in it.' He hesitated. 'What'll you tell old Suds?'

'Nothing. The fewer who know – we'll keep it between the four of us.'

'Suits me,' Billy said, and the rest of the ride passed in silence.

At the camp the fire was burning and Jo had boiled spuds and onions to go with the corned meat. Two fresh horses were tied behind the firebreak; Billy, leading the weary Slug into the paddock, paused to identify Peddler and Carnival.

'The first we came across,' Cub said. His right eye was swollen almost shut, the tender flesh beneath it grape coloured, and he moved stiffly, favouring his ribs. He'd be a mess tomorrow, Billy judged, when the bruising from the blows he'd sustained in the fight began to come out.

'You look like hell.' He forked potatoes onto his plate of meat and stabbed an onion. 'How's your face, Jo?'

'A bit tight. Like it's swollen.' Sitting beside her twin she looked both dishevelled and weary, shirt crumpled and sweatstained, the torn buttonholes gaping. She shivered as a mopoke called from the timber line. 'I wish I was home.'

Simon took a last swallow of his tea and glanced at the moon's position. 'We'd better get moving or we'll be seeing the dawn in from the saddle.' He took up Carnival's reins and looked at his brother. 'Come on, big fella. And remember, you two – as fast a job as you can manage then get out.'

'What's that supposed to mean?' Jo, hands tucked into her back pockets, stood watching the two riders dwindle in size across the moonlit flat.

'We'll try and smother a few tracks before we leave.' Billy tossed his empty plate into the pan of hot water and came to stand beside her. 'Are you all right, love?' Hesitantly he put his arm around her and instead of pulling away as he had half feared she surprised him by wrapping her arms tightly around his neck. Her voice came indistinctly, her face was hard against his chest.

'Hold me, Billy. Don't say anything, just hold me tight.'

He did so, moving one hand in soothing circles over her back until he felt the tension in her body slacken. He kissed her hair that smelled of dust and then her ear, rocking her gently against him until she sighed and pulled back.

'All right now?' He peered at her in the moonlight and she put up a hand and touched his cheek.

'You're so caring, Billy,' she said simply. 'It's why I love you.'

'You do?' It was the first time she had said it and his heart sang.

'Yes.' Her eyes were shadowed but he felt the intensity of her gaze. 'When Lucas attacked me today – I know it sounds crazy that I could even think about it when I was so scared but – I wished that we had made love. I mean, I was certain I was going to be raped and it just went through my mind that I couldn't bear it that he—' she shuddered and Billy held her again, rage against the dead man licking like fire through his veins.

'It's all right,' he repeated, 'it's all right. He can't ever touch you again. Come on. It's been a long day. Time to turn in.'

'Not before I've had a bath,' she said firmly. 'Come with me, Billy – just down the creek. I can feel his hands on me still. I *have* to wash.'

'Now?' He was startled. 'It must be past midnight.'

'So what? There won't be time in the morning. Besides,' she leaned closer, sniffing, 'you need a bath yourself. And I want – I want to be with you. Now, tonight – not later when maybe I'll have had nightmares of him. You know what I'm saying.'

'Well – if you're sure.' His heart was putting in the odd triple beat and to calm it he bent and pushed the fire together. 'It'll be cold.'

'It's the middle of summer, you old slowcoach,' she said, exasperated. 'Honestly, Billy!' Taking his hand she tugged him down the shelving bank below the shadow of the paperbacks. 'There's a pad here somewhere. Don't walk into Tinker.'

The horse, tied up for the night to ensure an early start, snorted softly as Billy, eyes full of fire shine, recoiled from its rump into a tree and lost his hat. Jo giggled and they bumped heads retrieving it.

'It's blacker than a coal face—' She gave a squawk as her boots shot out from under her. Billy fell too and tumbled, cursing, into a bush. They clasped hands and an electric tingle went through him as they pulled each other up.

'Where are we?' Peering blindly into inky shadows, he sniffed. 'What's that smell?'

'Paperbark blossom. The creek timber's in flower. Surely you noticed? This way – we'll go to the rocks.' She led and he was content to follow, hearing the squeaking and rustle of flying foxes in the warm air that was dense with the scent of nectar. They emerged suddenly from tree shadow to the sight of water gleaming like pewter under the stars. It was where he had swum with Cub on their last trip to the valley. Dropping his towel and hat he bent to pull off his boots, breath coming fast with his awareness of Jo similarly engaged beside him.

Stripped at last he turned towards her, seeing the pale glow of her body, shadowed at breast and crotch. Pulse quickening he reached for her, just as she tossed her hair back and jumped.

'Last one in's a rotten egg,' she cried. The water geysered high around her then covered her head.

305

In the long moments waiting for her to emerge Billy was seized with irrational terror. 'Jo!' He plunged after her, eyes wide, ignoring the cold shock of it, searching frantically through lifeless depths to find her. Nightmares gibbered at the corner of his mind. She had hit her head, impaled herself on a sunken branch – he surfaced with bursting lungs to find her an arm's length away, laughing at him.

'Old slowcoach!'

'Don't you *ever* do that again.' He flicked hair from his eyes and clipped a sudden arm about the silky skin of her waist. He held her, treading water as they kissed, the slide of her body like a brand against his skin. Then she twisted from his hold and duck dived, slick as an eel in the water.

His blood up, Billy went after her, snatching at an ankle that slipped through his grasp. When he came up for breath she was treading water behind him. 'Slowcoach!' The taunt sounded a little breathless but she was the better swimmer and easily evaded his lunge.

'You wait!' But each time his clutching hands fell tantalisingly short. Around them the flying foxes left and the creek hushed to their breathless cries until finally, spent from play, they lay side by side in the water, clinging to the rocky ledge while the night closed around them, soft as the stroke of owls' wings, filled with the scent of honey and moonlight.

Finning lazily, their lips met. He marked the liquid sheen of her eyes, the sleek curve of her skull where the wet hair clung. She was like a seal. He said with wonder, 'You're so beautiful, Jo.'

Her smile was wide and wonderful to see as, foreheads bumping, she nuzzled his nose with her own. Her hand strayed across his chest setting off rockets of desire. 'You're not so bad yourself, mate.'

'Come.' Hooking his fingers over the rock's edge Billy heaved himself up, strewed their clothes to make a bed on the sheet of sandstone, and knelt to help her out, their breath mingling as they began, tentatively at first, to explore each other's bodies.

His was wiry and strong; hers chilled from the water, nipples erect on the small breasts that barely filled Billy's hands, but they made their own heat as they loved with little cries and discoveries under the white face of the moon, past and present forgotten in the all-consuming now. Afterwards they slept close in each other's arms despite the hardness of their bed, and the occasional marauding mosquito.

Thirty-six

Billy woke as he always did in the camp to the bright sparkle of stars and the knowledge that dawn was not far off. In the west the moon had all but vanished behind the range, making it darker than it had been all night. He shifted on the rock, groaning a little at stiffened muscles and Jo woke and stretched, her elbow nudging his chest.

'Time is it?' She sat up, squeezing her arms to her naked sides. 'It's a bit cold.'

'Good morning, my love.' He kissed her, feeling tender and proud and on top of the world. 'You are, you know, and always will be. The morning star's up so we haven't much time but – will you marry me, Jo?'

'What?' She tugged at the clothing beneath him.

'I said, will you marry me. Please?'

'That's what I thought you said.' She was wriggling into her panties and feeling for the hooks on her bra strap. 'Why are you asking now? Because if you're feeling guilty about last night – I wanted that to happen, Billy – I needed it to – but you don't have to marry me because of it.'

Aghast, he stared at the dim shape of her. 'What do you mean?' Something that felt like a lead balloon settled in his stomach as he peered at her. 'But I *want* to. I want to spend my life with you. Have children with you. I want us to grow old together. I *love* you, Jo!'

'That's all right then.' Briskly she thrust naked feet into her boots and stamped them, standing before him in bra and panties. 'I just wanted to hear you say it. Of course I'll marry you but I just didn't want you to think you had to. Why didn't you ask me before, anyway, you old slowcoach, you?'

'Because,' he cried, as ireful as he was exultant, 'I spent three years finding the nerve to get the question out – that's why!' He reached to pull her against him and began a slow exploration of her mouth but after a brief contact she twisted away.

'Not now, cowboy. It'll be daylight soon and we've got to get moving.' She scooped up her shirt and jeans. 'I've got clean ones in my swag. Here's your socks . . .' She stretched and groaned, 'I feel like a herd's galloped over me. Next time let's find a bed.'

When the grey light broke over the range walls they had the packhorses loaded and tied up in the yard and were leading their own mounts from the paddock. Billy could not resist an apprehensive glance behind him as they set off. Daylight brought a return of the fears that their time together had banished. He remembered again the awful, dead weight of the body they had sunk in the dark waters of the spring. They would never be free of the guilt occasioned by Lucas's death – but, once dead, what choice had they had but to dispose of his corpse?

Nor he did deceive himself that it was over. It could never be over for the man's presence would haunt the valley. None of them, Billy imagined, would ever visit the spring again. And for the first time he wondered how the day would have gone had Jo elected to take her bath in the more public arena of the creek where they had swum last night.

Thankfully the horses were easy to find. They picked up most of the plant they had brought with them and eighteen or twenty fresh ones that, led by Butterfly, put their tails over their backs and gave Billy a merry chase before he turned them. Whiffling and snorting, heads high and tails bannering, he brought them streaming back into the main mob and without more ado they set out for the gorge.

By mid morning they were back at the gate on the horse pad, having picked up the packhorses en route. Their nerves were at full stretch and Billy found himself listening with all his being, straining to hear above the clop of hooves, the rattle of the packs and the buzz of flies, that first vibration in the air. The hum that heralded the approach of a vehicle.

'This bit's the worst,' Jo glanced nervously about. 'If they're coming they'll have to come this way because the road in follows along the fence. I'll lead the packhorses through. Don't worry too much about drafting the nags. Whatever comes will do.'

He nodded tersely. 'Soon as you can head down the ridge. That way we can stay in the scrub. If they come, they might miss seeing us.'

The hum he had been listening for sounded just as he dropped the gate lever behind the brown gelding Finn. The horse ducked his head and cantered along the fence trying to rejoin his mates on the other side and, cursing furiously, Billy grabbed his stirrup, swung up and went after him. Jo was bustling the rest along the slope of the ridge, the pack-horses blundering clumsily through thickets of witchetty and knee-high spinifex. It needed burning, he thought, as he crowded the recalcitrant brown after them. The ground fell away into a gully paved with layers of fractured stone, and there were patches of woolly butt and wattle to cloak their movements. The sound had deepened to a gear-changing growl. Just before his mount carried him into the timber he caught a brief flash of light on a windscreen a couple of ridges away and relaxed. They'd be well out of sight before even a driver who knew the road got anywhere near the gate.

It was well after midday before they reached their usual dinner camp, a little timbered flat that spread either side of a dry creek bed. The fresh horses had worked up a lather in the heat and were happy enough to pull up and rest. Jo raked a section of the ashy grey soil clear of fallen leaves and built a fire while Billy pulled the canteens off Bluebob to fill their quart pots. They ate, squatting on their heels, as they had done a thousand times before but although their hands touched and their eyes strayed constantly to each other neither had the inclination to lose themselves in their new-found passion.

'I feel as if there are eyes everywhere,' Jo complained. 'It's spooky.'

'I know.' Too jumpy to take his time, Billy's rushed meal lay heavily on his stomach. 'I wonder how good they are at reading tracks? For that matter I wonder who it is – Watson or the Stock Squad?'

'I guess Si—' Jo began then leapt to her feet and emptied her quart over the embers of the fire. 'They're coming back!'

The dinner camp was right beside the road. 'Get the nags into the creek,' Billy said. He dragged dirt over the steaming coals with the side of his boot and caught up the canteens in a controlled rush at the pack-horse. The hum in his ear had grown to a drone – this was the faster end of the road – that deepened steadily as he tossed the swag back on top of the canteens and yanked the surcingle tight. By the time he had got himself, the pack-horse and his own mount down into the creek bed, the vehicle was almost upon them. Safely out of sight with a conveniently placed conkaberry bush to screen their faces, they watched it pass. Two men in an unmarked Toyota with an aerial mast whipping about on the front.

'Not Watson.' Billy stared after it, a cold hand clutching at his vitals. 'Must be the Stock Squad. Not wasting any time, are they?'

Jo was frowning. 'Why are they back so fast? They must've turned round as soon as they got there, or they'd never be here so soon.'

'I dunno. Unless,' he said with sudden quickening certainty, 'somebody's already missed Lucas. I bet that's it! The station knows and Bennett's called a search. And being coppers they'd get dragged straight onto it. They had an aerial, remember? And they probably travel with the radio permanently on, the way the stockies do. So getting hold of them wouldn't be hard.'

'You're right.' She had paled a little. 'Oh, God! I wonder how long they'll look for him?'

'In this weather,' Billy palmed sweat from his face, 'four days? Maybe five if they think he's got water. Was there any on his horse?'

'I don't know.' She swallowed. 'I wonder if they'll even find his horse? It could've picked up with the brumbies by now. It's happened before plenty of times. There was a miner got lost one summer on Plover Creek. The search went on for a fortnight. Every man in the district was out but they did no good. He was a Swede. They said he got bushed trying to shortcut through the gidyea to another mine. It wasn't far – a mile at most – but he never turned up. The area's still known as the Swede's Scrub.'

'When was this?'

'Oh, a long time back – thirty or forty years ago.'

'Well let's hope that in another thirty they're saying the same about Harry Lucas.' Billy tied the halter shank up on Bluebob and turned to his mount. 'Come on, love. The sooner we get home, the sooner we'll know what's happening.'

They reached the ford on the Wildhorse as the sun was sinking, laying a band of fiery colour across the rippling water as the fresh horses pushed thirstily into it to drink. Bluebob tried to lie down in the water and Billy yelled and spurred his mount.

'On your feet!' He kicked him in the flank and the grey snorted and lunged upright, spraying them both. 'What d'you think this is,' he cried angrily, 'a picnic?'

Jo chuckled. 'You've been hanging round us too long, Billy, you sound just like Cub. I'll get the gate.' She stood in the irons and let the horse carry her up the steep bank at a trot. The others followed on the pad, snorting and shying away from a little mob of wild pigs that broke suddenly out of the pandanus to cross their paths. Billy hollowed his back and yawned. He seemed to have spent most of the last twenty-four hours in the saddle and he was looking forward to a few days' break. Time spent letting the events of the last two days settle to the back of his mind. Time just for Jo and himself to make plans for the future: where they'd live, when, and where, they'd marry – all the things he'd dreamt about for so long and were now, or soon would be, about to happen.

His mount carried him to the open gate, ears pricking at the sight of Jo leaning with exaggerated patience against it.

'Come on, slowcoach. The lead'll be in Western Australia at this rate.'

'Sorry.' He jerked himself back to the present, to the smell and sight of dust like a pale mist behind the trotting horses, vanishing into the darkness up the track. The thump of the diesel sounded faintly in the distance, mixed with the cries of black cockies winging late to roost in the carbean trees beside the homestead. Above the western range the first stars were pricking out while the day faded in a smudge of red along the range tops. There would be no storm tonight; the air was clear and dry, freighted only with dust and the smell of horse sweat. 'I'll get 'em,' Billy said, setting off at a canter as the gate squealed shut behind him.

Cub was waiting for them at the yards, sitting hatless on the top rail. He climbed slowly down as they reined in at the gate and came forward to swing it shut.

'God, you look a right mess.' Billy peered at his face. There was just enough light to see the bruising to his cheek and jaw, and that his eye was, if anything, bigger and blacker than before. 'What'd you tell Suds?'

'Yes.' Jo dismounted and stretched, 'What's the story?'

'I got thrown while we were mustering the valley. Off Tosser, just so you've got the yarn straight. A pig come out of a bush and set him off, but only Simon was there so you don't need the details. I was knocked cold. That's why we came on ahead – in case I had concussion. The Stock Squad turned up this morning. Coupla hard-looking coppers, Si said. He held them here as long as he could, looking for a map he said we had – I take it you got the tracks covered?'

'Yep.' Billy started pulling the load off Bluebob. 'They came belting back while we were on the dinner camp. Didn't see us but it was a close thing. We nicked into the creek bed with the nags just in time.'

'And they can only just have got there before turning back,' Jo added, 'there wouldn't have been time to even look around.'

'Yeah.' He dropped a hand on her shoulder. 'You okay, kiddo?'

'Yes.' She touched his cheek. 'Your poor face.'

'It'll heal.' He was peering at the loose horses. 'What'd you bring Stinger for? You know he's got a chronic back.'

'Listen mate, we didn't have time to pick and choose,' Billy said. 'We were at the gate drafting when we heard them coming. Incidentally, I'm going to marry your sister. We got engaged this morning.'

'Did you?' Cub gave a grin that turned to a grimace as his split lip cracked open. He whacked Billy's shoulder then stuck out his hand. 'Congratulations. When's the wedding to be, Jo?'

'I'll tell you when we know.' She yawned. 'I'm so tired. What time did you get back?'

'Pretty late. No sooner got to bed than it was daylight again.' He hoisted the last pack-saddle onto its rail and bent slowly to pick up a swag as the dinner bell sounded vigorously from the house. 'The rest can wait till the morning.'

'How's Blake getting on?' Billy slung Jo's swag over his shoulder. 'Any change?'

'Yeah, he's awake. But there's some damage to his legs. The doc said it's the motor nerves. It's like he's been paralysed.'

'Jesus!' Billy was shocked. 'Is he gunna get better?'

'Dunno. They said physio and time could make a difference. It's like stroke victims, he said – depends on the severity of the damage. He reckoned Blake's lucky – he coulda woken up as a vegetable. Or maybe never woken up at all.'

'Poor old bugger,' Billy said. Jo's fingers lay within his and he squeezed them encouragingly. 'We'll have to go and see him, love.'

'I don't think so,' her voice was suddenly cool. 'Simon will need to, for the business. You go with him if you want. He's nothing to me.'

Billy opened his mouth, then wisely shut it again.

Belle met them at the gate. They dumped their burdens and made for the bathroom where a large green frog squatted in the basin and two more clung like bright plastic limpets to the cor-rugated iron below the window. The water was cold and sweet.

Billy drank from his cupped hands while Jo, having flipped the frog through the window, lathered dust from her face and arms.

'My hair's filthy.'

'Looks good to me.' He flung his own towel carelessly at the rail and pulled her towards him. 'So do you.' She wound her arms around his neck, her hands caressing the nape as he drew her body to his. The kiss was long and lingering and they parted reluctantly.

'We'd better go,' Jo said at length. 'Apart from anything else, I'm starving.'

'Me too. I could fang a dead horse. And sleep for a week after.' There was a smile in his dark eyes. 'I never knew this getting engaged was so tiring.'

Suds had made one of his corned beef curries with a pot of fluffy rice to go with it. Cub had been before them with the news and the old cook greeted them with a broad smile.

'So you getting married, girl? When's it gunna be?'

'We don't know yet, Suds. Will you come to the wedding?'

''Course I will. You want me to make the cake?'

'We'll see when the time comes. But thank you, I love your fruit-cakes.' Smiling, she kissed his dark, seamed cheek.

'I'm pretty keen on them too,' Billy said, accepting a congratulatory handshake. '*And* your curries.' Whatever his failings with the bottle, Suds was highly skilled at his calling.

Simon was briefly congratulatory as he had other things on his mind. 'Did Cub tell you Harry Lucas has gone missing?'

'What?' Just in time Billy understood that he wasn't supposed to know anything about it. 'When did this happen?'

'Some fencing contractor found his horse in the range country west of Toby's Hole. Well, *a* horse. Dragging its reins and with the saddle half under its guts. Turned out to be Lucas's. They're getting a search party organised. I told Bennett we'd be there.'

'*What?*' This time his performance was natural, fuelled by an indignation as great as Cub's. 'You're seriously suggesting—' Billy began when Cub interrupted.

'Let the bastard stay lost. Best place for him.' With grim amusement he added, ''S'what Blake'd tell you.'

'Yeah. But he's not here – and seeing this has happened maybe that's a good thing. Think about it. You want the people round here treating us like pariahs for the rest of our lives? That's what'll happen if we don't help. I think it's time for us to start mending fences.'

Cub, looking mutinous, carried his part well. 'You're wasting your time. He's probably just been dumped from his horse. He'll make it back on his own feet.'

'Then if he does we've been seen to do the right thing anyway,' Simon said patiently. 'You don't have to go.' His eyes, steady on Billy, held a message. 'What d'you say, Billy? You up for it?'

'Yeah, I suppose.' There was no need either to feign his disgust or dispute Simon's choice. With the known bad blood between the missing man and the Reillys it was a duty incumbent upon Cub to stay out of sight until his injuries healed. Logically nobody could connect the two but you never knew what idle speculation could come up with. And Cub's face, Billy admitted to himself, more nearly resembled the results of a fistfight than a fall from a horse.

When he thought about it he was actually surprised that Suds had swallowed the tale. If indeed he had.

'Tomorrow?' he suggested hopefully, but Simon shook his head.

'Watson's already at Toby's Hole. The search'll be based there. The station trucked nags out today and they're aiming for a daylight start. We'd best get over there tonight.'

'No rest for the wicked,' Billy sighed, then bit his lip at the unconscious appositeness of the words. 'Never mind,' he touched Jo's wrist, speaking for Sud's benefit, 'shouldn't take more than a couple of days – if he hasn't already turned up, that is. I'll be back before you know it.'

It took a week. They camped, Simon and Billy, Watson and his tracker, the two Stock Squad men, of whom one was a sergeant and thus outranked Watson, and four station men. One of these was the mechanic who couldn't ride, so he stayed in camp to cook and man the radio. There was also Axel Cooper, Ken Walker, Henry Burch, Nev Farmer and, for two days until mild sunstroke took him home, Oscar Davies. Keith Guthrie also turned up but left three days later when a call came through from the pub to tell him he had a passenger clamouring for a ride south.

Lionel Bennett came and went but the rest of them stayed camped on the dusty flat near the long waterhole with the pink lilies down one side and the pandanus thicket beside the horse pad.

Billy thought he would never forget the place, nor the peculiar horribleness of riding pointlessly all day through baking heat, then sitting through interminable briefings as the men who knew the country best planned the search. Tempers shortened as the days wore on. Hopes of locating Lucas alive waned after the first couple of days but a dogged determination to find him, to cheat death, spurred them on. They argued about how long he could last without water, how far the horse might have travelled from the scene of the accident, and what that accident had entailed. He was known to be a fair horseman so the big question, Henry maintained, was whether he lost the horse while afoot – had him pull away, say – or was injured in the separation. Maybe he was physically undamaged and had simply walked in the wrong direction.

The Stock Squad sergeant had charge of the map Bennett had provided and spent more time in camp on the radio to the inspector in Harditch than in the saddle. They'd have done better, Billy thought critically, with Frank Watson in charge. He at least could read tracks, a skill, along with patience, that the sergeant didn't possess.

'He's dead,' he had declared on the morning of the fourth day. 'We're looking for a body now, not a man.'

'They don't reckon so.' Ken Walker jerked his head at a pair of kite hawks planing idly over the humped shoulders of the hills. Unshaven, wearing a grimy shirt, he perched on his heels, a sweat-stained hat pulled low over his brow. 'You ask me he was never here. We've rode every inch of this country – so's the tracker and he's seen nothing.' The black man, squatting apart at his own fire, gave no sign that he'd heard. 'An' like I say – if there's a body the birds would've found it.'

'The horse was picked up less than a mile away.' The sergeant snapped. 'You've gotta start somewhere.'

'He's right. A body would bring the birds.' Bennett stood up. 'Maybe we should shift the search. South, towards the Bindin paddock. I don't understand what he'd be doing this far out in the bush country. But he *might've* been riding the Bindin fence.'

Billy swallowed the last of his breakfast and exchanged a glance with Simon. Rainsford's manager, it appeared, had not been a party to the ambush that had awaited them in Verity Valley.

'We need a better tracker,' the sergeant blustered. 'If we'd had that—'

'It's not Jeddy's fault, sarge,' Frank Watson wasn't going to hear his man maligned. 'This is brumby country. Jeddy did well to follow the horse as far as he did. But he's a touchy animal; once the saddle turned he coulda galloped five miles in any direction.'

Henry Burch spat disgustedly and rose, heading for his mount. 'Stone the flamin' crows! It's the man we're looking for – we've already got the bloody 'orse. We going on with the search or not?'

'Yes,' Watson spoke before the sergeant could veto it. Billy and Simon, along with the rest of the station men, followed him across to where the horses waited. Only Ken Walker didn't.

'I can't stay no longer,' he spoke awkwardly, dropping the butt of his cigarette to grind it under the toe of his patched workboot. 'Agent's bringing a buyer out today to look at the place. Hope you find the poor bugger before it's too late.'

'It probably is already.' Bennett shook his hand. 'Thanks for your help, Ken. I appreciate your coming.'

'Anytime. Least a man can do. See you, boys,' he called to the rest of them, nodding to and naming, those closest, 'Axel, Frank.'

By noon the sergeant had had enough. The spotter plane that had spent two days overflying the country had, he announced to the assembled company, been called off and with it the official search. The locals could carry on but he personally gave them no chance of finding anything.

'I think I'll give it another day for all that,' Axel Cooper said. 'What about you, Frank?'

'I'll stay.' Watson's voice was clipped.

'We will, too,' Simon said and Billy, suppressing the desire to groan, nodded.

The sergeant's gaze flicked their way like the dart of a snake's tongue. 'Well then, we've a bit of unfinished business at your place. Maybe you'll want to change your mind and accompany us – we'll be checking your paddocks, you know.'

'You check what you want,' Simon's tone was cold. 'There's a man's life at stake here. I'm staying to help.'

'Good on yer, mate.' The unexpected support came from Henry Burch, who eyed the sergeant with dislike. 'Now we're getting rid of the dead wood we might even do some good.'

The Stock Squad man flushed and turned away to throw his swag into the back of the Toyota. The doors of the vehicle slammed behind the occupants and they pulled away without another word spoken. Billy, waiting for them to turn north towards the Brumby, saw the nose of the vehicle swing in the opposite direction.

'All bluff,' Simon murmured for his ears alone. 'Thought it might be.'

They weren't altogether fools, Billy thought. They knew the

twins were at home and forewarned of their presence. With four clear days to work in, the Stock Squad would know that returning was nothing but wasted effort. Supposing there had been anything to find in the first place, that was.

They rode the rest of that day and the next. Late in the afternoon, with storm clouds muttering in the west and their mounts' coats spiked with sweat, Lionel Bennett shook each man's hand as they gathered their gear together and left. Henry had come with Axel Cooper, and Nev in Frank Watson's vehicle.

'We gave it our best shot,' the latter said, massaging the back of his neck, 'but it's tough country to find a man in.'

'It's that,' Bennett agreed. Thanks for your help. And you, Nev. Good of you to take the time.'

'Been in the same boat meself, near enough,' Nev said. 'Trouble comes you rely on your neighbours. 'S'what we're here for. See you, lads.' The salute from his crippled hand included them all.

Bennett thanked Billy and Simon, adding civilly, 'Any news of your father?'

'Yeah. He's conscious, but there seems to be nerve damage to his spine. Early days but it might mean a wheelchair for him.'

'So,' Bennett's look was assessing, 'you'll be running the place then?'

'Yeah,' Simon said in the soft-voiced way he had, 'and maybe now, without Blake or Harry stirring things, we'll get along better. I'll tell you the once, Lionel: none of us were responsible for killing your horse. Whether or not you believe that's up to you – but it's the truth.'

Bennett nodded, though whether as a simple acknowledgement or acceptance of Simon's word, Billy couldn't tell. Thunder
growled to the west and he eyed the approaching storm. That's all
they needed now – a run in the creeks to stop them getting home
tonight. Bennett must have had the same thought on his own
account.

'Pity it couldn't have come three days back. Might've saved him
then. You'd best get off. It'll be pouring soon and you've a way to go.
Thanks again for your help. I shan't forget it.'

The truck with the horses had already left. Bennett stepped into
his own vehicle and a few moments later they followed him back
to the road pursued by blowing dust from the wind that preceded
the rain. Looking behind him Billy saw the flat where they had
camped, and the waterhole, blotted out by the onrushing storm. It
looked like being a regular gully washer – enough to fill the half-
empty lagoon and scour away every trace of the past five days from
the face of the land. Sighing, he wished that they could as easily
erase the memory of those days from all their lives.

Thirty-seven

It was good to be home again, with Belle padding to greet them at the gate and the yellow light spilling from the kitchen door onto the concrete walkway. Jo flew to greet him as Billy hung his hat and Cub, looking up from his half-eaten meal, spoke, for Suds' benefit.

'So you didn't find him?'

Simon shook his head. 'Hopeless. The more so with that useless bugger in charge. Sergeant from the Stock Squad,' he explained. 'Couldn't track a bulldozer in mud. They'd have done better to turn the whole thing over to Frank Watson. Officially they stopped looking yesterday.'

'We heard it on the news,' Jo said. 'And about the plane being recalled.'

'That was a bit of a long shot anyway,' Billy said. 'A lot of the country's been burnt so I dunno what you'd see from a thousand feet – or whatever they fly at.'

'They coming back – those johnnies in the Stock Squad?' Suds asked.

'No. Said they were – just trying to rattle us – but it's not likely.' Simon picked up a plate and sniffed appreciatively. 'That smells good, Suds – they had Les Finkel murdering the tucker down there. I hope he's a better mechanic than he is a cook.'

Afterwards in a quiet hour on the verandah with Jo, sitting in near darkness with only the dim glow from the office highlighting her features, Billy told her about the search in more detail.

'It was horrible. But Simon was right to go. Bennett even shook hands with us when we left. I think he's seeing possibilities of a fresh start between the two places.'

'Who? Simon or Bennett?'

'Bennett – but Simon too. He made it pretty plain he wanted to. And Bennett was definitely puzzled about what Lucas was doing. Said he shouldn't have been anywhere near where the horse was found. He can't have been in on it.' As a natural corollary, he added, 'How's Cub doing?'

'What? Okay, I guess. Sick of hanging around waiting – we both are. What makes you ask?'

'Oh, just – I have nightmares,' he confessed a little shame-faced, 'and I wasn't even there. Horrible,' he scrubbed his face. 'It must be worse for him.'

'Well, he hasn't said.' Her hand found his and squeezed. 'What sort of nightmares, Billy?'

'It doesn't matter.' Now that he'd raised the subject he was reluctant to speak of the dark dreams of sinking into lightless depths with Lucas's dead face for company. He said abruptly, 'The whole thing has made me see how – how *chancy* life is.' He searched for words to explain. 'Of course you *know* it but you don't really think about it. That one moment you're here and a second later you're dead. I mean it's so final,' he said, desperate to be understood and knowing that he wasn't. In the dim wash of light he could read the incomprehension on her face.

'What are you trying to say, Billy? That death is final? Everybody knows that! I haven't seen too many shot cattle get to their feet again.'

'I'm not talking about death as such. I mean that once it's happened it's over – it's too late for anything else. To – to finish a sentence if you like. To sort things out.' He drew a careful breath, his hand that had been caressing her wrist closing urgently about it. 'Like with Blake. If he'd died where he fell that day that'd be it. You'd never have the chance to talk to him. Don't you want to know about your mother? What she was like, why she left? If I had a father I wouldn't waste the opportunity. And he's the only one who can tell you those things. Don't you think it matters – finding out?'

She stiffened and pulled free of his touch. 'That's a bit two-faced, isn't it? Why should it matter to me if it doesn't to you?'

'It does.' He looked surprised. 'Only my mother's dead and I don't know who my father is so there can't be any urgency about it. Records last – but people die, Jo. Blake still could you know. That's all I'm saying – that now might be the only chance you'll have to sort things out.'

'Well, I don't want to – and neither does Cub. Besides, we already know. He brutalised her until she had nothing left for us. Even a dying cow will charge if you touch its calf,' Jo said bitterly.

'But she just dumped us, like we didn't matter. You can talk all you like, Billy, but that's down to him.'

'That's not what Simon says.'

In the half light her head turned and he saw on her face the mulish look more common to her twin. They were perilously close, Billy recognised, to quarrelling. 'So? What does he say?'

'He just remembers her differently – as being unhappy, not weak. He spoke of her goading Blake rather than being terrified of him. And when she left she wanted to take him with her. Apparently the man she was with said she could choose one of you – but she loved you enough to know she couldn't split you and Cub up. So she picked him.'

There was disbelief in her tone. 'That can't be true. If it was why wouldn't he have gone?'

'He told me he didn't want to. He's a lot older than you two, so he remembers Blake as he was before he went to prison. Your parents were destructive together, Jo. He'd worked that out for himself by then. From what Simon said I think he was glad she left. And he didn't go with her because he thought that, by staying, he'd find his dad again.'

Jo snorted. 'The more fool him. So why didn't he tell us – about her choosing him? All this time we've thought she just walked out on the three of us – and she didn't,' she said bitterly, 'it was just on Cub and me.'

'I suppose that's why,' Billy said, 'to protect you.'

She brooded over these words. 'That'd be Si. He always looked out for us. But even if it's right about Blake not driving her away, it

328

doesn't excuse his other behaviour.' Her hand rose to cover the scar on her cheek.

'No. But you said it was the last time – and he was drunk.'

'That's an excuse?' She was incredulous and angry. 'Why are you sticking up for him?'

'I'm not,' Billy spread his hands, 'only, afterwards, if he was ashamed of having done it, and there was no sort of – I dunno – bond between you and him, well, can't you see it how it might be hard for him to know how to make it right? And the longer it went on the harder it would be. I just think,' he said doggedly, 'that you should go down and visit him. The man's crippled, Jo – maybe dying. Couldn't you just give him one chance to tell his side? Even criminals get that.'

'Oh, you think so, do you?' She jumped furiously to her feet, her voice rising. 'Well I've got a better idea. Seeing you like him so much, you go! You can tell him Cub and I have better things to do, but that we hope he'll enjoy his wheelchair. He deserves it.' She whirled and ran then, her boot heels making an angry din along the verandah floor.

Billy made to follow then dropped back into his chair and punched the armrest. 'Ah, shit!'

When they met again next morning in the kitchen after what had been, for him, a largely sleepless night, she looked uncertainly at him across the room.

'Jo,' he crossed to her side, ignoring Suds at the stove, frying up fritters for breakfast. 'I'm sorry. It's not my business really – only everything that touches you is, and I just think—'

She put two fingers to his lips, stopping his explanation. 'I know what you think. Let's just leave it, shall we?' The fine skin around her eyes had darkened as if she also had missed sleep. 'I'm sorry, too. Don't let's quarrel, Billy – certainly not over *him*. Friends still?'

'You bet.' He kissed her eagerly, holding her tight. 'I love you,' he whispered fiercely into her hair, shaken to the core by the sudden surge of need that filled him.

Simon appeared with dew on his boots. He was dapper in town wear, brushing at the nap of his good hat before lodging it carefully on a hook beside his old sweatstained work hat. 'You all packed, Suds?'

'Yep.'

Glancing round Billy saw that the cook was shaven and spruced up for a journey, and was struck by a thought. 'Who's gunna feed us?'

'You work it out,' Simon grunted. 'Change in the weather this morning. Storms coming or I'm a Dutchman. We'll be gone about a week.' He considered, 'If there's big rain, or the river's up, you can leave a message at the flying doctor base. I can phone from the coast before we start back, see what the road's like.' He glanced across at Cub, who'd followed him in. 'What're you gunna do?'

'Airstrip.' He poured tea from the pot. 'That ground we looked at across the creek. I reckon if we shift a few rocks with the tractor and fell some trees we can get the distance we need by going sou-sou-west. I called the base while you were down at Rainsford, and talked to one of the pilots. He told me all that sort of stuff. Billy and me, we'll make a start on it while you're gone.'

'Sounds good. Soon as I'm back we'd better get the truck into town and pick up a Wet Season order. Maybe you could work one out, Jo? And, Billy, you might check the fuel. Count the petrol drums, measure what diesel's left in the tank, and if we're gunna need more kero for the fridges. I'll have to get into the bookwork soon as I'm back. There hasn't been a bill paid since Blake got hurt. I'll get him to sign a few cheques to cover the really urgent ones.' He drained his tea and put his palms flat on the table. 'That's about it?' His glance swept over them. 'Any messages to deliver?'

'Give the boss my best,' Billy said when the twins remained silent, 'oh, and tell him I'm marrying his daughter. I'll drop him a line later.'

'Right, then. We'll see you when we see you.'

'And keep me kitchen proper,' Suds warned as he followed Simon to the door. 'I don't wanna come back to no mess.'

'You just worry about keeping off the grog,' Cub retorted. He looked at his sister. 'Looks like you're it.'

'That's okay.' She yawned and stretched, arching her back and Billy's gaze was drawn to the thrust of her breasts against the thin cotton. She caught his glance and blushed. 'Better than grubbing up red hot stone and shifting it,' she told her twin.

They did a lot of that in the days that followed. It had sounded easy enough around the kitchen table but the reality under the searing heat, as the days passed into November and the humidity rose, was something else. The tractor was a useful workhorse but it had its limits. A bulldozer would have made child's play of the boulders that they pried painfully from their beds, then grappled into the bucket of the Fordson for removal.

Cub worked like a man possessed, throwing all his energies into the task. 'Because it's gunna take weeks, just to get the ground clear, let alone levelled,' he snapped one day when Billy asked what the hurry was.

They were taking their lunch break in the straggly shade of a patch of yellow jack and he tilted his hat to examine the sky, eyes screwed up against the glare. 'Look at those clouds. They're not gunna fart around forever. Coupla days and it'll be storming on us.'

Billy shrugged. 'So the creek'll rise and we shan't be able to cross it. All the more reason for taking it steady now – if we're not going to finish anyway.'

'No.' He balled the paper that had held his sandwiches and rammed it into his mug. 'We can ride out. We don't need the vehicle. Tomorrow I'll bring extra fuel for the tractor. We can work it on the ridge here even when the paddock's too boggy to drive over.'

Billy sighed. He'd been looking forward to the break the weather could have provided to spend time with Jo. Changing the subject he said, 'I've been thinking – about Lucas.' Pinching his sweat-soaked shirt between his fingers he blew down on his chest where his prickly heat burned. 'You know how we said he must've had help to get the cattle onto the place? Well, whoever it was must've known, when he went missing, that Lucas could've been in Verity Valley. But he didn't come forward. There was a stranger in Southbend waiting on a ride out on the mail while the search was actually on. I remember Oscar called Keith, who was with us, and told him he'd better get back because this bloke was threatening to report him for not running. Maybe it was him?'

'Who cares?' Cub growled. 'What's it matter now? If it was, he's long gone.'

'I suppose,' Billy said doubtfully. 'But if that wasn't him – if he was a local – well, what if his conscience gets the better of him and he talks? Funnier things have happened. And if he comes to believe we could've found Lucas just by his speaking up—'

Cub's face darkened. 'Shut up!' he flared. 'Will you just for Christ's sake shut up? You're like a bloody dog with a bone, Billy. You can't let it alone. He's dead, gone forever – let him stay that way. I don't want to hear another word about it.' Slamming the mug down with force enough to crack it he sprang to his feet and strode across to the silent tractor, revving it to life again.

Billy grimaced and took his time folding his own lunch paper, draining his mug. Try as he would he could not for long expunge the memory of that day in the valley. So how much worse was it for Cub, whose fist had struck the blow that led to the man's death? And while not talking about it wasn't going to stop his thoughts, his reaction to Billy's words went a long way towards explaining the driven way he was working.

Picking up the crowbar, wrapped in rags to protect his hands against the heat the sun transferred to the steel, Billy went across to join Cub. The tractor, motor idling, was in position. Now they had to lever the dug-out boulder from its bed and into the bucket.

'Sorry, mate,' Billy said.

Cub grunted an acknowledgement. Together they swung down

on their bars, the exertion causing the sweat to pop out on their bodies. The heat fell like a blow across his back as Billy set his feet so that his legs rose like iron pillars connecting his body to the earth. His muscles swelled; he felt the stone grate and lift and then topple forward into the bucket's maw. Gasping, he fell back from the bar, sleeving his brow as Cub was also doing, then returned his hard grin at an arduous goal achieved.

''Nother one down,' Cub panted.

'Yeah.' Which in his estimation meant there were only about five hundred more to go.

Thirty-eight

When they got home that evening Jo had two items of news picked up from the radio.

She kissed Billy, wrinkling her nose as she did so. 'Phew, you smell like a billy goat.'

'I know it. I'm gunna shower – if your brother doesn't beat me to it. Any news?' He meant of Simon's return but she took him literally.

'Yes. They had two inches at the Mount last night so the mail won't be running. Keith started out but he turned back at the Black Swamp. And old Misery's dead. The hospital wired Fiona.'

'He said he wouldn't see Christmas,' Billy remembered. 'Poor old bloke.'

'He was a miserable old wretch,' Jo said, 'but how will the town manage without a store? Fiona's not likely to run it, is she? Not now while she's nursing, or later when she marries Simon. And I suppose there's a good chance it'll come to her – or her mum.'

'Yeah.' Billy's mind was on food. He sniffed the aroma from the stove. 'What's cooking? I could eat a bullock. Labouring in this heat really takes it out of you. Shifting rock is worse than fencing.'

'I'll bet it is. How much longer to go?'

'About six flaming months,' he spoke gloomily, 'unless it rains first.'

It did, off and on over the next fortnight. Showers at first, then a proper storm on the headwaters of the Wildhorse that brought the creek down overnight. The following week the mail truck got through. Then Simon returned accompanied by a morose and hungover Suds, days later than planned, because they had stayed to attend Misery Jones's funeral.

'How's the boss?' Billy asked, sorting through the letters Simon had picked up from the 'Bend. There was one for him from Ivy.

'Having physio. They're building him up to manage a wheel-chair. He's lost a lot of weight and has got the shakes in his right hand. And his legs don't work. I took Fiona along to see him. We brought her back with us,' he explained.

'Did she say what's happening with the store?' Jo avoided Billy's eyes as she steered the subject away from Blake.

'She had other things on her mind. But the town needs it so I suppose it'll stay open.' Simon yawned. His eyes were bloodshot and he looked drawn and tired. It was a long trip back from the coast. 'I daresay the solicitor will work it out – she engaged one before the funeral.'

'So – what's the plan?' Cub asked restlessly. 'With Blake? How long before he's back? The way the weather is we'd better fetch a ration order pretty damn quick. And we need to get some killers into the paddock too.'

336

'Give us a chance,' Simon protested. 'The doctor said Blake'll be ready to leave there in a couple of months – which means after the Wet. That'll gives us time to make a few alterations. Paths,' he added in response to their blank looks. 'A ramp onto the verandah, wheelchair access to the bathroom. I've got a list somewhere from the physio bloke. Anyway, I stopped off in Harditch and saw Bob Atkins the builder. He'll come out in a coupla weeks and do the work. Said a day to set up, another to run the paths and the ramp, and maybe a third on the bathroom – but that depends on the floor.'

'And on the weather,' Cub said. 'I'll service the truck in the morning. If we don't get into town soon we might not make it at all.'

Simon ran a distracted hand through his hair and eyed the pile of mail Billy had disturbed. 'Not before I pay a few of those bills.'

Later that night when the evening meal was over and they were ensconced in the roomy cane chair on the verandah, Billy interrupted what he was doing long enough to say, 'Jo, how would you feel about a January wedding? Is it too soon?'

'Soon?' Laughter bubbled in her voice. 'By the way things are going we ought to get married tomorrow. Did I ever call you slow? You're certainly making up for it now.'

'Seriously. I got a letter from Ivy,' he fished it from his shirt pocket, 'here, read it later on. I've told you about her – she's got the farm on the Tablelands—'

'And Daisy, the grey mare,' he felt her nod against his cheek, 'what's that got to do with getting married?'

'She's invited us to visit. Said we could have the cottage

where I used to camp and I was thinking it'd be a great place for a honeymoon. It's pretty country. You'd love it – and you couldn't help but like old Ivy. If we were married in early January we could travel straight down, have the rest of the month there, and get back – weather permitting – before the Wet sets in. And if January doesn't oblige – if it rains,' he shrugged, 'I'll get a job someplace and we can come back afterwards. What d'you think?'

'Yes.' She licked his neck then blew softly on the wet patch, her breath like ghostly fingers on his skin. 'Don't you have to get papers – a licence or something? And where would we have it? Not in Harditch or we couldn't all go, somebody would have to stay behind, and I want us all to be there.'

'Southbend? We could ask the flying padre to do the job – and then get a lift back to Harditch with him and take a bus from there.' He grimaced apologetically. 'I'll have to get a vehicle – maybe after the wedding, when we're on the coast. They should be cheaper there. What do you think, love? If you want it that way I'll see Padre Barry when we get to town and find out what we have to do.'

'Weather permitting,' she said as they always did. 'It sounds great. We could have it in the hall. All I need is a dress – and a cake. Suds will make that and I'll get Heather Waring to ice it. She does beautiful cakes – when she's not cutting hair. I saw the photo of the one she did for Daphne Cooper's engagement. It was like something out of a bride magazine.'

'And you need a ring.' Billy carried her hand to his lips and kissed the bare finger that would wear it. 'Maybe we'd better wait to pick the actual day because that'll depend on the padre and how much paperwork's involved. But we can sort it all out in Harditch. You'll be my wife,' he marvelled. 'Weather permitting of course.'

For a while it seemed that the weather would not even permit the initial trip into town, intermittent storms raising the level of first one and then another of the waterways between the Brumby and the 'Bend. According to the Met reports the monsoon trough had made an early appearance across the northern tip of Australia and was generating the host of storms they were experiencing.

'Might be a wet old wedding at this rate,' Cub said.

But finally the skies cleared and they made a hurried dash through country made green and beautiful by the rain. Even the roads had improved, the bulldust patches firmed to hardness, the creek banks washed smooth by the passage of water, and gay with the flowers of convolvulus vines. During the frantic week that followed Billy chose an engagement ring – a thin white-gold band set with a minuscule diamond. He slid it onto Jo's finger on the final evening in the café where they'd been taking their meals. They kissed above the candle flame lighting their table, and were clapped and whistled at by the other patrons – truckies from the rigs waiting outside, an overalled mechanic, and a young family sharing a meal of fish and chips.

'She's marrying me,' Billy said proudly to the room at large.

Two days later they were home again, having been forced to wait in Southbend overnight for the Rainsford River to drop following a storm upstream. And a day behind them came Bob Atkins, his three-tonner loaded with cement and the tools of his trade.

'I dunno about this,' he said, shaking hands at the gate, 'a man's a mug – I never seen a sky with more rain in it.'

'Ah, it's only November,' Simon replied. 'How are you, Bob? Supposing we get your truck under cover first? Then come and have a feed. After that we'll look at the job.'

Atkins pulled off the baseball cap he wore, used it to mop the sweat from his face, then stared around him. 'Probably more to it than you reckon.' He sucked his teeth. 'That path from the gate there's too narrow for a wheelchair. It'll need fixing. Well, I brought extra cement so that's okay. Wish now I'd brought the lad too – job'd go the quicker and that's all to the good the way the weather is.'

'I'll off-side for you,' Simon offered. 'Just so we get it done.'

Billy and Cub returned to their labours on the airstrip while the dry spell lasted, but they took the precaution when the opportunity offered of running a few horses into the house paddock. Billy, latching the gate shut in the dusk, watched the five of them circle away through the timber, bucking and kicking. Carnival was in the lead, tail and head high. They hadn't particularly wanted her, or the bay pack-horse, in the paddock, but taking the lot had been the only way to get the other three, Banjo, Linnet and dependable old Brandy.

The work was going well. Despite his earlier pessimism another week should see the removal of the last of the large boulders and they could then begin the task of carting fill to even the ground. It was still a mammoth task giving the inadequacy of the Fordson, but then clearing fence lines with the tractor had been no picnic either.

It was like anything else, Billy thought, his mind straying as it usually did, to Jo. If you wanted it badly enough you could accomplish it – even getting married. In a little more than six weeks Jo would be his wife. Sometimes he woke in the night with the panicked certainty he'd dreamed it all. Then when he grasped it was all true, he'd feel weak with relief and lie revelling in the knowledge that soon Padre Barry would be out at the Brumby to finalise the paperwork and talk to him and Jo, and arrange a date . . .

'Hey!' Cub bellowed, his head out the cab window, 'Are you gunna get in or you wanna walk home?'

'Oh, right.' Feeling foolish, Billy scrambled to hook the gate chain he had forgotten. He had never been happier, filled with a sense of joy as new and fresh as the scent of the sappy grass underfoot.

Jo met them at the gate with the news that the creek was coming down. They went to look and found a stealthy tide of clear water swirling amid the pandanus stems.

'Clean,' Billy flashed the torch he'd brought from the kitchen. 'Must've come all the way from the headwaters. Should we shift the pump?'

'Nah,' Cub said, 'not yet, anyway. It's only a couple of foot. Probably run down overnight. Anyway we've got the nags in so it doesn't matter.'

But in the morning the creek was higher and Cub was late to breakfast, coming in at last wet to the knees from tramping through dew-sodden grass at the yards. Billy, who'd heard the 'Rover go out, looked up at his arrival. 'Get 'em okay?'

'No.' Cub scowled. 'Banjo's gone over the fence and Linnet into it. She's damn near ripped her leg off. I yarded her with the others – maybe you could look at her, Jo?'

She nodded. 'After breakfast. How did it happen?'

'A damn pheasant. Came out of the grass right under Banjo's nose and the silly bugger went into the fence just this side of the watering lane. Linnet panicked and followed him but stopped short of going over it. I'll have to take that chestnut of yours today, Simon. There's only her and old Brandy left. Anyone checked the creek?'

'Still rising,' Suds said. 'No need to shift the pump yet, but.'

'It's not likely to be a swim then at the ford,' Cub said dismissively and it wasn't.

Billy, sitting his saddle, watched the fast smooth roil of the water gliding past with the sunlight catching the ripples until they vanished into the shade of the tree-lined banks. He patted Brandy's neck then pulled his lunch from the saddle pouch and tucked it into his shirt. 'How deep you reckon that is?'

'Under shoulder height – a doddle,' Cub said, 'supposing I can get this bitch into it. I dunno what Simon sees in her.'

In the half-mile between the homestead and the ford Carnival had already fretted herself into a lather. She moved in bounds like a jumpy cat, nostrils flaring and ears alarmed, ready for trouble. Billy didn't envy Cub his ride.

'She might follow Brandy.' He kicked him into the stream and the old brown, after dipping his nose, forged steadily ahead. They were halfway across, Billy with his boots tucked high on the horse's flanks, when the mare passed him in a rush of surging spray. Her eyes rolled whitely and she bounded the last few feet, lashing out with a snort when her sodden tail touched her hocks.

Cub was soaked to the waist; Billy smugly lowered his own dry boots into the irons, and replaced his lunch. Then with the chestnut fighting for her head they set off at a canter to cover the two miles to the airstrip.

It was another long, sweat-streaked day. The horses drowsed and stamped in tree shade, tails swishing against the stinging bites of pestering march flies. They paid no attention to the rumbling tractor or the heat-slowed movement of the two men who returned from time to time to drink from the waterbag swinging near them. At midday the noise died and a thin wisp of smoke added its fragrance to that of dust, dung, and horse sweat.

'Definite change in the air,' Billy eyed the towering build-up of clouds to the west. 'God it's hot! There must be rain in that lot.'

'Yeah. Bob's probably wishing himself back in town,' Cub said as a sudden stab of lighting rent the monstrous pillar of cloud followed by the crack of the thunderclap. 'Could wind up being a poor season for all that.'

'How d'you make that out? We've had about ten inches already and it's still a week off December.'

'Yeah, sometimes it comes early,' Cub agreed, 'and stops early too. Sixty-eight was like that. We dry bogged the truck out near the main road in March. Anyway, enough talk. Let's get back to it.'

An hour before dark, the valley filling with shadows, they knocked off for the day, stacking the tools and capping the upright exhaust on the tractor. The horses were hungry, eager for the paddock, and Carnival suffered herself to be mounted without fuss. 'All the same,' Cub remarked, 'we run into any horses we'll take them back with us. I don't like being down to one mount.'

343

But they were out of luck, reaching the creek without seeing anything other than a wallaby crawling through the grass along its bank. It sat up as they passed, scratching at its chest, but Billy had eyes only for the Wildhorse and reined Brandy to a startled halt.

'Holy mackerel!' The ford was half again as wide as it had been that morning, and the heads of the shrubby growths that had stood proud beside the pandanus now streamed forlornly in the flood. 'Jesus! That storm must've been right astride the creek. It's risen a good five feet. Wonder if they got the pump out?' He slapped at the sudden burn of an insect bite. 'We'll have to wait.'

Cub was slapping too. Mosquitoes had descended on them in a whining, stinging cloud and the horses began to twitch and stamp. 'You got the matches?'

'Why would I have?' Billy stared at him. 'They're back on the job, inside the tea tin.'

'Great.' He swore, smacking viciously at his forearms. 'Well I'm not hanging around without smoke to hunt 'em. We'll swim it.' He reined about heading upstream to where the creek was considerably narrower. Following him, Billy's misgivings grew as he eyed the half-submerged line of pandanus lining the opposite bank. 'How are we supposed to get out through that?'

'We don't. Good God, you're never going to make it straight across! That's a strong current. It'll take us down to the ford. Some horses swim low – just hang onto the mane and let the water carry you and you'll be right. Don't worry, we've done this before.'

Billy eyed the prospect without enthusiasm. His only experience swimming a horse had been through the gorge in Verity, and that had been still water, not this swift-running current. 'After you then.'

It was almost dark; what light there was lingered above the roiling surface that was no longer clear but a rich, earthy brown dotted with spume, like piles of dirty soapsuds. The birds had gone to roost and the only noise was the rush of water, the whine of mosquitoes and the sound of Carnival's unhappy snorting as Cub coaxed her onto the pad. She inched her way down it, digging her feet in until all four were bunched at the water's edge. He clapped her shoulder with his open palm and instead of stepping forward as he expected, she gave a great snort and leapt, landing with a belly slapping thump in the creek.

Her head went under and she reared as the current seized her, whinnying shrilly, and spun back to face the bank. Cub's hat had gone and the splash of her landing had smeared wet hair across his eyes. Billy heard him curse. 'Stupid bitch!' He was trying to haul her head around but the press of the water forced her back against the bank. She found bottom for an instant for one foreleg struck suddenly clear, hoof and slender pastern darkly wet. Then the water had her again, pulling her down, and she screamed wildly.

'Leave her!' Billy roared, seeing her swing on her side. 'Swim for it!' Cub seemed to be trying to do so. His torso jerked as he tried to thrust himself clear but the mare completed her roll and he vanished beneath her, the two of them sinking into darkness.

Thirty-nine

Billy flung himself from his mount, tugging at his boots while yelling Cub's name. There was just light enough to glimpse the round of Carnival's rump and one flailing hoof before the terrified mare's head surfaced again and she was swept away, nostrils half submerged.

He dived, fear for Cub edging out any terror he felt. Instantly the water took him, tumbling him like a leaf, with careless brutal force that shocked the breath from him. The violent rush of the water showed the creek's true nature. Billy couldn't believe that they had ever been mad enough to think of swimming it. Even in daylight he doubted he could have seen anything in the rush of the silt-laden flood. Eyes wide and straining, he swam desperately in darkness, hands groping before him, his mind ticking off the passing seconds. Something touched his foot; he jack-knifed down, reaching, but was torn away, to surface and gasp air into his starved lungs.

Down he went again, despair building, it was too dark, the

current too strong, and he was too poor a swimmer to succeed. He couldn't quit. He couldn't even tell if he was near the bank or in midstream, but presumably his body would follow the same path Cub's had taken. He dived, and dived again, fruitlessly. Once a log touched him, or he it, and he grabbed the spiky roughness while a great gout of gladness blossomed in him. But it died fast as he swam on. Water burned in his nose and gullet. He coughed it up and kept diving, his movements becoming more laboured as fatigue whittled away his strength.

Soon his arms were too heavy to lift. He rested on his back, feeling himself borne along headfirst while the water lapped over his chin. In just a moment he would try once more. He could no longer tell how long he had been in the water. His chin sank lower and a great lassitude filled him as he lay in the rough embrace of the Wildhorse with the stars whirling by overhead; he was going to die. Cub had drowned and he would soon follow him. It didn't seem to matter – save that it was a pity he should do so when he was only a month or so from marrying Jo . . .

Her name galvanised him as nothing else could. The comfort of lassitude changed instantly to struggle and pain, and the burn of water in his nose. She had lost her twin – he could not, must not, leave her to carry such a weight of grief alone. Lifting his arm was an effort as great as single-handedly moving one of the airstrip boulders, but he did it, and again, and then again, his heart burning with pity and anguish for her. Stroking feebly on his back he forced his weary legs to move. The first downward kick touched something but the sensation took so long to register that before it did his head had already rammed into the obstacle to which the rushing of the Wildhorse had carried him.

He clung to the surface of the mass, which had the pliability of wet hay, hitching himself higher by degrees until his shoulders and upper chest were clear of the flood. He lay for what could have been minutes or hours while the burn of his muscles faded and he gradually came back to himself. By then he'd worked out where he was. Somewhere in the mess of debris on which he lay was the cable of the creek crossing on the eastern edge of the Spell paddock. The flood must have swept a tree down the creek, which the cable had caught and held, and the current had done the rest, tumbling everything in its path into the solid mat of debris against which he had been caught. He was, Billy realised, a couple of miles below the point where he'd entered the creek. In its normal state the water here would be no more than knee deep. Numbly he wondered if Cub's body was also lodged in the trash below him.

Careful not to disturb the unstable structure that had saved him, Billy explored until his questing hand found a sturdy branch. He worked the belt free from his sodden jeans and used it to create a loop through which he thrust his arm. Should the mass disintegrate he would still have an anchor point. He could only wait for the flood to subside.

Through the long hours of the night Billy lay in a stupor of grief and physical exhaustion, his arm through the strap, drifting in and out of sleep and watching the stars wheel overhead. At one point, feeling his legs chill, he grasped that the cause lay in his wet jeans. It took a moment for the significance of this to sink in, and a cautious examination of his surroundings confirmed it. The creek was dropping.

By the first grey light when the mosquitoes found him the water had sunk to thigh deep with only the tide line of sticks and dried grass, and the muddy marks on the trees, to show where it had been.

Before leaving his unlikely sanctuary Billy located the cable and re-buckled his belt about it. He felt the need of something to hold onto, and the pull of the water as he lowered himself into it justified the precaution. Wincing his way across the pebbly bottom, for he'd somehow lost his socks, he staggered, dripping, up the gentle curve of the bank. His insides cleaved together over his empty belly; he'd eaten nothing since the previous midday, and his head felt light as a result. The mosquito bites on his arms and neck burned and he scooped a handful of mud to cool them, found the horse pad further up the bank and began the long walk home.

Bob Atkins picked him up at the ford. He was there armed with a long pole with which he was prodding through a collapsed tangle of pandanus, the station Land Rover, abandoned with the driver's door hanging open, parked on the flood bank above him.

He gave a shout and dropped the pole, bounding up the slope in great strides. 'Thank Christ!' His gaze went past Billy down the paddock. 'You okay? You look bloody awful. Where's your mate?'

'He drowned. The mare—' Billy shook his head, too weary for explanations. 'Where's Simon?'

'Looking for you. We come down here at daylight and there was a saddled horse lying over there,' he nodded at the far bank. 'Had the reins caught in a log. Simon waded over and took off on it.' Face creased with concern he grasped Billy's arm. 'You musta had a crack on the head; there's blood in your hair. Let's get you back.' He coughed awkwardly, 'You're sure about your mate?'

'Yeah.' Billy resisted his effort to take his arm. 'And Jo – does she, is she—?'

'Oh, she knows,' Bob said. 'Knew last night – well, that something was wrong. One minute she's standing at the table and the next she let out this god-awful cry—' he shivered in the bright morning. 'I tell you the hair fair stood up on my neck. Next thing she's got us out on the creek bank for all the good it did in the dark. I seen Simon took it serious enough for all that.'

Yes, Billy thought, he knew the twins and the bond between them. Jo had told him how Cub had come at a breakneck pace to the spring, because he felt her terror. Surely it would be the same for Jo. He could only imagine the anguish of having that knowledge ripped from her as Cub died. Staring numbly at the other man, Billy saw the shadow of fatigue in Bob's ruddy face from the long night's labour. The soles of his feet left bloody marks on the grass as he climbed into the cab. 'Take me to her.'

The sun was over the range, stretching long shadows of shrub and tree across the paddock. Smoke curled from the kitchen chimney and a subdued Belle came to meet him, picking her way through Bob's half-laid boxing. He found Jo huddled on a bench in the kitchen, hands gripping her upper arms as if to stop herself flying apart. Her pale face held such a look of suffering that his heart broke over again and in the long moment it took for her to raise her head and see him standing framed in the doorway, he wished that it had been he that had died instead of Cub. Then she started up, her cry breaking on a sob of gladness.

'Billy! Oh, Billy – you're safe. I thought – I was sure I had lost you too.'

'I'm okay, Jo. Fit as a fiddle,' he tried to smile for her and could not. They met in the middle of the room. He held her to him, resting his head on her shoulder while her hair tickled his ear. 'I'm so sorry, love. Carnival – she panicked in the water and fell on top of him. I couldn't find him.' By the stove Suds was watching, dark eyes pouched and stricken. He had helped raise the twins and had loved Cub too. Billy's voice shook. 'He was my mate – my best mate.' Outside, beyond the garden still damp with the night's dew, a ground pheasant called and he felt the wet scald of Jo's tears against his throat.

'The copper's coming.' Suds spoke for the first time since Billy had arrived, placing a mug of tea in front of him. He was beating eggs by the stove and making a pile of toast. 'Simon called him last night. He's gunna organise a search. He's out getting 'orses in for 'em – Simon, I mean.'

Billy drank the tea, forcing his brain to concentrate. 'Which – Bob said one of them was still on the bank, with the reins caught – was it Brandy or—'

'Yeah. He shot t'other. Her leg was broke.' He tipped the omelette onto a plate and slid it across the table along with the toast. 'Eat it,' he commanded gruffly. 'You too, girl. Even if it's just a bite o' toast.'

Billy's hunger had died to a vague emptiness but the first mouthful brought it roaring back. He finished the eggs and coaxed Jo into trying a slice of toast when they heard hooves thundering up the paddock and behind it the rapid approach of a vehicle.

'I'll go.' He got up and went out, thinking Frank Watson hadn't wasted any time, but it was a Toyota that pulled up by the engine shed and it carried, not the policeman, but Rachel Cooper. In her haste she all but fell out the passenger side, leaving Alex to follow at a more moderate pace.

'G'day, Billy.' His eyes flickered over him and away, taking in the homestead and Belle at the gate. For a Cooper he seemed remarkably ill at ease. 'We half heard a call Simon made to Frank Watson – something about you and his brother being missing? I came because there was no stopping Rachel, but it's obviously a fool's errand—'

'Oh stop it, Dad!' The girl's voice cracked. Her eyes were wild, the delicate skin of her cheeks pale as bone. 'Is he all right, Billy? Where—' Something in his own haggard mien must have warned her for her eyes darkened and she gave a heartbroken cry. 'He's dead, isn't he? Oh Cub!'

She'd never been other than small but reading the silent confirmation in his face her body seemed to shrink. She sagged and Axel sprang forward to catch her. He rocked her in his arms and as the sobs wrenched her body, his face was riven with the grief he had never shown for Ben. 'There, lass,' he crooned, 'there, there.' And over her head, 'There's no doubt?'

'None.' Dully, Billy turned back to the gate. 'You'd better come in.' It was only just eight o'clock. He wondered how much more sorrow and pain the day could bring.

The hours and days that followed seemed like fragments in a dream, a kaleidoscope of images running into each other until it was impossible to make sense of any of them. Billy remembered the way his swollen feet hurt as he helped in the search. And the bloated body of Carnival wedged between a rock and the big river fig below the crossing. Somebody – he thought it might have been Henry Burch – had hooked a tow chain first to the rock, and then to the mare, and dragged her away up the paddock.

Frank Watson had wanted the full details of the accident. Billy recalled it for him and the little ring of neighbouring men who had come to help, made awkward by sympathy and laden down with their wives' cooking. He had sat for hours on the side of Jo's bed, holding her as she slept, soothing the whimpers of her troubled dreams. And he had rested briefly himself, head on the table, to wake with an aching neck to the sight of Rachel fiercely chopping onions that were salted by her tears.

Afterwards he found Rachel pacing in the garden, different in rage from the girl he thought he knew. She had railed at Cub for leaving her, for letting death take from her the only thing that mattered. Thinking her in the grip of hysteria he had slapped her, expecting her to collapse. Instead she had slapped him back, a full-handed angry blow. Cheek smarting, he apologised.

'I'm sorry – I thought—'

'I know what you thought! What everyone thinks – I've got no business making such a fuss, have I? It's not like he even loved me – but he might've done if he'd lived. He might've! I have to believe that because I loved him. I loved him and now he's gone. And all because you couldn't wait until it was safe to cross a stupid creek.'

The accusation was so true that Billy could find no answer.

Next morning as he sat on the verandah edge with his feet dangling into the boxing where Bob had knocked the steps away, Simon padded up silently to join him. Billy had scarcely seen him since the accident; he shifted over to make room and the other man sighed and ran his hands through his hair.

'We're not gunna find him, Billy.' His cheekbones were gaunt, the skin about his eyes bruised and tired looking.

'No.' After a moment he added, 'Will you stop the search?'

'I think we have to. We're just drawing it out – going over the same ground. Better for Jo if we quit.'

'Maybe.' Billy teased at a splinter of wood with his thumbnail. If they found the body of her twin would Jo demand to see it? Could they prevent her doing so? It had been five days now. Better, he thought, not to have that as her final horrific memory of him. He remembered something. 'Has anyone told Blake?'

'Suds wired him – the day after. We haven't heard anything back. I suppose I'll have to go down again.' He sighed. 'There's so much to see to. And the Wet's almost on us—' It had stormed again the previous night and thunder muttered behind the dawn.

'I'll go,' Billy said. 'Jo needs to get away. I've been thinking – if she'll come – that I'll take her across to the Tablelands to stay with

Ivy until – well, for as long as she needs. It's no distance from there to Townsville. And I always planned to visit him anyway. He'll be my father-in-law after all.'

Simon nodded. 'I'd forgotten about the wedding. What'll you do?'

'Leave it till Jo's ready. It doesn't matter.' He had never thought to utter such words but his whole being was gripped with anxiety over Jo. She scarcely ate and grief wrapped her like a cloak. He could almost see the bleeding wound Cub's death had made and there seemed no way to stop the pain, or to fill the emptiness it had caused in her. Facing his greatest fear he said, 'She may not want to now anyway. I'm not much of a substitute for Cub.'

'Don't be bloody stupid, man,' Simon said roughly, 'you were never that.'

Face despairing, Billy kicked the boxing. 'None of it had to happen. If Linnet hadn't cut her leg he'd never have been on that damn mare in the first place.'

'That's no good. You might as well say if I hadn't put one over on Bennett all those years back and sneaked her dam into his stallion, Carnival wouldn't have been here to kill him. You make choices in life – and then you have to pay for them. Like Lucas. If he hadn't been in the valley that day—'

'Well Cub's paid for that, hasn't he? So has Jo. And even Rachel, though she doesn't know what she's paying for. Not to mention you, and me, and old Suds – where does it end?'

'I don't know.' Simon sighed again as he stood up. 'But it will – one day. And in the meantime we just have to get on with it. That's all anyone can do.'

Forty

Everyone had left and the four of them were alone again, in rooms that echoed to their boot heels, when Padre Barry arrived the following day. He had Fiona with him. Simon and Billy met them in the garden where Belle still whined and searched restlessly for Cub. Staring blankly at the padre, whom he'd met only the once before, Billy suddenly remembered that he'd been coming about the wedding and apologised for the wasted journey.

'That's all right.' The padre was short and tubby with thin, sandy hair and pale eyes. 'I'm not here about that. Miss Forrest wanted to come, and,' he looked at Simon, 'I thought at some future time you might like to consider a memorial service. Here, or in Southbend – just as you like.'

'We'll think about it,' Simon, who was gripping Fiona's hand, seemed hardly to be listening. 'It's too soon—' He broke off to touch her cheek, 'I'm glad you're here. Come inside, we'll have some tea – you too, Padre.' To Fiona he said, 'I don't suppose you can stay?'

'No.' Her hazel eyes were regretful. 'Matron's taking a week off from Wednesday. She's going to Harditch before the Wet sets in, and Melanie's on holiday. So it's me and the wardsman holding the fort. I'll have to go back with Barry. I just wanted to see you, and Jo. How is she?'

'About what you'd expect.' He opened the screen door. 'Billy wants to take her away from here and I think it'd be best. Maybe you could tell her so too?'

'Of course. And Barry might be of help there.' She arched her brows, 'I know you're not a church-going family but one thing a minister gets, Simon, is experience with grief.'

'I suppose you're right.' He hooked his hat next to the empty space where Cub's had hung and turned. 'Come and meet Suds.' In an abrupt aside he added, 'He's feeling it. He helped raise the twins.'

'Poor old man,' she said softly. 'Such a dreadful thing to've happened. Have you told your father yet?'

'Suds did – the next day. He sent a wire.'

'I'll ring him – if the phone's working.' Southbend only had the one, in the post office side of Misery's shop.

'What'll you say?'

'I don't know – what one does when tragedy occurs. That's three gone from the district in one hit,' she said sombrely, 'first young Ben Cooper, then Harry Lucas, and now your brother. It's tragic. And strange – that there should be two men lost so close together and their bodies not found, don't you think?'

'Yeah.' Wanting to change the subject he said, 'What about you? How are things going? Have you had any luck locating old Mal's will yet?'

'Oh yes. He did have a solicitor after all. He saw the death notice and got in contact. I didn't want to mention it on the air because of his creditors, but he's left everything to me – the shop and whatever money he had. I didn't go into it over the phone. It was the day after I heard about Cub and it just seemed – unimportant. He said he'd be in touch by mail. Everything's tied up until probate has been granted anyway, but I did get permission to keep the store running in the interim. His name's Evans and he practises in Townsville. He was polite but I don't think he really believed me when I explained it was the only shop in town.'

'They haven't a clue,' Simon said. 'They think it's all bitumen and grid power out here. Well, I'm glad the old boy remembered you.' He smiled, 'Means I should be right for a free tin of bully beef if I lob into town without tucker someday. Hey, Suds,' he called to the cook, who had been studiously ignoring them, 'this is Fiona. She and the padre're dying for a cuppa.'

'Well I already figured that out and made it.' The old man carefully wiped his palm and held it out. 'Howdo? I dunno,' he said, eyeing her, 'you look too pretty for a ugly mug like him.'

Fiona laughed and shook his hand. 'I can see we'll get along just fine. Why do they call you Suds?'

A week later Billy tossed his rolled swag into the back of the Land Rover alongside Jo's canvas bag, and solicitously held the door for her as she climbed in beside Simon, who was already behind the wheel. Her shirt and jeans hung on her frame and her face was thin and pale within the curtain of her hair. She wore boots but had left her hat. She shook her head when Billy asked if he should fetch it.

Belle howled as they drove off, a spine-prickling cry that soared above the engine noise. At the ford the water, now only a few inches deep, sparkled prettily in the sunlight, between banks still torn and raw. Jo stared straight ahead as they crossed but the hand lying on her lap trembled and Billy covered it with his own. Simon was driving them as far as Harditch and would return the following day – weather permitting. Billy's eyes stung at the phrase, the ghostly echo of Cub's voice trickling through his mind. *Up here everything's always down to the bloody weather.*

From Harditch they would catch a bus to the Tablelands. He had wired Ivy the bare news of Cub's death and followed it with a letter the padre had promised to post, explaining the circumstances of their visit. He turned unseeing eyes upon the country, automatically bracing himself against the inequalities of the road. He had succeeded in getting Jo away but the battle was far from won. Grief rode with them like a fourth presence in the cab and his helpless anxiety for her was a weight, like a stone, in his chest.

'Any idea when you'll be back?' Simon had asked earlier. Bob Atkins had finished the job and gone but eventually the road would close, putting a stop to all travel, and that was what he was really querying – would it be before the road closed.

'I don't know. When she's ready. It might take till after the Wet.' He had spoken confidently as if grief was just a fever from which you recovered. But watching her now, marking the jut of her wrist bones, the dark smudges beneath her eyes, he felt a superstitious frisson of fear, a reminder that some fevers killed.

Forty-one

Promising himself a ten-minute breather, Billy leaned on his hoe and looked across the gentle slope at the cleared area behind him. The stems and crowns of bracken lay upturned by his efforts and he thought he could just about call it quits for the day. His gaze, following the slope, found the gully where the kookaburras congregated and noted the regrowth of lantana there. Something else that needed attention.

The gully marked the boundary of the property and behind it ran the narrow lane that serviced the farm. It would, he judged, be close enough to five o'clock, going on the angle of the light that fell in golden shafts through the canopy of the tall timber, so different from the scrubby forests of the Gulf. They'd be back anytime. Shouldering the hoe he started across the paddock to meet them at the gate.

They were there before him. He heard the clop of hooves and the murmur of voices, and caught a glimpse of Daisy's suddenly tossed head across the lantana, and then the sound of Jo's laugh.

Billy smiled. She was coming back to him at last, although it had taken a couple of months. Time had done it, and Ivy, and the horses. He'd been right to bring her here, to the haven of the farm and the kind old woman who'd taught him his trade. Of course she was not fully over her twin's death, he doubted she would ever truly lose the pain of that loss, but she was eating properly again and taking an interest in things, and that contented him for now.

'How'd it go?' She'd got off for the gate, and smiled at him as she led the grey mare through, Ivy following behind on Magic, the old black gelding. Jo still had no hat but wore a long-billed navy baseball cap instead. There was a logo for farm machinery stitched into the front and a scouting badge pinned to one side. Billy wondered where Ivy had found it.

'No problems. The cattle are so quiet you could yard them on foot.' They'd been mustering the agisted steers from the top paddock. 'They walked into the truck like lambs.'

'Yeah, I heard it go past a while ago.'

'We've been riding.' She reached up to pat the mare's neck and Daisy whickered and nipped at her hip pocket searching for treats. 'It was great.' There was colour in her cheeks and the bruised look had gone from beneath her eyes. 'And Ivy's been telling me a few things about you.' The blue eyes held the glimmer of a smile.

He said cautiously. 'Oh yes?'

'How taken you were with Daisy, for instance. And how the first time you chased a beast on her you fell off.'

Billy looked reproachfully at his hostess. 'Why'd you have to bring that up?'

'It just happened.' Her eyes twinkled at him out of a face that had grown more seamed and weathered since he'd called her boss. She reached to take the reins from Jo's hand. 'I'll see to her. You walk up with Billy. And I'll tell you what, I wouldn't say no to a cuppa.'

'I'll put the kettle on,' Jo promised. He shut the gate and when he returned to her side she linked her arm in his and leaned suddenly to kiss his cheek.

'What's that for?' He was pleased, but surprised. Since Cub's death she had accepted his embraces and murmured endearments but initiated none of her own. She no longer even wore his ring, but he comforted himself with the fact that she had not worn it at the Brumby either, not wanting, she'd told him then, to either lose or damage it working.

'Oh, just for – everything. And she *is* a lovely creature; I can see why you fell for her, especially as she was the first stock horse you'd ever ridden.'

'Grass couldn't have been greener than I was,' he agreed ruefully. 'She propped to follow a beast and I just kept going.'

'Well if it's any comfort Ivy claims you showed a natural ability for stock work right from the start.' Her gaze roved over the paddock beyond the split timber fence where a handful of cows browsed in the golden light. 'It's lovely, isn't it? And so's Ivy. Better than the grandmother I never had. She's so wise and – accepting of things. I suppose she had to learn to be, losing her husband like that, and having to sell up. Thank you for bringing me here, Billy.'

'I'm just glad you're feeling better.'

She touched his cheek, blue eyes sombre again. 'It's down to you that I am. You can't know how much you've helped me. There were times when I really wanted to die – just to end the pain. But you were always there.' He moved his arm to put it around her then and they continued to walk in silence, their shadows like poles before them. When next she spoke it was to ask a question. 'Are you still going down tomorrow to see Blake?'

'Yes, but I shan't be long away. There and back, love, that's all.'

'I was thinking,' she had come to a stop, forcing him to drop his arm as she turned to face him, 'about what you said that night on the verandah. It didn't mean anything then but now with – since Cub—' she swallowed, 'I've decided you're right. I *do* want to know the truth – about our mother. So,' she finished in a rush, 'I'll come with you.'

'Are you sure, Jo?'

'No,' she said baldly, 'but without Cub—' the tears started and she sniffed them back 'Don't you see, Billy? *He* made me complete and I – we – didn't need anyone else. Not parents, not even Si really. But I'm alone now and I need to know. So – I'm going.'

'I'm glad.' Billy knew there was no point in telling her she wasn't alone. Twinship was a different bond. He turned the peak of her cap so it wasn't poking his eye out and kissed her instead. 'And what say we find you a proper hat while we're at it?'

Ivy made them sandwiches and filled a flask with tea. 'You can't be boiling a billy on the side of the road down here,' she said firmly. 'And I put in a tin of gingerbread for smokos.'

'Ivy, we could buy something,' Billy protested.

363

'You need to be saving your money,' she countered firmly. 'You're getting married, aren't you?'

Today even that seemed a possibility for Jo was again wearing his ring. She hugged Ivy and they climbed into the new-looking but used Toyota Billy had bought when they arrived, and drove off, pausing at the gate to shut it and wave back at the lone figure on the verandah steps.

Billy looked across the cab at Jo as she pulled her seatbelt on. 'You okay, love?'

'Yes.' She gave him that glimmer of a smile. 'A bit nervous. I don't think I've ever talked to Blake, not a conversation anyway. I'm not sure I know how.'

'Just think of a question,' Billy said, 'and take it from there. And I'll be with you – unless you want to do it alone?'

'No. Stay with me, please.' She fell silent and after a while he twiddled the radio dial to find some music and then let his mind drift to the relaxing strains, enjoying the drive as much as the novelty of having bitumen beneath his wheels.

The public hospital was in North Ward. Billy, proceeding by direction alone, found himself at a set of lights in the wrong lane during the five o'clock rush, and stalled the motor. Flustered and swearing he took the first exit into a quieter street and had to resort to the map in a phone book to orient himself again.

'Crazy damn place,' he grumbled, pulling back into the traffic. 'I'd find it faster on foot.'

When they did eventually locate the hospital visiting hours were in full swing and the car park was crowded. He drove around until a vehicle pulled out just in front of them and scooted firmly into the vacancy.

'Big place,' Jo said as he locked the door and pocketed the key. She swallowed and gripped the small clutch purse she carried. 'I wonder how we go about finding him?'

It was Billy's second visit. 'I got bushed last time. It's easier just to ask.'

'Second floor,' the woman at the desk in Reception told them. 'Take the lift – down the corridor there. When you get out turn right and follow the arrows to the nursing station. You'll find Mr Reilly in Ward Three.'

There was a smell of floor polish and antiseptic, and seemingly miles of brown polyurethane-floored corridors with doors opening off them to either side. A woman pushed a trolley by them, pausing to collect trays from the rooms, and nurses passed with quick, professional smiles for the visitors. Ward Three had a western aspect; pausing at the door Billy could see the light of the declining sun patterning the floor with the shape of the vertical blinds. He looked at Jo.

'Ready?'

She nodded and they entered.

There were three beds in the room. One, unoccupied, the sheet folded neatly over a tightly drawn cover. The second rumpled but empty and the third, the temporary property of Blake who sat in the wheelchair beside it. He was facing the window but looked around with the quick instinct of the bush bred at their approach.

'Well,' the hard, pale eyes flickered over them and something moved in their depths. Billy, snatching a brief glimpse, almost thought it was pain. 'I didn't expect this.' Blake cleared his throat, his voice the only part of him unchanged. His eyes were on his daughter. 'Jo – I'm more sorry than I can say about the lad.'

Her throat spasmed and her 'thank you' was brittle. The silence stretched and Billy stepped into it, pulling the visitor's chair out from beside the locker.

'Here, sit down, love. So, how are you, boss?'

'As you see,' Blake said dryly. There was a water jug on his locker and a glass, beside a radio and a crumpled newspaper. 'Breakfast, bath, physio – the days don't change much in here. How're things on the place?'

'We haven't heard anything from Simon bar the rainfall since the cyclone.' Cyclone Ted had hit the western Gulf in the middle of December, unroofing half of Southbend and bringing unprecedented rainfall. 'Be a while before he gets a letter out. By the sound of the river heights quoted on the weather news the council'll probably have to rebuild the road before the mail runs again.' He looked at the crumpled paper, 'How're you doing for reading matter? We could bring you some books or fruit—?'

Blake shook his head. 'Red Cross come round with the library trolley. And the tucker's okay. Why'd you come?'

Billy glanced at Jo. She had been studying her father as if he were a stranger – and he looked it. The flesh had melted from Blake's bones and the colour leached from his skin. The accident had aged him, put a stoop in his shoulders and a tremor in his

366

hands. Only his fierce, guarded gaze was unchanged, that of the monster of her childhood. It rested on her now and with surprising gentleness he repeated, 'Why have you come?'

'To hear about my mother.' She spoke baldly. 'Simon remembers things that we – that I don't. So I want to hear it from you. Why you drove her away from us.'

Blake's gaze moved from her to the window and the verandah beyond where the ambulatory patients liked to spend time, then came back, almost reluctantly, to her face. 'It wasn't quite like that, Jo. She wanted to go.'

'Because you knocked her around!' Jo's left hand had gone to her face. The stone in her ring glittered briefly as the sun's rays caught it.

'Yes, I did.' His eyes dropped for a moment before her accusatory glare. 'And I regret it – more than anything. Except,' he nodded at her cheek, 'for that. I was drunk, but it's no excuse. You needn't believe me but when I sobered up and understood what I'd done – well, I'd have served another five years not to've been the cause of it.' He swallowed, his Adam's apple moving jaggedly in the thinness of his throat. He looked, Billy thought, like a puff of wind could blow him away as he began speaking again, the words seemingly torn from a reservoir that had been dammed for years.

'Things shoulda been different. Christ knows I *wanted* 'em to be – but somehow we never got the chance. Or I had it, and blew it. Too late now. But for what it's worth, I'm sorry.'

Jo blinked. It was the last thing she had expected but her

attitude didn't soften. 'Tell me about my mother then. If she wanted to leave, using her for a punching bag wasn't going to make her stay, was it?'

'No.' He stared past her, down the years, the defeat in his eyes suddenly so plain that Billy looked away. 'When they sent me to prison – that finished it. We'd been happy till then, but she couldn't stand the disgrace.' A corrosive bitterness charged his voice. 'She believed 'em – the cops. Harped on it ever after – how I was a crook, a failure she'd thrown her life away on. She never let it rest – every row we had she'd bring it up. Jesus! It's no wonder I took to the drink.' He shook his head. 'You kids were the only good thing I had going, and I crooled that too. Then she left. Hadn't been for Suds I dunno how I'da managed.'

'What about the man who took her away?'

Blake shrugged. 'Some bloke from a copper mine out of town. There were still a few miners poking about then, gunna make their fortune from it, even though the real mining had finished. She'd been seeing him all that droving season. I didn't care by then.'

'With things that bad between you,' Jo said bluntly, 'it's a wonder we were even conceived.'

As far as it was possible to do so Blake looked embarrassed. He cleared his throat. 'Ah, well, I wasn't always camping on the verandah, girl. Not when I first got out. Maybe we were even happy for a bit. It just didn't last. By the time you two were toddling she had the blame thing going at full throttle, saying I'd trapped her. Got her pregnant so she'd never be free—'

Jo's stricken expression stopped him. He shook his head then reached tentatively with his trembling hand to lay it on her knee. 'I'm sorry.' The words were husky, uncertain, 'I didn't mean to hurt you, girl. Truth is she wasn't cut out for kids. Some women aren't.'

Jo froze at the touch. Billy held his breath for what seemed an eternity while she stared down at the hand that had marked her face. The skin of it was pale now and soft, but it was still broad and scarred across the knuckles, the thumbnail ridged and broken where a shoeing hammer had once split it. Slowly, hesitatingly, she put her own hand down to cover her father's. Her breath went out in a long sigh and with it much of her hostility.

'It's all right,' she said. 'I suppose at the back of our minds we always knew that if we'd mattered to her she'd never have left us. Billy told me what Simon says *she* told him the day she left. That he could go with her. And he wouldn't. He said he wanted to stay with you. If he'd ever told us maybe we wouldn't have clung onto the idea of her for so long.' Pain and regret shone in her eyes and a touch of anger re-entered her voice. '*You* should have told us. Cub – when we were kids, he wanted a father so much. If we'd known he could've – and now it's too late.' With the directness that characterised her she said, 'It's why he hated you – that you weren't what you should have been. What he *needed* you to be.'

Blake winced. 'But also for this,' he said sadly. His touch on her cheek was light enough to be imaginary. Then a switch clicked behind them and the corners of the room sprang out of the dimness that had, unnoticed, overtaken them.

'That's better,' a nurse said heartily. 'Now, Mr Mackworth, let's get you settled.' A sturdy girl in her twenties, she was pushing a wheelchair containing a double amputee towards the other bed. 'Time you were in bed too, Mr Reilly. You've been sitting too long.'

Billy cleared his throat. 'We'd better go.'

'Yes.' Jo stood like one waking from a dream. 'I – we'll come back tomorrow.' She looked at Billy and he nodded. 'Yes – tomorrow.' Her hand moved uncertainly towards Blake before she let it fall again. 'Goodbye.'

Blake nodded brusquely. 'I'll see you then.' As they turned away he gripped the wheels of his chair and began manoeuvring it towards the bed.

The lights were on in the car park. And high above them, black shapes against the city's glow, a host of flying foxes flew north. Billy turned on his heel to watch them. 'Must be a big park somewhere. Or maybe they've got a Botanical Garden.' He unlocked the vehicle. 'You okay, Jo?'

'Yes.' She got in, moving as if still in a dream. 'It's just – well, like suddenly everything's backward to what you thought. I wish—' she stopped uncertainly then began again. 'Don't expect me to suddenly start loving him – because I don't. But—' she stopped again as if unsure about how she felt, and he helped her out.

'. . . there's always tomorrow.'

'Yes.' She shifted in the seat to lean against him. 'I feel – I don't know – changed somehow. All mixed up – angry that we didn't know, and sad too, because things could've been different. But mainly relieved – like putting down a heavy load, you know? Only this was more like a – a shadow, a blackness. But suddenly it's – gone. Just like that. Because I believe him, Billy. That's the thing – I do believe him.' She sat up and buckled the seatbelt, her old practical self. 'Where to now?'

Billy started the engine. 'Find a motel. There's got to be budget places out from the centre of the city.' He hesitated for they had slept apart at Ivy's place – she in the spare bedroom, he in the little cottage he had used before. 'A twin room'll come cheaper than two singles. What d'you think?'

'That's my old cautious slowcoach.' She laughed suddenly, not the full-throated laugh he had always loved – he had not heard that since Cub's death – but a little gurgle of amusement. 'I've got a better idea. Why don't we just get a double instead?'

His heart leapt. Abandoning the gearstick he turned to her.

'Then – you do still want to marry me, Jo?'

'Of course I do. Why—? Oh, poor love,' she was suddenly remorseful, 'did you think—? But it was nothing to do with *us,* Billy.'

'I know. You needed time to grieve.' Dark eyes haunted, he squeezed her hand. 'Only I was afraid you'd never find your way back from it, Jo. But now we can make plans again. Let's get married straightaway. It's what everyone's expecting anyway.'

She rubbed his lean cheek with her thumb. 'Why not? I need you so much, Billy. I don't ever want to lose you.' Then with a return to her old manner, 'Who's everyone?'

'Well, Rachel I guess, and I suppose that means the 'Bend. I had a letter from her last week – Rachel. She must've called Simon for the address. Seems that since the cyclone they're been flying the mail into town. She's got a job now – running the store for Fiona.

You know she did an accountancy course? Anyway she sent her best wishes for the wedding.'

'You didn't tell me.'

'I didn't think there was going to *be* a wedding,' Billy was honest.

'Well there is. And that being so let's find this motel and do some planning.'

'Just planning?' Billy affected disappointment.

Her eyes crinkled at the corners in the way he loved. 'Well, we might ring Ivy first and tell her. Then we'll see.'

Forty-two

In the kitchen at the Brumby, Suds was cooking mango chutney, the smell of the simmering vinegar sharp in the moist air. February was generally a cooler month and this one had followed the rule, not surprisingly when scarcely a day of it had passed without rain falling. The vegetable garden, lying fallow over the summer, was waist deep in weeds, the waters of the Wildhorse a permanent turgid brown. The homestead walls sprouted mould, and dampness clung to everything capable of absorbing it. Even the damn table, Suds thought, eyeing it morosely, was growing a crop of mildew.

He was sick of the Wet Season. He wished the endless rain would stop. They needed sunlight and heat to dry things out. The ground was growing *moss* for chrissake! It had to be the biggest Wet they'd had in forty years. And while he was on the job he wished he had a bottle as well – he was drier than a year-old bone.

Simon entered the kitchen and hung his hat. Belle's toes clicked on the concrete behind him and when the door shut on her she lay down with her nose almost touching the screen, following him with her eyes. Lonely, Suds thought, like the rest of us.

'There's a telegram come,' he said grumpily, nodding at the sheet of paper on the table.

'Yeah?' Simon picked it up. 'So,' he said when he'd read it, 'they're getting married. What'll next Thursday be?' He looked at the calendar. 'First of March then. Registry Office in Townsville, it says. We could send a telegram to them there, I suppose. The wedding present'll have to wait a bit though. But maybe you can have the cake waiting for them when they get back?'

'When's that gunna be?' Suds stirred the boiler angrily, eyes watering in the pungent steam.

'Not till the roads open, that's for sure. Maybe April. Cheer up, mate. It means Jo's getting over losing him – and for a while there I was afraid she wouldn't.' He looked at the stove, 'What's that you're cooking?'

'Mango chutney. Their – her favourite.' Suds sniffed furiously. ''S'last of the late mangos – what the flying foxes didn't get that is.'

Simon rubbed his jaw and re-read the telegram, thinking about Fiona. He hadn't seen her since Padre Barry's visit and wasn't likely to for another month – and that depended on the rain stopping today. Billy was a lucky bugger . . . 'Yeah,' he said absently, 'any chance of a cuppa?'

Oscar Davies leant on his bar and through the door surveyed the green of the police paddock, a slice of which was visible between the school and the store. The grass was higher than he'd seen it in years. It completely hid the fence. On his shoulder Bluey bent his head and nibbled gently at his ear. He raised a hand to scratch the cocky's crest.

'All this rain might be good for the stations, old mate,' he rumbled, 'but I can tell you it does bugger-all for business.'

'Bastard,' Bluey agreed sociably.

'Who's that you're talking to, Oscar?' Keith Guthrie had come unseen along the verandah and now moved his beanpole frame through the door and eased it onto a stool.

'The bird.' Without being asked Oscar set a beer in front of his only customer. 'You won't be doing a run this week then?'

'Not likely. The river's dropped a bit though. Might get through to the Mount in a fortnight say – if it don't rain again.'

'Chance'd be a fine thing,' Oscar grunted. 'It's for sure you won't get past it. Rainfall for the summer to date's fifty-nine inches. A record for the district. They'll be talking about the big Wet of seventy-six when you and me's history.'

'Yeah,' Keith agreed. 'Cyclone Ted left his mark on the country all right.'

'Too right. There's Rumhole homestead drowned. Every windmill within cooee minus its head and Gawd knows how many cattle lost. Not to mention that slip of a Cooper girl running the store.'

'Can't see how you can blame the cyclone for that,' Keith demurred.

Oscar ignored this. 'Took me roof, didn't it?' he said inarguably. Both men peered up at the heavy tarpaulin pulled over the bare rafters in place of the missing iron, while Bluey, sensing opportunity, descended to the bar and Keith's unguarded beer.

'Coulda been worse,' the lanky mailman observed. 'And about what you'd expect from this bloody country. Didn't I – get your damn beak outta me glass!' He swatted the bird away. 'Makes you wonder, but. There's poor old Ken slogs his guts out for years on Rumhole and winds up worse off'n when he started. While the only rich girl the town's ever seen gets snapped up by Simon Reilly. Old Blake must be laughing himself into a hernia.'

'They've had their troubles too,' Oscar said fair-mindedly. 'Weddins must be in the air. His sister tied the knot last week. Her and that young Martin – I wouldn't mind marrying half a station meself.'

'I wouldn't mind a beer that bloody parrot of yours hadn't dribbled in,' Keith retorted. He thrust his drink across the bar, startling the bird into retreat. 'How about it?'

Bluey ruffled his feathers and veiled one eye then bent to inspect the scaly skin of his feet. 'Who's a bastard?' he murmured sadly to the bar top as Oscar replaced the glass.

At the farm Billy loaded the swag, grunting as he lifted it. 'Oof! Proper married man's job that, weighs a ton.' He placed it on top of the box of fruit and pulled the rope tight. 'That's it?'

'Everything,' Jo agreed, 'if you've got the shovel.'

'It's on.' He checked as he spoke, running his eye over the load for the essentials – the axe, tow chain, cable, water, tuckerbox, spare tyre, tyre lever, jack, tools, extra fuel. According to Simon the road was open – just. He knew what that meant; they'd probably need everything they were carrying before they got there. He re-fitted his hat, dusted his hands and turned to hug Ivy, planting a kiss on her wrinkled cheek. 'You take care.'

'My, you're a lot bolder than you were when you worked for me, son,' her old eyes twinkled at him. 'Marriage agrees with you.'

Billy laughed. 'Five week's practice. Thanks, Ivy. More than you can imagine. For everything.'

'Send me a telegram when you get there. And you, my dear,' she folded Jo into a close embrace, 'I shall miss you both. Come back soon.'

'We will,' Jo promised, eyes very bright. 'Send word when Daisy foals.'

'Of course I will. Safe journey, and a good season.'

She watched Billy reverse the vehicle and when he glanced back from the gate she was still there, by the steps, waving to them. He waved back and then Ivy and the old farmhouse were hidden from sight by the lantana. The engine ran sweetly as he drove along the narrow lane, making for the road that would take them north-west. Already the summer seemed half a dream away, a collection of fragments unspooling behind them.

Billy reached for Jo's hand and squeezed it. His heart sang. He who had been adrift most of his life could feel it now, just the way Ivy had once described it, the strong mystical tug of country – in his case the Gulf country – calling him home. 'We're on our way, love. Harditch tonight. Maybe Southbend tomorrow?'

'Weather permitting,' she smiled bravely and for an instant Cub was there with them in the cab.

'We'll pick up the mail,' Billy planned, 'must be a ton of it by now. And a six-pack for old Suds. We've got fresh fruit and vegies. Anything else we're going to need?'

'Just dry roads.' Jo smiled at him, the yellow feather bright against the fawn of her new hat, 'and what's waiting at the end of them.'